THE NANNY TENURE

A SINGLE DADS' CLUB NOVEL

SOPHIE ANDREWS

Digital ISBN 978-1-957580-56-2

Paperback ISBN 978-1-957580-66-1

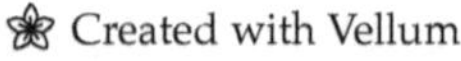 Created with Vellum

THE NANNY TENURE

Wanted: Nanny for preschooler. Must love dinosaurs, silly songs, hand puppets, and will definitely not fall for his single dad.

After my three-year-old terror on two feet turns my live interview into a viral joke, I'm crowned the internet's favorite "zaddy." Whatever that means. But when my newfound fame threatens my shot at tenure, I know I need help to keep my academic career on track.

In saunters Kennedy Novak, an effervescent ray of sunshine. With her megawatt smile and endless patience, she is a godsend, exactly what my son, Finn, needs.

Exactly what I need to stabilize my home life.

Which makes my attraction to her all the more problematic. Even though she's twelve years my junior, I can't ignore her lush body, the playful way she calls me "professor," or how she moans my name when we almost kiss.

Yet I know I can't cross that line and risk losing the best thing that has ever happened to Finn and me.

Until her ex comes back.

Then all bets are off. Because there is no way I'll give up Kennedy, internet fame or tenured position be damned.

CONTENT NOTE

Although The Nanny Tenure is a delicious slow burn romance, please note there are some serious topics discussed inside, including epilepsy, the death of parents, and domestic abuse. But, as always, you can be guaranteed a happy ending for this hot professor and his son's nanny.

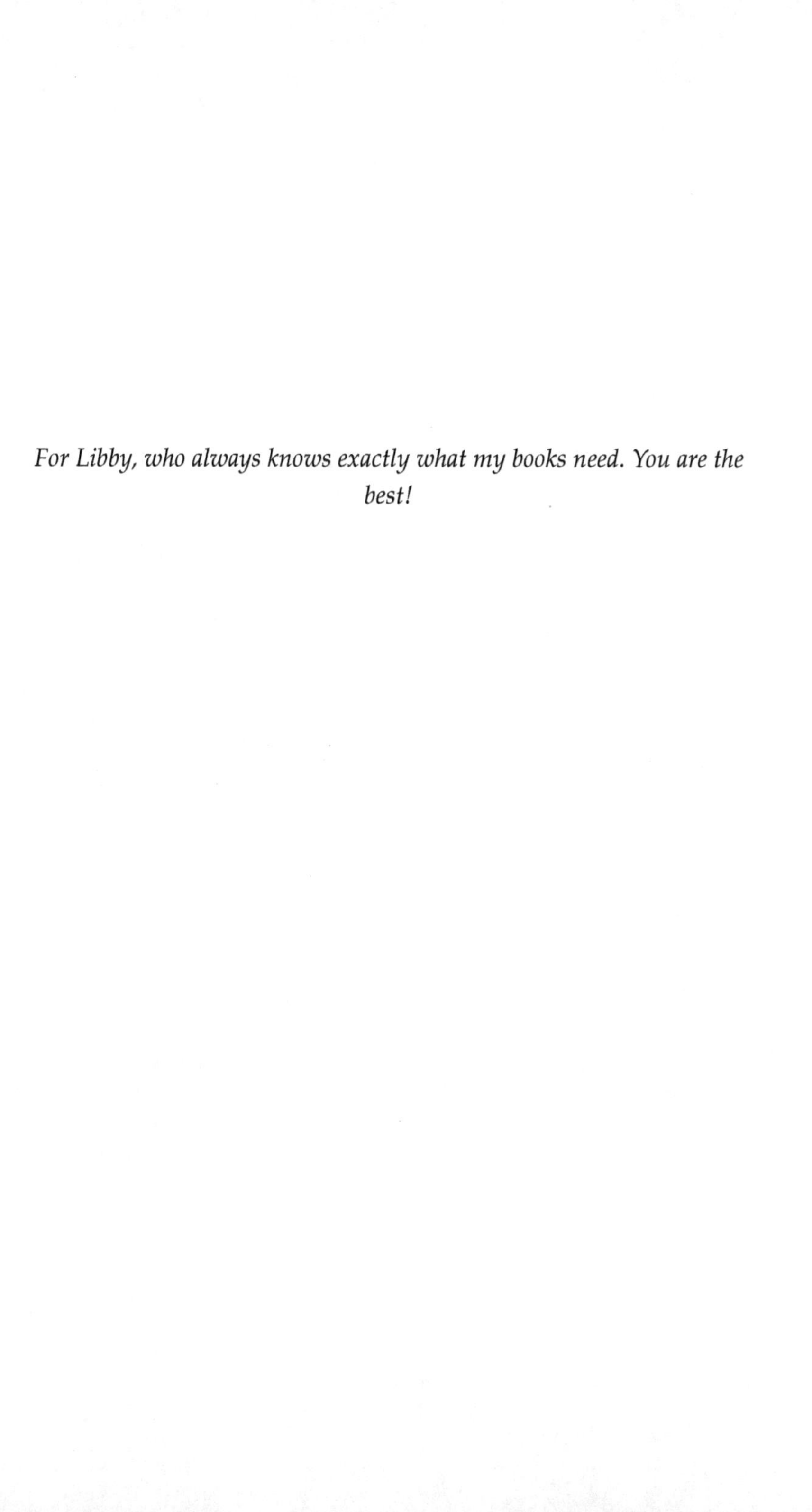

For Libby, who always knows exactly what my books need. You are the best!

ONE

LIAM

"I love my child. I love my child. I love my child," I told the clear sky above me. It was an unseasonably warm Saturday in September, and I was already overheated from losing my patience with Finn.

He yanked on my hand. "Oh! Oh! Oh!"

Go. Go. Go.

"Yeah, go get run over by a car. You won't like it," I mumbled, holding tighter to his fingers as he tried to rush off through the parking lot at the same time a car pulled out in front of us.

He whined in frustration. "Ooooooh!"

I bit back the string of curses that had been threatening to release for the last few days and sighed. "You can wait."

"No!"

Those speech lessons *had* been working. If only for one word. "No."

I fought to keep Finn at my side as we made our way to the sidewalk, and then I let him loose. He sprinted to the doors of Imagination Station and Play Center, where he was too tiny to grab the handles of the door, so like any feral three-year-old, he attempted to jump for them and ended up smacking his forehead.

"Oh Christ," I muttered, rushing to help him up, checking that he didn't display any signs of a concussion. I knew them so well with how often my child willingly leaped off or climbed on furniture.

"I it," Finn told me with eyes watering behind his glasses.

"You hit your head, I know. You shouldn't be jumping around."

He leaned into me, silently asking for a kiss, and I rubbed the reddening spot before kissing it. Then he was off as soon as I had the door open.

"There he is!"

I turned toward Jude's voice, and he had his to-go coffee mug held aloft in a salute.

"How's it feel to be famous?"

I trudged over to the bench we always sat on and plopped down at the end.

Dylan acknowledged me with his usual nod, though his shit-eating-grin was new.

"Shut up," I grumbled before he could say anything, and both of my so-called friends laughed. "Seriously. I've been getting so much shit the past forty-eight hours, I can't..." I pushed my hands through my hair and bent over, exhausted, embarrassed, angry...everything. It was too much.

"Here. Figured you could use this." Dylan handed me a coffee. I'd forgotten mine, so I accepted it gratefully.

Jude passed me a box of brownies. He never went anywhere without something sweet. Not only was I pretty sure he was addicted to sugar, but his family owned Gray's Candy shop. I helped myself to a brownie, nearly shoving the whole thing in my mouth, as I watched my third of what was essentially one big floor filled with imaginary play centers. Among them were a doctor's office, a grocery store, a salon, and an auto shop. The kids loved it.

Well, most of them.

Jude's eldest, Sebastian, mostly hung by himself in the corner playing some video game or chatted with us if he was feeling particularly friendly. The other ones—Amelia, Seb's sister; Dylan's kids, Scarlett and Tucker; and, of course, Finn—were like puppies with the zoomies. They raced from one end to another, and we played zone defense to make sure no one needed a trip to the ER.

Jude, Dylan, and I had been meeting once a month for play-dates, ever since I'd first brought Finn here when he'd started walking. Because, even then, he had been a handful who needed to run off his energy. The three of us kept bumping into one another and noticed our kids all got along well. Not to mention that we did too.

"Seriously, though," Jude said, "how're you doing?"

I swiped a hand over my prickly jaw. I hadn't bothered to shave since the video clip of my interview on a national news program had gone viral. "I had to turn my phone off. Everyone and their mother's calling me," I said, frustration lacing my words with my hometown accent. "I'm getting all kinds of shit from my colleagues and an email from the provost telling me that it was an embarrassment. Meanwhile, the dean of admissions is calling me, telling me it was fantastic because so many people are interested in the school now."

Jude sucked air through his teeth. "That's rough, man. Sorry."

Dylan leaned forward, eyeing me over Jude. "If it makes you feel any better, I totally got what you were saying with the… history and political parties…and stuff."

"Thanks." Dylan gave zero shits about my job or what I taught, and I huffed a laugh then gulped down a bit of the coffee. "All anyone's talking about is Finn or—"

"The Hot Professor," Jude interrupted with an elbow to my side.

"Don't remind me," I muttered, sinking down to hide in case anyone here recognized me.

In the spring, I'd signed a deal with a publisher. My nonfiction book, *Donkeys, Elephants, and the Two-Party System*, was going to be my first printed work outside of an academic press. It was a big deal for me. I received an advance and everything.

Up until now, I'd quietly taught my university classes and attempted to parent my son, but now my face was *everywhere*. I was splashed across social media platforms, written up in online articles, and talked about how I was the Hot Professor. I was getting messages from random strangers calling me *Zaddy*, whatever that was. The past few days had been a nightmare.

My segment on the six-o'clock news hour was supposed to be an easy seven minutes, discussing how America's current politics were transforming. I was in the middle of drawing parallels to early America's political parties and the struggle to form our constitution when Finn, who was supposed to be playing quietly on an iPad in his bedroom, came waddling into my office with his pants down around his ankles, holding his diaper as he told me in his Finn language that he had to go potty. The hosts of the show were gracious and took it in stride, laughing about funny stories with their own children, but in the moment, I froze. I obviously couldn't continue the interview with Finn crawling all over me, and the producer in my ear cut the interview short.

But by then, the damage had been done. My frozen face had become a meme, the video of my son shuffling around with his pants down was a GIF, and no one cared about all the work I'd put into my PhD or the book I had coming out next year. No, all they cared about was that I was a "hot dad" and that my kid was adorable. Which he was.

He was also a real asshole sometimes. Like when he ruined his father's segments on live television.

"I need help," I told my friends, confessing what I knew had been true for months. But it wasn't until two days ago, when my mother called and told me she was packing her bags to come down, that I decided I needed to do something.

I loved my mother, but I wasn't about to invite her into my house for the foreseeable future.

"You need a babysitter," Dylan said, while Jude shook his head.

"You need a full-time nanny."

I jerked back. "Like Mary Poppins?"

"I've been to your house," Jude said with a wince, and he didn't need to continue, so I put my hand up.

My house was a mess. I ordered out more than I cooked, and between my job and Finn's preschool and appointments, let alone his constant need for attention, I was really struggling to get into a routine.

Finn's mom, Tessa, was a professor in the science department, and we'd been good friends for a few years before we decided to give dating a shot. We'd only been together a few months when we found out she was pregnant. It was a happy accident, although we very quickly realized we were better off friends and decided to split amicably and raise Finn together. We had a wonderful partnership, got along great, and never argued, but she had accepted a yearlong sabbatical to study climate change in Antarctica.

Four months in, and I was drowning.

When Tessa had first informed me about the research grant, I was so proud of her, though it would have been a lie to say I wasn't worried. The program had been her dream for a long time, and I couldn't keep her from it just because I was afraid of being a single dad for a year. So, I'd assured her over and over again that I could handle it.

I genuinely thought I could.

Yet here I was, in the middle of a veritable child circus, running on two hours of sleep, my life having been turned into an internet joke.

"I don't know anything about hiring a nanny," I said.

Jude retrieved his phone, typing on it for a few moments. "How to hire a nanny," he read aloud. "A nanny can be a great addition in your household to help make the transition of returning to work an easy one for new parents."

"I'm already working," I mumbled.

Jude kept reading. "While finding the right nanny may seem like an overwhelming task, it doesn't have to be. Depending on your comfort level, time, and budget, you can do a lot of the work yourself, or if you need help, employ an agency to find one for you."

"More work," I said, pointing my finger at Jude's phone screen. I didn't have time, and I wasn't really looking forward to adding more to my plate in order to take it off. That didn't make sense to me.

Jude shrugged. "So let us help you."

"Yeah." Dylan crossed his ankle over his knee. "It can't be that hard. There's got to be, like, a Tinder for nannies."

Jude and I both chuckled. Dylan had been a frequenter of online "dating" apps for his hookups until he met Gen, his one-night-stand-turned-girlfriend. She was off touring the world as a dancer on a cruise ship, and I knew how he hated being parted from her. Although, he didn't struggle much with his kids since he had a big, blended family with his ex-wife. Jude, while widowed, had his family and was still very close with his late wife's family.

On the other hand, my mom and brothers were all up in Boston, and Tessa's family was across the state in Erie, Pennsylvania. I *could* ask them for help—hell, my mother was chomping at the bit—but I didn't want them to disrupt their lives to take on the full-time gig that was Finn.

"Why don't we go to Walt's?" Dylan suggested.

Walt's was our regular haunt, owned by our friend Nate. I hadn't been there in ages because of Finn, and when I shook my head, Jude waved his hand. "Come on. Drop Finn off at my house. I'll have my parents come over."

Finn was a handful, and I didn't trust any random babysitter with him.

"We'll have a few beers and come up with a list for your Mary Poppins," he added, and the temptation to get away for a night was a big one.

"All right." I gave in, powering my cell phone back on, the screen immediately filling with alerts for new text messages, voice mails, and emails. I ignored them all and opened my calendar. "Everybody good for Thursday night?"

"I'm good," Jude said, and Dylan agreed.

"Me too."

I plugged it into my calendar and slid my phone into my back pocket right as Finn tried to climb into one of the shopping carts. "Hey! Finn, no!"

"Tucker!" Dylan stood because his four-year-old son had his hands wrapped around the handle of the cart, appearing as if he was going to take Finn for a ride. "I don't think so."

They both ignored us, and Dylan ran to stop them, the shopping cart ramming into his shins. Tucker grinned impishly with a "Sorry!" then scampered off while his dad's face turned bright red, and I could imagine the string of curses he was holding back as he limped in a tight circle.

Jude covered his laugh with his hand as I hopped up to take Finn out of the cart. "Whatdya think you're doing? You coulda taken a header right out of here and busted your face. You wanna go to the hospital for stitches?"

He shook his head.

"Stop climbing on things. It's not safe." I set him on the floor and fixed his glasses with the rubber band around his head. "You do it again, and we're leaving."

He only wrinkled his nose then took off again.

I caught up to Dylan and clapped his shoulder. "All right?"

He grunted as he closed his eyes for a moment, inhaling. "I love my children."

I agreed. Sometimes you just didn't like them.

TWO
KENNEDY

"Hey Nate, could I get another?"

My sister, Taylor, arched her brow. "You really need *another*?"

"Yes. I really need *another*."

Every third Thursday of the month, I tagged along with her to Walt's to watch her boyfriend, Dean, play in his cover band. When I went out, I almost never had more than one or two drinks because of my meds. I couldn't mess with them and chance a seizure, but today was shit and called for alcohol.

Nate, the cute, bearded, and tattooed owner of this delightful little dive, appeared in front of me with a refill. "How's it going, ladies?"

Taylor, as per usual, offered him a nod.

My sister was great. Loved her to the moon and back, but she had a raging case of resting bitch face. She knew it and wore it well. It was part of her charm.

"What about you?" he asked me, satisfied with Taylor's silent answer.

"It's been a day," I said, swiping my hand through my hair.

"Yeah?" He leaned his forearms on the bar. "What happened?"

That was what I liked about Nate. He was a genuinely nice guy. You could tell he really cared about people. My sister often called me naïve, said I was too trusting, and maybe I was, but Nate? He was one of the good ones.

"I got fired from my job," I told him.

"That sucks. I'm sorry."

"Because I got into a car accident."

"Oh shit." He reared back, his hands on the glossy bar top. "Really? Are you okay? Is your car okay?"

I sipped from my refilled beer and started to set it back down, but Taylor intercepted it and placed it in front of herself.

"You're kidding," I snapped, and I *never* snapped at anyone, let alone my sister.

"No, you're kidding," she said with a tip of her chin to my fingers, which were still a little shaky from earlier.

Barely.

No one would even notice. Except for her.

Of course.

My sister noticed everything.

Nate toggled his eyes between the two of us, clearly sensing something off, then tapped the bar and turned to help other customers.

"What's your problem?" I asked once we were alone.

"My problem is that not even two hours ago, you were crying because you were so upset, and now you're here trying to drown your sorrows in alcohol."

I twisted on my stool, my gaze landing on Dean. He was in the middle of fiddling with his guitar strap, but I raised my hand for his attention. He would definitely side with me.

When he spotted me, he set his guitar down and hopped off the little stage in the corner, waved to some people he knew—wives of the other guys in the band—and made his way to us.

"What's up?" he asked, draping his hand on the back of Taylor's chair while meeting my gaze.

I pointed at my sister. "She took my drink away."

"Of course she did. She's a thief of joy."

Taylor and Dean had met years ago in law school and hated each other. Coincidentally, they'd ended up working together at my family's law firm, where they still hated each other. Until recently. Now, I had the big brother I never knew I wanted.

"Hargrove," my sister said, jaw tight.

He slanted his head toward her. "Yes, Satan?"

She rolled her eyes. "Don't give in to her."

"Don't baby me," I bit out, and he nodded at me in solidarity then told her, "Don't baby her."

"I'm not babying her."

"Yes, you are." I tried to keep the whine from my voice but failed.

My sister huffed and lifted the small glass of whisky that she and Dean always shared before one of his gigs. He watched her drink a bit of the amber liquid then took the glass from her so he could finish it off.

"She's had a rough day. She's gotta let off some steam," Dean murmured once he set the empty glass on the bar, talking about me like I wasn't right here. And yeah, *that* did make me feel like a baby.

Then he curled his hand around the back of Taylor's neck and kissed her jaw. "We can take her home if she ties one on. Don't worry."

My sister gave in when he kissed her mouth, and he tossed a victorious smile my way. But I didn't even want the drink anymore.

It was difficult to be not only *a* little sister, but *Taylor Novak's* little sister. Brilliant esquire and overprotective Cancer, she was six years older than me and had been more mother than sibling since our own mom hadn't always been present, mentally or emotionally.

Taylor had assumed that she'd shielded me from the brunt of it, that I didn't notice how Mom had fallen into a deep depression after our father had passed away and then bounced back into a manic state. She'd evened out eventually with the help of medication, but I knew. I'd always known that it was Taylor who was cooking my dinners and making sure I got to all my extracurriculars. And it was my sister who was there when I had my first seizure at fourteen.

My relationship with Taylor had always been out of balance, with her need to take care of me and with my need to be taken care of. But I was tired of relying on my sister all the time. I was twenty-four years old, a grown woman.

And right now, playing on our typical seesaw wasn't as comforting as it usually was.

"I gotta go." Dean squeezed my shoulder before sauntering to the stage. Taylor pushed the beer back in front of me with her index finger, though I already felt like a child who'd had her toy taken away for being naughty and left the glass where it was.

Onstage, the Anchormen started in on their first number after the lead singer introduced himself and the rest of the band. They were good for a dive bar cover band. They played a variety of songs, from the Rolling Stones to Shawn Mendes. I mostly scrolled on my phone, ignoring my ex-boyfriend's text messages.

Jordan and I had broken up in the spring after a fight had turned…bad. I knew he wasn't a violent guy, but he had smacked my wrist, which caused me to spill my pills all over the floor, and then he wouldn't let me pick them up because he was so dead set on keeping all of my attention. He wouldn't let me go. Wouldn't let me do anything besides listen to him explain in his shouted words that he loved me and he couldn't understand why I was talking to some random guy at the bar we were at. I believed him when he said he hadn't meant to hit my wrist—he was trying to grab my arms to keep me in place—but it didn't make me feel any better about how he had basically trapped me in the bathroom.

Dean and Taylor had had to come and get me because I was too shaken up to drive. It was always about the driving!

Jordan and I hadn't spoken through the summer, but he'd

recently started texting me again. Telling me he was working on himself. Apologizing. And while I hadn't yet been able to text him back, I also didn't delete his messages or block him, because I had loved him. I just didn't know if I *still* loved him. I had too much of my own stuff to work through to figure that out.

Namely, finding a job, a place to live, the money to fix my car, and, of course, the courage to drive again.

After my diagnosis, my doctors had wanted me to wait until I was at least eighteen to get my license. But by then, I was so in my head about it, it took me two years before I passed the test.

It wasn't that I was a bad driver. It was that I was a nervous driver.

I didn't like driving in big cities or at night. Or to places I wasn't familiar with. Or anywhere that required parallel parking. Or in the rain. Or on, like, really long drives.

But other than that, I was totally fine.

Until some college kid had run a stop sign and T-boned me five hours ago.

My sister was right. I was still trembling, and I curled my hands into fists, tucking them under my arms when I crossed them over my torso. I ignored how Taylor was practically eye-fucking Dean next to me and bobbed my head along to "Something to Talk About" as I swept my gaze around the bar to the group of gray-haired guys with their eyes on the television while eating baskets of chicken wings. To the few tables in the front of the stage which were mostly taken up by the girlfriends and wives of the guys in the band. To the group of women in matching T-shirts like they were on some kind of sports team. To the preppy white guy making his way out of the bathroom.

I canted my head.

I knew him.

How did I know him?

Leaning into Taylor to make sure she heard me over the music, I asked, "That guy sitting catty-corner to us, thick head of curly hair… Does he look familiar to you?"

She peeked over her shoulder and shrugged. "Not really."

I turned and lifted my drink as an excuse to check him out again, and at that very moment, he pushed the sleeves of his sweater up his forearms.

"Oh my god!" I slapped at my sister. "That's the Hot Professor!"

She narrowed her brows at me. "Who?"

"The Hot Professor. You have to have seen it. The video's everywhere."

"What're you talking about?"

I exchanged my still-full beer for my cell phone, scrolling through my social media for the viral video. "He'd been in the middle of an interview about something or other, and his toddler interrupted. It was hilarious. And hot. He'd pushed his sleeves up his forearms in the video too. Just before his kid came in."

I found said video and played it for Taylor. "Oh yeah, yeah. I've seen that. So funny."

"That's him!" I whisper-shouted, setting my phone down and swiveling back around on my stool to full-on stare at the Hot Professor. "He's actually cuter in person."

Taylor followed my line of sight.

"But what's he doing?" I asked, mostly to myself.

Taylor tapped her fingers on the bar, guessing, "Working?"

Hot Professor was seated between two other guys. On his right was a man in a baseball cap, holding a pint, occasionally nodding along at whatever they were saying. On the left was a guy with a beard and man bun, pointing at the paper, talking a lot as Hot Professor...took notes?

But I didn't know how anyone could think over the Anchormen's version of Britney's "Toxic."

I continued to watch the trio. Hot Professor had a habit of sucking his lips between his teeth in thought, his eyes glazing over for a few seconds, and then he'd write furiously. To say my interest was piqued was an understatement.

When Nate made his way back to Taylor and me, checking in, I tipped my chin in their direction. "Do you know them?"

Nate glanced back. "Oh yeah. They're my good buddies. Why?"

"Is that the guy from the hot—"

"Please don't go up to him. He's mortified."

"So, he is the Hot Professor?"

Nate rolled his eyes. "He's not that hot."

I snorted a laugh. "Yes, he is."

Nate struck a pose, popping his triceps. "More than me?"

"Well, you've got different vibes. It's apples and oranges."

"Yeah, but oranges are much hotter than apples, aren't they?"

"If you say so." I shook my head in amusement. "What are they working on?"

Nate glanced over his shoulder again then leaned his forearms on the table. Because I was pretty much a regular here, I'd learned Nate was a bit of a gossip. It's why we got along so great. "Those are my boys, okay? The hairy one on the end there? We go way back to high school, and the other two have been coming here for a while. They're all single dads, and they come here to hang out and relax."

"So you're saying I shouldn't go up and ask him for a selfie?"

He laughed. "O'Neil's not dealing with his newfound fame real well, and we're trying to help him."

"You?" I deliberately splayed my hands out in front of me, encapsulating the bar.

"I'm providing free drinks while they come up with a list for his nanny search."

"His nanny search?"

Nate stood, stacking a few coasters in the corner of the bar. "He needs help with his kid. He was on the national news for a reason. The guy's brilliant, but Finn's a tiny terror."

"Finn's his little boy?" I asked, thinking of the bespectacled toddler charging into his father's interview with the gusto of a marching band.

"Yeah. With everything going on, he decided he needs some help. So the boys are coming up with qualifications for the application."

"Seems like you got the easy end of the deal. You provide the drinks while they do all the work."

He slapped his hand on the bar, grinning. "Made it through thirty-three years kid-free and plan on making it through the next thirty-three the same way."

Behind me, the band finished up their set, and Taylor turned, listening in on my conversation with Nate as I asked, "Do you know what he's looking for?"

"In a nanny?" When I nodded, Nate shrugged. "Why? You interested?"

"I might be," I said, and Taylor stuck her finger in the air.

"Wait a minute. Wait a minute. What did I miss?"

"Hot Professor needs a nanny," I said, and Nate propped his hands on his hips, surveying me seriously as if I was in an interview.

"Do you have any experience?" he asked.

"A bit. I worked in a day care for a while."

"And you're really interested?"

"I lost my job. I need money."

Out of the corner of my eye, Taylor's head was on a swivel between Nate and me. "Wait just a goddamn second, Ken. You want to be a *nanny*? Since when?"

"Since I got into a car accident and was fired for not showing up at my job."

"You say that as if you were fired out of the blue. You were warned not to be late on multiple occasions."

I waved away that detail. "I didn't like the job anyway."

"You don't like any job. That's your whole issue."

"I like kids, though," I said.

Here I was, trying to problem-solve on my own. And here she was, trying to interfere. She should've been happy. Proud of my initiative. "And how hard could it be?" I went on. "I need a job and money to fix my car."

"How are you going to get to said job without a car that works?" she asked like she was cross-examining me.

She had me there, but when I glanced to Nate and then over his shoulder to the Hot Professor diligently writing, it hit me. I zipped my attention back to Nate. "You think he's offering room and board?"

That would kill *three* birds with one stone.

"No idea." Nate lifted his hand to acknowledge another patron, who needed a refill, then rapped his knuckles on the bar. "You guys let me know if you need anything." He pointed at me with a smile. "Including a job."

My laugh was cut off by Taylor grabbing hold of my wrist. "What the fuck are you talking about? You suddenly want to be a nanny and live with a stranger?"

"I was already living with a stranger."

"What do you mean *was*?"

I dropped my head back on my shoulders, blowing out a breath. I would really love it if my sister didn't pick up on Every. Little. Detail.

"Kennedy. What do you mean was? You're not living with Carol anymore?"

Carol was a woman in her sixties who rented me a room in her house. I'd found it on an apartment-hunting website a few months ago, after I'd been living in Philly with my family for a few weeks post Jordan breakup. I had needed a place to live, and it was cheap. Carol was nice and minded her own business. But the sly minx had gone and met a man online, and she was moving across the country to be with him. I told my sister the condensed version of the story, and she groaned my name.

"*Kennedy*. Why didn't you tell me?"

"Because." When my sister scowled at me, I added a petulant, "I don't have to tell you everything."

"Yeah, but you should've told me this."

"Why? You couldn't do anything about it."

"I could help you."

I whirled on my stool to face her. "Titi, I love you, but I'm tired of feeling like..." I coasted my gaze around the bar, mentally searching for an explanation. "I'm not like you. I'm not book smart and haven't known what I wanted to do from the time I was five."

She opened her mouth to argue, but I needed to get this out and held up my palm to quiet her.

"Please don't patronize me and tell me I can do whatever I set my mind to. Because I don't even know *what* to set my mind to. And yeah, I know I've wasted a lot of time, but I'm tired of being so dependent on you. I'm tired of not knowing what I'm doing every day. I'm tired of just not knowing, period."

Dean appeared then, his eyes flickering between us. "What's going on?"

"Kennedy wants to be a nanny," Taylor explained, and without looking in Hot Professor's direction, she aimed her index finger at him. "He's Nate's friend and needs one, so she thinks she's going to walk up to him—a stranger—and ask him for a job *and* housing because she's avoided telling me that Carol's moving and now she has nowhere to live."

Dean shot his gaze to me. "Kenny, seriously?"

"I was going to figure it out on my own," I said, my voice rising in annoyance.

Dean narrowed his brows. "And your new plan is to be a nanny for some random guy?"

"Well, he's not some random guy. He's the internet's Hot Professor."

They both rolled their eyes at me.

"And he would have to hire me first, but...yeah. I could be a nanny."

"Are you sure that's what you want?" Dean asked at the same time my sister said, "You can't."

And that was the word I hated. *Can't.* I'd heard it since I was fourteen.

There are a lot of things a person with epilepsy can't do. Can't have too much caffeine, can't have too much sugar, can't be around strobe lights or intense music, can't have too much stress, can't go swimming by myself or play certain sports. Can't climb tall structures or operate heavy machinery, which I guess would really piss me off if I wanted to drive a bulldozer.

I'd been ruled by *can't* for the last decade.

It was the reason why I hadn't settled for *can't.* I did what I wanted now because I needed to have some control in my life. Whether it was staying out late with friends or quitting a job I didn't love, I wasn't going to be ruled by something I couldn't control. I'd spent too much time being afraid of blacking out and never waking up again, but I'd eventually realized I couldn't live like that. I had to live for today, right now. And I took *can't* out of my vocabulary.

Which was why I stood up, sent my sister a withering glare, then set my shoulders and marched to the other end of the bar.

"Excuse me?"

Three pairs of eyes slanted to me.

"My name's Kennedy, and I hear you're in need of a nanny."

THREE
LIAM

"**M**y name's Kennedy, and I hear you're in need of a nanny."

It took me a second to realize those words were directed at me. Dylan elbowed me in the side and leaned back, allowing me a view of the woman who'd been hidden behind him.

"Excuse me?" I asked.

"My name is Kennedy Novak, and I was just talking to Nate —" she motioned to my friend, currently leaning against the bar "—and he told me you were in search of a nanny. I would like to apply."

I faced Nate, who smiled, chagrined. "You telling everybody my business?"

"Of course he is," Dylan said from behind his pint of beer.

Nate held his hands up in innocence. "Kennedy's great."

"We're looking for a nanny," Jude told him. "What do you know about her besides that she's great?"

"You can ask her since she's standing right here," the woman said, though *woman* was pushing it. She looked young, early twenties. She could've been one of my students.

Jesus, I hoped she wasn't one of my students.

Jude craned his neck to meet her gaze. "I'm sorry. I didn't mean to be rude, but our friend has a habit of—"

"Being a gossipy dick," Dylan interrupted, and Nate shot his fist out, punching Dylan's shoulder. Nate also happened to be Gen's brother, so he and Dylan had a real love-hate relationship.

I sighed. "Can we get back to business here?" Then I looked at the woman. "You said your name was Kennedy?"

"Yes."

"Are you an undergrad?" I asked, and she shook her head. *Thank God*. Though I couldn't pinpoint why I was so relieved.

"I'm happy to send you a résumé," she said with a hopeful smile.

"What experience do you have working as a nanny?" I asked, and her hope faltered with an almost imperceptible frown before she wiped it away.

"None," she said eventually, "but I do have experience working in a day care."

I tapped my pen on the list we'd drawn up. A few years' experience was our number one requirement. Finn needed someone who could handle him. Not some girl who appeared barely old enough to drink and had, what...? "How long were you with the day care?"

There was that slight dip of her lips again. "A few months."

Dylan stayed silent, his hat pulled down low over his brow, but I could tell he was suspicious of her.

Jude was the one to ask, "Did you go to school for education or...?"

"No," she answered, and I blew out a breath, scrubbing my hand through my hair before taking her in. She was on the shorter side, with a golden complexion and long, shiny hair the color of black coffee that waved around her shoulders. Her eyes were dark too, surrounded by long lashes and makeup. Her face was round with apple cheeks, and from the little I could see of her, still mostly hidden by Dylan, she didn't strike me as a Mary Poppins type. Not that I expected Finn's nanny to wear some turn-of-the-twentieth-century getup, but I expected to hire someone older than me. Someone who wore thick cardigans and had tissues stuffed up her sleeve.

This girl was certainly *not* that. With her hoop earrings, multiple necklaces, including one with a K that lay on her collarbone, and her plump lips painted dark pink, she wasn't what I'd imagined at all.

"Do you have a degree?" I asked, and she shifted, revealing more of herself. Her dark green top sat wide on her shoulders and seemed to be holding on for dear life, threatening to slip down at any moment. Especially with her voluptuous cleavage trying its best to win the battle.

I forced my eyes up as she answered, "I attended cosmetology school."

Before I could tell her thanks but no thanks, she went on, clearly padding this so-called résumé. "Most recently, I was working the front desk at a hotel, but before that, I spent time volunteering for a nonprofit in Philadelphia. The day care I worked at is in the Poconos, but I could give you references. I've also worked in food service and sales."

I was a pretty easygoing guy. Up to a point. And most of the time, that point was my son. He was everything to me. I couldn't hire some random stranger from a bar.

Literally.

"No offense," I said, "but what does any of that have to do with taking care of a child?"

"Customer service," she said without missing a beat. "I'm good at it, and that's basically what taking care of children is, dealing with really tough customers. You have to keep them happy while keeping them safe and healthy. I can do that."

I had to hand it to her; that was a creative answer for someone with basically no experience in education or childcare. I skimmed my notes again. "Are you certified in CPR and first aid?"

"No. But I can be."

With a deep breath, I asked, "What are your water safety skills like?"

"I graduated out of dolphin level in my swim lessons," she said, and it was more than her shirt that was fighting for its life. It was her optimism too.

She held up her hands, palms out to me. Her fingers were small and dainty, and she wore a bunch of thin gold rings. "I'm twenty-four and motivated. I have lots of energy, and while I don't have a lot of experience, I make up for it in my ability to adapt and learn. I'm more than willing to get any certifications you require."

Again, I was about to tell her thanks but no thanks when Jude leaned his elbow on the bar and asked, "How's your cooking?"

Kennedy met his gaze and smiled.

And, goddamn, that smile.

It was like the Fourth of July.

"My mother's Italian. I'm a great cook." She flicked her eyes toward me. "You like lasagna? I have a recipe passed down from my great-grandmother."

Actually, I did like lasagna.

"You mind a little cleaning up?" Dylan asked, and I couldn't believe my two friends were lobbing questions at her like we should truly consider her.

"I don't mind cleaning," Kennedy told him and turned to me. "Do you need help with that too?"

I hated to admit it, so instead of answering her, I explained, "My son is three, and I've had trouble keeping up with him and with all my work."

"I would be happy to help around the house. In fact, while we're talking about your house…"

I huffed. We weren't talking about my house. She and my friends were talking about my house. I was trying to find a way out of this "interview."

"Are you offering room and board?"

I tipped my head back. "I'm sorry. What?"

She shifted her attention to the paper beneath my hands. "Are you offering room and board?"

"Like a live-in position?"

"Yes." Her audacity was both startling and confounding.

I hadn't originally planned on making this a live-in position because it had never occurred to me to have my gray-haired, cardigan-wearing, tissue-carrying older nanny living in my house.

"I would be very interested in housing," she said. "In fact, I would take a pay decrease for it. I'm currently renting a room from a woman, but she's going to be selling her house to move, so…"

No qualifications and in need of a place to live? Kennedy wasn't painting a real great picture of responsibility and maturity here.

Dylan hummed quietly on one side of me, while Jude nudged my other side. I twisted on my stool toward him, and he raised his brow, silently urging me on. I shook my head. He frowned.

"I'll vouch for her," Nate said, and I'd almost forgotten he was here. Although I wasn't sure how. He was the one who'd gotten me into this mess, bringing this girl to me, offering her up on a platter to be my son's nanny. "She's Taylor's sister."

"Who's Taylor?" I asked, and he pointed to a woman on the other side of the bar, watching us with a shrewd gaze. Beside her was the guitar player from the band. I'd spoken to him on an occasion or two. If you came to Walt's enough, you got to know people, and since Nate knew everyone and liked to make connections, he was always introducing people.

Exhibit A, Kennedy.

"Listen," I started, only to be interrupted by her, as if she knew I was going to dismiss her.

"I don't want to give you a whole sob story, but I could really use a break. I *need* this job."

Next to me, Jude, the patron saint of soft hearts, asked, "What happened?"

"I was in a car accident today, and because of that, I was fired from my job."

"Really? Are you okay? Here, sit," he said, and Dylan laughed into his beer.

"What?" I muttered under my breath.

He stayed silent, though his smirk was awfully telling. I was getting steamrolled. He knew it, and I knew it.

Jude stood and waved Kennedy over to take his place next to me. That was when I realized just how short she was and how she smelled like a mix of sugar and fresh flowers. And it wasn't only her breasts that were voluptuous, but the rest of her too. Her stomach was round and looked soft under where her shirt was tucked in at her waist. Her thick thighs were covered in dark denim, ripped at the knees. Brown boots capped off her legs, and she crossed them once she was seated.

"I'm sorry about your car accident," I started, "but—"

"So, it sounds like you're pretty flexible," Jude said then caught himself. "With your schedule, I mean."

She laughed, a frothy, cheerful sound. "Yes, my schedule's very flexible." She met my eyes. "I'm willing to work when you need me. All I ask is that I have two nights off a week."

"That sounds more than fair," Jude said, and I wiped my hand down my face. Was she working for me or everyone else?

Dylan, surprisingly, was the voice of reason. He leaned forward, eyeing her. "You said you're twenty…?"

"Twenty-four," she filled in.

"Why does a twenty-four-year-old want to be a nanny? You don't know anything about Finn, so what would make you walk right up to Liam and ask for a job?"

This exact question was in the back of my mind, and I folded my arms, waiting for her answer. Afraid to hear what I knew to be true.

She licked her lips, shifting her attention across the bar to her sister then to Nate in front of us and finally back to me. "I recognized you. But that's not why I came over." At my apparent expression of doubt, she shook her head. "I recognized you and was curious at what the Hot Professor could possibly be working on at a bar. You looked so serious."

"I am very serious about my child," I said.

"As you should be. And I am very serious about this job." Her dark eyes turned a little glassy. But I wasn't going to fall for it. I took a deep breath and settled my gaze somewhere over her shoulder as she said, "The thing is…"

She paused long enough that I focused back on her. She blinked her eyes clear and tipped her chin, confident now. "I've spent a lot of my life being underestimated by everyone around me. I even underestimate myself. I make excuses and let people think less of me because I think less of myself. But I don't want to do that anymore, so I'm not going to give you excuses. I know I'm young and don't have experience, but I am good with children. I'm good with *people.* I'm patient and a good listener. I'm creative and know that I can have fun with your son."

"He doesn't need fun. He needs someone to keep him from inadvertently killing himself."

Her lips trembled with a threatening smile, and I found myself giving in to one of my own. "Go ahead. You can laugh. I know it's funny. My son is basically the Tasmanian Devil."

"The who?"

"You know, the cartoon?" I waved my arms around like the whirling cartoon animal.

She shook her head. Jesus, she was young.

"I need someone to drop him off and pick him up from preschool. I need someone to be around for his speech therapy appointments and to occasionally be home with him if I have a function at school. And like my ex-best friends pointed out, I need help with a little housework. Oh, and potty training. It's been a struggle, so his nanny has to be able to handle that."

"I can do all of that. Whatever you need, I'm your girl. I promise, if you give me a chance, I won't let you down."

I stared at her for a moment. She didn't blink or look away, and it took a lot of self-assurance to hold eye contact. When I silently asked Nate his opinion with a questioning stare, he nodded his approval. Jude was obviously in. I glanced over my shoulder to Dylan, and he shrugged. "She seems sweet."

Too sweet, maybe.

When I faced her again, the corner of her bottom lip was trapped between her teeth and her fingers were knotted together. Whatever was going on with this girl, it did seem like she needed a break. And hell, it couldn't get any worse than it was now.

"Okay," I said. "When can you start?"

She gasped and grinned, bringing her hands up under her chin. "Whenever you need. There's just one thing—"

"Hi." Kennedy and I both twisted around to find her sister stepping up next to our stools, the guitarist right behind her.

"Oh. Hi," Kennedy said, her cheeks flaming a little. "This is my sister, Taylor."

"Taylor Novak," she said, sticking her hand out to me.

I shook it. "Liam O'Neil."

Taylor motioned behind her. "This is Dean Hargrove."

I shook his hand too.

"Kennedy's lawyer," he said, and I shot my brows up.

She had a lawyer?

"Oh my God," Kennedy intoned, angling her body as if she could block them out. "We were just wrapping up."

Taylor's piercing gaze shifted between us. "Looked like it was going well here, and I thought I would see what you were chatting about."

Kennedy appeared flustered with her sister, so I explained, "Kennedy and I were about to work out the details of when she would start as my son's live-in nanny."

"Live-in nanny?" Taylor repeated, and Dean's hand curled around her shoulder, as if holding her back.

I dipped my gaze to Kennedy, saying, "Dependent on references and a background check, I was hoping you could start as soon as possible."

She opened her mouth, but Dean cut her off. "Have you discussed salary?"

Kennedy started, "I can handle—"

"Let Dean hash out the details with him." Taylor tugged on Kennedy's arm. "I need to talk to you."

Before Kennedy could answer, her sister yanked her off the stool, and Dean swiftly took her seat, opening up his notes app on his phone, asking for all of my information.

Jude and Dylan lost interest now that the entertainment of Kennedy was gone, and they started some conversation about baseball while Nate headed back to the kitchen, leaving me to "hash out the details" with some guy I'd only met in passing.

"I'd really rather do this with Kennedy," I said, and Dean leaned back, brushing his hand over his short beard.

"I'm a contracts guy, and I know you'd like to make sure you have all your Ts crossed and Is dotted when it comes to this position since it's for your child, right?" He didn't give me time to respond. "I'm happy to outline the parameters and send it to both of you, so everyone is clear on the terms." When I didn't respond, he glanced over to where Kennedy and Taylor were in the corner, apparently arguing. "Kenny's like a sister to me, and while Nate says you're a good guy, I want to make sure this transaction is on the up-and-up. I assume you were planning on using some kind of service to hire someone?"

"Yeah, I was." Until Kennedy sauntered up with her eyes and smile, promising me she was my girl.

Dean kept his attention on his phone as he typed on it. "If there's one thing I can say for Kenny, it's that she has the biggest heart of anyone I know. She loves hard, and it's impossible not to fall in love with her right back."

That sounded a lot like a warning, but I wasn't going to be falling in love with her. She was going to be my employee, my son's nanny, and, for all intents and purposes, my roommate. Not to mention that she was twenty-four and most likely had a boyfriend or something. I was twelve years older than her and a single dad. We had nothing in common.

I was *not* going to be falling in love with her.

But then Dean lifted his gaze to me and said, "Your kid's going to love her."

And yeah, *that* made a lot more sense.

"Hopefully," I agreed, and we spoke another few minutes about payments and length of term and days off, but I wasn't paying a whole lot of attention because my eyes were on Kennedy as she argued with her sister. Kennedy, who was a few inches shorter but a lot more animated, seemed to be holding her ground, even if something about the way Taylor was speaking to Kennedy bothered me.

I could tell she was the younger sibling from the way she was both defiant yet still compliant. I was the third in a line of four boys and knew what it felt like to be unhappy about being told what to do, while still giving in because they were in charge.

At some point, Kennedy rolled her eyes and tucked her arms underneath her ample breasts, and I forced my gaze to Dean, who was saying, "All right, I'll write this all up and email you and Kenny, and you two can take it from there."

He stood and nodded to Taylor, who eyed me then said one last thing to her sister before stalking off toward the front of the bar, where Dean gathered up his guitar. Kennedy's shoulders rose and fell on a deep breath, her gaze slow to meet mine.

She strode to me, smile back in place. "Sorry about that."

I stood, which meant I was looking down at her because she was almost a foot shorter than me. And I could basically see down the dark valley between her breasts.

Son of a bitch. I was going to have to be careful to keep my eyes up above her neck.

"It's all good," I told her. "They were looking out for you. As they should." I held my cell phone out to her. "Why don't you add your number in here? Dean's going to be emailing us the contract, but until we get everything sorted, we can at least have each other's contact information."

She took my phone in her hands, tapping in her name and number with fingernails that were painted a soft orange. Once she finished, she called her own cell phone, which she pulled from her back pocket. I watched as she programmed it with my first name while laughing.

"What?" I asked.

"Nothing. I…" She bit into her lip as she slipped her phone back into her pocket. "The internet's calling you Hot Professor. I kinda wanted to put that as your name."

"Yeah. That whole…thing. It's been…terrible."

She briefly touched my arm, bending forward with a giggle. "What an absolute *tragedy*. The world thinking you're hot."

I refused to laugh with her. Even if I wanted to. It was easy to do around her. Be a little looser than I was normally.

She caught Dylan's and Jude's attention with a wave. "I'm sorry. I didn't even get your names."

"Tweedledee and Tweedledum," I said, and Kennedy stepped around me, gently brushing up against my side to get to my friends, and I was momentarily stunned by her scent and softness. My friends introduced themselves, and Nate reappeared, grinning like a fool.

"Glad it's all worked out."

Kennedy hopped a little on her toes, all cute and innocent. "Me too."

She whirled to me, eyes sparkling with emotion again, and I had a hunch this girl got whatever she wanted. A few smiles or shiny eyes threatening tears, and people probably wilted at her feet. I had, and I'd always thought I came from stronger Southie stock.

"Thank you," she said quietly, her hand back on me. "Really, you saved me."

I shrugged, not used to being such a pushover. "I think it's the other way around. You're saving me and Finn."

She grinned up at me. "We'll save each other."

Then with a squeeze to my forearm, she was off, and I was frozen staring after her. Finn had a nanny, and I… I had a beautiful and effervescent twenty-four-year-old girl about to move in to my house.

It was going to be fine.

Probably.

FOUR
LIAM

A week and a half later, I opened the front door to Kennedy and her big dark-pink rolling suitcase. Behind her were Dean and Taylor, each of them carrying two bags.

"Hi, Professor!" Kennedy chirped as I opened the door wider for them to enter.

"I didn't realize you were all coming," I said as Taylor and Dean followed Kennedy in.

Dean set down the bags he'd been holding. "Didn't think you'd mind."

I shook my head. "I don't." But I also didn't know Kennedy would arrive with so much stuff. "How is everybody?"

"Fantastic," she answered as Taylor looked me up and down.

And damn, she had the mean mug down pat.

"Can I get anyone something to drink?" I offered while staring at Taylor. When she didn't answer, I tried, "Did you want a tour of the house or…"

"Nope." Kennedy nudged her sister away. "No, they don't."

"No." Taylor finally relented. "We only came to drop Kennedy off."

Kennedy pushed Taylor toward the door. "Thanks for your

help, but I can take it all from here." She piled up all her bags then hugged Dean and Taylor. "I'll text you later."

"Love you," Taylor said.

"Love you," Kennedy replied, and Dean tossed her a look. "You too, Deanie Weenie."

"Let me know if you need anything." He playfully tugged at a lock of her hair, and she batted his hand away.

"I will."

Taylor and Dean each shook my hand, and I walked them to the door, noting how they both got into the same car. There was not another in the driveway or parked on the street.

"Where's your car?" I asked after shutting the door. "I have the second car seat. Do you want me to put it in, or do you want to do that yourself?"

She did that quick frowny-face thing again. "Uh, yeah, well…"

I braced myself. "What?"

"Remember that car accident I was in?"

I nodded.

"My car's still getting fixed."

"So you don't currently have a car?"

She shook her head.

"Kennedy," I said, my disappointed teacher voice coming out, though I didn't even know where to begin. "Why didn't you tell me?"

"I thought it would have been done by now."

"How do you expect to get Finn to and from school?"

"I looked over all the information you sent me, and his preschool is only two miles away. That's totally walking distance."

"Two miles as the crow flies," I corrected.

She ticked her head to the side. "The *what*?"

I groaned and combed my hands through my hair. "A straight line. As the crow flies means in a straight line."

"Oh. Is that, like, a history thing or something?"

"Jesus," I muttered, rubbing at the back of my neck, feeling the tension creep back up my spine and into my head. I'd need a few painkillers, stat.

"I'm sorry. I really thought I'd have it back by now, so I—"

"Stop," I told her, holding up my phone. "Where's your car at?"

"Jeff's Auto—"

"On Sutton Street?" I shook my head. "He does shit work. And never on time."

"Yeah, apparently," she mumbled, toying with her shirt nervously. "I'm sorry."

"It's fine," I said, even though it wasn't. But at least this was something I could fix.

Hopefully.

I normally texted, but this was a time-sensitive emergency that couldn't wait on Dylan getting back to me, so I called him. "Hey," I said when he picked up. "I know it's Sunday, but is there any way I could get you to look at Kennedy's car today if I get it towed to your shop?"

He grunted softly like he was moving on the other end. "What's up with it?"

I turned to Kennedy. "What's wrong with it?"

"The whole passenger side is dented," she said, moving her hand back and forth like the car was right in front of us. "And the axle is off…or something."

My irritation spiked, and I refrained from rolling my eyes as I relayed that information to Dylan. He responded by saying, "I could fix the axle, but I can't do the body work. Where does she have it?"

"Jeff's."

"That fucking guy?" He scoffed. "She's exactly the type he takes advantage of. He's gonna take his sweet time and over-charge her because she won't know the difference."

I met Kennedy's gaze. She was watching me with those big

doe eyes of her, her cheeks pink, her hands playing with her hair now. I sighed. "Yep."

"I can't help you, but I'll stop in to talk to Jeff myself. Let him know he can't fuck around with her car."

"Thanks. I appreciate it."

"No problem."

We hung up, and I slipped my cell phone into my back pocket. "Okay, Dylan's going to try to speed up the process. In the meantime, you can use my car. Since I'm at campus all day, I won't need it."

"But how will you get around?"

"Uber or something."

She waved her hand in the air, like the idea was ridiculous. "Oh no. You keep your car."

"Then how will *you* get around?"

She shrugged. "The bus."

"Kennedy," I started, attempting to soften my voice from the razor-sharp point it was at now, "while I appreciate you trying to make this work on your own, that's not safe or feasible. I'll contact my insurance and add you as a temporary driver."

"You don't have to do that."

"Yes. I do. I should have asked before if you had reliable transportation." But it was too late now. At least the background check came back clean. "We'll get it sorted out."

She worried her bottom lip between her teeth. "Are you sure? I don't want to inconvenience you or anything."

She absolutely was inconveniencing me, but I didn't like how anxious she seemed.

"My main concern is Finn's safety. And yours, of course," I added as an afterthought, and her answering smile was tepid at best.

"Okay. Thank you."

"Let me show you to your room so you can get settled. Finn's still napping, so I figured we could go over his schedule."

She grinned, the sun coming out again, and grabbed hold of

her suitcase to follow me upstairs. "I really appreciate you doing all this. Not just for the car, but for giving me a chance."

I nodded but didn't reply otherwise. My house was a bi-level with two smaller sets of steps leading to the top floor, and when Kennedy struggled with her suitcase on the carpet, I nudged her gently out of the way. "Let me help you."

I heaved it up the staircase. "What do you have packed in here? Bricks? Jesus."

"No bricks or Jesus packed in there."

I gave in to a small smile and set down her suitcase. "This is your room," I said, waving my hand to the plain bedroom. "I figured it might be a little…"

"It's perfect." She dragged her luggage inside and sat on the bed, kicking her legs.

I hadn't painted the walls or anything, and she was a rainbow bursting through a gray cloud with her makeup and jewelry, not to mention her colorful clothes. "You can decorate or whatever you want. I want you to feel at home here."

She stood and struggled to lift her suitcase onto the bed, so I helped her. "Do you want me to get the rest of your bags?"

"You don't have to. I can do it."

"Can you?" It was a serious question. She was only a few inches over five feet, and I doubted she had much wiggle room in those dark jeans that were basically a second skin. I imagined her dragging each bag upstairs.

As if she could see inside my head, she tried on an angry face, but it melted into a giggle. "No, actually. My weightlifting regimen consists of my hair dryer and brush."

When I quirked my brow, she tossed her sleek dark hair over her shoulder. "It's a workout to tame this mass." Then she unzipped her suitcase and pulled out a large orange hair dryer and a bunch of attachments, along with a few brushes. They looked professional-grade. "Try holding your arms up in the air for twenty minutes while you dry and curl two feet of hair."

I tipped my head to the side, giving up the impossible task of remaining stoic around her. "Yeah? You got muscle?"

She tossed down her hair tools and lifted her arms, flexing the little biceps she had. I shook my head in amusement, and she shrugged, motioning her hands down the length of her body, her leg extended out to the side, posing. "It's okay to admit you're jealous."

My smile faded, and I cleared my throat, as I forced my attention up from where it hovered around her thighs. They were thick and lush, and I blinked away the picture of my fingers pressed into her soft skin there.

I couldn't fantasize about Finn's nanny that way.

"Yeah, so…" I pointed to the room across the hall. "You and Finn will share a bathroom. I have one in my room too, and there's a half bath downstairs next to the laundry closet."

"Do you need help with laundry?" she asked, unpacking her things from her suitcase, starting with clothes, which she placed into the empty drawers of the chest by the window.

"Please. That would be really great."

"And what about cleaning?"

"I have someone come in once a month for a deep cleaning, but it's the day-to-day stuff that I feel like I can't catch up on."

"I noticed your dining room table."

"Yeah." It currently held dirty dishes that were I didn't know how old, my laptop and charger, a bunch of random puzzle pieces, and glitter slime. Because some parent in Finn's preschool class apparently hated the rest of us and gave each kid glitter slime for their daughter's birthday. "I need help tidying up."

She smiled over her shoulder as she shut the drawer. "Got it."

"I don't expect you to—"

A sharp cry from Finn's room interrupted me, and I checked the time on my watch. He should have still been asleep for another half hour or so.

"Et-Et-Et-Et!"

I held my hand up to Kennedy, half apology-half wince, then headed into the next room. With his hands wrapped around the bars at the end of his toddler bed, my son jumped up and down like a tiny prisoner hopped up on sugar.

"Guy, why aren't you asleep?"

"Et!"

"Get," I corrected him. "Get me up, please."

I put his glasses on him and slung him to my side. "I want you to meet someone who's gonna help take care of you. Her name's Kennedy."

As we rounded the door of her room, she finished hanging something in the closet then pivoted to us, her face lighting up.

"Finn, this is Kennedy. Kennedy, this is my son, Finn."

She closed the distance between us, so close I got a good whiff of her sugar-and-flowers scent. With our height difference, she and Finn were nearly eye to eye.

"Hi, Finn. I like your T-shirt."

He patted his shirt then held his hand out to Kennedy, and she stepped close enough that he could pat her shirt too. It was loose-fitting with frilly sleeves and tassels on the front, where it gaped a bit, displaying just enough of her cleavage that I had to keep my head up so I wasn't staring down at her tits.

"You like my shirt too?" she asked. "I wore it today because purple's my favorite color. What's your favorite color?"

Finn didn't answer. Merely flopped around until I put him down. Then he ran around what was now Kennedy's bedroom, knocking over a floor lamp.

She gasped and kneeled on the floor at Finn's side, but he popped back up and took off again.

"Like a wild animal," I mumbled and righted the lamp before helping her to stand.

"I Googled that Tasmanian Devil cartoon you mentioned, and I see what you mean."

I ignored that reminder of how young she was—so young

she had to Google the Tasmanian Devil—and gestured to my son. "Uncanny, right?"

She laughed, and I explained, "He doesn't talk much. When he does, most of it won't make sense to you until you start to understand his vernacular. He's in weekly speech therapy. Or, I should say, it's supposed to be weekly, but with how everything's been going lately, I haven't been able to keep up with it very well. Which is why you're here."

"Does he sign?"

"Like ASL?" I asked, and when she nodded, I said, "No. Why? Do you?"

"I've picked up a few words here and there, but I know a lot of kids who struggle verbally sometimes do really well communicating with ASL."

"It's never something we tried."

"Well..." She held her hand out to Finn. "Want to show me around your house?"

He took her hand and pulled her into the hallway.

"You don't have to do anything tonight," I told her, following them downstairs. "You don't officially start until tomorrow. I figured you'd want to get settled."

"I'm settled enough. Besides, there are so many things I want to know. Right, Finn?"

When we landed in the living room, she plopped down in the middle of the mess with my son and righted his glasses. "I need to know so much about you. Like your favorite animal and color and toy. So much we have to talk about, huh?"

Finn didn't answer, of course, but he did hand her a stuffed horse while he held a plastic zebra.

"Ooh, you want to play zoo? I used to love going to the zoo when I was a kid."

I watched them for a few moments, Kennedy rambling sweetly while Finn played silently, and I found myself grinning.

Maybe this would work out after all.

Lack of transportation, notwithstanding.

FIVE
KENNEDY

Finn was a wild animal. And an amazing little boy. Funny and full of energy, he never spent more than a few minutes on one thing before he was on to the next. I knew I'd have my hands full with him and that I'd really have to get creative in finding ways to keep him in line and on track, while still allowing him freedom to expend all that horsepower.

Liam had ordered pizza for dinner, and we'd sat at the small kitchen table, chatting a bit about what exactly had happened with that viral video. He'd said he had prepared for a long time and that he was really disappointed those ten seconds of bad timing took over the whole interview. I'd told him the upside was he looked great and now the country knew he was a wonderful and patient father. He'd frowned at me and explained the downside, that it apparently wasn't great for an academic to have his face plastered everywhere for being hot as opposed to being smart.

A shame. Because he had a great face.

Prior to moving in, I had spent a good amount of time Googling Liam and learned he'd grown up in Boston and attended American University in DC for undergrad then received his PhD from the University of Pennsylvania. I was never big on academics, but if my teachers had looked and sounded like Liam O'Neil, I might have been more interested.

He was tall, over six feet, with a head of caramel-colored curls and blue eyes that could be both inquisitive and kind. Like he was interested in knowing everything about the world around him, but he also didn't hold grudges. He was slow to smile, so when he did, his mouth would pull lazily at the right corner until his lips finally parted, revealing two rows of perfect teeth. I'd had braces as a kid, and even my teeth weren't that straight.

I could only conclude he had really good genes.

Finn was dark-haired but had a smile like his dad, slightly crooked and so addictive. I wondered what his mother was like —and what the story was with her and Liam, although I didn't think I knew him well enough yet to ask. I kept my questions to Finn and my new job, which I believed I could really excel at, despite my lack of experience.

I knew Liam had taken a chance by hiring me, and I didn't want to let him down. Let alone myself.

So when he called my name in that *tone*, I immediately went on high alert. This voice let me know that underneath that charming and handsome professor front, he was stone.

I'd only been on the job for a few hours, and already, I was in trouble.

"I need to talk to you," he said from the top of the first staircase, his eyebrows narrowed, his hands on his trim hips.

"Okay." I smiled at Finn and made sure he was occupied with jamming on a plastic drum set. I could feel Liam's sharp gaze on me as I took my time crossing the living room and up the six steps to where the kitchen and dining room were laid out with the second set of steps up to the top floor. That was where Liam stood, holding an orange prescription bottle.

My prescription bottle.

"I was double-checking that there were enough towels in your bathroom when I saw multiple bottles around the sink." He held the one in his hand out toward me. "Want to explain what these are and why you have them around my three-year-old's sink, where he can reach them? Open them?"

His jaw was tight with so much tension in his body, I reflexively backed up, my heels hanging off the edge of the step, and I fell backward. He lunged for me at the same time I caught myself with my hand on the railing.

"Christ almighty," he murmured. "You okay?"

"Yeah. Sorry."

He exhaled harshly and wrapped his hand around my elbow to pull me into the dining room, where we could still clearly see Finn banging around downstairs. Then he set the pill bottle on the table. Like it was more evidence of my disqualifications for this job. "I need you to explain."

"I have epilepsy," I said quietly.

I swore I saw pity flash in his eyes before they hardened again. "You have epilepsy? As in seizures? Why am I just now learning you have seizures?"

My shoulders had unconsciously hiked up to my ears, and I reminded myself to drop them. "I didn't intentionally keep it from you, but it never came up."

"Like your car?"

"I, well—"

"You didn't think to mention you had a serious medical condition before accepting a job looking after a toddler?" he snapped and lifted his hand, causing me to flinch instinctively, and he froze. "Are you— I'm sorry. I didn't mean to scare you."

He stepped back from me, and I shook my head, forcing a smile past my embarrassment and shame. Embarrassed that I couldn't seem to get on the right foot to start this new job, and ashamed that I was actually afraid of him. Even for only a moment. "It's okay."

"It's not," he said. "I apologize for raising my voice. It's not okay." Then he lifted his hand once again and raked his fingers through his hair. *That* was what he'd meant to do, brush his hand through his hair. "I'm really anxious about all of this. About my work and the aftermath of the video and now this..." He circled his hand, pointing to Finn, me, and then himself. "It's been a big adjustment with Tessa away, and I feel like I'm failing. I—" He huffed out a sound of irritation. "I don't fail. Ever."

I chanced a step closer to him. With his chin down, his hands laced together at the back of his neck, it was obvious he'd been put through the wringer. Like he needed a week's worth of good sleep to begin to recover. In an attempt to lighten the mood, I offered, "I fail all the time."

He raised his head, eyeing me, the hint of a smile at the corner of his mouth. The tension easing. "That's supposed to make me feel better?"

I shrugged. "You can't control everything. I learned that lesson pretty early, so it's easy to forget I'm supposed to be upset when I fail at something. Even more when I quit."

He sat on the edge of the round dining table, pushing the random items aside to make room. "You've quit a lot?"

"I wouldn't say *a lot*, but I was in the 'if it doesn't bring you joy, get rid of it' camp long before it became popular. When you could possibly black out at any moment, it kinda forces you to reevaluate things."

"You're not making me feel any better about this." He rubbed the heels of his palms against his forehead as if I was giving him a headache, and I felt terrible that I was disappointing him. "How can I trust you to be with Finn? What if you have a seizure around him? What if you have a seizure while you're driving?"

I sat on the table next to him, so close I could lean my head on his shoulder if I wanted. Not that I wanted to. Or could. He was my boss. And this was a serious conversation. "It's managed with the medication. I haven't had a seizure in a long time."

"How long?"

I tipped my head back, doing the math. "Three years."

"But you still could have one now?" he asked, though it sounded more like an accusation.

I'd spent the last decade of my life on a pendulum. First, living life as a shell of myself, then taking too many risks. I'd swung from fear to rebellion, and I was ready to find balance. To find what made me happy and to learn what I was good at. I'd never given myself the opportunity, and now that I had it, I wouldn't let it go.

I met his steady gaze. "You don't need to worry about me caring for Finn. I would never do anything to put him in danger."

"But I need to worry about you," he said, and it was a punch in the gut.

"You don't."

"What do I do if you have a seizure?"

"I won't have one," I said, but he only shook his head.

"You're living in my house. I need to know what I should do if you have one."

I stared down at my feet. "Put me on my side and make sure I'm not near anything that I could hurt myself with. Nothing sharp, nothing I could fall off, or near water."

"Okay," he said quietly. "And then?"

"And then I eventually wake back up. They've never lasted all that long. Usually less than a minute."

"What would be the procedure if you have a seizure and Finn's the only one around?"

"That won't happen."

"Humor me," he said with a scowl.

I thought for a minute. "I guess I could make up a chart for emergencies. It would probably be good to have one anyway. Like how to dial 9-1-1."

"That's a good idea. There's a first aid kit under the sink in the kitchen and one in every bathroom."

"But it's a really, *really* slim possibility I'll have a seizure, even slimmer that he's the only one around when it happens."

Liam still appeared unconvinced, so I tried again. "I wanted this job because I knew I was capable of it. Please, give me time to prove I am."

He considered me for a few seconds and gave in with a terse nod. "Fine. But no more surprises, all right? I need to know I can trust you with my son. And you need to put the pills somewhere Finn can't get to them."

"Right. Of course. And no more surprises. I promise." When I crossed the tip of my index finger over my chest, his gaze drifted down then he immediately blinked away. That was when I realized I'd accidentally shifted my peasant top over a bit, so my cleavage was on display.

He stood. "I, um, I'm gonna get Finn down to sleep and then try to get some work done, so…"

I gestured vaguely to the kitchen. "I'll clean up a bit in here."

He made his way downstairs, calling, "Come on, guy, time for a bath."

"No!"

"Yes."

"No!"

"Yes." Liam picked up Finn and tossed him over his shoulder. "Like a sack of lobsters."

I bit back my laugh at his sudden accent on "lobsters" and waved to Finn as they passed me to head upstairs. "Night night!"

I spent about twenty minutes cleaning up the kitchen, learning where everything was in the cabinets, and taking stock of the food situation before scrolling through my social media while nibbling on animal crackers. Although I loved to cook, I had always lived with other people and was self-conscious about asking to take over. But since that was expected here, I found a few ideas for dinners and jotted down a grocery list while quiet voices upstairs filtered down to me.

At one point, when I figured Finn was supposed to be in bed, I heard a lot of quick stomps, and I smiled to myself, guessing he was dancing or trying to sneak out of bed. Then, finally, about a half hour later, Liam reappeared. "He's asleep. I'll be working in the dining room."

"Will I wake him up if I go upstairs and in the bathroom?"

"No." He waved his hand. "He's got a sound machine and music on. He won't hear a thing. The only time he's quiet and still is when he's asleep."

"Okay, then I'll be upstairs."

He sat down at the dining room table, shifting his laptop around toys and clothes and mail. I would definitely need to come up with some kind of chores system. For myself and these two messy boys I lived with now.

"G'night," he said, his attention already on his computer.

"Night."

Upstairs, I finished putting all my things away and crept to the bathroom. Just in case.

I swallowed down my pills, put them in the closet on the top shelf, and changed into my pajamas. Even though it was still early, I wasn't comfortable enough to help myself to hanging out downstairs, especially after our little confrontation. It seemed like everything was okay, but I didn't want to push my luck. I needed this job, and I really liked Finn, so instead of stationing myself in front of the television in the living room, I did some research to see what kinds of local activities there were to do with toddlers.

After texting a bit with Taylor, I called our mom.

"Kenny!" she answered. I usually FaceTimed with her, but she was loud, and I didn't want her voice carrying. "How are you? How's the new job?"

"I'm good. It's good."

"Yeah?"

"Mm-hmm. How's it going with you? I saw the photo you posted this morning. I like your new hair color." She lived in Las Vegas with her professional-poker-playing boyfriend, and it was easier to talk to my mom about insignificant things. Taylor was the one I had serious conversations with. Which was exactly why I was going to be communicating strictly through text messages for at least the next week, or else she'd be a helicopter-sister.

"Thanks," Mom said. "I wanted to be more like you."

My mom and I were basically twins, in personality and appearance. Both of us wore our emotions on our sleeves and were sometimes a bit flighty—I was confident enough in myself to admit that. But I'd also inherited my appearance from my mother, what we affectionately called Italian grandma chic. Short, squat, and a mustache we had to wax. Taylor, on the other hand, with her slender figure and tall height, took after our father.

"I can't believe you cut it," I said, referring to how my mother had always had long hair, almost down to her waist. Now it was above her shoulders.

"I'm too old for long hair."

"You're not too old for long hair. Who told you that?"

"Society," she said with a laugh.

"Society's stupid. Wear your hair long. Besides, you're not even sixty yet."

"Speaking of. I was thinking you and your sister should come out here for Thanksgiving. It's Duke's birthday, so I thought we could go out for a big dinner. He's turning fifty this year."

Though it wasn't a big difference in age, my mom was older than Duke. I often teased her about being a cougar, although I couldn't tonight. Not when she accidentally brought my focus back to my boss and the crappy first impression I'd made today.

"Um, yeah, maybe. I'll have to work it out with Liam. We haven't discussed holidays."

"I haven't seen my babies in so long. I miss you."

"I miss you too."

"Text me tomorrow and let me know how everything is going, okay? I gotta run. Duke just got home.

"Okay. Bye, Mom. Love you."

"Love you so much, babe. Talk later."

After we hung up, I stared at my cell phone, thinking about the last time my sister and I were both with our mom at the same time. It had been a while, and it would be nice for all of us to be in one place again, though I'd probably have to drag Taylor there by her hair.

I lay in bed a bit, tagging Dean in posts for me to win hair and makeup products because I knew it annoyed him, then eventually turned off the light and settled into bed with my sleep podcast. But not even the man with the soothing English accent, reading a bedtime story about walking through a meadow, could help me sleep.

I tossed and turned, unable to shut off my brain and forget about how Liam doubted my abilities. I didn't like disappointing people and especially didn't like being a burden. I was supposed to be making things easier on him, but I was adding to the weight he already carried.

In the short time I'd known him, it was clear Liam was a devoted dad, and when he'd confessed he felt like he was failing, my heart broke for him. He was anything but a failure, and I would do whatever I could to help him.

Rolling over yet again, I stared up at the ceiling in the dark and sang softly to myself. But as I hit the chorus of "Popular" from *Wicked*, I heard music coming from somewhere, pounding drums and a fast guitar. I waited for it to go away, thinking it might have been a car, and when it didn't pass, I waited another minute before I got out of bed to peek through the window. There was no one outside, and it didn't sound like it was coming from any other house on the street.

I tiptoed out of my room and pressed my ear against Finn's bedroom door. Besides the white noise and instrumental lullabies playing, there was no sign he was awake. I supposed he really did sleep through anything.

But I wondered if Liam could hear it and if it was bothering him. Although, when I checked, the dining room and kitchen were both empty. I followed the music, AC/DC's "Back in Black," but it wasn't only the song that I heard now. There was also a series of dull thuds.

Curious, I made my way to the bottom floor and stopped midway down the wooden staircase, my attention coasting around the mostly unfinished basement.

My mouth fell open at the sight before me. Liam was shirtless with a sheen of sweat covering his back and arms as he unleashed a barrage of punches on the large black bag hanging from the ceiling. I couldn't look away from the power and grace of his movements, the way his muscles flexed with each swing, making the intricate design of a family crest ripple along his shoulder blade. When he shifted to the right, I spotted another tattoo, this one lower on the side of his ribs. Two tiny footprints and "Finn" below it in cursive.

I hadn't realized I'd sunk down to the step until Liam spun, evidently having seen me out of the corner of his eye. Surprise flashed across his features, and he slowly lowered his fists, but it was a long time before I could haul my gaze up to his face.

Looking *respectfully*, I took in the ladder of muscle along his abdomen and another tattoo. This one of an infinity symbol over his heart. He had light-brown chest hair sprinkled across his defined pectoral muscles, which narrowed to a line down the middle of his stomach, eventually sinking below his blue shorts. And dear God in heaven, he had those deep grooves at his hips.

The music shut off, and I shot my attention up to where Liam had his hand lifted, aiming a tiny remote control at the speaker in the corner. His chest still heaved with his breathing, and he swiped the back of his wrapped-up hand over his mouth. "Everything okay?"

I forced my mouth closed. "Mm-hmm."

"Kennedy."

I, once again, zipped my gaze up from where it'd been tracing his biceps and the veins in his forearms. "Yeah. Hi."

I swore a look of satisfaction crossed his features before they shuttered.

My cheeks flushed with embarrassment. "Sorry. I heard the music and…"

He sniffed and wiped his face with his forearm, propping his other hand on his hip, not at all detracting from his level of hotness. If the internet knew the hot daddy professor was also a hot boxer, it would collectively lose its mind.

"I didn't wake you, did I?" he asked, and I shook my head.

"Couldn't sleep."

"I usually work out down here at night."

"It's after eleven," I said. "I figured you'd be asleep by now."

"It's the only time I get." He took a step closer to me, and I made sure to keep my eyes on his.

Because I was his son's nanny. I couldn't be attracted to him. That was, like, rule number one in the nanny handbook.

If there was a nanny handbook.

"Maybe now that I'm here, you'll be able to find a different time."

He shrugged. "I don't mind. I like tiring myself out before bed. Helps me relax."

"Yeah. Right." I absolutely did not think about other ways he could tire himself out. "That makes sense." I motioned to him, still walking toward me on the steps. Him in only shorts, sneakers, and hand wraps. Me in gray cotton pants and a Minnie Mouse T-shirt with no bra. "I didn't expect…"

He challenged me to finish that sentence. "What?"

"For you to be like…"

He was outright grinning now, standing next to me, his fingers on the edge of the step my feet were on. I had the height advantage here, and he had to tip his head back to meet my gaze. "Like what, Kennedy?"

"You know…"

He shook his head. "I don't."

I peevishly crossed my arms. "I didn't expect you to look like that under your old-man sweaters."

He huffed. "They are *not* old-man sweaters."

"Okay, Mr. Rogers." I slanted my eyes to him, and he laughed.

"You know who Mr. Rogers is, but you don't know the Tasmanian Devil?"

"Everyone knows Mr. Rogers."

He flicked his gaze over me so quickly I wasn't even sure he was aware he did it. Then he backed up two paces. "You're so young, I don't know where your pop culture references start."

"I'm not *that* young. I'm twenty-four."

He faced his punching bag again. "Twelve years younger than me."

And I wasn't sure why that seemed to bother him so much.

"I'll leave you to it," I said and stood as he jerked his chin in acknowledgment of my words. A moment later, his music was back on, and I shuffled to my room with visions of Liam boxing in my head.

SIX
KENNEDY

My first week on the job was great. I met up with Finn's preschool teachers to introduce myself, scheduled appointments with the speech therapist, and signed him up for a music class since he loved to bang around so much. I'd even had my car returned to me in top condition because of whatever Dylan had said to Jeff. I liked to think the grumpy-looking mechanic went in there like a mafia boss and threatened to break kneecaps. Though Liam, always the voice of reason, assured me that definitely did not happen.

We had slipped into a good routine, Liam and I. He came home between five and six, depending on what he had to do, and by then, dinner was ready. We'd all eat together, and then I'd have the night off to do what I wanted, which up until tonight had been lazing around. But I had plans to meet up with friends for drinks later.

The front door opened, and Finn lifted his gaze from where he'd been studiously watching me paint his nails. His mouth opened wide, eyes curious.

"That must be your daddy," I said, and I could tell he wanted to race out of the chair, but I shook my head. "The timer didn't go off yet."

He glanced at the red circle on my phone and then to me. "No off et."

"Not off yet," I corrected with a smile. "Here. Go like this." I softly blew over his nails, and he did the same, even as I heard Liam's muffled steps on the carpet behind me.

A moment later, he announced himself. "What's going on here?"

Finn hopped around on his chair, holding his hands up. "Ook! Ook!"

"Careful, babes," I told him. "You don't want to get polish everywhere."

Liam held Finn's hands up to get a look at them. "Playing nail salon for real, huh?" Liam kissed his son's head. "I like that purple."

Even though I should have been used to it by now, every time I witnessed Liam's ease as a dad and his healthy masculinity, my heart fluttered. I didn't know very many men, and of those few, not a whole lot of them were comfortable in themselves or progressive in their attitudes. There was Dean, but he was, like, one in a million.

Though, I supposed, Liam made two.

"He saw me doing my nails and wanted his done too," I explained. "I set the timer and told him he couldn't move until it went off."

Liam shucked off his blazer and slouched into the chair next to his son at the dining room table. "That's a good way to keep him still. Huh, guy?"

I liked when he called Finn guy. A hint of his natural accent lacing the single syllable.

I bent, blowing air over Finn's nails. "Almost done. Twenty more seconds." Finn sat up, craning his neck to watch the timer count down, so I counted out loud. "Eighteen, seventeen, sixteen..."

The corner of Liam's mouth rose, and my cheeks heated.

"His speech therapist said we need to narrate Finn's day. I was—"

"No, you're good." Liam leaned forward, his eyes on my cell phone, and then he joined me. "Ten, nine, eight, seven…"

Together, we counted down until the timer went off, and Finn leaped from the chair, running in a circle around the dining table as if he needed to stretch his legs before throwing himself at his dad, who caught him.

"I always have trouble with that," Liam said, "the narration thing. I'm not generally a talkative person, and it's hard to know what to say."

"Don't worry." I waved my hand. "I do enough talking for the both of us."

"Yeah. I got that."

I smiled and started to put the nail polish away, but Finn pushed Liam's hand toward me. "You!"

"Me what?" Liam asked.

He grabbed at my polish. "You!"

"You want me to paint my nails?"

He nodded, and Liam raised his gaze to mine in silent question.

"I am a professional," I said with a flip of my hair, which earned a lazy smile.

"Okay." He placed both of his hands flat on the table, fingers splayed. "Do your worst."

I pushed my container of polishes to Finn. "What color should Daddy get?"

He dug through, finding a bright blue, and I took it from him. "Nice choice."

Finn sat in his father's lap as I painted Liam's nails, both of their heads bent at the same angle, watching like it was the most fascinating thing they'd ever seen.

"I'm only gonna do one coat," I told Liam, who remained silent, which made me laugh.

That was when he slanted his gaze to me. "What?"

"It's funny. The two of you," I said with a tilt of my chin. "You're both so cute together."

Finn took the opportunity to squeeze his dad's cheeks. In return, Liam pretended to bite at his son's shoulder until Finn shrieked in laughter and took off toward the living room, leaving me to finish painting Liam's nails alone.

His fingers were long with atrocious nail beds. "You have to stop biting your nails."

"How do you know I bite my nails?"

I dragged the pad of my thumb over the jagged and reddened nail of his middle finger. "Not good, Professor." Then I tapped his callused knuckles. "I'm sure it splits a lot if you're boxing. Does it bother you?"

He lifted one shoulder, his eyes still on my hands as I finished up with the polish.

"I'm not sure you're going to impress anybody with these dry hands."

That got his attention. He stared at me as I put the cap back on the bottle and set it down. "It's not my hands I hope to impress people with."

I playfully rolled my eyes. "I'm sure everybody else loves your big brain. But I like a guy with nice hands."

It took me a moment to realize what I'd said, but before I could take it back, he smiled, the quirk of his lips walking a fine line between humor and flirtation. "I don't impress you?"

I was stunned into silence as the air between us crackled, and since the earth didn't open up and swallow me whole, it took me a long time to recover. "I-I didn't mean—"

"What should I put on my hands?"

"Hm?"

"What should I put on my hands so they aren't dry?"

"I, uh…" I dropped my gaze to the table, where he tapped his thumbs a few times. "I have some good lotion if you want."

"Yeah. I'll try it."

Without looking at him, I slunk away from the table,

pretending like I wasn't tingling everywhere from a combination of mortification and temptation.

I couldn't be attracted to him.

Absolutely not.

Rule number one.

I grabbed my CeraVe lotion and returned to the dining room table, where Liam was checking out his new nails. I set the bottle down in front of him, and he squirted some into his palm then rubbed his hands together, focusing on his knuckles before holding them out to me. "Better?"

When I didn't move, he arched his brow, like he really did need my approval. Wrapping one hand around his wrist, I dragged the pads of my fingers over his knuckles. "Better. You keep using that and Finn's mom should be very happy when she comes back from Antarctica."

This time, he frowned. "Finn's mom?"

"Yeah, I figured… Are you two not together?"

"No."

The awkward silence that descended was like that time in cosmetology school when Jade ended up turning her client's hair pink by accident and everyone was staring, afraid to say anything to make it worse.

Liam eventually cleared his throat. "Tessa and I knew each other for a long time before we started dating. It wasn't anything serious, and by the time she found out she was pregnant, we were both sure we were better as friends."

It was my turn to clear my throat. "So, you and Tessa are… friends?"

"Yeah. Great friends." The corner of his mouth kicked up as he tugged at his sweater, this one thin and light green. "We have to be to make sure we're doing right by Finn."

At a loss for what to say, I went with, "That's really mature."

As I began packing up my nail polish, Liam leaned forward, locking his fingers together, eyeing me seriously. I imagined he did that a lot when speaking to students. "Are we going to talk about why you aren't driving?"

I paused. "What?"

"Your car hasn't left the spot it was parked in since Wednesday night."

"How do you know?"

"I have two working eyes."

Lost for an explanation that didn't make me sound unreliable, I sputtered out a few syllables. "I...uh... Well, the thing... um..."

I was already a nervous driver to begin with, and ever since the accident, thinking about getting behind the wheel again made me a tad nauseous. Even though Liam had left me his car for Monday and Tuesday, I didn't use it, instead sticking Finn in the stroller to walk him to and from school. It was good exercise, and I was learning my new neighborhood. Plus, it gave Finn and me time to explore nature. He was a big fan of collecting blades of grass.

I didn't think anything of continuing our little jaunts. But I'd never guessed Liam would notice I never actually moved my car.

"Kennedy, I need you to talk to me."

I swallowed down my trepidation and started at the beginning. "I was fourteen when I had my first seizure. I have juvenile myoclonic epilepsy, and it was a complete surprise when it happened. It was close to Christmas, and my sister was home from college. Our mom was out, and I was in the kitchen getting a drink. The next thing I knew, I woke up in a pool of blood." With my gaze down, I couldn't see him, but I heard his audible intake of breath. "I'd dropped the glass I'd been holding and inadvertently cut my arm when I fell. I even peed myself at some point. I was confused, in pain, terrified...embarrassed."

I finally raised my head, lingering emotions of that night clogging my throat.

Liam moved seats so he was next to me, though he kept his

hands to himself. But his being nearer helped. "What happened?"

"My sister called 9-1-1, and I was in the hospital for a couple days until all the tests were run and my diagnosis was sorted. Then it was a lot of appointments with neurologists and years of experimenting with medication for the right combination."

"You're on the right combination now?" he asked, and I wagged my head side to side.

"It's hard because everyone's body is constantly changing, which affects how they respond to meds. The last two or three years have been in flux for me, and some of the pills don't have very nice side effects. Like this one that they recently changed because studies have shown it causes heart problems. And there was one I was on in high school that made me depressed." I heaved a sigh. "It's hard."

"I'm sorry," Liam said, his knee resting against mine.

"I'm used to it."

"Still sucks, though."

I nodded, even as it was awkward to describe my medical condition to the man who entrusted me with his son. I was supposed to be impressing him, not making him more suspicious. "I've mostly gotten over my fear of blacking out and not waking up. But really—" I curled my hand around his forearm because I needed him to believe me "—I haven't had a seizure in so long. It won't be an issue. It won't affect my job."

He blew out a small, annoyed puff of air between his lips, and I both hated and loved that irritated little breath. Because I didn't *want* to annoy him, but it also felt the tiniest bit thrilling to earn that stern look from him. Especially when he said, "This past week has been one of the best weeks in recent memory, and it's because I'm not stressed and anxious over Finn. You're doing great. But I am worried about *you*."

I pretended I wasn't at all affected by that. "I'm fine."

"Then why aren't you driving?" When I refused to answer, he shifted closer, looming over me. "Kennedy."

I gave in with a shrug. "Even though I am *perfectly* fine now, it's hard to ignore the little voice of fear in the back of my head. I didn't get my license until I was twenty, and I'm a nervous driver. I get, like…" I shook my hands, trying to think of the word for whenever I attempted to merge on the highway. "It's nerve-racking for me to begin with, and ever since the accident, I haven't been able to talk myself into driving again."

Liam squinted, sucking his lips between his teeth. A habit, I'd learned, that he had when in deep thought.

After a moment, he cleared his throat then met my gaze. "What I said to you on Sunday, about not trusting you to drive with Finn, I'm sure that made it worse, and I'm sorry."

I couldn't lie and tell him it didn't add to my hesitation, so instead, I offered him a small smile. "Thank you. I appreciate that."

"And I want to go driving with you this weekend. You can practice with Finn and me in the car. I want you to be comfortable."

"No, I don't—"

"I could bribe you like Finn." He squinted, assessing me. "For every four hours of practice, I'll buy you something special."

"Ooh, Professor," I said, laughing. "You don't know what you just promised."

"Has to be under five dollars."

I leaned into him, my chin in my hands, both of my knees on the inside of his. "You've never been to Ulta before, have you? There's quite a bit you can find for under five dollars."

"What's Ulta?"

I stood up, slapping him on his unsuspectingly muscular shoulder, and grinned. "You'll find out tomorrow. But I have to go get changed now. Dinner's on the stove. It's pasta fagioli, my mom's recipe. Finn tried a few bites of it, but I'm sure he'll want snacks later."

"Thanks," he said and turned to call for Finn while I skipped upstairs.

Two hours later, I had on my old reliable: sky-high nude heels, my favorite pair of jeans, and a black top that showed off the girls. I slipped my purse over my shoulder and texted my friend.

Liam had already put Finn to bed. I knew because they'd knocked on my bedroom door about an hour ago. Finn didn't want to go to sleep without a hug from me, and I'd melted into a puddle, which took about twenty minutes to recover from.

When I finally made it downstairs to the living room, I needed to pick my jaw up off the floor *yet again*. Liam "hot daddy professor who secretly boxed and had tattoos" was lying there on the couch in gray sweatpants, a worn T-shirt, and wire-rimmed glasses.

It was like he'd researched all the things heterosexual women loved and set out to accomplish them one by one.

But this time, he didn't notice how I was staring. Because he was staring too.

Starting at my feet, his gaze crawled up my legs, hovering somewhere below my waist before journeying up for a long look at my breasts—I mean, I didn't wear this shirt for people *not* to notice them—then finally, he met my eyes. The tops of his cheeks were ruddy, and he shifted on the couch, crossing his legs at the ankles.

"Where are you headed?" he asked after a while.

"Drinks with my friends."

"In that?"

"Yeah." I glanced down at myself. "Why?"

"Won't you be cold?"

I laughed. He didn't.

My shirt was deceptively sexy. From the back, it looked like a loose T-shirt, but the cowl neckline drooped low in the front, held together by one tiny strip of material. It was a pain to tape my boobs up, but this shirt had a 100% success rate.

"You don't need a cardigan or something?" he asked, and I shook my head.

"No, Mr. Rogers, I'll be okay."

He shook his head, mumbling something I didn't catch.

"It's not that cold out," I told him, but he ignored me.

"Are you driving?" he asked.

"No, my friend's picking me up."

He stood, closing the distance between us. "Let me know if you need a ride home."

"Why?" I asked with a laugh, absently placing my hand on his chest. "You aren't going to wake up Finn to put him in the car."

"I would if I had to."

"You won't," I said, gently pushing back, but he didn't budge. He merely stood there, barely a few inches of space between us, his eyes burning a trail across my face and my hand on his hard chest.

"Are you coming home tonight?" he asked, and I wasn't sure if it was his soft voice, the word *home*, or that it was Liam questioning me, but whatever it was made my insides warm.

I normally would have balked at being so fussed over by anyone else, though I indulged in his overprotectiveness. Smiling, I moved my hand to squeeze his arm. "I'm coming home tonight."

My cell phone vibrated with a text, and after seeing that my friend was outside, I backed away from him. "I gotta go."

He followed me to the front door. "Have fun."

"Don't wait up," I said, yet as I walked to the car, I glanced over my shoulder to find him watching me.

And I hoped he would wait up.

SEVEN
LIAM

"Don't forget your turn signal," I reminded Kennedy as she switched lanes.

She threw me a look of exasperation, and if I hadn't spent this last week getting to know her, I would've thought she was actually angry. But I was starting to believe under all the hair and makeup, she was an angel in disguise. And too damn sweet for her own good.

I had yet to see her lose her patience. Even when Finn spilled juice all over the floor after she'd repeatedly told him to keep it on the table. Or with me, when I'd put her on the spot multiple times. Instead, she had smiled and stood up for herself, even if it came with an apology.

She apologized a lot. Too often.

Last night, as she'd told me about her diagnosis, I couldn't help but think I had completely underestimated her. I had assumed she was immature and irresponsible, and it might have been true to a *very small* extent, but she'd been living with a black cloud over her for the last decade. She lived with fear and uncertainty every day, yet she remained strong and confident. Or, she was faking it well enough to walk up to a stranger at a bar and convince him to offer her a job. To top it all off, she was sincere about her good attributes and unselfconscious about her faults. It was refreshing to deal with someone so honest.

Whatever had been plaguing her, either about her disease or things holding her back in the past, she was ready to move on from it.

And I was inexplicably proud.

"You're worse than a driving instructor," she said, playfully scolding me. "You're here for moral support, not backseat driving."

"Technically, it would be passenger-seat driving."

She pressed her pink lips together, a valiant fight with her smile. Which she eventually lost. I was glad of it.

"Whatever you say, Professor," she murmured, glancing to the rearview mirror. Finn was strapped in his car seat, fast asleep.

While he napped in the back, we'd driven aimlessly for the last hour and a half, so she could get comfortable behind the wheel again. She'd spent a good amount of that time cruising around different neighborhoods because she wasn't willing to get on the highway, but I'd eventually talked her into it, encouraging her the whole way by saying, "Stay relaxed," or "You're doing so well," and "That's it."

I hadn't realized until Kennedy had flushed red and asked me, "Are you doing it on purpose?"

"What?"

"The sex talk. Are you deliberately trying to throw me off?"

I'd rewound my words and promptly shut my mouth. "Nope. Sorry."

She'd loosened her white-knuckle grip on the steering wheel, and took a deep breath before relaxing her shoulders infinitesimally.

Now, I watched her profile as she focused intently on the road. The afternoon sun lit up her flawless skin and highlighted the dark hair she had tied up on the top of her head. I'd gotten used to how stylish she was, with her clothes and jewelry, but I liked her like this. Casual with no makeup, in an oversized hoodie and leggings.

Although, last night had been like a slap to the face, seeing her in those painted-on jeans and the top with her tits practically spilling out. She'd gone from cute nanny to siren, and I hadn't been able to stop staring.

Which was a problem. A *big* problem.

As she'd sauntered down the sidewalk, glowing from the lights along the path, my eyes had been glued to her ass, big and round, and I'd had the very ungentlemanly urge to bite it. My mouth had literally watered, especially with her sugar-and-petal scent trailing after her.

I had spent the rest of the night attempting to forget the dark-red color of her lips. I'd reminded myself that she was Finn's nanny and far too young for me to be thinking about sinking between her luscious thighs and kissing her there, talking her through it in a totally different environment.

Shifting in my seat, I willed my dick to chill the fuck out and turned up the volume of the radio. Some pop song I was unfamiliar with played, but Kennedy sang along to the lyrics about being jealous of the pillow against your cheek and the steering wheel under your fingers, and it felt like she was speaking my thoughts aloud.

"You have a really good voice," I said when the song ended.

"Thanks." She shrugged. "I hadn't realized I was singing."

"No? I wonder what you'd sound like when you did it on purpose."

She double-checked her mirrors before changing lanes again. "The same but louder."

I chuckled and rested my forearm on the door. "You like to sing?"

"Yeah. It relaxes me, keeps me company."

"You ever perform anywhere?"

She waited until she took the exit off the highway to answer. "When I was a kid, yeah. I love musicals, and I used to do this theater camp in middle school, but once I started having seizures, I stopped. I was afraid of what might happen."

I nodded in understanding. She had given up a lot for a long time, and I didn't want her to do that anymore. "You should do it again."

She turned to me at a red light. "Do what?"

"Sing, act, perform."

She laughed off my suggestion.

"No, really. If you love it, you should do it."

"I doubt I could."

"Coming from the same girl who stomped over to me at Walt's, demanding I hand my kid to her."

"I did *not* stomp or demand."

"Politely persuaded," I said, earning a smile. "You should do it. Join a choir or something. You'd be great."

The light changed to green, and she drove through it. "I don't know."

"Come on, be brave." I motioned out of the windshield. "Like now. Conquering your fear."

"I'm only doing this because you promised to take me to Ulta."

"I'll double the money," I offered, and she wolf whistled.

"Ooh, Professor. You know just what to say, don't you?"

I absent-mindedly reached over to her leg. I meant it to be a supportive pat.

Or, maybe not.

I didn't know. I wasn't thinking.

Because, suddenly, my fingers were pressed into her thigh, squeezing, and Kennedy's lips parted slightly, like her legs did. A few seconds passed before I realized what the hell I was doing, and that I was 0.1 seconds from taking advantage of what appeared to be her unintentional welcoming gesture. Her widening legs gave me room to move, allowing my fingertips to roam and explore the heated place between them, but I knew she didn't mean for it to happen, and I jerked my traitorous hand back.

"I'm sorry," I said, and she shook her head, her lips wet from licking them.

Not sure where to go from here, I stayed silent, hoping I hadn't insulted her. But besides her quickened breath, she displayed no outward signs of being offended, and I rubbed at the back of my neck, knowing I needed to get a hold of myself.

Mentally promising to keep my hands to myself and my thoughts pure enough to make my mother proud, I rolled down the window.

The cold September air didn't help my imagination, but it did wake up Finn, and he whined, grabbing at his straps, wanting out.

"Almost there," Kennedy told him as she turned down another street, heading straight for the strip mall. She said to me, "I know you weren't serious about the bribe, but I really do need to get a few things. I hope you don't mind."

"I don't mind, and I was serious. I don't go back on my word."

Her brows rose, and I hated that something as minor as a guy keeping his promise would impress her. Whoever had lowered the bar for her needed to get the shit kicked out of him.

She pulled into the lot in front of Ulta and shut off the ignition before facing me. "I wanted to talk to you about something."

Finn whined, and I tossed him a snack bag of chips, which would keep him busy for a minute or two while I waited for her to continue.

"We never discussed holidays, and I didn't know if you already had plans or not, but I was wondering if it would be okay for me to visit my mom for Thanksgiving?"

"Yeah, of course." I waved my hand. "You didn't even need to ask."

"I don't want to leave you high and dry."

I shook my head. "You're not."

"Are you sure?"

"Yeah. And don't give me those eyes. Contrary to popular belief," I said with forced amusement, "I am quite capable of fathering my son on my own for a bit."

"Please," she said all dramatic as she unbuckled her seat belt, "it's not only me who knows you're a capable father. The entire internet knows."

I huffed and stepped out of the car to get Finn from his seat. He wiggled for me to put him down, and I grabbed his hand, as usual. What wasn't usual was how Kennedy took the snack bag of chips from him so she could hold his other hand.

And I swear to God, my heart actually skipped a beat.

"You say contrary to popular belief, but you're the only one who thinks you're not a good dad." Kennedy stared at me as the three of us walked toward the store. "If I have to be brave, then you have to be more confident."

She had me there, but even at thirty-six, I found it all too easy to dwell on my mistakes. It was part of the reason I worked out before bed, so I would be too tired to go over everything I'd ever done wrong in my entire life. But I didn't have time to psychoanalyze that at the moment because Kennedy swung open the big black door, and I was hit with a kaleidoscope of colors and scents. Finn danced around, desperate to run free.

"I know," she said to him in a quiet voice of awe, "that's how I feel whenever I come here."

I let go of his hand, watching as the two took off. At the nail polish section, he showed her some shimmery color.

"That's very pretty, isn't it?"

He nodded eagerly, captivated by the pink and purple sparkles.

Then she gazed up at me from where she kneeled, as if my opinion was important too.

"It's nice," I offered, blinking away the indecent images of us in this same position but for a very different reason. "Very… sparkly."

"Et-et-et!"

"Get," Kennedy corrected. "You want to get this one?"

He jumped up and down, and she once again slanted her face up to me. I tipped my chin to the basket she held. "Well, looks like we're painting our nails with sparkles next time."

She grinned and dropped the tiny bottle in then resumed wandering the aisles. I followed, hands tucked into my pockets, happy to watch her in her element. She paused to test a perfume, dabbing it on her wrist and lifting it to her nose. She toggled her head side to side then held her arm out to Finn. "Give it a whiff, babes. Tell me if it smells good."

My three-year-old had no interest in smelling the perfume and decided the shiny hair clips across the other aisle were more entertaining, so she offered me her wrist instead. "I need a signature scent," she informed me. "What do you think of this one?"

I bent my head, barely touching my nose to her skin. Though I was tempted to drag my face along the length of her arm. She was so soft. "I like it," I said, straightening, "but I like whatever you use better."

"I don't have any perfume on now."

"But…" I sucked my lips between my teeth, knowing I was about to give myself away.

"But what?"

I lifted a casual shoulder. "You smell good. Like sugar and flowers."

Her smile was so sweet it made my chest constrict. "That's only my lotion and hair products."

I spun to grab hold of Finn, mumbling, "It's nice, whatever it is."

We continued to weave through displays of makeup as Finn touched everything, putting them in the basket while Kennedy cheerfully explained each item to him.

"This mascara is the absolute best…"

"And that is an eye shadow palette. It's like a rainbow, isn't it?"

"That goes on your lips. It makes them wet and shiny."

I closed my eyes, taking a deep breath.

She was Finn's nanny.

I couldn't think of her wet and shiny lips.

Wrapped around my cock.

No.

Absolutely not.

Finally, in the hair products section, she perused a few tubs and bottles for a couple of minutes until deciding on one.

"What is it?" I asked, peering over her shoulder.

"Hair mask. It's for deep conditioning and helps damaged hair."

Her hair didn't appear damaged to me, but what did I know? I took it from her, adding it to the basket. "You ready to check out?"

"We're not getting all this stuff," she said, yanking on the handles of the basket as if to take it from me.

"Yeah, we are."

"You told me you'd get me one thing. The hair mask." When I didn't let go of the basket, she tugged on it again. "That's way too much."

"You like everything in here?"

She bit the corner of her lip like she didn't want to admit she obviously did.

"Let's go." She opened her mouth to argue, but I waved her off. "You earned it. For the great job you're doing with Finn and for conquering your fear." Then I impulsively tucked a loose lock of hair behind her ear.

Her answering pleased little smile did dangerous things to my already impaired self-control.

As we made our way back to the car, Finn in between us with a few butterfly clips in his hair, I had a feeling one hundred bucks in makeup was nothing compared to what I was willing to do to see her smile.

EIGHT
LIAM

A few days had passed since I'd spent the afternoon driving around with Kennedy, and the more she settled in at home, the better I felt at work. I felt energetic during my classes, my lectures were informative—at least I hoped, but Mike in my US Political Thought class fell asleep this morning—and I was getting all my grades in on time. Not to mention, my publisher was really happy with my book, and advanced copies were being sent out to readers, mostly academics, librarians, and any media personalities interested in the history of America's political landscape.

As I opened the front door to my home, the scent of something savory hit my nose, and I inhaled deeply. Whatever was cooking smelled amazing.

I shrugged off my jacket and made sure to hang it on the hook by the door, lest I miss out on my sticker. Yes, Kennedy had all three of us filling out chore charts with stickers. I hadn't thought she was Mary Poppins when I'd met her, but these last two weeks had proven me wrong. She had Finn on a schedule, made me pick up after myself, and I was positive she was made of magic.

I followed the scent of the food and the sounds of music to the kitchen. I unbuttoned the cuffs of my shirt, rolling them up to my elbows as I paused in the doorway, taking in the scene before me.

Kennedy and Finn bopped around together, both of them wearing what looked like homemade hand puppets. Kennedy wore a raccoon, or maybe it was a skunk. And I was pretty sure Finn's was some sort of dinosaur with its teeth and tail.

I released the top two buttons of my shirt and rubbed at my chest, loosening the sudden tightness there. Oblivious to my presence, they spun in a circle, Kennedy belting the chorus of some peppy Top 40 tune while Finn shrieked and occasionally shouted a few syllables here and there. He'd been making a lot of noise lately, not quite whole words, but more attempts at expressing himself, and it was because of Kennedy. She was working with him, following all of the advice and information from the speech therapist, and talking to him, singing to him every single day.

I had no idea Finn loved to sing and dance so much. But there he was, grinning wide and wonderful. Kennedy looked so carefree with her sparkling eyes, hair tumbling around her shoulders, skin flushed. She was breathtaking.

The song ended and morphed into something slower, and she swayed them side to side. That was when she spotted me leaning against the doorframe.

"Oh!" She straightened abruptly, her pink cheeks darkening to red. "Hi. I didn't hear you come in."

Finn leaped at me. "Addy!"

I caught him and kissed his head as I hugged him close. "Hiya, guy. Did you have a good day?"

He nodded, and I looked back to Kennedy. "Having your own private dance party, huh?"

She smoothed her hair back from her face. "I got tired of *Cocomelon*."

"Yeah." *Cocomelon* was the absolute worst. "I get it."

"I told him we'd make our own puppets and have a dance party with them if we could turn it off."

Finn thrust his puppet in my face. "Rahh!"

I pretended to be scared, and he laughed happily. "Ti-tah!"

I quirked my brow at Kennedy for translation. "Triceratops."

"Right." I studied the puppet made out of a little brown paper bag, construction paper, and some googly eyes. "But triceratops have three horns on their heads," I said to Finn, and Kennedy tossed her arms in the air, a silent reprimand. I immediately told him, "It's really good, buddy!"

He kicked his legs, a sign for me to put him down, and as soon as I did, he snatched Kennedy's…zebra?…and started attacking it with his triceratops.

"Welcome home," she told me with a laugh, tying her hair up on her head before waving her hands on either side of her face in an attempt to cool off. "Or should I say, welcome back to the circus?"

"Depends. What role am I?"

"Juggler."

I crossed to the stove and lifted the lid from the big pot. Inside, spaghetti sauce bubbled. "I thought I'd be the ringmaster."

She shook her head and stood right next to me to dip a spoon into the pot. She tasted a bit of the sauce then offered some to me. We didn't break eye contact as she lifted it to my mouth and my lips surrounded the spoon. The sauce was thick and flavorful.

"How is it?" she asked, dropping the spoon in the sink.

"Delicious. Another family recipe?"

"Not so much a recipe as a trick." She tipped her head to the pot. "You cook the meatballs in the sauce."

"Well, it's really good." I licked my lips to make sure I hadn't missed any, and she mirrored me, her own tongue skimming to the corner of her mouth. I gripped the edge of the counter and fought to hold on to the last string of our conversation. "If I'm the juggler, who are you?"

She propped one hand on her hip, cocking her leg out to the side, posing. "Lion tamer. Obviously."

"Obviously," I repeated, giving in to a smile.

"Dinner'll be ready in about ten minutes."

I backed away as she shifted pots around on the stove, turned up the heat on the burner. "Can I do anything to help?"

"Nope. Only need to boil the spaghetti."

"Is it homemade?"

"I'm a good cook but not *that* good."

"Coulda fooled me." While she finished up dinner, I set the table then corralled Finn to sit in front of his plastic plate and fork. She served each of us heaping portions of spaghetti and meatballs, along with cut-up cucumbers for Finn and bowls of salad for her and me. I wasn't used to anyone else taking care of these domestic chores, and it was…nice.

The three of us at the table together, eating and chatting. It was comfortable, like we've been doing it a lot longer than a few weeks.

Kennedy asked me about my day, and she filled me in on their trip to the park after she'd picked Finn up from school and their plans to go to story time at the library tomorrow.

I savored another mouthful of the tangy tomato sauce, watching Finn make more of a mess than actually get any food into his mouth. Kennedy reached over periodically to wipe his face or scoot a stray meatball his way. She made it all look so effortless. The food, the dance party, her communication with Finn. It was like she was meant to be here.

"So," she started, once we'd both finished our food and Finn had taken off from the table again. "I decided I'm going to audition for a show."

"Really?" I tossed my napkin to the table. "That's great. When? Where?"

"First round of auditions is tomorrow. For a local theater production of *Hairspray*."

I knew my smile was ridiculously broad, but I was so happy for her. "You'll do great."

Her own smile wavered. "I'm not sure I'll get cast at all, but if I do, even for the chorus, I'll need a lot of nights off, especially when it gets closer to the show."

I waved away her unspoken concern. "Don't worry about it. I want you to do this. I want you to be happy."

"Yeah?"

Honestly, whoever led her to think she owed everyone around her something made me want to cause violence.

"You may work for me, but I don't expect you to chain yourself to Finn."

"He'd probably like that," she said with a laugh, and I pointed at her with my glass of water.

"He probably would."

"He's funny. I love him so much already."

I gulped down the rest of my drink and set it on the table, thinking back to Dean's words the night this had all started at Walt's. *She loves hard, and it's impossible not to fall in love with her right back.*

I nodded at Kennedy. "Yeah. I think he loves you too."

Her answering grin was pure joy.

"Why don't I do the dishes?" I offered. "You go hang out. Prepare for tomorrow or whatever you need to do."

"It's fine. I can do it."

"I insist."

"Well, if you *insist*." She theatrically and deliberately took her time finishing her glass of water.

I gathered up the plates to drop them in the sink. Kennedy was two steps out of the kitchen when her cell phone buzzed on the windowsill. A text message appeared on her screen from someone named Jordan, and it read **I miss you, baby**.

I hadn't realized that I was still smiling like an idiot until I felt it slip, and whatever had been inflated inside my chest popped. I cleared my throat. "Don't forget your phone."

"Oh yeah. Thanks." She stood next to me, typing, as I rinsed off the plates and set them in the dishwasher. I didn't know who Jordan was, nor did I care. Because Kennedy's personal life was none of my business, and someone calling her *baby* made no difference to me. Because she was Finn's nanny.

And wanting to know who the hell Jordan was and why they were calling Finn's nanny *baby* was most definitely some kind of ethics violation.

After a few moments, she slid her cell phone into her back pocket then asked me, "Wanted to run it by you first, but I know Finn really likes whipped cream, so I was thinking we should use that as an incentive for him to go on the potty. I know you said you tried naked day, and it didn't work."

"No." I huffed. He didn't care that he was naked and took a dump in the corner of the living room. I think he felt more connected to his animal side. "It definitely didn't work."

"He's good with bribes, and he's been doing great with the sticker chore chart. I figured a treat might be good to try. What do you think?"

"Makes sense."

She pivoted away, calling out, "Hey Finnie, want to try to go to the bathroom before tubby time? If you go on the potty, you can have squirt!"

He came roaring into the kitchen. "Irt!"

"Yes! Squirt!" She sank down to her knees. "Let's try to go now. Then you can get squirts, okay?"

He held her hand, and Kennedy winked at me as they pranced to the bathroom while I put away the leftovers, scrubbing the pots a bit harder than necessary.

But at least they were squeaky-clean by the time I finished, and Finn was bathed and in his pajamas.

"So, how'd it go?" I asked, once they reappeared in the kitchen. "Did you go potty?"

Finn stayed silent as Kennedy shook her head. "But he did try, so I said he could have a little squirt."

She opened the refrigerator for the can of whipped cream. Finn danced in place as she shook it. "Just a little," she repeated and squirted a bit into his mouth.

He swallowed it and made the ASL sign for "more." Another thing Kennedy had taught him, a few ASL words.

She raised her brow at me in question.

"All right. A little more." I took the bottle from her and shot a bit into his mouth then sprayed a big glob in mine. Finn laughed hysterically at my chipmunk cheeks. I swallowed it all down and held the bottle up to Kennedy, a silent invitation.

Instead of taking it from me, she tipped her head back and opened her mouth. I squirted some of the white cream between her lips, and she giggled, her mouth so full, it seeped out of the sides when she swallowed.

And I was officially in hell.

She wiped her mouth with her index finger and licked it clean.

Fucking hell.

I'd have to throw away every goddamn bottle of whipped cream. Finn would simply have to learn to pee another way.

I capped the can and placed it back on the door of the refrigerator. "Okay, guy, say night to Kennedy. Time for bed."

She lifted him up, hugging him tight with her eyes closed, whispering, "Sleep tight, babes."

Finn and I completed the nightly routine: brushing teeth, filling up a water bottle, reading a story, and tucking him in before I lay next to him for a few minutes, staring at the light-up stars on the ceiling.

"What do you think of Kennedy?" I asked. "Do you love her?"

"Uv her," he said.

"Yeah. I thought so." I sighed and scrubbed my hand over my face and hair. "It's an uphill battle." I rolled over to power on his sound machine and his music then kissed his forehead. "I love you. Sleep well. I'll see you in the morning."

I gave him one last squeeze and stood, quietly and *quickly* making a getaway. I shut his door right as Kennedy reached the top of the steps. "You going to bed already?" It wasn't like we ever hung out or anything. Or that I would suggest it either. But... "It's only eight."

"Yeah, I thought I'd go over my audition piece a few times. Don't worry, though. I'll use my headphones. You won't hear a thing."

I met her by her door, keeping my voice down as I said, "I don't care. Do what you need to." I could tell she was nervous by how she plucked at her shirt, so I gave her shoulder an encouraging squeeze. "You're going to do amazing tomorrow."

"I hope so. When I think about it, I feel like puking. You got any tips, Professor?"

"Picture them naked," I offered with a shrug.

She bent her head, biting back a smile. "I don't know if I want to picture them naked."

"No," I agreed, but I didn't think it was funny. Not when I was standing so close to Kennedy I could feel her body heat. "Naked is bad. Very bad."

"Yeah." She lifted her head, her gaze slow to meet mine, and her throat worked on a swallow. A few pieces of hair had fallen out of her bun, and she curled them behind her ear, her fingers lingering at her neck. "That's...not what I want to picture."

"You should picture someone you want to perform for," I said, my voice barely above a whisper.

She let her hand fall, her knuckles brushing mine. "Good idea."

We stood there like that, breathing each other in, her head tipped up toward me, my attention split between her mouth, soft and inviting, and her eyes, almost black in the low light of the hall. "Show them who you are. There's no way they won't fall in love with you."

She licked her lips, starting to speak, but a thump sounded behind Finn's door, followed by clomping footsteps. It opened, and he poked his head out. "Addy!"

I blinked away from Kennedy, the moment evaporated, and brushed past her. "Yeah, buddy. I'm coming."

It was for the best anyway.

Somebody named Jordan was already calling her baby.

NINE
KENNEDY

After the first *Hairspray* auditions Thursday night, I'd been called back, and while I hoped I had a good chance, I was up against an undergrad in musical theatre. I'd spent the better part of the last two days a ball of nerves. Finn even seemed to understand how wound up I was because he was at a level five when he normally ran at a fifteen.

Last night, Liam had put Finn to bed then sat in the living room to be my audience while I'd rehearsed my song over and over again. Though, his feedback wasn't all that useful, because each time I'd finished "I Can Hear the Bells," he'd smile and say, "That was better than the last time," or "You sound so good."

This morning, I'd been too nervous to eat breakfast and had arrived to the callbacks hopped up on two cups of coffee, but I thought it had added to my performance as the "pleasantly plump" and bighearted Tracy Turnblad, the star of the show. Now, I was back at Liam's, tucked up in my room, trying to keep my mind off the audition by talking to my sister and mom.

Every Sunday, Liam and Finn FaceTimed with Tessa. She was living in Antarctica, doing research for some big-time academic study, and I stayed away, not wanting to intrude on their time together. I'd briefly "met" her last week, and she'd seemed perfectly nice, with porcelain skin, shoulder-length chestnut hair, brown eyes, and freckles, like some well-aged star of a teen drama who was now retired and living on the coast. No wonder Liam had made a baby with her.

Two beautiful, nerdy people and their beautiful, nerdy little kid.

And I wasn't jealous at all.

Liam was the hot daddy professor I was nannying for, and she was the mother of his child. In the hierarchy of this family, I was in last place. Or, really, not listed at all. Which was why I hid myself away whenever they had their scheduled call. Because I didn't want to be reminded of what was real—they were a family, and I was merely on the outside.

This was exactly what Taylor had warned me about. She'd told me over and over again that I needed to remain unattached. This was my job. "Don't go falling in love," she'd said, only half joking, and I'd laughed it off because that was what I did.

I fell in love. A lot.

If it was because my father had died when I was young or because I'd never felt safe, I couldn't tell. I didn't go to therapy like a well-adjusted person, although I *did* know I fell in love easily. Too easily sometimes.

But I liked it.

I liked the butterflies and smiles and flirting. I liked the feeling of coming home to someone waiting for me and not having to ask for a hug. I liked being in a relationship.

And after my *moment* in the hallway with Liam Wednesday night, I knew I had to be careful. It would be easy—so easy—to fall in love with him. But I couldn't.

Not only because he was paying me to take care of his child, but because I had promised myself that this was a new chapter in my life. One where I worked on myself and stayed away from men who were bad for me.

This was my new leaf. I was going to make good choices.

Falling for Liam was *not* a good choice.

Lounging on my bed, I texted my mom a few emojis since she'd sent me a cute picture of her and Duke then messaged my sister to see if she had talked to Mom about Thanksgiving.

It'll be fun.

TAYLOR

If your version of fun is hanging out in the desert.

You're cold-blooded. I'm sure you'll like it.

TAYLOR

You need to stop hanging out with Dean. I don't like it.

TAYLOR

Pleeeaaaase. Come on.

TAYLOR

I don't know. Dean and I haven't had the whole holiday conversation yet. I have no idea where we're spending them.

You're spending turkey day in Vegas.

OMG THEN YOU CAN ELOPE OMG OMG

TAYLOR

No.

YOU CAN DO IT IN ONE OF THOSE FAKE GONDOLA THINGS

TAYLOR

Just what I've always wanted. To get married on one of those fake gondola things.

Just a thought.

TAYLOR

Not one of your best.

I was about to reply that I'd look into wedding packages when a phone call came through, the name of the show director on the screen.

My stomach flip-flopped, and I immediately started sweating. I sat up from my prone position and took a deep breath before jabbing the green button to answer. "Hello?"

"Hi, Kennedy. It's Cathy."

"Hi, Cathy. How are you?"

"I'm wonderful. I'm calling about your audition," she said, and I didn't realize I'd been holding my breath until it rushed out of me as she told me, "I think you'd be perfect as Tracy."

"Oh my god," I half cried, half whispered. "I'm Tracy?"

"Yes, and I can't wait to get started."

I stood, pacing my bedroom and waving my hand around my face to keep from crying. It was useless. "Thank you so much!"

"Truly, thank *you*. We'll be sending out packets shortly with the schedule and show information. We're going to be starting tomorrow night. You're still okay with that, right?"

"Yes!" I realized I'd shouted my answer and repeated it quieter. "Yes. Yes, I'm still okay with starting tomorrow. Cathy, thank you so much. I won't let you down."

"I know you won't. All you have to do is be your bubbly self, and you'll do great. I'll see you tomorrow."

"Yes. Yes, you will. Thanks again!" I hung up and promptly let out a happy squeal before skipping out of my room.

Liam and Finn were already running to me as I bounded down the steps.

"What?" Liam held me by the shoulders. "What's wrong? What happened?"

I couldn't answer, too busy screeching and jumping up and down. So was Finn.

Liam tried again. "*What?*"

"I did it! I'm Tracy!"

His worried expression melted into a dazzling grin. He swept me into his arms. "You got the part? Amazing! I knew you could do it."

Laughing breathlessly, I threw my arms around his neck. "Thank you."

His solid strength enveloped me, warm and steadying, with one hand on the back of my head and the other wrapped tight about my waist. "I'm so proud of you."

For a blissful moment, I let myself sink into his embrace. "I wouldn't have done it without you. So, thank you."

He squeezed me tighter, lifting me off the floor a few inches, and I squeaked out a giggle before he set me back down. His hands lingered at my waist, our eyes locked, faces inches apart. "Don't thank me. It was all you. Your talent. Your courage."

I grinned, lighting up from the inside out at the pride in his voice. Liam O'Neil, professor, author, and parent, was proud of *me*. The nanny.

His attention dipped to my mouth, and my heart skittered to a momentary stop at the way his eyes widened ever so slightly. I held my breath, leaning in, wanting to close the space between us, fearing what it meant that I couldn't back away.

Until Finn bounced into us, shouting, "Me! Me! Me! Me!"

Liam released me and ruffled his son's hair. "You! You! What?"

"Up!"

"Lift me up, please," Liam said, then picked Finn up. "You hear that, guy? Kennedy got the part. Give her a big hug."

Finn jumped out of Liam's arms for me, and I laughed, spinning him in a circle.

"Um, hello?"

"Oh shit," Liam muttered. "Sorry, Tess. Sorry." He scooted

back over to the couch and motioned to the iPad settled on the coffee table.

"What's going on?" Tessa asked. "What was all that screaming?"

I sucked in a breath, suddenly embarrassed at my over-the-top reaction. "Sorry," I called out in the direction of the iPad. "That was just me being silly."

"Kennedy auditioned for a local show and got the part she wanted," Liam told her.

"That's great," I heard Tessa say, and then he lifted the iPad, turning it so we could see each other on-screen. She smiled. "Congratulations."

"Thank you." I hitched Finn on my hip and wiped the remaining wetness away from under my eyes. "I was just so excited."

"As you should be. What show is it?"

"*Hairspray*. I'm going to be Tracy."

"I'm not very familiar with theater," Tessa said. "Is it a play or…?"

"A musical." I stepped closer to Liam so I could explain it to Tessa. "It's based on the John Waters film from the '80s but takes place in the '60s, about a white girl in Baltimore. She makes friends with a bunch of Black kids, and they end up desegregating an *American Bandstand* type show. By singing and dancing, obviously."

Tessa nodded. "I like it. A musical with political intention."

"And Kennedy's the star," Liam stated, smiling at me.

Honestly, if he continued to look so proud of me, I would have no other choice but to kiss him.

"But don't worry," I said Tessa, "it won't interfere with me taking care of Finn."

At his name, he shifted, starting to climb me like a monkey, and I puffed up my cheeks to make my monkey face. He giggled and squished my cheeks between his hands.

On the iPad, Tessa waved her hand. "I'm not worried at all.

Liam told me how Finn adores you, and I can see that. I'm happy Liam made the decision to get some help, and I'm really grateful it's you."

Her appreciation was touching, and I teared up again. At this rate, I'd be going to rehearsal with puffy red eyes. "Thank you." I sniffed. "That's very sweet of you to say."

"Well, I'm sure you'll want to celebrate, and I don't want to stop you," she said. "Liam, same time next week?"

"Yeah, sounds good, Tess."

"Finn, sweetie, I love you."

I bent so Finn could lean into the screen. He banged on it a few times.

Liam prompted him. "Can you say 'I love you, Mommy'?"

"Wuv, Ommy."

Tessa pressed her hands to her heart, appearing like she might cry. "Aw, buddy. I love you too. So much. I miss you. I'm gonna take lots more pictures to send to Daddy so you don't forget me, okay?"

Finn kicked his legs. "Guin!"

"Yes, and penguins too," she agreed, laughing. "I won't forget pictures of the penguins." She blew a few kisses. "Talk later."

I waved as Liam held the iPad aloft so we were all in the frame. "See you."

Then with a press of a button, the FaceTime call ended, and I set Finn down. "She's so kind."

"Yeah," Liam agreed. "She is. It's what attracted me to her, even just as friends. It can be real dog-eat-dog sometimes in academics, but she was never like that."

"Well, I really like her. Not that it makes a difference."

He turned to me after putting the iPad away. "It makes a difference."

I tried not to read into that and bent to Finn. "What do you say? Should we celebrate with some squirt?"

He raised his arms, hopping up and down, but Liam offered another choice. "How 'bout we go for ice cream?"

That really got Finn going, and he took a few laps around the room. "Yeeeaaaahhhhhhh!"

The three of us piled into Liam's car, and he insisted on blasting the *Hairspray* soundtrack so I could sing, which I found hopelessly endearing. By the time we arrived at the ice cream shop, I was out of breath from laughing and singing so much.

We ordered and sat at a booth in the back, with Finn next to his dad and me across from them.

"You two are twins," I noted, tipping my chin at how they both had their hands curled around their bowls, heads tilted when they raised their spoons to their mouths, like they didn't want to miss one drop. "Copy and paste. Too cute."

"You hear that?" Liam elbowed Finn. "She thinks we're cute."

"Mostly just Finn," I corrected, and Liam eyed me behind his glasses, a teasing lilt to his mouth.

It was funny how I was learning all of his habits. Like the way he crumpled up paper napkins and tossed them on the table when he finished eating. Or how he cracked his knuckles with his thumbs, like he did now.

"Thanks for treating me to ice cream," I said, and he frowned.

"You really have to stop thanking me for things."

"Why? I appreciate you."

"Yeah, but it makes me feel like you think you owe me something. You don't."

I lifted a shoulder. He wasn't wrong. "I owe you for giving me this job when I know you could have easily hired someone else."

"Yeah, but someone else isn't you."

I pressed my cool hands to my hot cheeks and attempted to douse the butterflies in my belly. I know he didn't mean anything by it. He was only being nice. Because that's what Liam was, a nice guy.

A supportive guy.

A thoughtful and decent guy who would never cross any lines. Including the one that started with the little boy next to him.

"Addy!" Finn rotated his hands up and down, signing that he was all done.

"You're all done," I said and wiped at his mouth. "You gobbled that down quick. I can't even finish mine."

Liam pointed to my Oreo sundae. "You don't want the rest?"

I shook my head. I was still too amped up from my good news and a little self-conscious about how I couldn't seem to stop assigning meaning to Liam's words and actions. I had to stop, or I'd be headed for heartbreak.

The ice cream I'd eaten sat in my stomach like a boulder, and I pushed what was left of it toward Liam. "You want it?"

He didn't need to be asked twice and scooped up a bit to shove into his mouth. I definitely didn't read into him using my spoon without a second thought.

He was merely hungry. The man was tall and lean, probably burned more calories than the average person using all of his brain power. Not to mention the boxing.

The boxing.

But, whatever. None of it mattered.

Not our easy friendship. Or that sometimes I caught him staring at me.

Because I was most definitely not falling for Liam Hot Professor Zaddy O'Neil.

TEN

LIAM

t was the Friday before midterm break, so I let my last class out early and canceled my office hours. No one was going to show up when all the students were either headed home for a long weekend or off to get plastered somewhere. I had big plans to hang out with Finn for the next few days, including a trip to the pumpkin patch, all-you-can-eat pancakes, and meeting the guys at Imagination Station, while Kennedy could enjoy some well-deserved time off.

Opening the front door of my house, I heard music playing in the kitchen, but when I popped my head in, it was empty save for more hand puppets. These were Halloween-themed: Frankenstein, a jack-o'-lantern, a bat, and a scarecrow. At least, I thought it was a scarecrow.

Checking the time, I figured Finn was down for his nap, and I smiled. I was looking at a four-day weekend, so I'd treat myself to a beer. Right after I changed.

The carpeting muffled my steps as I took them two at a time, my forward momentum speeding me past Kennedy's open bedroom door. Until I saw something out of the corner of my eye and backtracked.

And *fuuuuuck.*

I immediately spun away, heading straight to my room, with the image of a naked Kennedy burned into my retinas. I couldn't blink the picture away. Not of her long, wet hair hanging halfway down her back. Or her dimpled thighs. Or the dark brown birthmark on the top of her ass, a slightly misshapen heart that I wanted to bite.

Fuck me.

I jammed my fingers into my eyes, but there she was in the front of my mind, golden and dewy. I doubted anything short of a lobotomy could make me forget the curve of her hips or her round belly.

Every person had physical attributes they were attracted to. Some liked a certain eye color or height. A lot of guys liked big asses or pouty lips. Me? I liked women to be *soft*, and there was not one inch of Kennedy that wasn't supple.

Suddenly desperate for a soft place to land, my cock stiffened almost painfully.

I shut my door, leaning heavily against it as I shook out my hands. As if I could rid the tingles in my fingers, the desire to dig them into her skin, leave marks on her hips as I drove into her.

"Fucking shit," I muttered, unbuttoning my pants and ripping my zipper down.

I hated myself. Hated that I couldn't control my instincts. Hated that I now knew exactly how much my son's nanny affected me, and that I couldn't even wait five goddamn seconds until I had my hand wrapped around my dick.

"Christ," I hissed, gripping it tightly. I turned and slapped my hand against the wall, letting my chin drop toward my chest as guilt and shame warred with want and need. "This is what you do to me."

I thrust once into my fist before lifting my hand to my mouth and spitting on my palm. I wrapped it around my cock again, completely disgusted with myself and yet unable to stop.

She was my son's nanny.

And I was jerking off to her.

My exhales were harsh, and I squeezed my eyes shut, dying to finish and still trying to hold off.

I held all the power over Kennedy, and it wasn't right.

But… "Fuck. Fuck. Fuck me." It felt right.

I gritted my teeth and pumped faster, imagining Kennedy under me. Staring up at me with those big, dark eyes, licking her perfect lips, sighing and moaning so sweetly like I knew she would.

"Good fucking Christ." I couldn't stand it.

Couldn't stand myself.

Couldn't stand that she was living in my house.

Couldn't stand that I couldn't ever touch her.

It was wrong on so many levels, but I worked my hand harder, thinking of her legs wrapped around my neck, of pressing my face to her pussy, of breathing her in and kissing every centimeter of her body.

"Shit," I growled, dropping my forearm to the wall, resting my forehead on it, as if I could pretend I wasn't erupting like a teenager after seeing his first real-life pair of tits. But I was.

I was absolutely losing it.

At the last moment, I snatched a T-shirt from the hamper and released my orgasm into it, sighing with relief before wincing in regret.

I'd violated Kennedy's privacy and dignity. Whether she would care or not, *I* cared. I had seen her naked without her consent and then masturbated like some creep.

I had to tell her. Not the masturbating part, but the me getting an eyeful part. It was the respectable thing to do. *Right?*

I shook my head as if I could knock some sense into my brain and stripped off my clothes. Pulling on sweats, I weighed the options of admitting what had happened. Make it weird for both of us and possibly lose the best thing to happen to me in a long time, *or* keep it to myself and wallow in shame.

"You're such a goddamn idiot," I muttered, scrubbing my

hands through my hair before spinning in a tight circle, like I could find the answer on my walls.

A knock sounded, interrupting my breakdown, and I froze. There was only one person who could be on the other side of my bedroom door, and I sure as shit wasn't ready to face her.

Still, I swung it open to find her smiling up at me. "Hey, Professor. I didn't know you were home, but I heard some noise in here."

Did she hear me fucking my own hand?

Did she know I saw her naked?

Did she understand that I was a man at her mercy?

I cleared my throat. "Uh, yeah. Left school early. Thought I'd get a jump on the long weekend."

She clapped, hopping on her toes. "I don't have rehearsal tonight. Do you wanna do a movie marathon? I've been trying to talk Finn into watching *Toy Story*."

"Oh no." I tried to play it cool. "You don't want to hang out with us. You have off until Tuesday."

She pursed her lips, narrowing her eyebrows as if she didn't comprehend my words.

"You don't have to stay here. Go out. Go have fun."

Her confused—and maybe a little hurt—shrug hit me in my solar plexus. "You don't want me here?"

"No, I…" I rubbed at the back of my head, keeping my focus on the floor. "I figured you'd have better things to do than hang out with a three-year-old and his dad."

"But I like that three-year-old and his dad."

My chest ached. Actually fucking ached, and I couldn't say no to her. Slowly, I raised my gaze and attempted a smile, though it felt wonky. Her answering grin was not. It was pure sunshine.

"Finn should be up in a few minutes. I ran him ragged at the park, so he could barely keep his eyes open this afternoon." She waved for me to follow her down the hall. "I'll make pizza for dinner, but how do you feel about mixing M&Ms in your popcorn?"

"I like whatever you like," I told her, because I was a spineless single-celled organism, who apparently could do nothing but follow this girl around.

———

I'd been so messed up in the head over what happened with Kennedy that two days later, I was still thinking about it. When Finn had smacked his hand over and over on the car's window in the back, saying, "Pop! Pop!" while I was in the drive-thru at Starbucks, I'd ordered without being conscious of it, so we'd arrived to Imagination with a handful of cake pops for all the kids.

As they happily munched on the treats, Jude and Dylan eyed me. I slugged my coffee down in an effort to ignore them.

I finally gave in after a minute. "*What*?"

Jude was the one to answer. "You look…wound up."

If I could laugh, I would. But I was indeed wound up with too much anxiety to find my situation humorous. "I am."

"What's going on? I thought everything was going great."

Jude, Dylan, Nate, and I had a group text thread for occasional check-ins and random links to stuff. Like the beer brewing thing Nate invited us to or the TikToks Dylan sent us that were of this woman with a really big mouth—like, an unhinged jaw big—and she was basically trying to find restaurants with the tallest sandwiches and eating them. Originally, Dylan had opened a TikTok account to troll me with videos about *me*, but he'd fallen down this sandwich-lady rabbit hole. Though it was rare, we did sometimes ask how the others were doing. Which was why Jude thought everything had been going well since Kennedy had moved in.

"It was going great," I said, leaning over to place my elbows on my knees, "until I saw her naked."

Dylan choked on a gulp of coffee. "Bro, *what*?"

Jude slapped his back, eyes on me. "You saw her naked?"

I set my coffee cup on the floor and dropped my head into my hands. "I didn't mean to."

"How'd that happen?" Jude asked.

"I came home early on Friday, and Finn was napping, so I guess she took a shower and didn't think she had to close her door. I walked past and…"

"And what?" Dylan asked. "I don't get why you're so upset about it."

"Yeah," Jude agreed. "You didn't do anything wrong."

When I didn't respond, they both stared at me. This time, it was Dylan who asked, "What'd you do?"

"I, uh…" I kept my eyes on the floor as I admitted, "I immediately went and jacked off."

There was silence, and when I finally straightened, lifting my gaze to my two friends, they both broke up. Loud, obnoxious guffaws. Falling into each other laughing.

I felt my face heat in embarrassment, and I crossed my arms over my chest, leaning against the wall.

"Ooh, look at him," Jude chuckled. "All red."

"It's not funny," I muttered.

"It really is, though," Dylan said, catching his breath. "You got an eyeful of your nanny's ass and couldn't handle it. What are you? Twelve?"

I blew out an aggrieved breath. Because, yeah, that was what it had felt like then. *Now*, I felt like an asshole. "I violated her privacy. But on top of that, I can't have the hots for Finn's nanny. That's, like, rule number one."

"I didn't know there was a rule book," Dylan said after taking a sip of coffee.

"Oh, you can fuck off with that shit, Mr. Everyone-knows-the-rules-and-won't-catch-feelings."

Dylan raised his brow for a moment then inclined his head, accepting that he was full of shit. Up until he'd met Genevieve, he'd lived by a certain set of rules with women, no repeats and no feelings. He'd had one-night stands only. But he'd gone and torched that code of honor when we'd walked into Walt's that night last spring and spotted Gen.

Jude knocked his elbow into my side. "Seriously. You have a fair point about her privacy, but it was an accident, right? Stop beating yourself up about it."

"Beating off about it," Dylan said under his breath, and I leaned forward, scowling at him around Jude.

"I'll deck you."

"All right. All right." Jude spread his arms out, physically putting more distance between us. "Dylan's already been clocked by one of us. Let's not go for two."

Dylan was a grumpy son of a bitch, but he could also be quite the smartass, and after he'd unintentionally broken Gen's heart in June, Nate had come out fists blazing in defense of his sister.

I earned my PhD and looked the part of an academic, but I also had been trained to fight by my prize-winning brother. And I didn't have a problem laying somebody out.

"Listen," Jude went on. "Don't be so hard on yourself. It was an accident you saw her. It happened. Now, move past it."

"That's the thing," I grumbled. "I can't move past it. I can't get her out of my head." I glared at Dylan's knowing look. "And stop smirking."

He held up his hands, trying and failing to school his expression. Honestly, hanging out with my friends was like living with my brothers. Then again, that was probably why I enjoyed it so much.

"I know you don't want to hear it from me, but since I was sorta in the same boat with Genevieve—wanting her and not knowing how I could have her—it seems to me like you have two options." Dylan flicked his index finger up. "One, stop fighting it. If this thing between you and the nanny is—"

"Kennedy. Her name is Kennedy."

He smirked like the son of a bitch he was. "If this thing between you and Kennedy is mutual, then—"

I cut him off with an incredulous noise. "No. No. That's not an option. She's my son's nanny. She's a dozen years younger than me. Plus," I said with a frustrated grumble, "I think she's with somebody. I saw a text message from a person named Jordan. She's been texting a lot more lately and…"

I trailed off, raking my hands through my hair before rubbing at my neck.

"That brings us to option two." Dylan stuck two fingers up. "Quit thinking with your dick and remember what your priorities are."

I huffed. "That work for you?"

"No, but luckily, Genevieve likes my dick."

Jude shook his head. "You're real great at this, man."

Dylan shrugged and chucked his empty coffee cup into the nearby trash can on his way to redirect Tucker, who appeared as if he was about to get into a fight with his sister.

Jude patted my back. "I can tell you're really stressed over this situation, and if you're dead set against anything happening between you two, I think the best thing to do would be to stay as far away as you can. You know? Like you said, she's Finn's nanny."

"Yeah. I know. I know. I have to keep it professional. No matter what."

But that was easier said than done with how she was around all the time. Even when I didn't want her to be. "This whole weekend, I thought she'd take off since I don't have school tomorrow and Tuesday," I told Jude. "But she insisted she wanted to stick around. She must have things to do, but she said no. She wanted to hang out with me and Finn."

My friend hummed then went quiet for a while. "On the upside, it sounds like she's doing wonders for Finn."

"Oh yeah. She's phenomenal. It sucks to admit that I was having such a hard time being a single parent, that I was failing him, but Kennedy's a godsend. She's patient and sweet and… I can't lose her just because I can't control myself around her."

He shrugged. "Maybe you need to find someone else to get your mind off her. Go on some dates or something."

I threw him a dubious look, and he laughed in return. "Yeah. Yeah. I know. Pot calling the kettle."

Jude had been a widower a few years now, and every couple of months, he was talked into going on a date, which he would either cancel or go on and promptly make up an excuse to leave. He should've been the last one to tell someone else to go on a date as a distraction.

"In the meantime…" He pointed over to where Finn had his head stuck in the plastic mailbox. *Again.*

ELEVEN
KENNEDY

"Five, six, seven, eight!"

I danced along breathlessly as Andie, the choreographer, took us through the energetic number, "You Can't Stop The Beat." My shirt was soaked with sweat and my ponytail hung limply off the side of my head, but I couldn't keep the smile off my face.

Cathy, as usual, sat at a six-foot-long table with her notepad and script, watching intently, giving notes and direction. She was fun and well organized, but I guessed with only about two months until the show, she had to be. Rehearsals were three hours every night, Monday through Thursday, broken down by scenes, songs, or chorus numbers. The cast was huge, and Cathy liked to work with the major roles at the beginning of the week, while Andie took the chorus through the big numbers, and then, we'd put it all together on Thursday nights.

The whole cast got along really well, and even the few kids who were in the show were trying their very best. While this wasn't Broadway, it was wonderful to find a community that accepted me. For once, I didn't feel out of place or like I was lagging behind. That was what made theater so great. We all were here because we loved it, which made it so much easier to keep going even as my feet ached.

"All right, let's take ten!" Andie called with some clapping.

Cathy smiled, offering us a thumbs-up. "Great work."

I gulped down some water from my aluminum water bottle, covered with dinosaur stickers from Finn, then mopped my face with my T-shirt before collapsing at the end of the stage.

A shadow fell over me, and I focused my sight up to find Christian smiling down at me. "You're killing it, Ken."

He offered me a fist bump as he sat next to me, his long legs dangling off the edge of the stage. He was about my age and playing Seaweed, one of the main Black characters, who sang my favorite song in the whole show, "Run and Tell That." Christian was a great singer, but an even better dancer, so for him to compliment me made my insides all gooey.

"Thanks. I'm trying."

"It shows. But listen," he said, lightly backhanding my arm, "I'm trying to get something together for this weekend. See who's available to grab dinner and a drink. You in?"

"I have to double-check that I'm free, but I should be."

"Nice." He pulled out his cell phone and started typing, so I dropped my head back and closed my eyes, my mind wandering to Liam, as it had been doing all week.

He seemed to be avoiding me, and I didn't know what to do or how to feel about it. He'd been coming home only a few minutes before I had to leave for rehearsal, so the little time we had together was a quick rundown of the day and a handoff. I'd say, "Dinner's in the oven," and he'd say, "Okay. Thanks. Have fun and drive safe." Then I was off to rehearsal, and by the time I got home, Finn was asleep and Liam was in his room. Until I'd hear him sneak downstairs and the raging music would start a minute later, so I knew he was boxing.

It was almost as if he didn't want to be around me.

I shouldn't have been upset about that. Because we weren't…

friends or anything. I worked for him. That was it. There was no reason for me to stay awake at night, waiting to hear any sound or movement, letting me know he'd finished his workout. And I definitely shouldn't have been imagining him stripping his shorts off and stepping naked under the spray of his shower, his hands raking through his mess of hair or skimming over his long torso, down to those muscles at his hips, to the impressive—

"Somebody's calling you," Christian said, nudging my leg for my attention.

I blinked a few times, confused and flushed from the journey my mind had taken. Next to me, Christian gestured to my cell phone, which was on silent and sitting on top of my script. I reached for it, finding Liam's name on the screen. Daydream of the devil…

"Hey," I answered. "Is everything okay?"

"Oh yeah, yeah," he assured me quickly. "It's Finn. He won't settle down for bed and keeps asking for you. I don't mean to inter—"

"Put him on," I said, smiling. My sweet boy missed me.

Finn's voice filled my ear. "Ken-dee! No seep."

"Babes," I cooed. "You have to sleep. It's night-night time."

"No!"

"Yes. If you don't go to sleep, you won't be awake to play with me tomorrow. You want to play with me, right?" When he didn't respond, I went on, "Tomorrow is Friday, and I wanted to go to the store after school and pick out a special treat for the weekend. What do you think?"

"Reat! Reat!"

"Yeah, you want treats. So, go to sleep, and we'll go to the store tomorrow, okay?"

"Reat!"

I laughed. "Yeah. Go night night and get treats tomorrow. I'll see you when you wake up, okay? I love you."

"Wuv you."

Liam came back on the line. "Thanks for that, and sorry about calling you."

"No big deal. We're on a break right now."

"Okay, well, I'm gonna put him down. I'll see you later."

"See you," I said and hung up as Cathy started to assemble us back to center stage. "Help," I whined, and Christian chuckled, holding out his hand to hoist me up.

"Let's get back to it, Tracy."

When I returned home two hours later, I was surprised to find Liam lounged out on the couch in the living room. He lifted his hand in silent greeting, and I gave him a small smile in return. I toed off my sneakers, setting them on the shoe rack, and hung my coat up before crossing the room to the couch, making sure to keep to my end.

I could've sat on the recliner, which I would have all to myself with plenty of room, and yet…

"How was it?" Liam asked.

"Great." I tugged my scrunchie out of my hair, letting the strands down. I was a mess and needed a shower, but he didn't seem to mind my sweaty locks, his gaze trailing over me.

He nodded after a while. "And, again, I'm sorry for calling during your rehearsal. That's your time and—"

"Liam, it's fine. Really."

He crossed his arms, his focus going back to the television and some news show with a panel of people discussing something about Congress. I watched for a moment, though I might as well have been listening to them breaking down sports stats for all that I understood. Or cared to understand.

"*This* is really what you're into?" I asked, and the corner of his mouth ticked up.

"Yep. This is really what I'm into."

"Why?" I waved my hand in a circle. "I think it's all so… boring and, like, nonsense. We're supposed to vote for these people, but they don't do anything for us. I mean, you know how many people still can't afford medication because the insurance system is so messed up?" Unfortunately, I had a ton of personal experience with the hell that was medical insurance. I took a lot of pills, and they weren't cheap. It was nutty to me that people were dying every day because they couldn't afford life-saving treatments. "Isn't the whole point of the government to help its people?"

On the other side of the couch, Liam turned to me, extending his arm along the length of the cushion, pulled up his right leg, bent at the knee, and grinned. "You want to have a philosophical discussion about the government? Now you're speaking my language."

I bit back a laugh. "I don't. I really, *really* don't, but I am curious why you want to."

He raised his gaze somewhere above me and squinted in thought. "I can't tell you why I find it so fascinating, but I always have. While other kids were staying up late to watch *SNL* or movies or something, I was staying up late to watch C-SPAN."

"Oh my god," I mumbled behind my palm, hiding an outrageously wide grin. "You are *such* a nerd."

"Right?" He met my eyes, his own full of amusement behind his glasses. "I'm interested in how countries came to be, how government plays a role in that. Almost all of politics is deciding what the government should or should not provide for its citizens."

I pretended to fall asleep, letting out an obnoxious snore, and he poked my thigh with his finger. I woke up to his smiling face. "Okay," he started, trying again, "I know you're into *Hamilton*. I've heard you singing it in the shower."

My brain only momentarily stuttered at the fact that he'd heard me in the shower. I wondered if he'd thought about me in the shower, like I'd thought about him. I brushed my fantasy aside. "Of course I'm into *Hamilton*. Who isn't?"

He inclined his head to me in agreement. "Okay, so the whole second act is basically summarizing how the different parties fought for control to decide what the government would do, who it would protect, and as much as that show makes it seem like Hamilton was right all the time, I think it would surprise people to know how he really felt about *our* government."

"Which was what?" I asked, surprising myself that I was interested in the answer.

"He basically wanted the British government part two. Strong central power with a permanent ruling class, and do you know who he thought that ruling class should be?"

I shook my head, involuntarily leaning in.

"The upper class. So—" Liam stuck his fingers up, counting off points "—he wanted a strong central power, see king," he stage-whispered, "and electors who were only made up of the wealthy, aka Parliament. In essence, he wanted to recreate England's power structure with one guy in charge and his personal advisers making all the decisions."

"Which is bad?" I guessed.

He shrugged. "That's up to you to decide. Or I should say, for the citizens of each country to decide on their own. But if we're talking about our country and its political origins, it's more nuanced than people make it out to be. Hamilton was all for a monarchy without calling it a monarchy, while Thomas Jefferson—"

"Was a definite bad guy," I interrupted, earning a repressed smile from Liam.

"This is about nuance, Kennedy. *Nuance.*"

I pretended the way he said my name didn't give me chills and motioned for him to continue.

"Jefferson enslaved people, yes, and we know that's a moral blight. He also believed in upholding the rights of the minority, not in terms of race but in the ruling party. He wanted the people and states to hold the power and believed that abolition shouldn't be a declaration from the federal government, but as a part of the democratic process, which would involve all slave-owners eventually voting to eliminate slavery."

"So you're saying he's a good guy?"

He tipped his head. "Is anyone a good guy?"

"I feel like this is a trick question."

"Not a trick question, but one for everyone to decide on their own. What qualities make a government work or not work, what makes it good or bad, that's what I find interesting. History isn't really history because we're still trying to figure it out. Our country, like most, is still fighting over what the government should and shouldn't do. America's having the exact same conversations that we had in 1787, but with different terms. Get it?"

"Not at all," I said, and he dropped his head back to the couch, chuckling.

"You really know how to wound me."

"No, I'm kidding. I'm sure your students love you. Animated lectures from a hot professor, what else could they ask for?" I grinned like an idiot begging to have her heart broken and playfully whacked his leg.

Which, of course, made him turn to stone. His smile dropped, and he cleared his throat, scooting back into the corner of the sofa like I had cooties.

I put on the acting performance of a lifetime, like I wasn't one bit affected by the last five seconds. "I was invited out this weekend and wanted to make sure you didn't have anything on your schedule that you needed me for."

He paused with a frown. "Go and enjoy your date."

"Date?" I repeated, a little annoyed at his tone. Like he was bitter about it. "I was invited out by one of my castmates, but why did you say 'date' like that?"

He raised his brow. "I figured it was a date since I've seen you texting someone named Jordan. I put two and two together." Though now his bitter tone was replaced by an apologetic one. "I didn't mean to sound a certain way about it or pry into your personal life."

I waved it off, my mind spinning with the conclusion he was drawing. He wasn't far off. "Jordan's my ex-boyfriend. I don't know what you saw or…"

"Not much, really, and I'm sorry I brought it up."

"It's okay."

He shook his head, his gaze down and unfocused, and I felt the need to explain myself. As absurd as it was, I blurted it all out anyway. "I was living with him in the Poconos, but we broke up in April."

Liam curled his bottom lip up between his teeth and squinted at me, as if I was something to study as I went on.

"We've been texting for the past few weeks, had a phone call the night I found out I got the part. I was really excited, and when he texted me, I told him and…" I let out a long breath. "Anyway, he wants to get back together, but it didn't…end well, and I'm trying to figure out how I feel about him. He's telling me he's changed, that he's working on himself, which I'm happy about, but I'm not sure I can trust him, you know?"

Liam stared at the floor for a while, his jaw ticking, and right when I thought I should excuse myself, he leaned toward me, covering my hand with his so I had to stop scratching at the material of the couch. "He hurt you?"

I only nodded, afraid to answer and admit more than I was ready to. That it wasn't only an emotional hurt, but a physical one too.

Liam gazed at me like he was trying to imprint his words on me. "You deserve so much better than that."

My nose stung and my eyes watered, and before I consciously thought about it, I turned my palm up, wrapping my fingers around his hand. He brushed his thumb over my knuckles, and the tender touch made my pulse stutter.

After a long moment of me finding my breath and his thumb continuously stroking, he squeezed my hand then slowly backed away. "I think I'm gonna go hit the bag for a while."

I aimed for a smile, hoping the distance between us from the past week had finally dissipated. "Thanks for…everything."

He offered me a single tip of his chin then pivoted away with a quiet, "Night, Kennedy."

"Night, Liam." I watched him walk away, wondering what or who he thought *he* deserved. I suspected whoever eventually caught his eye wouldn't ever deserve him.

TWELVE

LIAM

shifted my feet, resisting the urge to loosen my tie as I made idle small talk with the other professors. Occasional events like this were part of the job—special ceremonies, academic conferences, lectures. Tonight, it was a cocktail party, which was really an excuse for the faculty to schmooze with the wealthy alumni during homecoming weekend and remind them how grateful we were for their donations.

So far, I'd had not one person ask me about my classes, but I did have over a dozen people tell me how funny the viral video was, four people ask if I would ever be invited back on television again, and one bold woman slip me her phone number.

Super.

After obtaining a fresh drink, I found a quiet corner from which to people watch. It wasn't as if I hated being with my colleagues or attending important events for the school, but I didn't have the easiest time making conversation. I'd grown up with three outgoing brothers, while I was the more introverted one. It didn't help that I'd been a tall and lanky geek in a neighborhood filled with guys who didn't think twice about pushing others around. I had often found it easier to hide in corners than put myself out there.

It wasn't until my brother Seamus took me under his wing and started to teach me how to box that I became more confident. I was finally able to stand up for myself.

Still, twenty years later, sometimes it was easier to fall into old habits.

"There you are."

I shot my focus up from where I'd been scrolling on my cell phone to Dr. Lang. "Hi, Nadine. How are you?"

"I'm good. I was wondering if you had a moment to chat." She motioned to where I attempted to discreetly slide my cell phone into my pocket. "And it looks like you do."

I let out an embarrassed laugh. "Uh, yeah. Sorry."

She merely pressed her mouth into a thin line, a sort of smile, and my neck heated. Nadine Lang was the chair of the department, and she was a straight shooter. I liked her a lot, though she was a bit intimidating.

I followed her outside, where a few people milled about. The fall night air was bracing after being in the stuffy party so long, and Nadine took a deep breath, almost like she needed a break too.

"Are you enjoying yourself?" she asked after a few seconds.

"Yes, thanks. Are you?"

"Haven't been able to get my hands on one of those stuffed mushrooms that are being passed around."

"Oh yeah. They're delicious. One of my students is working, so he made sure to stop by me first with the tray."

She let out a puff of air from her nose, her version of a laugh. "I wanted to catch you alone because your tenure review is coming up."

I swallowed thickly. Receiving tenure wasn't easy. It took a lot of time and effort, proof of research in the academic field and continued educational development. Tenure represented a significant long-term investment for the university, so the process was lengthy and intense, involving multiple stages and committees to vet a candidate's added value to the school. It was what most professors worked toward, and while it wasn't necessary to continue teaching, it was a big accomplishment to receive tenure.

"The faculty committee has been very impressed with your work," Nadine continued.

I allowed myself to smile, proud. "Thank you. I'm glad to hear my effort hasn't gone unnoticed."

"Far from it. You are exactly what we hope for in a tenured professor, and I expect your review to go smoothly," she said, and I relaxed. Until her expression morphed from one of support to a warning. "There is one point of concern."

My palms went clammy even with the chill, knowing what she was about to say.

"The video from your television interview this summer," she started quietly, almost sympathetically. "You've gained a lot of notoriety since then."

I nodded because it was true. It felt like my so-called fame was finally coming to a tail end.

"It's attracted a lot of interest in our school. I think I remember hearing you say Dean Herring spoke to you about it."

Again, I nodded. Janice Herring was the dean of admissions and was ecstatic that my face was everywhere. She called me a walking, talking billboard for the university, but I also knew some people were unhappy about it, particularly the provost.

"Wendall's concerned," I guessed, and she inclined her head.

Wendall Assman—yes, that was his actual last name—wasn't a fan of my newfound fame, and he'd made it known in a curtly worded email, informing me that if I was going to represent the university on national television, I needed to do a better job. The problem with Wendall, besides his terrible last name, was that he had the final word on tenure.

I couldn't piss him off.

"I'm on your side here," Nadine said, "but we have to be certain there won't be further...incidents that could jeopardize your position or the school's standing."

Read: don't have any more stupid videos of you go viral.

"I'm not planning on allowing anything like that to ever happen again. It was an anomaly."

She patted my arm. "I know you're dedicated to your job, and you're an asset to this university. As far as I'm concerned, you deserve this tenured position, but you have to help yourself. Do you understand?"

"Yes. Absolutely. I'll be a choirboy."

"Well, I don't know if you have to go that far," she said with a smile then turned to head back to the party.

"I appreciate your giving me a heads-up, Dr. Lang."

She waved over her shoulder and disappeared inside.

I stayed a moment longer, processing our conversation. Her direction was clear, keep my nose clean and tenure was mine. Simple.

Now that I had Kennedy to help me out with Finn, everything was smooth sailing.

With renewed motivation, I sauntered back into the party and rubbed elbows for another hour or so before I made a polite exit.

At home, I yanked my tie loose as I trudged upstairs. It was after ten, and the house was quiet. At the top of the steps, I could see Kennedy's door cracked open, light spilling into the hall. I took one step forward, planning to check on Finn, but my body made the decision before my mind consciously did. And suddenly, I had one hand on the doorframe, the other quietly knocking and inadvertently pushing Kennedy's door open.

She was on her bed, hair splayed out across her pillow and her phone in her hand like she'd fallen asleep in the middle of using it. A twinge of jealousy momentarily coated my senses. Just the other day, she'd told me this ex-boyfriend of hers had hurt her, but maybe she'd decided she wanted to get back with him and was up texting until she fell asleep.

Or, maybe, she was talking to someone else. The guy from her cast who'd invited her out for drinks.

Maybe she was on a dating app, looking for a hookup.

Or, very possibly, I was losing my mind and needed to get a grip.

Even though I was exhausted from having to be *on* all night, I decided I needed to hit the bag for a while.

Tiptoeing into her room, I lifted the comforter over her and then forced myself to turn right the fuck around instead of tucking her hair behind her ear, dragging my finger over the apple of her cheek, or bending to kiss her mouth like I wanted to.

"Hey, Professor."

I froze halfway to the door at her scratchy, sleep-filled voice. Every day, I was called professor, but Kennedy was the only one to give me goose bumps when she said it. Like she was deliberately, sensuously trailing her fingernails down my spine.

I was slow to face her, fearing I might not be able to leave.

And I was right.

Because her smile was drowsy, and I couldn't deny her when she sat up and patted the mattress in front of her. "Come tell me how it was."

She might as well have offered me a bone for how well I followed her direction. I sat on her bed, though I kept a foot of distance between us. "It was fine."

"You're like a middle schooler when their mom asks how their day was." She rolled her eyes up to the ceiling and shrugged theatrically, dropping her voice when she droned, "Fine."

"Was that supposed to be me?"

"No, this is you. *Hey, guy, you look wicked hungry. You want a grinder? Or should I go to Dunkin'?*"

I refused to laugh at her ridiculous Boston accent. "First of all, it's Dunks, not Dunkin', and second, I don't sound like that."

"Sometimes."

"Nah. I lost my accent a long time ago."

"Not when you're angry or upset. Or when you say 'lobster.'" Of course, she said lobster like lobstaaah.

"I never say 'lobster.' I never have the occasion to."

She nodded, all full of herself. "Uh-huh. Last month, you picked Finn up and said he was like a sack of lobsters. Do lobsters even come in sacks?"

I narrowed my brow in thought because it wasn't like I said that all the time. And I couldn't believe she would remember such a tiny detail. "Lobsters are transported in crates, not sacks."

This small piece of knowledge seemed to delight Kennedy, her eyes bright and awake now. She shifted closer to me. "How do you know?"

"My dad was a fisherman."

"Really?"

I nodded. "Family business."

"How come you didn't go into it?"

"My dad died when I was ten, and my brothers and I weren't interested in it without him, so…" I slanted my gaze to the wall as I shrugged. I'd had a lot of years to deal with my grief, and while it still hurt, it was more like a tender bruise as opposed to the open wound I'd had when I was younger. "My uncle took it over completely. A couple of my cousins are still doing it."

"I'm sorry about your father," she said, scooting even closer to me so her thigh was right up against mine. "Mine died when I was eight." Surprised, I met Kennedy's eyes, and she offered me a tiny, sad smile. "It's like our own little club."

I gave in to a rough laugh. "The dead dads club." When her fingers curled around mine, squeezing, I squeezed back. "Mine was a stroke. What was yours?"

"Cancer."

"You seem well-adjusted," I noted, and she outright guffawed.

"If you think choosing all the wrong men to fall in love with and fearing they will leave, so you walk on eggshells around them, then yes, I'm very well-adjusted. What about you?"

I didn't like her sarcastic answer, especially because of the rage congealing in my chest, imagining Kennedy giving in to assholes. But I responded to her question anyway. "Well, I fight with a heavy bag almost every night because sometimes it feels like the only way I can safely feel anything, so…maybe?"

She leaned her head on my shoulder, her other hand wrapping around the top of mine as if I needed comfort. I didn't. *She* did. She was the one who basically admitted to struggling.

But she had me telling her more of my story. "I live in my head, for the most part. Great with facts and figures, not so great with letting out emotion. When my dad died, I saw what a rough time my mom was having. My eldest brother, Seamus, was pissed off all the time. Brian cried a lot, and Collin was only five, so he didn't even fully get it. I made sure not to do anything that would require anyone to give me any extra attention. I went to school, got good grades, was never in trouble, and after a few years, it was easier for me to just keep my mouth shut about everything. Even when the neighborhood assholes started to pick on me. I never told my mother because I didn't want to worry her, but Seamus figured out what was going on, and by then, he'd already been training for a while, so he took me into the ring."

"That's why you box?" She lifted her head, her face so close to mine, I could see the distinction of gold and brown in her irises. "Because of your brother?"

"He was on the amateur circuit, and it was a safe space for me to let it all out. All the things I kept inside. I learned to take it out on the bag. Plus, you know, assholes."

"I can't believe you were bullied."

I lifted one shoulder. "I was an easy target."

She huffed. "I hate them. Where are they now?"

"No idea."

With another cute little annoyed huff, she laid her head back on my shoulder.

"Tell me more about these eggshells," I said, my lips dragging over her hair.

"When my dad died, my mom went into a deep depression.

The can't get out of bed or shower kind of depression, and my sister pretty much became my mother for a few years until Mom pulled herself out of it. Sort of like you, I saw what was going on around me, and I didn't want to make it any harder or upset anyone. And then I was diagnosed with epilepsy, which was kinda inconvenient for everyone. It doesn't just affect me. It affects everyone around me because I'm a liability."

I stayed quiet, sitting in the guilt of how I might have contributed to her feeling like she had to walk on eggshells around me and Finn.

"I don't ever want to make anyone feel like they have to do anything special for me. I don't want to be extra work," she said, and I forced my jaw to unclench.

"You're not extra work, Kennedy."

She lifted her head, meeting my gaze. "I am, and don't try to deny it to make me feel better. I know I pissed you off when I showed up here without a car."

"Yeah, but—"

"I'm a people pleaser and avoid rocking the boat so they don't get mad when they realize I come with so many instructions."

"Instructions?" I repeated with a reluctant chuckle.

"Yeah. I'm like new clothes that come with a tag of tiny directions."

"Wash on cold and dry on low?"

"Exactly." She breathed out a laugh, her breath fanning over me. "I'm high-maintenance. I know that about myself."

Having a medical condition and requiring intervention for it was *not* high-maintenance. It was life. And once again, I found myself curling my fingers into fists at the idea that anyone made Kennedy feel less than or unworthy. That she'd believe simply living her life the way she needed to was somehow bad.

"I hope you know you don't have to walk on eggshells around me." When she nodded, I told her, "And if the people in your life really love you, they won't care about you being extra work. You're epileptic and have a penchant for bad luck, so what?"

"*So what?*" She jerked upright. "So, you sat with me in the car for a day while I drove around, and you put up multiple signs around the house for what to do in case I have a seizure."

"Yeah. So what?" Never mind that those signs could potentially save her life, and I wouldn't care if they were turned into wallpaper and glued on every inch of the house. "What you need doesn't affect anyone else. If they argue otherwise, you let me know who they are, and I'll take 'em out back to teach 'em what's what."

"My knight in shining armor."

"I wouldn't go that far," I said, pulling away from her and her warm sunshine essence. "I don't like horses."

She stayed on the bed, her head tipped back to look up at me. "Who needs a horse?"

I crossed to her bedroom door, leaning against it. "You do. If that's what you want."

"I'm not *that* high-maintenance."

With her hair down, her face clear of makeup, and a well-worn sweatshirt on, she didn't look high-maintenance at all. But... "For the record, I like you exactly the way you are. Dry cleaning required or not. Don't change for anyone."

Her answering smile lodged deep beneath my ribs. So deep I didn't think it was ever going away.

I dipped my chin in her direction. "Night, Kennedy."

"G'night, Professor."

THIRTEEN
KENNEDY

'd just finished pouring a mixture of candy into a big bowl when a creature roared behind me a moment before something bit my butt. I screeched, playing at being hurt, falling to the floor as the small dinosaur kept attacking me.

"Ken-dee! Rah!"

"No, don't eat me, T-Rex!"

Finn giggled, pawing and nibbling at me.

"Hey, whoa. No eating Kennedy." Liam wrapped his hands around Finn, detaching his son's mouth from my shirt, and I got my first look at father and son together.

In matching plush dinosaur costumes with big heads, teeth, and the tall scales along their spines.

My heart threatened to burst out of my chest.

"Bad manners," Liam told Finn, who snapped his jaw in my direction.

"It's okay." I laughed and accepted Liam's hand to help me stand up. "I know I taste good."

And the world stopped. All the air sucked into a vacuum. Everything was so still, I thought I could even see the particles of dust floating around me. Because I'd made a dumb joke about how I tasted.

Because Finn was "eating" me.

But now, all I could think about was Liam tasting me.

All I could see was the way Liam's eyes flared.

All I could feel was his hot gaze as it strayed from my face down my throat, over my chest, covered by my "Good Witch" T-shirt, and down to my black leggings and eventually to my bare feet. It felt like a century before his gaze journeyed back up, taking the same scorching path to my face.

He didn't crack a smile or even offer some one-liner in return. He merely cleared his throat then turned away from me, and I nearly passed out.

Liam sank down to his knees in front of Finn. "I know you're excited to trick-or-treat, and you love dressing up as a dinosaur, but I need you to remember you're a human, okay? You can't go around biting people."

I fanned at my face and piled my hair up on the top of my head. "Yeah, babes, it's okay because you know me, but it would be really bad if you went around biting strangers. You won't be invited back to their houses to trick-or-treat anymore if you bite them."

Finn batted at his dinosaur head, which was falling into his face, disturbing his glasses. I reached out to help him at the same time Liam did, and we bumped hands.

"Oh, sorry. I didn't…"

"No, go ahead. You can…"

We glanced at each other then at Finn, and both of us backed away, leaving his dinosaur head slumped down over his forehead.

We were a mess. Ever since last Friday, when Liam had come home from that cocktail party he'd attended at school then snuck into my room while I was sleeping.

At first when I'd woken up, I'd worried that something had happened, until I'd quickly realized everything was fine since he'd been trying to creep back out after placing my blanket on top of me. Then I'd been overcome with the warmth of his tenderness and my own blaze of desire.

I'd fallen asleep reading an article he'd written in some academic journal. I didn't understand a lick of it and was actually quite bored, but I'd wanted to read his words. Even if I fell asleep before I finished it.

I was both thrilled to know he cared enough to cover me up and desperate to know if he could tell I was fighting this attraction to him.

When he'd actually accepted my invitation to sit on my bed, I'd found out we had a lot more in common than I'd realized. I'd always assumed we couldn't ever find a level playing field. He was too smart, too much older, too good for me. But after last week, it was hard to draw those lines anymore. It didn't matter that he was more than a decade older than me, that I'd never gone to college, or that I was his son's nanny.

This pulsing energy between us wasn't going away. In fact, it was growing. Every single day. In the lazy smiles he offered over breakfast, the way he placed his hand on my back when he passed me in the house as if to let me know he was there, and how he always told me to be careful and to text him throughout the day. It had started with updates about Finn, but now Liam texted to see what I was up to while Finn was at preschool or to find out if he needed to stop at the grocery store on the way home or if my headache had gone away yesterday.

He cared about me. And even though I suspected that was simply the kind of man Liam O'Neil was, caring and gentle, it did nothing to allay my yearning for more.

His lingering stare now? Definitely wasn't helping.

Even in his ridiculous costume.

"The guys should be here soon," Liam said as he fixed Finn's costume, and I was grateful for the change of subject.

"Hold on. Wait, wait," I said, retrieving the bag of goodies I'd squirreled away. "Look what I got."

When Liam had informed me he'd invited his friends and their kids over to all go trick-or-treating together, I'd said I'd get some special treats for them. They could all come back and have a little party for the kids, and even though Liam had tried to talk me out of it, told me I didn't need to go through all the effort, I could tell he was happy. These were his best friends, and while I'd only met them for a few minutes at Walt's, I knew they meant a lot to Liam. And if they meant a lot to Liam, they meant a lot to me too.

"Kennedy," Liam said with a delicious smile that started in one corner of his mouth and slowly crawled to the other. "You're too much."

I grinned up at him, bouncing on my toes. "I thought you'd get a laugh out of them."

Liam held the four stainless-steel tumblers in his hands with the custom-printed dad jokes on each. "Why didn't the vampire bite Taylor Swift? 'Cause she's got bad blood."

I giggled. "Good, right?"

"Yeah. Terrible but good."

The way he stared down at me with amusement shining in his eyes, like I was the cleverest girl in the world, made butterflies spring free from their cocoons inside my chest.

He read the next one. "Why did the ghost go to the bar? For the boos."

"I thought that could be Nate's."

"He's not coming," Liam said, setting the tumblers down on the counter while Finn lay on the floor, kicking his feet in the air.

"Oh, why not?"

He shrugged. "Needs to work at the bar. Big night there."

"I just figured he'd tag along. He seems the type to enjoy trick-or-treat."

"For sure, he is, but he doesn't have kids, and who wants to hang out with a bunch of single dads and their children?"

I raised my hand, pretending to be shy about it, winning a chuckle in response.

"If he weren't going to be at the bar tonight, he would definitely be here. I think—"

"Knock! Knock!"

Liam and I both peeked out of the kitchen and down toward the front door, where we could see multiple pairs of feet walking through the living room. Finn growled and took off in their direction.

"Dinosaur attack!" someone shouted.

Liam and I hit the steps in time to see Finn launch himself at Jude, who caught him in a tight hold.

"Hey." Liam greeted Jude's two children with a shoulder pat for the little girl in a unicorn costume and a high five for the boy in some kind of light-up skeleton jumpsuit. Then he towed Finn off Jude and gestured to me. "Kennedy, I'm assuming you remember Jude."

"Yeah, hi." I smiled, and Jude held his arms out for a hug, which I happily obliged, though it was tough around the slice of pizza he wore.

"How are you?" he asked.

"I'm good. Thanks."

Jude, with his sun-kissed hair and rosy cheeks, seemed perpetually happy, though from the very little bit Liam had told me about his friends, I knew Jude's wife had passed away suddenly a few years ago.

"You seem like you're right at home here," he said.

I tried not to let my eyes flicker to Liam, tried not to think about this house being *my home*. But I lost to my stupid imagination running away again, and I blinked back to Jude. "I am. Finn and I are getting along great, and Liam's a terrific boss."

"Terrific, huh?" Some look passed between the two men, which had Liam's jaw ticking and Jude laughing. Then he turned back to me. "These are my kids, Amelia and Sebastian."

"Hi, it's nice to meet you. Can I be the first to give you some candy?"

Amelia hopped around while her brother merely offered me a nod and small smile.

I rushed upstairs to the kitchen for the candy and filled up the tumblers with the pumpkin beer Liam had bought a few days ago. By the time I returned to the living room, Dylan, dressed as a vampire, had arrived with his two kids in tow. I was introduced to Scarlett and Tucker, who were Ariel and a Teenage Mutant Ninja Turtle.

"If any kids want candy, they have to keep their weapons and teeth to themselves," I said in a singsong, holding out the bowl. Finn and Tucker immediately stopped play fighting and scurried over to me, so I could put candy in their bags and pumpkins, along with the others.

"And for the big kids…" I held out the tumblers to the dads. "It's pumpkin beer. I have some snacks for later when you come back."

Dylan acknowledged me with a salute of his *vampire puns suck* cup. "Thank you."

Jude held up his mug, his lips moving as he silently read *What happens when pumpkins drink alcohol? They get smashed.* Then he snorted a laugh. "You didn't have to go to all this trouble for us."

"That's what I told her," Liam said, his attention hot on my face, even if I did my best not to look at him. Because if I looked at him, I was afraid I wouldn't be able to hide exactly what I was thinking.

That I would go through a lot of trouble to make him happy.

Special-ordering some stupid personalized drink tumblers was nothing.

The five kids started getting antsy, and Dylan pointed to the door. "We should get going before we lose one."

"Real quick!" I scooted around by the door, holding up my cell phone. "Let's get some pictures."

They all bunched in together, and I snapped a few then told Liam and Finn to move over by the pumpkin clings Finn and I had slapped on the wall. "We can send these to Tessa. Finn, look at me. Smile!" I took a dozen photos, because why not? "So cute."

Jude tapped my shoulder. "You get in there, and I'll take some."

"Oh no, that—"

"Go ahead," Dylan said in a weirdly stiff tone at Jude's side, while jutting his chin at Liam and Finn.

Liam's only reaction was another tick of his jaw. I swiveled my head back and forth, failing to translate the silent conversation going on between the three men. But I marched over to Liam and Finn anyway.

"Move in together," Jude directed as Dylan held his hands up, pushing them together, motioning for us to squeeze in.

Liam grumbled behind me but pulled me into him, his hand at my waist, so my whole right side was against his torso. I didn't think I'd be able to feel anything under the dinosaur costume, but I was wrong. I felt every sinewy inch of him. I put my hands on Finn's shoulders and smiled.

"Everybody say boo!"

Finn and I both shouted, "Boo!" while Liam stayed silent.

"Ah, come on, O'Neil. Where's your Halloween spirit?" Dylan asked, and I didn't expect Liam's voice to drop two octaves, almost menacing.

"I don't need a knife or axe to murder you."

Dylan smirked into his tumbler. "That's the spirit."

Jude finished and returned my phone to me. "All right." He clapped his hands so all the kids spun toward him. "Rules are, we stay together, use our manners, and stick with a buddy."

Tucker and Finn paired off, along with Amelia and Scarlett, while Sebastian lunged for Dylan, leaving Jude and Liam to pair up.

"I hate you," Liam murmured to Jude, who tossed his head back, laughing.

"Man, you're *so* welcome. 'Kay, team, let's head out."

I stood at the door, waving. "Have fun and be safe!"

Liam was the last to leave. "Last chance. You can still come with us."

I shook my head, the bowl of candy at my hip. "I'll be here, watching *Hocus Pocus* and handing out candy."

"You absolutely sure?"

"Positive."

His hand skimmed my hip as he reached for the door. "See you in a bit."

FOURTEEN
KENNEDY

was barely able to sit for the first hour of trick-or-treat, but once the rush was over, I flopped down on the couch just as Winifred, Mary, and Sarah put all the townspeople under a spell at the dance.

Jordan and I had been texting me pretty regularly ever since I'd told him I got the role of Tracy. He kept telling me how proud he was, and over the last few weeks, it had been harder and harder to ignore his requests. Earlier, when he'd asked if we could FaceTime tonight, I'd agreed.

If only to help me get over…whatever this was I felt for Liam.

"Hey, baby," he said with a smile when I answered his call. His dark hair drooped over his forehead as if he was leaning over his phone.

"What are you doing?"

"Folding laundry."

"Look at you." I laughed because Jordan would rather run to the closest Walmart for a new package of Hanes T-shirts than do a load of laundry.

"I told you. New leaf."

I brought my cell phone with me as I answered the door for a trio of older kids, probably in middle school. "Hey, happy Halloween!"

The kids all held their bags up to me, thanking me once I'd dropped candy into them before scampering off. That was when Jordan chuckled.

"What?" I held my phone up to find him grinning on my screen.

"You're so peppy. It's adorable."

That was the thing about Jordan. He handed out compliments like candy to trick-or-treaters. Never stingy and always sweet. It was why it was so hard for me to understand his fits of jealousy or rage. Like the flip of a switch.

"You know I love Halloween," I said, and he let out a smug sound.

"That's right. I do. I know a lot about you."

I walked upstairs to the kitchen and turned the camera around. "I put these bags together for the kids." I held up the little decorated cellophane sacks filled with treats from the dollar store. "I went a little wild," I said, toying with the ribbon I'd tied around each. "Could barely close them."

"I thought you were just watching the one kid."

"I'm *nannying* for Finn, yes, but Liam invited his friends over with their kids, so I thought it would be nice—"

"Liam's the dad, right?"

"Yeah." I situated the bags back in place, then propped up my cell phone to take the cupcakes out of the refrigerator.

"How much longer do you have to work tonight?"

I lifted a shoulder as I licked a bit of orange icing off my finger. "I'm not really working now. I'm just getting everything set for when the kids come back."

"I don't get why you're doing so much." His voice was edged with something familiar. Something I didn't like.

"Because I want to."

He clucked his tongue, and when I glanced over to my phone

screen, he was lying on his bed, his one hand behind his head, highlighting his biceps.

I'd met Jordan at a party a friend of a friend was throwing. He'd been standing in the corner of the patio, chatting to a guy, with a beer bottle hanging loosely from his fingertips. It had been the middle of fall and cold enough to see our breath in the night air, but he'd only worn a plain gray T-shirt, jeans, and black boots. I'd noticed him, of course, with his olive skin, dark hair, and aloof air, but I didn't think he'd noticed me. Especially since some girl was hanging all over him. She was slim and blond, and I was the exact opposite.

So, it'd surprised me when I'd turned later that night, heading for one of the coolers, and walked right into him.

"I'm so sorry," I'd said, holding on to his forearm to balance myself.

"S'okay." He'd smiled and pointed to the cooler. "Can I get you something?"

"White Claw, please." When he'd offered me an amused shake of his head, his gaze sweeping over me, I had shrugged, joking, "White girl White Claw."

"What flavor you like?"

"Surprise me."

He had straightened with a can of raspberry in his hand and opened it before passing it to me, then he flicked the cap off a beer for himself.

"Aren't you cold?" I'd asked, tugging at the scarf around my neck.

"Not really. I'm a snowboard instructor. Basically cold-blooded at this point."

"I'm freezing just looking at you."

He had gestured behind him then, to the fire pit. "Let's get you warmed up."

He'd looped his arm around my shoulders, and that had been it. Love at first White Claw.

We were hot and heavy for a while, but I had needed a break.

I couldn't stand his distrust or bouts of irrational anger toward me, telling me I was going out of my way to flirt with other guys. It wasn't true, and I'd needed time apart. Last December, I'd headed back home to live with Taylor and sort things out.

But weeks later, I was back with Jordan, and he was back to accusing me of things I wasn't doing. *That night*, we'd gotten into a fight after he'd ripped me away from his friend, whom I'd given a friendly hug to. Apparently, I was "pressing my tits up against him like some slut."

I'd seen red, and we'd started yelling at each other. Then he'd knocked my hand out of the way as I'd tried to take my pills. A part of me had thought it was innocuous. While another part, one that sounded a lot like Taylor, told me it wasn't a harmless accident. That it was on purpose and violent.

But how could he be so sweet and yet…not?

Now he asked, "Your boss gonna let you off so you can go out with me tomorrow?"

He said it in that half-joking, half-serious voice he always used when he didn't want to let on to his true feelings.

"We're going out tomorrow?"

"Yeah. Why not? I haven't seen you in so long, and I promised to take you out to celebrate getting the part in the play."

"Musical," I corrected, and he sniffed a laugh.

"Yeah, whatever. Lemme take you out."

I finished placing the cupcakes on the plastic mummy tray I'd bought. "I don't know about tomorrow. I've got rehearsal."

"On the weekend?"

I nodded. "It's just me, the music director, and Will. He was sick last week, so we need to go over one of our songs since he's been out."

"Who's Will?"

"The guy playing my mom."

"Huh?"

I looked at my screen with a raised brow.

"A guy is playing your mom?"

"Yeah. The character is based on a real-life drag queen."

Jordan snorted and tousled his hair. I didn't like his flippant response, a mixture of disgust and disinterest.

"So, I don't think I'll be able to go out tomorrow," I said, but he was undeterred.

"Okay, how about Sunday?"

"I don't know," I hedged. "I have some errands to run."

"Okay. I'll run errands with you."

"Since when?"

"Since now."

"You're going to drive down here to take me to the grocery store and Target to buy food and Pull-Ups?" When he didn't answer, I lifted my shoulder like *See?*

He rolled his eyes. "Come on, Ken. You're killing me."

I wanted to remind him that I wasn't the one who'd brought up the idea of us going out. He was getting annoyed at me, but it wasn't as if he ever asked what my schedule was like.

"I'm trying," he told me, and I knew he was. He was trying to show me he could be a good boyfriend. I just wasn't sure how interested I was anymore.

Although, I supposed, I'd have to spend time with him to know that for sure.

He tried again. "Next week?"

"Yeah. Maybe."

"Maybe." He huffed. "Don't you want to see me?"

"Yeah," I said, injecting as much enthusiasm as I could because I didn't want to hurt his feelings, "but you know how busy I am. With the show and Finn and—"

"I miss you, baby. You tell me when and where, and I'll be there."

I bent over, leaning my forearms on the counter and met his gaze through the phone screen. "You'll really come down here?"

"Yes, of course. That's what I'm tryna tell you. I miss you, and I want to be with you."

I considered him and his soft, pleading brown eyes, wanting —needing—me to forgive him. "Okay. How about next weekend?"

He grinned. "Definitely."

The doorbell rang, and I picked up my cell phone, bringing Jordan with me as I handed out more candy. We talked about the coming winter season and his work schedule, about him buying tickets for my show, and a party he wanted to bring me to.

"You can stay at my place for the weekend," he suggested, and I offered a shrug. Not because I was afraid or didn't want to, but because I would rather be *here* instead of a party.

Twenty minutes later, the door opened, and Finn came roaring in. "Hey, babes!"

"Who's that?" Jordan asked.

I set the phone on the table and positioned Finn in front of me. "This is my friend Jordan. Can you say hi?"

He ignored my introduction and instead held up a king-size Kit Kat bar.

"Whoa." I laughed. "Who's giving out candy bars this big?"

"Mrs. Feldstein from down the street," Liam answered, holding the door open so his friends and their kids could enter the house.

Jordan leaned forward as if to see who I was talking to, but I angled the screen away. Though, I wasn't sure if it was because I didn't want Jordan to see Liam or the other way around.

"Hey, I gotta go," I said to Jordan, and he crimped his brow. "But—"

"I'll text you later." I hung up without another word and faced the chaos of Halloween costumes, candy, and three exhausted dads. They each threw themselves down on the living room furniture, Liam closest to me on the couch.

"Who was that?" he asked, motioning toward my cell phone.

I waved my hand. "Just a friend."

He seemed suspicious, but I offered him a smile, knowing for sure now that it was guilt that had me pushing my phone away so Liam didn't see it was Jordan I was talking to. I didn't want him to know I was talking to my ex. The same ex who Liam said didn't deserve me.

Under his steady gaze, I felt ashamed. I had always been quick to forgive and forget. Life was too short to hang on to anger. But knowing Liam, living with him, seeing and under-standing what it was like to be with a *man*, it was impossible not to think that maybe I was giving in too easily.

"You okay?" he asked.

"Just tired. Should I put on a pot of coffee?"

We both looked to the kids, all five of them splayed out on the floor, trading candy, and ripping wrappers off.

"Might as well," Liam said and followed me to the kitchen while Jude leaned over Dylan's shoulder, watching some video that appeared to be a guy fighting a kangaroo.

"How was it? Did you have fun?" I asked, putting on the pot and filling it with water.

He stripped off his dinosaur costume, leaving him in a T-shirt and thin pair of sweats. "Nobody got lost or hurt, so I'd say it was a win."

"Pretty low standards there, Professor."

"My objective in life is to keep Finn happy and whole. Other than that, the rest is gravy." I glanced over my shoulder right as he pulled his T-shirt away from his body. It lifted a few inches, revealing his deceptively muscular torso. "Jesus, that costume was hot."

I blinked a few times and focused on filling the filter with coffee grounds. He stood behind me, plucking at the goodie bags. "You made these?"

"Yep."

He waited until I met his gaze to say, "Thank you."

"It's only plastic bags and some dollar store stickers and bubbles."

"It's incredibly thoughtful is what it is."

I lifted my shoulder, biting back a smile.

"How was your night?" he asked, leaning in close to me. "Were any little asshole kids rude to you?"

I barked out a laugh. "You going to defend my honor against eight-year-olds?"

"If I have to."

I pressed my hand to my heart and rested my head against his chest, swooning. "My hero."

He offered me a lopsided smile as he smoothed his hand over my spine. With the near foot of height difference between us, it really did feel like he could protect me from anything—eight-year-olds, plush dinosaurs, or the voices in the back of my head telling me that I was a burden or too much work or not good enough. Because when he stared down at me with his fingertips curling into my lower back, I was enough.

This was enough.

He didn't seem in any rush for me to straighten up, and I had a hard time pushing away, yet I forced myself to take a big step back from him. "Can you see if Jude and Dylan want coffee?"

He gaze swept over me once before he turned away, murmuring what sounded like "Sure thing, angel."

But that couldn't be right.

Because I wasn't an angel. And Professor Liam O'Neil would certainly never have a nickname for me.

Right?

FIFTEEN
LIAM

A week into November and things were really starting to look up. Finn was finally potty trained and making big strides with speech therapy, while I'd received a call that I was being invited back for another television interview. This time, I knew it would all go well.

I hung up my coat and bag then hopped up the steps to the second floor, where I heard Kennedy and my son in the kitchen.

"Hey," I said, bursting around the corner to swing Finn up into my arms, kissing the top of his head.

Kennedy spun around, a bit of something on her chin. She smiled at me. "Hi."

Without thinking, I wiped the white powder off her jaw, and she froze, her eyes wide, wisps of hair curling around her temples. "Sorry." I motioned toward her chin. "You have…"

"I promised Finn we'd bake a pie with the apples we picked."

I surveyed the ingredients on the counter and the chili simmering in the pot on the stove. After so many years of living on my own, I was truly spoiled by coming home to this.

"You're amazing."

She snorted a laugh. "Not really."

I set Finn down and gently nudged her out of the way to wash my hands in the sink, my forearm skimming hers. "You are. You're so good with Finn and…" I dried my hands then held them up, encompassing everything she'd done for me, for Finn, for the house. "You're incredible."

"It's not that big of a deal."

"It's a very big deal," I said, because even as she argued with me, she reached for a bowl and filled it up with chili, placing a toasted piece of crusty bread on top. I took it from her with a pointed stare, but she only offered a lighthearted giggle, as if she hadn't completely changed my life within the last two months. As if I didn't need her.

I sat at the table and Finn joined me, so I asked him, "Did you eat already?"

"Dino nug!"

"Dino nuggets?"

He nodded, playing with a few plastic dinosaurs on the table.

"Did you have a good day today?"

He nodded again but didn't answer verbally.

"Tell Daddy how you helped me," Kennedy said, back to doing whatever she was doing with the pie.

"I yeet apppppples!"

I chuckled, his apples sounding like "a-pools."

"Yes, you ate lots of apple slices, but you also helped me make the dough, right?"

He answered by holding up one of his dinosaurs in her direction. "Roar!"

"Yes, Rex helped too. We all got our hands and claws dirty mixing everything up."

I swallowed down a bite of chili then grinned at her. Didn't she see how I'd still be flailing about with a three-year-old running wild without her? Now, I was settled, confident, and so goddamn excited to tell her, "I got some good news today."

"Yeah?" She washed her hands and turned to fully face me as

she dried them on one of the checkered dish towels she'd bought with an embroidered pumpkin on the bottom.

"I'm going to be on the news on Thursday."

"On TV?" When I nodded, her happy gasp morphed into a screech. "On that same show with…what's her face?"

I laughed. "Yeah. I'm booked for another segment."

She threw herself at me, practically sitting in my lap to hug me. "Oh my god!"

I wrapped my arms around her middle and didn't deny myself the opportunity to curl one of my hands into her hair. "I'm sure they'll bring up what happened last time, but now that you're here—"

"I won't let anything ruin your interview." She backed away, her fingers on my shoulders, her eyes drifting back and forth between mine. "I promise. Finn and I will be far, *far* away."

"Not that far, I hope. You're my lucky charm."

The tops of her cheeks reddened, and she stepped out of my grasp to place the pie in the oven. "What're you going to wear? Are you gonna get your hair cut?"

"I haven't thought about what I'm going to wear," I said after another bite of dinner. "And is your asking if I'm going to get my hair cut a clue that I need to get my hair cut?"

"Well…yes." She laughed as she slipped into the chair next to me, and Finn immediately crawled up into her arms. "I'm not saying I don't like your look, because I do. Most of BookTok, GayTok, and MomTok likes your look, but—"

"I'm sorry. *What* Tok?"

She absently handed Finn one of his dinosaurs when he dropped it then waved her hand in the air. "You know… They're the different, like, divisions of TikTok, according to what you're into. Those are the three I'm into."

"MomTok?" I repeated because that was the one that stuck out to me, and the way she leaned her cheek on Finn's head sent my heart fucking galloping away.

"I peruse it to see what advice there is for me. I'm not Finn's mom, but…" She lifted one shoulder and smiled down at him. "It's not like I come up with all these games and schedules on my own."

"I never would have guessed you didn't."

"You have too much faith in me."

"You don't have enough faith in yourself," I shot back, and she inclined her head, agreeing with my point.

It was so natural for her to hold Finn as we chatted, and I was suddenly too warm. After pushing the sleeves of my sweater up my forearms, I nudged my bowl of chili away and caught my breath.

Kennedy appeared to notice my mini panic attack as she grinned at me.

Killing me. She was killing me slowly. Every day, little by little, stealing pieces of my sanity and heart.

I dropped my gaze to the table. "So, about this haircut…"

My hair was a mix of waves and curls, and I'd long ago given up on styling it. Unless I basically shaved it down to a crew cut, there was no way it didn't look a mess, but any time I did cut it short, my mother about had a heart attack. She loved my hair. Told me I was blessed with a great mane, and it was a mistake to ever buzz it.

"Do you want me to do it?" Kennedy offered. "I could shape it up for you."

"You would?"

"Of course." She set Finn down when he wiggled, and he ran to the living room. "It is the one thing I'm actually trained for."

I considered her offer with a tilt of my head. "Do we need to go to a barber shop or something?"

"No. I've got everything I need. We can do it here, whenever you want."

I sucked my lips between my teeth, thinking for a moment. I couldn't remember the last haircut I'd gotten. It was before Kennedy had arrived. Maybe even before Tessa had left. Single parenting severely cut into my personal time. "Yeah. Okay. Let's do it tonight."

She clapped a few times, bouncing in her chair before reaching out to my head. "I've been wanting to get my hands into your hair for ages."

Then she immediately clammed up, as if realizing she'd said something inappropriate. Not that I'd minded.

Though I absolutely should have. I was her boss. She was my son's nanny. I shouldn't have felt a hot fissure of desire split my stomach. Yet, here I was, staring at her round face and those big eyes, my blood pumping straight to my dick at the mere thought of her touching my hair.

She cleared her throat and stood. "I'll let you finish your dinner and get Finn ready for bed while the pie bakes."

Two hours later, the kitchen was cleaned up after dinner and dessert of pie and ice cream, and Finn was all tucked into bed. I quietly pulled his bedroom door closed and poked my head into Kennedy's room. "Hey."

She peeked over her shoulder at me. "Hey."

"You ready to…" I snipped my fingers by my temple.

"Yep." She held up a small bag. "All set."

"Where should we do it?'

"I want to wash your hair, so somewhere with a sink. The kitchen or bathroom."

I gestured toward my room. "Is my bathroom okay?"

She nodded a little jerkily, her smile a bit shaky. I trusted Kennedy, and I didn't think she'd give me a mullet, but I could feel her nervous energy as she followed me to my en suite bathroom.

"Sorry," I mumbled, as I scooped up a towel and yesterday's clothes from the floor to toss them in the hamper. "Lemme just…" I put away a few of my personal items, my toothbrush and razor, wiped the toothpaste out from the sink, and put the toilet seat down before turning sheepishly to Kennedy.

She raised her brow at me. "Do you need a sticker chart for in here?"

"That'd probably be good, yeah."

She visibly relaxed and set her rainbow bag down on the counter. "Can you pull a chair in here?"

I popped back out into the hall to snag a chair from the kitchen. It was small enough that it wouldn't take up much room. My house was a good size, but my bathroom was…cozy. With the shower, toilet, and double sinks at the vanity, there wasn't a whole lot of walking room.

By the time I returned, she pointed to the space in front of the sink and had a clean bath towel in her other hand. "Sit, please."

She pinned the towel around my neck like a cape after I sat then guided me to lean back, my head over the sink I didn't use. She ran the water over my hair, and it tickled behind my ears and down my spine, her fingers barely skimming over my skin. Yet, I felt it *everywhere*.

"How's the temperature?"

"Fine." I cleared my throat. "Good."

Once my hair was completely soaked, she squeezed some of my shampoo into her hand and massaged it into my hair and scalp. "So, what do you think? You want a trim or to go shorter?"

"Whatever you decide. You're the professional."

She moved over me, reaching for I don't know—a cup or something similar—and I had to bite my cheek when her breast briefly skimmed the side of my face. She either didn't notice or did but didn't want to say anything. When I glanced her way, I'd bet my entire paycheck on the latter, from the way her nipples were hard underneath her thin navy top and how she so dili-gently avoided eye contact with me.

I cleared my throat again because, damn, I had a boulder lodged there, and she worked in silence, conditioning, rinsing, and then drying my hair with a smaller towel. Standing in front of me, she raked her fingers through the wet strands, pulling and pushing it this way and that, before taking a matching iridescent comb and scissors from her tool kit. Then she got to work, snipping away, occasionally shifting to either side but always back in front of me to study me, the corner of her mouth quirked to the side.

"You're cute when you concentrate," I said like a total asshole.

She bit back a smile. "Well, I'm concentrating hard. I need to make you look good."

"I know. It's an almost impossible task with this face."

Her fingers slipped from the hair at my temple to my jaw. "Absolutely hideous."

She smiled. Then I smiled. And I wasn't sure how much longer I'd be able to control myself around her.

She was in front of me, smelling so sweet and looking so comfy with her hair pulled back in a loose knot, strands falling carelessly around her face and neck. She stood between my legs with bare feet, coils of my hair clumped on the floor, and as she ran her fingers over the back of my neck, brushing off clippings, I gave in.

I curled my hands around her hips, letting out a breath and closing my eyes. Like I'd finally finished a race.

One that I'd lost.

Kennedy halted, her gaze dipping to mine, and I swallowed thickly, any words of apology or explanation gone from my head. There was only her and my fingertips dragging down to the outsides of her thighs.

Her pretty mouth opened and closed, her warm breath fanning over my face, and I knew I should let her go. But I didn't.

I didn't fucking want to.

She licked those plump lips of hers and removed the towel from around my neck, and I tightened my grasp on her, squeezing her thighs. They were exactly as lush as I'd imagined.

"Liam," she whispered, and I dropped my forehead to her

stomach. She so rarely used my name. It was always a playful "Professor" or speaking about me in front of Finn so she called me "Daddy," but hearing my name rolling off her tongue, it was almost painful.

I took a deep breath, ready to stand up and apologize, but suddenly, one of her hands was wrapping around the nape of my neck, the other burrowing into my hair, urging me to lift my head, meet her gaze.

And I did. I met those brown eyes, wide and wondering and maybe a little fearful, but even more than that, they shone with something that looked an awful lot like lust.

"Kennedy…" I was exhausted from trying to hide this from her…from myself. I couldn't do it anymore. "I—"

I was interrupted by her phone ringing. We both whipped our heads to the side, where her cell lay on the vanity, between the two sinks. And all I needed to see was one name on the screen: Jordan.

I dropped my hands and released a ragged breath. It took her a long moment to step away from me. "I…um…"

I shook my head and stood, pulling at my shirt, releasing more stray strands of hair to the floor. "I'll clean up in here so you can get that."

"It's not—"

"It's fine."

"No, it's not," she said weakly.

"It is," I told her. "I shouldn't have…" I vaguely gestured to the chair then to her. "You're Finn's nanny, and your boyfriend's calling. It's my fault. I never should have touched you."

She shook her head, her brow crimping, mouth turned down, but I pivoted away before I could see her eyes fill with tears. I knew they were coming. I could tell from the way she wrung her fingers together, bit the corner of her lower lip.

When she didn't move, I picked up her cell phone and held it out to her, tipping my chin to the door. Jordan was FaceTiming her, and I honestly didn't know how long I could hold on to it before I chucked it into the hall, but she eventually took it from me.

She spun around and headed to the door, where she paused, glancing over her shoulder at me, but I'd already started to clean up. "He's not my boyfriend."

I finished zipping up her tools and handed them to her too. "I'm not either, and that's why I shouldn't have touched you. I'm your employer."

Her throat worked on a swallow, and she turned away from me, her shoulders sunken. A few seconds later, I heard a male voice saying, "Hey, baby," and then Kennedy's bedroom door closed.

With a silent curse, I tossed the towel down, giving up on cleaning. Instead, I changed and headed downstairs to hit the bag.

SIXTEEN
KENNEDY

I fluffed my hair a few times then looked over my outfit in the bathroom mirror. Jordan was picking me up in a couple minutes, and I still wasn't sure how exactly I felt about going out with him. We had talked every day, but I didn't quite feel…anything.

Working and living with Liam had changed me. I was more confident in who I was as a person and in what my abilities were, and I wasn't sure if I wanted to go backward. Which was what it felt like by agreeing to go out with Jordan. Like I was moving in reverse.

Especially after Liam and I…had whatever we'd had in his bathroom. I'd given countless haircuts, and never once had I been turned on while doing it, but there was a first time for everything. And being in that quiet, small space with him did funny things to my nervous system. It was difficult to concentrate with the body heat wafting off him and his thighs immovable as I'd tried to carefully step around them. Until he'd simply dragged me between his legs, gripping my hips like I was his lifeline. I could feel how badly he wanted me.

And god, I wanted him so badly too.

I didn't think it was possible for a thirty-six-year-old

professor to desire *me*. But I couldn't deny it after I'd noticed the bulge in his pants and the hunger in his eyes.

Yet now I was going out with my ex-boyfriend, and it just didn't feel right.

With a deep breath, I turned off the lights and made my way to the living room. Without ever lifting my gaze from the steps, I knew Liam was watching me. I could feel it.

I only looked up once my high-heeled boots hit the floor, and I offered him a smile, small as it was.

"You headed out?" he asked evenly, with one long leg perched on the sofa and the other extended out, taking up a lot of space in his gray sweatpants.

I nodded and looped my purse over my shoulder.

His blue eyes swept over me from under his glasses, then he gestured to Finn. "Kennedy's going out. Say g'night night to her."

When Finn threw himself at me, I lifted him up in my arms to hug and kiss him. "Love you, babes."

He giggled and kicked his feet, and after I set him down, he ran right to his father, who stared up at me. "Have a good time."

I hadn't told Liam I was going out with Jordan. I didn't know if I should, but even if I wanted to, I didn't have the right words. *Remember that ex-boyfriend I told you about? The one who you said didn't deserve me? I'm going out with him. Even though I can't stop thinking about you.*

Instead of saying anything, I stood there, awkward and insecure.

And because Liam was perfect, he asked, "You okay?"

I nodded, swallowing the lump in my throat.

"Do you need me to—"

Whatever question he was about to ask was cut off by two loud beeps outside.

"That's for me. I gotta go."

His nostrils flared slightly, and he stood up, following me to the door.

"I won't be late," I told him.

He shrugged. "It's fine."

Ever since he'd seen Jordan's name on my phone screen three nights ago, he'd been standoffish and short. Still polite, but at a distance. Even after his television interview yesterday, which had gone so well I couldn't help but hug him when it was over, he'd merely stood there, arms at his sides. As if he didn't want me touching him.

He opened the door for me, murmuring a quiet, "Be safe."

I tried for one more smile before heading outside to settle into Jordan's passenger seat. As I clicked my seat belt, I noted Liam still standing at the door, watching.

"You look sexy as shit," Jordan said, drawing my attention away from Liam.

"Sexy as shit. Always what I'd hoped to hear," I joked, and he toyed with a lock of my hair, tugging on it.

"You want a love poem instead?"

"It wouldn't hurt."

"Sorry, baby. You know I'm not good with words." He pulled away from the curb and settled his right hand on my thigh. "I'm starving. If you woulda taken any longer, I would've gone inside and thrown you over my shoulder."

I ignored that comment and asked, "How was the drive down?"

Jordan lived in the Poconos, about two hours away. I still couldn't believe he volunteered to make the drive. "I can't wait until you're done down here, and you can move back with me."

I'd given him no indication that I wanted to move back to the Poconos, let alone in with him, but instead of starting this date off on the wrong foot, I avoided the topic entirely and asked him about his upcoming snowboarding season on the mountain. Over dinner, he asked about my show and sat patiently while I showed him pictures of Finn from my phone.

"Who's that?" he asked, pointing to Liam. "The kid's dad?"

"Yep." I quickly swiped left to the next picture of Finn and me at the park.

"You're gonna be a good mom," he told me once I put my phone away.

I wrinkled my nose. Jordan and I hadn't talked a whole lot about the future, but when we did, it was never about kids. "I'm not sure I want to have kids."

He jerked back. "Since when?"

"Since…" I shrugged. "A long time, I guess."

"Why didn't you ever tell me?"

"It never came up."

He sighed as if I was the cause of all his problems. "Wow."

"That a deal-breaker for you?" I asked, trying not to sound hopeful. I wasn't good at breaking up with people…not that I was breaking up with him. We weren't even in a relationship, but I didn't like hurting anyone's feelings.

Jordan shrugged and stood up. "You wanna go to a bar or something?"

"I should head back."

His brow crimped. "Really? It's not even ten o'clock."

"Yeah, I know, but I'm really tired."

"From doing what?" He huffed. "You didn't do anything today."

It was true. I'd spent the day lazing in my bed while Liam and Finn ran errands. I always had the weekends off, and while I knew I could do whatever I wanted, I liked being there. Being *home*.

"I have a lot going on, and I'm tired."

Jordan rolled his eyes. "Too tired to spend time with me? Come on, I've been waiting so long, and now you're gonna ditch me? After I came all the way down here?"

Rather than answer and piss him off more, I put on my jacket, and swung my purse over my shoulders. We walked out to the car in silence, but by the time he was back behind the wheel, he seemed in a better mood, talking about his friends and a party they threw the other week that got out of hand. The cops ended up being called. He thought it was hilarious. I thought it was stupid.

Pulling up to Liam's house, Jordan leaned over the console. "So, you mind if I come in?"

I tensed. "That's not a good idea."

"Why not?"

"Because it's not my home." While that was technically true, I didn't think Liam would ever mind if I had friends over. *But* I did think he'd mind Jordan at his house. "I can't invite random people over."

"I'm not a random person. I'm your boyfriend."

"Ex-boyfriend," I corrected, and the way his eyebrow slowly arched told me I was in for a fight.

"Wow. You really gonna keep treating me like shit, huh?"

"How am I treating you like shit?"

"You keep me hanging on for all these weeks, and now you're gonna ice me out?"

I recoiled at his bitter tone. "I'm not icing you out."

"No? Then what do you call all this?" He waved a hand in the air around our heads. "You leading me on this whole fucking time. Telling me I had a chance."

"That's not fair for you to accuse me of leading you on. I did no such thing!" I knew I shouldn't have shouted, but he always did this. Turned everything around like it was my fault. My eyes burned with tears.

"You're such a little liar, you know that? First, you tell me you never wanted kids, and now, you're refusing to admit you've been jerking me around this whole time. You've been jerking me around for fucking *months*."

I didn't need to put up with this anymore. With my hand on the door handle, I told him good night and hopped out of the car, wiping at my face. I didn't want to cry in front of him. I didn't want to give him that power over me.

But a moment later, Jordan was stomping around the hood.

"Don't pretend like you didn't lead me on for weeks, texting and flirting." He grabbed my wrist, hauling me back to him with a bruising grip. "Everyone thinks you're so sweet, but I see through you. You're nothing but an attention whore."

I tried to pull away, but he held me tight, his fingers biting into my skin. "Let go. You're hurting me."

His other hand sank into my hair, pulling it savagely so I was forced to meet his gaze. "Who is it?"

I attempted to wrestle away from him but only managed to bring myself more pain, the nerve endings on my scalp screaming from how tightly he held my hair. "I don't know what you're talking about. Let me go," I practically whimpered. "Please!"

"Who're you fucking? Somebody from your show? That guy you're always talking about?" He sneered, pulling my face closer to his. "Or your boss. Getting paid to fuck him while living in his house, huh?"

"Shut up!" I batted at him, desperate to get away. But before I could say anything else or push away from him again, a muffled noise came from behind me, and suddenly I was wrenched backward.

"I believe she told you to let her go."

When I realized who it was, I very nearly wept in relief. *"Liam."*

SEVENTEEN
LIAM

The last few days had been weird. More than weird, it was uncomfortable. Wanting to touch Kennedy, make her smile, spend time together with her and Finn, when I couldn't. Not after what'd happened in the bathroom.

Not after I heard the need in her voice then saw Jordan calling. No matter that she said he was still her ex, she wasn't fooling anybody. I knew she was going out with him tonight. Her sweet face was terrible at keeping secrets and lying. Those dark yet sparkling eyes were an open book.

I knew she wouldn't want to hurt my feelings and actually admit she was getting dressed up in those godforsaken knee-high boots and her tight sweater dress for *him*. But I knew.

I just didn't know why she was still attracted to him. From the little she'd told me about him, he'd broken her heart before.

Strike one.

And he didn't even get out of his car. Instead, he beeped his horn for her to come out of the house.

Strike two.

Even if she weren't out on a date with him right now, I still wouldn't like him.

I'd stood at the door, watching him drive off with her until the taillights disappeared, then I'd spent the next few hours putting Finn to bed and keeping myself busy. But even forty-five minutes of boxing didn't help. And I couldn't care less about the documentary I'd randomly put on, something about military tanks. But at least I could sort of convince myself I wasn't watching the door for Kennedy to come home.

Because this was *her home.*

As I swallowed a sip of beer, I noticed headlights out of the corner of my eye. I set the bottle down on the table and strolled to the door, crossing my arms like some angry dad, waiting for their kid to walk in past curfew.

But Kennedy was no kid, and she had no curfew. She was all woman, and I hoped to god she wasn't planning on bringing that asshole inside.

With his car parked in the driveway, I had a hard time making out Kennedy and Jordan, even with the porch light on, but it appeared as if they were having a heated discussion. I adjusted my glasses and squinted for a better focus, leaning in, as if I'd be able to hear them. It was ridiculous, but this was what I was reduced to now. Creeping on my son's nanny, driven mad by jealousy and lust.

After a few minutes, the passenger side door opened, and Kennedy got out. I could see the clear frown on her face. I didn't like that.

Jordan was out of his car too, racing around the hood to hold her wrist. I couldn't hear what he was saying to her, but I understood it was nothing good with how he spun her back to him. Every muscle in my body went rigid as I watched him snarl in Kennedy's face.

She tried to twist away from him, but he didn't let her go. In fact, he pulled her closer with his fingers in her hair so her face was tipped up to him. And I think I blacked out for a second. Actually lost myself in space and time.

Then, all of a sudden, I was on the move, my vision focused on the pinpoint of Jordan's hands on Kennedy.

"Let me go," I heard her saying, her voice cracking, and I jumped down the three steps from the front door.

"Who are you fucking? Somebody from your show? That guy you're always talking about?" Jordan practically spat, and it felt like I was blazing a path of fire across the grass. I was surprised the earth wasn't ash under my feet.

This asshole was still talking. "Getting paid to fuck him while living in his house, huh?"

"Shut up!" Kennedy shouted, smacking at Jordan, and I was close enough to see the side of her face, the tears streaking down it.

I was going to murder him.

Snatching hold of his left wrist, I made sure he released her hair, then with my other arm, I towed Kennedy away from him. "I believe she told you to let her go."

I stepped in front of him, blocking his path to her, and the heart-wrenching sob she let out when she said my name had me momentarily losing my focus.

"Get in the house," I told her.

"Kennedy!" Jordan pushed past me, his hand reaching for her, but I was on him in an instant.

We were about the same height and build, both of us a bit over six feet and lean, but with the adrenaline coursing through my veins, I think I could've tossed him into a cement truck and then pushed the whole fucking thing into the ocean. I wrapped my hands around his collar, stopping him short so our heads almost crashed together. "Take one more step toward her, and I will end you."

He pushed at me, and *this* was what I'd been training for. I spared one glance over my shoulder. "Kennedy, get in the house."

"But—"

"Now!"

I heard her breathy gasp again, but I was too fixated on the son of a bitch in front of me to worry about her right now. I had to deal with him first.

"Get your fucking hands off me!" He attempted to twist in my hold, pivoting his hip to throw an arm around my neck, but I expected that and landed a hook to his kidney on the other side. He reflexively started to double over, but I didn't let him. Instead, I held him up by his collar.

"Yo! I told you!" He brought his right fist up, telegraphing his move, and I shoved him back so his punch didn't connect. "Don't fucking touch me."

"I watched you put your hands on Kennedy. So, yeah, I'm gonna put my hands on you since you clearly need to be taught a lesson."

He charged forward, his shoulders down like he was going to tackle me. When he was close enough, I hit him with an uppercut, followed immediately by another hook. I didn't even feel the pain in my knuckles with each strike.

He stumbled back, clutching his side, but I took hold of him again, driving him back until he was up against his car. "If you ever come near Kennedy again, you won't just be seein' me, but I'll be bringin' my brothers, too," I said, low and slow to make sure he understood my words. Fury wrapped around each syllable, tighter than my fists in this asshole's shirt, and it was impossible to keep my hometown accent from coming out. "I got one who's good with knives, another who pours cement, and one's already been to prison. You get me?"

He opened his stupid mouth to answer, so I shook him, ramming the back of his head against the car to shut him up. He winced, and I leaned in, speaking the next part close to his ear. "You even think about comin' near Kennedy again, you're fuckin' done."

Then I aimed a jab to his stomach, and when he bent in pain, I hit him with an uppercut to his jaw to finish him off. His head snapped back as he grunted, falling to the macadam of my driveway. "Only cowards lay their hands on a woman. Next time you wanna fight, pick on someone your own size."

I shook my hands out, backing away but keeping my gaze on him. "You got one minute to get in your car. Or I'm calling the police. You attacked someone on my property, and I was well within my rights to defend her."

By the time he scrambled up from the ground, I was at my door, though I waited and watched until he sat his ass back in his car and drove away.

Only then did I finally walk into my house. With a deep breath, I turned around and was immediately knocked against the door by Kennedy wrapping her arms around me.

"I'm sorry," she cried against my chest. "I didn't mean to drag—" her breath hiccupped "—you into my mess."

"Look at me." I carefully cupped her face between my hands and urged her to tilt her head up. She did, her eyes red, her cheeks stained with mascara and tears. I brushed wetness from the corner of her mouth. "None of that was your fault."

She sniffed. "But I—"

"No, Kennedy. Nothing you ever do or say is an excuse for a man to put his hands on you." I swept my palm over her forehead, pushing her hair away from her face then wiped her cheeks, though with how much she was crying, it wasn't helpful. "Come here."

I tugged her against me, holding her tight, smoothing one hand up and down her back, whispering soothing words about how she was okay, that he would never hurt her again, that I would protect her, no matter what.

Once her crying subsided to sniffles, I curled my fingers around her shoulders and bent my knees to meet her gaze. "Let's go sit in the kitchen. I could use a drink, yeah?"

She nodded and let me keep her against my side as we ambled upstairs. I sat her down at the table then poured us each a bit of the Jameson I kept in a top cabinet.

I slid a glass in front of Kennedy and slumped down next to

her with my own. I swallowed almost all of my whiskey in one go, working on calming my nerves and relaxing my muscles. Although, it would be a long damn time before I could forget the sound of Kennedy's cries, shouting for him to stop touching her.

We sat in silence for a few minutes. Until she finally looked at me. Her face was clear of tears, but the pain in her eyes broke my heart.

"Are you okay?" she asked, and I hated that after everything that had happened to her tonight, she was worried about *me*.

I gestured to her drink. "If anything, at least it'll help you sleep."

She raised her glass, swallowing a sip, then winced with a cough. "Burns."

"Let me put some ice in it," I said, reaching for her glass, but she stopped me.

"Oh my god! Your hand!"

I yanked it out of her grasp, but she bent, taking both of my hands in hers to examine them. "Your knuckles."

"Are fine."

"No. You need ice."

"I'm fine."

"You're not." She stood, busying herself with wrapping up ice cubes in a dish towel. When I attempted to tell her to sit down, she shook her head, her lips puckering like she might cry again. "Please. Let me take care of you."

I gave in with a sigh and let her fuss over me. But, really, I barely felt my split knuckles.

"I'm so sorry," she said again. "I—"

"Stop apologizing."

"You got hurt."

"Kennedy." I waited until she raised her eyes to mine, paused in her ministrations of rubbing Neosporin on my knuckles. "I know you think you're a burden, that you don't want anyone to go out of their way for you, but I will. What happened out there?

I would do it again—and worse. I don't care about a few stupid cuts, not when your well-being is threatened."

She sniffed and swiped the back of her hand across her nose. "I don't want you to get in trouble because of me."

"I'm not going to get in trouble. But even if I did, I would do it again in a heartbeat to protect you." I wrapped my hand around the back of her head. "Please stop apologizing." I let my fingers linger by her neck, toying with a few strands of her hair. "Are you okay? How bad did he hurt you?"

She absently touched her wrist, and I dropped my attention to the reddening skin, the pieces clicking into place. When we'd talked about Jordan previously, it was in vague terms of him hurting her. But he had *physically* hurt her before.

"This isn't the first time he's laid his hands on you," I said. Not a question but a statement, and she nodded. I moved my chair closer to hers, gently nudging her legs so they were between mine. With one hand on the back of her chair, I cupped my other around her face. "What happened?"

"He'd always been sort of…possessive, and I thought, *wow, he must really like me*, and blew it off. Because it made me feel good." She laughed at herself, though it cracked, her voice watery. "It was nice to have someone so into me when I spent such a long time angry at myself and the world, you know?"

I dragged the pad of my thumb across her cheek, and she continued.

"Of course, it only got worse, so I told him I needed a break. I moved back here with Taylor for a few weeks but eventually got back with him. I loved him, and I wanted to give him another chance when he said he was going to be better. I moved in with him…and then one night, we got into an argument." She dropped her chin toward her chest, obviously the story difficult for her to relay.

I dragged my hand over the back of her head. "He won't ever touch you again. I swear it."

After a few moments, she lifted her face, her teeth sawing into her lower lip.

"What happened when you got into an argument?"

She knotted her fingers together. "I was in the bathroom, taking my pills, giving him the silent treatment, and he kept getting angrier and angrier, louder and louder. I continued to ignore him, so he grabbed me, and I had my hands up..." She held her fists up in front of her, demonstrating. "I had my medication bottle, and he slapped my wrist, yelling at me to listen to him. My pills went everywhere, and he wouldn't let me pick them up. Wouldn't let me do anything, really, except listen to him. Eventually, I pushed him out of the bathroom and locked the door. I called my sister, and she and Dean came to get me."

I swallowed, my blood rushing in my ears, my temper needing release.

I should have killed him.

I might have been exaggerating a bit, but I could make Jordan disappear. Collin was a chef and was obsessive about his knives, and Brian worked construction, so he could get his hands on cement. I wasn't lying about Seamus. He was the one who'd taught me to fight, and he did spend time in prison. Though I was sure he wasn't looking to go back, I knew if I needed help, he'd be there, no questions asked.

The idea of anyone physically hurting Kennedy made me fucking ill, and I slid my hands over her shoulders and neck to her jaw. She wrapped her fingers around my wrists, holding me in place, and that tiny signal exploded the last of my resolve.

It had been gradually disappearing when it came to my growing feelings for her, but now it was gone.

Evaporated.

Because she wanted me here. Wanted my comfort. Wanted my hands on her.

And while I would never take advantage of her trauma, there was no way I was letting her go now.

"Why did you go out with him tonight?" I asked, and she offered me a sad little shrug.

"He said he'd changed. Told me he was working on himself, and I wanted to give him the benefit of the doubt, but I guess… I should have known."

With my palms bracketing her face, I stroked my thumbs under her eyes. "You are sweet and good and far too fucking trusting, but that's what I love about you. You're kind and honest, willing to see the best in everyone." I grimaced, trying to rid the image of Kennedy at Jordan's mercy from my memory, with his hands on her, as he yelled in her face. "I would…" I opened my eyes to her, promising, "I will do whatever it takes to protect you, always. I'd do anything for you."

Her eyes glistened with unshed tears, and she tilted her head, pressing a featherlight kiss to my palm. "I don't deserve that."

"You're right. You deserve a lot more."

Our gazes locked, and tension coiled between us. My senses heightened and with my adrenaline still soaring, it would have been so easy to give in. To pull her into my lap and make us both forget about tonight, but I knew we couldn't. We had so much more to say to each other, yet neither one of us was in the right state of mind to get into it.

"Liam, I—"

The sound of Finn's whining split the air, and we shifted apart, saving me from coming up with an excuse not to kiss her.

"I'll get him," I said, but she stood.

"Let me. I need… I think it would help if I could cuddle with him for a little bit."

I stood up too. "Okay."

She gripped the bottom of my shirt, a wry smile passing over her features.

I was just grateful she wasn't crying anymore. "What?"

"You never even lost your glasses."

I fixed said glasses on my nose. "I can do more than write a few research papers."

She giggled, and it was a literal balm to my soul.

I bent and kissed the top of her head. "I'm going to shower and probably stare at the wall for a while so I don't find out where that asshole lives. But I want you to get some rest tonight, okay?"

She scrunched my shirt in her fist, keeping me close. "Don't let—"

Finn's voice called out a moment after the creak of his door interrupted Kennedy, and she leaned over, peering at the staircase. "I'm coming, Finnie!" She let go of me, and I forced myself not to follow and wrap her up in my arms again. With a hopeful arch of her brow, she asked, "We'll talk later?"

"Yeah."

Her shoulders rose on a deep breath, as if she was finally satisfied. She offered me a tiny smile and spun away, heading upstairs, her soft, sweet voice carrying palpable affection. "What's wrong? Come here, babes."

I crept over, peeking around the wall of the kitchen so I could see Kennedy pick up my son, kissing his temple. He rested his head on her shoulder as she carried him back to his bedroom. A few moments later, his door closed, but not before I heard her singing to him.

Yes, she was an angel. *My* angel.

EIGHTEEN
KENNEDY

t turned out Finn didn't only have trouble sleeping; he was sick. It had started with a stuffy nose, but became worse with a fever a day later, and when I eventually took him to the doctor, it turned out to be RSV. For the last week, the poor kid had been miserable, and Liam and I had taken turns lying with him during the night, alternating between plying him with popsicles and his medication. It had been extra rough on Liam at bedtime since I was at rehearsal every evening, and that was when Finn hacked and coughed until he cried, which only made the hacking and coughing worse.

Whenever I'd come home, I always popped my head into his room to relieve Liam since neither one of us seemed to be able to leave the little guy alone when he was so out of sorts. But he was finally feeling better, and I took the opportunity to sprawl out on the couch in the living room with my favorite movie while Liam put Finn down.

I was about forty-five minutes into it when Liam plodded downstairs.

"How is he?" I asked, and Liam offered me an exhausted half smile as he combed his hand through his hair.

"Fast asleep. I stayed to make sure."

"You need anything?" I sat up, planning to get him a drink or a snack, but he held out his hand, staying me.

"Just need to sit." He reclined next to me with a sigh, extending his arm along the back of the sofa as he relaxed his head against the cushion. "What a week."

Not to mention last weekend when Liam had white-knighted me, coming to my defense with Jordan. I didn't know what exactly had gone down between the two because Liam had been completely tight-lipped about it, and I'd finally blocked Jordan's number. But whatever it was, I believed Liam when he said Jordan would never be contacting me again.

The day after my date with Jordan, I'd spent a long time on the phone with Taylor, explaining what had happened, and even though she'd demanded I meet with her in person, I didn't want to leave Finn while he was sick. So, she'd taken to texting and FaceTiming me multiple times a day.

"Your sister?" Liam asked, motioning to my cell phone now.

I sent off the message about being ready for her and Dean to pick me up tomorrow morning. "Yeah. About the flight."

We were headed to Vegas to spend Thanksgiving with my mother and her boyfriend. And it couldn't have been at a worse time. Not when everything between Liam and me felt so precarious.

We hadn't been able to finish our conversation from the kitchen and another almost-kiss.

"You excited to see your mom?"

"Yeah." Matching Liam's position, I let my head fall back to the sofa and turned to meet his gaze. "But I do feel bad about leaving you and Finn for the holiday."

He waved his hand in the air. "Nah. We'll be fine. We're going to Dylan's. His ex-wife has the kids Thursday, and he's bumming with his girlfriend gone, so Finn'll keep him busy."

I gave in to a laugh. "I'm glad he'll have fun, but I will miss you guys."

His eyes softened. "We'll miss you too."

He shifted closer by a hair's breadth, and I was hyperaware that I was in sweats while he was still in his work clothes, having stayed late at school for some meeting. My hair was piled up on the top of my head, and I didn't have a bra on underneath my sweatshirt that read *This girl runs on musicals and tea* like the theater nerd I was. But he stared at me like I was the best thing on earth.

And damn, did I want to be.

Not sure how to bring up what had happened between Jordan and me, then Jordan and Liam, *and then* Liam and me, I faced forward, concentrating on the movie.

Next to me, he scooted over a few inches, his knee almost touching mine. "What're we watching?"

"My favorite. *Cinderella*."

"This isn't *Cinderella*."

I snorted. "It is according to Rodgers and Hammerstein."

"Is that George from *Seinfeld*?"

"Yep. Jason Alexander."

"He sings?"

"Yep."

"I've…" He looked to me then back to the TV like his mind was blown. "I've never seen this."

"No? It's the best movie musical ever made."

He blew out a breath, tucking his chin in. "Bold statement."

I laughed. "What do you know about movie musicals?"

"Not much, but that seems like a real bold statement to make."

I counted off the names on my hands. "It's got Whitney, Brandy, Bernadette. It's got the best music from Rodgers and Hammerstein, and," I said, circling my hands at the television, encompassing everything about the movie, "look at those colors! It's so vibrant."

"You could write a thesis on this, huh?"

"Sorry to say, it'd probably be more entertaining than yours, Professor."

He quirked a smile in my direction. "Oh yeah. For sure."

I leaned toward the center of the couch, my head near his shoulder, and we both watched the movie in silence for a while. Until Brandy, as Cinderella, arrived at the ball, captivating the prince. Then Liam tilted his head down, and I tipped my head up, bringing us even closer together.

He closed his thumb and forefinger around a lock of loose hair at my temple and tucked it behind my ear before skimming his fingers down my jaw. And then we were kissing.

For a moment, neither of us moved, our lips merely touching as if waiting to see who would give in first. I opened my mouth, letting out a breath, and he pressed the advantage, gently angling my head back, the heat of his body invading my space. He curved his hand around my cheek, and I met his lips once, twice, three more times before his tongue slid along the seam of my mouth. I didn't hesitate to meet him there too, indulging in the feel of his fingers raking into my hair, messing up the already messy style.

When I pushed up onto my knees, he pulled back, blinking at me. Then he licked his lips and released his hold on me. "I…I'm sorry."

Because my first instinct was always to apologize, I nodded and swallowed thickly, even as my hands curled into his shirt. "Me too."

"You don't have to be sorry. I was the one who kissed you."

I shook my head. "No, I kissed you, and I'm—"

He silenced me with another kiss, this one more aggressive than the last, like he couldn't get enough of me. I wrapped my arm around his neck, digging my fingers into his hair, licking into his mouth, tasting the wild need that matched my own.

The tug of his lips on mine softened, his words barely audible. "Tell me to stop. Tell me to stop, and I'll walk away right now."

I shook my head and spoke my answer against his mouth. "No."

He groaned as my tongue slid against his, and goose bumps broke out all over my skin. Almost three months of working for this man, admiring him but never thinking I could ever actually have him, and here I was, nearly delirious from his kisses.

His mouth drifted from mine, blazing a path to my throat as his hands explored my body, roaming over my shoulders and breasts, down my sides to my thighs, which he squeezed roughly. "Jesus, Kennedy."

I groaned at the pained sound of my name. "Mm-hmm."

"We need to talk about this," he murmured against my ear before nipping it, and I gasped.

"Yes."

With little more than a muttered, "Come here, angel," he hoisted me onto his lap, clamping his hands on to my hips and ever so slightly thrusting up so his erection slotted between my legs.

I rolled my hips over the hard length of him, and both of us moaned.

"I've wanted you for so long," he said, his fingertips digging into me, urging me on, and when I widened my knees, sinking lower, he angled his chin out to me. "Take off your top."

I hesitated. First, because I was uncomfortable undressing in front of other people for the first time. I'd always been on the chubbier side, but since I'd started a new medication a few years ago, I'd gained a lot of weight. I wouldn't say I had low self-esteem, but knowing my body could betray me, at literally any moment, I wasn't super confident in it to begin with. Plus, this was Liam "Hot Professor" O'Neil. Of course I was intimidated by him.

"Let me see you." His blue eyes went dark and heavy-lidded, even as the corner of his mouth kicked up sinfully. "I've been dying for it."

And that's what did it.

Crossing my arms over my middle, I held the opposite hem with my hands and lifted my sweatshirt over my head, baring myself to him because he wanted me. If I couldn't believe it before, I did now.

Slipping his hand up my spine, he pushed against my back, positioning my breasts closer to his face so he could suck one of my nipples into his mouth. He let out a hungry sound, and it reverberated through every single cell in my body then pooled deep in my belly. I was hot and wet and already swollen. "Liam," I breathed, placing my hands on his shoulders to rub my clit along his cock, "I need…"

"What? What do you need, angel?"

I licked my dry lips, my chest heaving with each breath. "More."

"Of my mouth?" he asked, then licked at the tip of one nipple while he rolled the other between his fingers. "Or my hand."

"Both," I answered on an exhale.

His warm breath ghosted across my breasts when he laughed. "My greedy girl."

A moment later, he sank his fingers below the waistband of my leggings and toyed with not only the material of my under-wear but my sanity as well.

My blood pulsed thick in my veins, settling between my thighs, and I ached for relief, arching my back in an attempt to get him to touch me. I could feel him smile against my breast-bone when he kissed me, rasping, "I love how needy you are. Writhing all over me."

I whimpered. "Liam, please, *please*, touch me."

"Hearing you beg makes my dick so hard," he practically growled, a moment before he angled me back, providing him room to stroke his fingers down my slit, teasing at my opening. "I would never refuse you anything, you know that?" He pressed his fingers against my clit, circling lightly, as he licked and sucked his way across my chest.

"I have a confession," he said after releasing my nipple from his mouth, my skin glistening from his treatment, and I had a hard time following his train of thought. How could I concentrate on anything besides his fingers and mouth torturing me so sweetly?

"Huh?"

With his hand in my hair, he dragged my head closer to him, forcing me to focus on him. "Last month, on that day I came home early because of midterm break, I saw you."

"What? What do you mean?"

Drawing two fingers down the length of my pussy, he brought more of my wetness back to my clit, circling and circling until I was quivering in his hold. "Finn was taking a nap, and you had taken a shower but left your bedroom door open. I saw you naked, and I had to go lock myself in my room to masturbate."

"You…saw me…naked?"

"I saw some of you. Enough to drive me out of my goddamn mind. I was hard instantly, and then I stroked myself off, imagining you under me and over me, and letting me touch you and kiss you and fuck you."

His words were gasoline on a fire, devastating the working part of my brain, and I struggled to find my words. "I never thought… I didn't think you would ever be attracted to me."

He held me down, right over his thick bulge. "You're ridiculous."

"And you're the Hot Professor."

"And I've been jacking off in the shower any chance I got so I could try to pretend I didn't want to bend you over every flat surface in his house."

Well…I couldn't argue with that and, instead, kissed him. I curled my fingers into his hair, the locks that I'd personally cut and styled a few weeks ago and now delighted in messing up. Pulling me flat against him, he pushed two fingers inside me and latched his mouth on to the side of my throat. He didn't speak while he found my G-spot, gently and firmly stroking it.

"Oh god," I moaned.

"How is that?"

"S-so good. Please, don't stop."

"I'd never stop. I'll *never* stop." He readjusted his hand so his palm rubbed against my clit while his long fingers brought me closer and closer to the edge. I tipped my hips, finding the angle that worked for me, and the sound he made was nothing short of pleased. "That's it, angel. Ride me."

With a few deep breaths, I was able to parse together a couple words without sounding like a wanton creature on the verge of losing her mind. I even managed a smile. "Whatever you say, Professor."

His response was downright feral. He raked his teeth over my bare shoulder, eliciting a gasp of surprise from my throat, before sucking at my nipple again. His fingers were no less gentle, working me over, urging me on.

"You close? Tell me what you need."

"My clit. I can't come without touching it."

He hummed and removed his fingers, and I could feel how soaked I was, not to mention the sound—downright obscene. Then he was there, where I needed him, pressing and massaging until I fell over the edge.

"That's it. You look so pretty when you come. You're pretty all the time, but especially like this." The hand he had in my hair smoothed down my neck and shoulder to my breast, squeezing it. "Open your eyes, angel. Look at me."

It took a few seconds, but I eventually fluttered my eyelids open to find Liam staring at me, color high in his cheeks, his index and middle fingers in his mouth. When he removed them, no longer wet from me but from his tongue, he pushed back my hair, which had come loose, over my shoulder, and I shifted, staring down between us, where I saw the bulge in his pants.

"Will you show me?" I asked, playing with his belt. "How you touch yourself when you think of me?"

His mouth dragged up in the corner as he nodded. I slipped to the floor, kneeling in between his legs, still topless, and he didn't take his eyes off me as he undid his belt with one hand while he traced a circle around my areola with the other. I helped him tug his pants down enough that he could take hold of his erection. I leaned forward, appreciating the beauty of his hand wrapped around his cock. I'd never thought the male genitalia was especially pretty, but Liam gripping himself hard enough that the veins in his forearm stood out was a sight to be admired.

"Teach me, Professor. Show me what you like."

"I need it wet," he said, and I obliged him, tapping on the back of his hand so he'd move it, allowing me to lick up the length. And when he grunted, I did it two more times before spitting on the head.

He hissed a curse and caught my hand in his, fisting it around him, demonstrating how hard he liked the grip and how fast he wanted me to pump, spreading the wetness up and down.

"You're a dream," he rasped, letting go of me once I got it, and widened his knees, so I had more room and he could more easily touch me, hold my breasts, stroking his thumbs over my nipples.

"Feel good?" I asked, and his eyes burned into me.

"Feels better than good. Feels better than I imagined."

I licked my lips, trying on my most flirtatious smile and tone. "Am I a good student?"

He answered by bending forward, kissing me, licking into my mouth so I lost my breath and the rhythm of my strokes. He curled his hand around mine again, both of us working him, our kisses turning sloppy.

"You're gonna make me come soon, angel."

Our lips brushed, breaths mingled.

"Gonna let me paint your pretty tits?"

"Yes," I practically moaned, and he sped up, making me speed up too, both of our hands pumping from root to tip. After a moment, he nudged my fingers out of the away and took over. I sat up tall, watching in fascination as he breathed hard out of parted lips, his cheeks going ruddy, the head of his cock a bright reddish-purple, and for one second, Liam winced like he was in pain before he flicked his eyes open to me, his pupils blown wide. And then he was coming, spurting over my breasts.

He groaned, slowing his movements as his orgasm came to an end, both of us staring at the haphazard lines across my chest. "Fucking killing me, Kennedy," he said eventually, and he trailed his index finger through it, smearing it like he was finger painting. "A work of art."

He brought his finger to my lips, and I sucked off the salty taste before he kissed me again. Yet when I assumed he was going to pull me onto the couch to continue what we were doing, maybe strip naked, he didn't. Instead, he leaned back and asked, "Did you pack yet?"

I frowned in confusion. "What?"

"Did you pack for your trip yet?"

When I blinked and blinked again, obviously not following his train of thought, he explained, "I don't want to stop, but you've got to be up early, and if you still have stuff to do..."

He glanced down between us, me covered in his come, and his cock, not quite flaccid yet, and, *of course*, he was being mature and considerate about all this. Always thinking ahead.

I shook my head. "I was going to pack tonight."

He pointedly turned to the clock by the television. It was after eleven, and I needed to be up at four. "I guess I need to..."

Though I swore I saw disappointment in his eyes, he nodded and, with a fleeting look at my breasts, reached for my sweatshirt. I slipped it over my head then gingerly stood up from the floor. I shook out my legs while he tucked himself back into his pants. "I'm gonna change and go hit the bag for a while."

We both fought through the awkward moment of *what do we do now?* and walked upstairs next to each other. At my bedroom door, he offered me a sluggish half smile and a kiss to the temple before continuing on his way to his bedroom. While I started packing, he changed and stopped at my door again. "You going to bed soon?"

I tucked another pair of jeans into my suitcase. "Probably."

He pulled at the old and stained T-shirt he wore. "All right, I'll see you tomorrow morning, then."

"You don't have to wake up."

He arched his brow with a slight roll of his eyes then knocked on my doorframe. "Sleep well, angel. I'll see you tomorrow morning."

I didn't bother responding since he was already making his way down the hall. I worked on finishing up so I could shower and go to sleep and not think about how we'd just given each other an orgasm and he'd shot his come on me.

Except that was all I could think about.

But the melatonin gummies worked great, because in the blink of an eye, my alarm was waking me up. I changed into matching leggings and sweatshirt for the plane ride, brushed my teeth, and threw on a bit of makeup, then dragged my suitcase to the steps, where Liam was waiting.

He carried it all the way to the front door then met me in the kitchen, where he'd started a pot of coffee, even had my pink travel mug out and ready for me.

"How long did you box last night?" I asked, adding cream and sugar to my coffee.

"A while."

I laughed, and he wrapped his hand around my hip, lowering it to my thigh. It was so casual, like he'd been doing it for years, touching me like this.

"I peeked in your room to check if you were asleep," he said.

"I took some melatonin."

"Afraid you were going to stay awake for some reason?"

I set down my mug and traced my index finger over the logo of his Upenn T-shirt. "I don't know what you're talking about."

He arched his brow. "You're a terrible liar."

When I started to step away, he stopped me, lacing his fingers with mine. I didn't even have time to question it before he'd hauled me into him, hugging me tightly, his face pressed into my hair. "Text me before you board and when you land."

"I will," I said against his pec, wrapping my arms around his waist.

"Be safe."

"I will."

"Have fun."

I snickered. "I will."

We held each other for a little while longer, and when we finally let go, he tenderly swiped his thumb over my bottom lip. He bent as if to kiss me, but my cell phone buzzed. "They're here."

In the living room, I layered on my vest, knit hat, scarf, and purse, then caught how his mouth curved. "What?"

"Nothing." He grinned, positively boyish. "You're cute is all. Come on, I'll carry this out for you."

Outside, he met Dean at the trunk of his car with a hand-shake then loaded my suitcase in before exchanging a few pleasant words with my sister.

"Have a safe flight," he said with a raised hand to all of us, and I twisted around in the back seat, watching Liam's form fade in the distance as we drove away from the curb.

It wasn't until we were halfway to the Philadelphia airport that I realized Liam and I never did have that talk.

NINETEEN
LIAM

Thanksgiving at Dylan's was a less-than-traditional dinner with burgers and grilled vegetables instead of turkey and mashed potatoes, but I wasn't complaining. Finn had already finished his cheeseburger, which meant he picked off the cheese to eat and tore up the bun into tiny pieces, only munching on about half. Now, he watched some YouTube video on the iPad that was probably going to rot his brain, but at least Dylan and I got to eat in peace.

"You have the kids tomorrow?" I asked after swallowing a bite of my burger, and he nodded.

Dylan and his ex-wife, Paige, shared custody of Scarlett and Tucker. While it was a good arrangement, I knew Dylan felt bad about being alone, without his kids or Genevieve. He could be a surly asshole, but he was one of my best friends.

"Thanks for having us over," I said around a sip of beer, and he lifted a shoulder, mumbling around food in his mouth.

"No problem."

"You—" My cell phone buzzed next to my plate, interrupting me, and I wasted no time flipping it over to find a text from Kennedy. It was a picture of her with her mom, both of them wearing some ridiculous party glasses with turkeys on them.

"You ever hear it's rude to answer your phone at the dinner table?" Dylan said, checking his own cell phone, and I leaned back in my chair, typing out a reply, only to receive another photo. This one was of Kennedy and her mother, still in their glasses, but with Taylor and Dean behind them, in matching turkey hats. Dean was grinning. Taylor was sneering.

I chuckled, assuming that had to be all Kennedy's doing.

"Sorry," I mumbled absently, texting that I hoped she was having a good time.

"Is that the nanny?"

"Yes, it's *Kennedy*," I corrected, even though he called her *the nanny* just to get under my skin.

"You two seemed pretty cozy at Halloween."

I stayed silent, not wanting to give myself away, but he ticked his head to the side, studying me. After a while, his brows shot up. "Did you fu—" He stopped himself, glancing to Finn, before continuing more carefully, "Did you…do something with her?"

I scratched at my stubble. "We might have, uh, crossed a line."

"What kind of line?" he asked with a knowing, amused glint in his eyes.

I cleared my throat and scratched at the paper napkin next to my plate, not looking forward to getting ragged on again. Like I'd been when I'd confessed I ran to my room to masturbate after seeing Kennedy naked.

"A physical line," I hedged, and this prick laughed.

"I knew it. I knew you wouldn't be able to stay away."

I rubbed at my forehead. The last thing I wanted to do was agree with him. "It… Yeah." I sighed. "I couldn't stay away. Even though I should've. I mean… She's my kid's nanny. She's twelve years younger than me. I'm not—"

"Hey, man." He waved his beer bottle at me like he was swatting at a bug. "None of that stuff matters. If you have feelings for each other, none of those details matter."

"Since when are you such a romantic?"

He shrugged.

"Gen's made you soft, huh?"

He rolled his eyes. "So what are you gonna do?"

"No idea. She flew out to visit her mom yesterday, and we've been texting back and forth a bit, but we never talked about what happened."

"What exactly happened? Did you…?" We both looked to Finn, who was laid out on his back, holding the iPad above his face while kicking his legs up and down. "Did you fuck her?" Dylan mouthed at me.

I shook my head then took a long swig of my beer. "Didn't go that far."

Before I could change the topic, Dylan's doorbell rang, and he frowned as he stood to make his way to the front of the house. I craned my neck, angling to get a view of Dylan opening the front door, and he asked, "What are you doing here?"

"Nice to see you too," I heard Nate say cheerfully, and then he kicked his boots off. He tossed his coat on the couch, earning a grumble from Dylan, before patting Finn on the head and beelining to the dining room with two six-packs of beer and a reusable shopping bag.

He held them up, grinning at me.

"What are you doing here?" I asked, and he huffed.

"You two make a guy feel real welcome." He sat in Dylan's chair. "I'm here for dessert, obviously." He placed the bag on the table, gesturing for Dylan to open it as he said, "It's pumpkin pie. Evie told me I had to come check on you. Make sure you weren't too brokenhearted over her being away." He smacked Dylan's arm. "You're welcome."

Dylan let out a long-suffering sigh but stalked off to the kitchen, returning with clean plates and utensils a few moments later.

"You had dinner somewhere?" I asked him, helping myself to unwrapping the pie.

He popped the top off a beer. "Lunch at my mom's."

I turned to get my kid's attention. "Finn, you want some pie?" When he jumped up, I pointed to the chair next to mine, and he hopped onto it, immediately reaching for the whipped cream Nate had retrieved from the bag before folding it up.

Finn flipped when he spotted the can. "Quirt!"

"Your mom's in Jersey, right?" I asked, cutting a small piece of pie for Finn.

Nate nodded and shook the can then squirted a massive amount of whipped cream onto Finn's pie. I thought my son's eyes might have actually rolled to the back of his head in ecstasy. I handed him a fork, and he dug in like a feral animal.

Nate helped himself to his own dessert. "My stepmom invited me over there too, but… Hard pass. Especially without Evie."

"You sure you aren't here because you're missing your sister?" Dylan asked from his new seat at the other end of the table.

"No. Her text message specifically said, *I know Dylan is crying. Go pet his head.*" He reached out to Dylan—I assumed to pet his head—but Dylan swatted at Nate, who merely chuckled. He asked, "What have I missed?"

"Cheeseburgers and grilled squash," Dylan said around his beer bottle.

Nate arched his brow my way, pointing his fork at me. "What's up with you? How's it going with Kennedy? She's in Vegas, right?"

"How'd you know?"

"Dean told me he was going with Taylor and Kennedy."

Right. Because Nate knew everybody.

"It's fine," I answered flatly.

"That sounded convincing."

Dylan didn't say anything as his gaze ping-ponged between Nate and me, basically all but holding up a neon sign that I was hiding something.

"What?" Nate shoved the last bit of pie in his mouth. "What is it?"

"Nothing," I mumbled.

"*Dude.*" He eyed me. "Did you fuck her?"

"Oh my god," I muttered, meaningfully jutting my chin toward my three-year-old, although he was too busy literally licking his plate to notice Nate's curse.

"You did, didn't you?"

"No. No, I didn't."

"So, what *did* you do?"

This time, Dylan shifted forward, elbows on the table, ready for story time.

I knew there was no way around it, so I told them, "Tuesday night, we were watching a movie and…"

They both waited.

I rubbed my palm over my mouth. "I may now know what she sounds like when she comes."

Nate chuckled. "You dog!"

Dylan smirked.

I ignored them both when my phone buzzed.

KENNEDY

I miss Finn.

I snapped a picture of Finn, his mouth covered in remnants of whipped cream, and sent it back to her.

He misses you too.

"Look at him smiling," Nate stage-whispered. "Must be her."

"Definitely," Dylan agreed.

So do I.

So do I?

Christ. She's going to think I'm some love-sick idiot.

Which may have been correct, because my stomach dipped at her next text.

"Hey… Uh…"

The guys gazed at me, brows arched.

I cleared my throat and set my phone down. "What do you think it means if you tell someone you miss them and they respond with purple hearts but nothing else?"

Dylan tossed his head back and howled in laughter. The prick.

"You really like her, huh?" Nate rubbed his hands together. "Emoji analysis, that's what I'm here for."

"They're hearts," Dylan said, lingering amusement still on his face. "She likes you. What is there to analyze?"

"I don't know." I threw my hand out. "She's in a whole different generation than us. Maybe it means something different. Like, what if she's trying to let me down easy instead of calling me her pervert boss."

"What have you two been texting about?" Nate asked.

"Nothing big, just good morning and good night. She checks in on Finn a lot. I ask her what she's up to."

He shrugged. "So, everything sounds solid. She's definitely into you. Hearts are a good thing."

"But why wouldn't she say it back?" I asked, rolling my beer bottle on its edge across the table. It wasn't like I *couldn't* express myself verbally; I *didn't* because feelings were hard for me. I'd spent most of my life even-keeled, happy with the status quo, but Kennedy'd upended that. She felt so much, and like I'd been warned, loved so hard, it was impossible for me not to want to be the same way. I texted her that because not only was it true, but I needed her to know.

I missed her.

And it sucked to be vulnerable with somebody. Especially when you didn't know what the hell emojis meant.

"You really like her, huh?" Dylan asked, and I met his gaze.

"Yeah. I do."

Finn hopped down from his chair and scurried back to the living room, where he tore into Scarlett and Tucker's toy bin. Nate smiled at him then turned back to me. "So, are you dating now or…?"

I curled my lips over my teeth, thinking about what I wanted out of this. I felt more for her than I ever had for Tessa, but I didn't know how to go about making the transition. "How do we go from me being her employer to her being…someone important to me?"

"Might be messy," Dylan offered completely unhelpfully, and Nate pinned him with a scowl.

"Oh, like you weren't messy with my sister."

Dylan pointed his beer bottle at Nate. "I told you I'm going to marry her. You know I love her. There's nothing messy about it."

"*Now*," he said, all beleaguered, then faced me. "What are you going to do? Pretend like it never happened?"

I shook my head. "Impossible."

I could never pretend I hadn't tasted Kennedy's perfect lips, felt her tight pussy squeezing my fingers when she orgasmed, heard my name like a prayer from her mouth.

I'd come all over her tits, for Christ's sake.

I'd never forget anything, especially that.

Not to mention her smile greeting me every morning, her everlasting patience, the sound of her singing through the house. I was partial to when she sang in the kitchen, swaying side to side, occasionally using a utensil or some food package as a microphone.

I could live the rest of my life with only Kennedy's voice as my soundtrack.

Then again, I wasn't sure I was prepared to live the rest of my life without her. For as much as she shook me up, she calmed me down. Kept me steady. Let me be honest and brave enough to tell her I missed her. Even though I hated waiting to hear it back, I was sure she missed me too.

I felt it. Because Kennedy wore her emotions on her sleeve, and that was the greatest gift of all. More than how she took care of Finn and me, she opened her heart to us and was unafraid to show it.

I would do whatever I had to in order to keep it that way.

Nate scratched at his beard. "Okay, so you can't go over it, can't go under it, ya gotta go through it."

"Bro…" Dylan's brow crimped. "*What?*"

I brought my beer to my mouth, stifling a laugh. "That was such a dad thing to say."

Nate shook his head. "Don't give me that shit. Evie tells me that all the time."

Dylan held his arms open. "You ready to join the club?"

"No way, man. But watch this… It came up on my feed this morning, but I forgot to text it to you guys." He held out his cell phone screen to Dylan and me, pressing play on a video. I squinted because it took me a moment to understand what I was looking at. "Is that a raccoon?"

"Oh shit," Dylan said under his breath. "It's going after that little girl."

"Yeah, wait for it," Nate said, and a few moments later, the video showed a woman, probably the girl's mom, run out and grab the raccoon by the scruff of its neck. Absolutely no fear.

"Look at her." Nate's voice was filled with awe. "Threw that thing like a shot put. Moms are amazing."

Dylan and I agreed, but then the next video popped up, and Dylan motioned to the screen. "Oh, no wait. Was that a snake in a car engine? Play that one."

And that was how my friends and I spent Thanksgiving. Watching people versus wild animal videos.

TWENTY
KENNEDY

'd arrived home from Las Vegas at almost midnight on Sunday and found Liam waiting in the living room. I had texted him earlier that day about the flight issues—three times delayed!—but I hadn't expected him to still be awake.

Without any words, he had opened his arms to me, and I all but collapsed into him. Between the time change and the hours I'd spent in the airport and then in the plane, I was beat. He'd held me tight, his hands locked at my back, as he kissed the top of my head then rested his chin against it. "Hi."

"Hi," I'd mumbled into his chest, earning a low laugh.

I wasn't sure how long we'd stood there, hugging each other, but at some point, he had helped me upstairs, and I'd fallen face first into my pillow to sleep.

Days later, I was still exhausted, but for a whole other reason.

I'd spent the week in a blur of tech rehearsals, dress rehearsals, and last-minute issues. In one number, I'd had a costume change onstage, but the zipper had broken, and I'd missed my cue for the finale of the song, so I'd needed to stay late last night to make sure it was fixed.

Liam and I hadn't had much time to talk in person over this last week because of my schedule, and a lot of our communication happened over text messages, letting each other know where we were and what time we'd be home. There were moments when I wanted to strip naked and kiss him, but I feared it would be too much and not enough, at the same time.

Sure, when he had pulled me into his lap and demanded I remove my shirt so he could see me, I knew he wanted me in that moment, but that didn't mean he wanted me for the long haul. I was afraid to voice how I felt, only for him to tell me that it was a one-time thing. I was, after all, Finn's nanny, and Liam was paying me.

I was sure Professor O'Neil had slides made up about the ethics of the situation. Although, I wasn't all that interested in the ethics. I didn't care.

Because I was falling for him.

And I didn't think I could bear it if he fired me.

Because I loved Finn too.

So, I'd made sure to keep all of our conversations short, even though I could tell he wanted more time, especially this morning. I'd been up early, too nervous about opening night to sleep in, and was voraciously cleaning the cabinet under the sink…as people do.

He'd patted the back of my knee since I'd been lying down on my side, scraping gunk off the back wall…as people do.

Taken by surprise, I'd darted up, smacking my head in the process, which of course, led to a fair amount of whining from me and a few mumbled curses from him as he pulled an ice pack from the freezer for my head.

Conversation averted.

Now, minutes before the show, I stared at my cell phone and the last text from Liam on my screen.

PROFESSOR

Break a leg out there tonight! Finn and I will be in the front row to cheer you on.

Knowing they were here was more nerve-racking than

anyone else in the audience because I wanted to put on the best performance for them. I wanted to impress them. Even though Finn would probably be more excited by a Blippi video.

I slipped my phone into my bag and shook out my clammy hands as I made my way to the stage. I peeked out at the packed theater from backstage, and my heart swelled when I spotted Liam and Finn, in the front row, as promised. Finn was bopping around in his chair, a packet of goldfish in his hand, while Liam casually tossed his arm across the back of Finn's chair, leaning down to say something in his ear.

I grinned.

And then Cathy gathered us all together because it was showtime.

Everything went perfectly, even my onstage costume change. The audience laughed in all the right places and gave Evelyn, the woman playing Motormouth Maybelle, a standing ovation after her song, "I Know Where I've Been." But when the cast came together at the end for bows, it was the sight of Finn jumping and clapping that had me wiping away tears. Next to him, Liam beamed with pride, alternating applause and cupping his hands around his mouth to holler words I couldn't quite make out in the noise.

The cast took a final bow and waved as the curtains closed before we all flew into one another's arms. Christian swung me around, chuckling, Will swatted my butt, and Joanie laid a smacking kiss on my cheek.

I was floating on air by the time I changed and trotted out to the lobby. My sister promptly threw herself at me, hugging me tight.

"Kenny! You were amazing!" She rocked me side to side. "Even if I had to sit behind some asshole who wouldn't stop sniffling the whole time." She pulled away from me. "I mean, Jesus, use a tissue. It was disgusting. He—"

"Hey, superstar." Dean cut her off, throwing his arm around me. "You were great up there."

"Thanks." Still flushed from the lights and excitement, I couldn't bear to keep my zip-up on anymore and dropped my bag to the floor before stripping off my sweatshirt, leaving me in only leggings and a tank top. "I'm so hot."

Taylor fanned me with her program. "You want to go out and celebrate?"

Dean nodded. "Grab a drink or something?"

I stretched up onto my toes, searching for Liam and Finn. "I don't know…"

My sister followed my gaze. "Who are you looking for?"

When I spotted them across the room, I grinned and waved. Liam did too.

"Oh," Taylor said next to me.

I tilted my head back at her tone. "*What*?"

She intentionally widened her eyes. "What's that about?"

"What's what about?"

She crossed her arms. "Don't play dumb. What's going on with you two?"

"Nothing." But I answered too quickly, and she clucked her tongue. Behind my sister, Dean shook his head. He knew I was caught.

"I've got twenty-twenty vision and an above-average brain," Taylor said, to which Dean rolled his eyes.

"By one point. Above-average by one point. It's really nothing to write home about."

Without looking behind her, she held up her middle finger to her boyfriend while I bit back a laugh. "Okay, so you're really smart. Good for you."

"Don't be coy. For someone who just sang and danced her way through two hours, you're a terrible actress. Might as well staple a note to your forehead that says you love him."

I whacked at her arm. "Will you shut up! He's coming over here."

"So, you don't deny it? You do love him?"

"No, of course not."

She sighed. "Kennedy."

"What?"

"I should have known. He was who you were constantly texting and smiling about while we were in Vegas."

I folded my arms. "I wasn't constantly texting him."

Dean toggled his head side to side and pressed his thumb and index finger together.

"Traitor," I hissed in his direction.

He shrugged in response. "You know I hate to agree with your sister, but all evidence suggests you have a hard-on for this guy."

"Will you two knock it off? I don't need you in my personal business all the time."

Taylor huffed. "That's what you said last time."

I jerked back. "Low blow."

"I'm sorry, but—"

"I don't need you throwing Jordan in my face. It's not fair to keep treating me like I'm going to make the same mistakes over and over again. Liam would never hurt me."

"Maybe not physically but… I worry about it."

"I'm a big girl, and I am going to make my own choices, so will you shut up," I whisper-yelled as Liam strode up to me, Finn in one hand and a giant bouquet of colorful flowers in his other.

He held them out to me. "You're really something special, angel."

I took the flowers from him and pressed up onto my toes to throw my arms around him. "Thank you."

He bent, circling me with his arms and lifting me up off the floor. I laughed, unable to contain the giddy fever racing over my skin. "I'm proud of you," he said from where he'd tucked his face against my throat. "So goddamned proud."

He'd told me he was proud of me before, and each time he did, it was another crack in the wall of self-doubt I'd built up over the last decade. I'd spent so long being afraid of what might happen if I found something I was good at, if I found something I loved, because I could lose it at a moment's notice. I never wanted to find a purpose and, instead, took the easy way out. Every single time.

But now, with Liam and Finn, I think I knew—deep down—my purpose was to be with them. To love them.

And hearing Liam's confident words of praise, I realized that I was hiding once again. I had to tell Liam how I felt. I had to let him know this was more than just a job for me. Liam and Finn—they were everything.

"You were brilliant." Liam kissed my cheek, lowering my feet to the floor, only for Finn to hop up and down, grunting because he wanted up too. "You want to give Kennedy a hug?"

At his son's nod, Liam hoisted him up, but instead of letting go of his dad, Finn kept one arm around Liam's neck and reached the other out to me, hugging us both at the same time.

And my heart went careening out of my chest, straight to these two boys, who in a few months had become my whole world.

"Uv you," Finn squeaked out against my cheek, and I swiped at a tear in the corner of my eye.

"I love you too, babes." I kissed his forehead then gently pushed him into Liam's arms.

"Oh my gosh! Is this your family? Your son is so cute!"

I spun to find Cathy, the director, behind me, smiling at Liam and Finn. She waved at Finn, who was busy gazing excitedly around at the crowd, while Liam attempted to control his feet so he didn't get kicked in the ribs, even as he stared at me.

My attention drifted from Finn, who was *not* my son, to Liam, who seemed to be delighting in my need to traverse these waters, then to Dean, who hid his grin with a fist, to my sister, who smirked in arrogance.

Honestly. I couldn't stand her.

I cleared my throat and avoided answering the question of who was my family by looping my arm around Cathy's shoulders. "Finn's not my son, but he is cute, isn't he? Guys, this is Cathy, my phenomenal director."

She waved her hand. "You're the phenomenal one," she said then looked to Taylor, Dean, and Liam. "Isn't she?"

They all agreed.

"Well, I'll let you get back to chatting." She waved at us. "See you tomorrow, Kennedy."

"See you." I smiled then counted to three in my head, knowing what was coming.

"Well, isn't this precious," my sister cooed. "Your little family here."

"You are the absolute worst," I told her as I picked up my bag and sweatshirt from the floor.

"So, you don't want that drink, then?" Taylor teased, and I threw her an annoyed glare.

Liam pinged his focus between the two of us. "You want to go out, Kennedy?"

I shook my head, zipping my sweatshirt.

"You should. Go out and celebrate," he said, and Taylor not so subtly elbowed me.

I elbowed her right back. "No. I don't want to."

"Are you sure?" He pointed at Finn. "I've got to put him down, but it's not like you need to—"

I held up my hand, stopping him there. "I don't want to go out. I want to go home."

I could basically hear my sister's silent thoughts as she huffed next to me. *See?* she said to me through brain waves. *You're in love with him.*

So? I mentally shouted back. *So what if I love a man who makes me feel confident and seen and has never once treated me like I'm a burden or like I owe him anything? Of course I love him.*

Instead, I placed my bag on my shoulder and offered both Taylor and Dean quick hugs and thank-yous, before taking Finn's hand in my own when Liam put him down so the three of us could walk out of the auditorium.

"What was that about?" Liam asked once we reached his car.

"Nothing." I smiled at Finn as I strapped him in the car seat. "Just my sister not minding her own business."

When I shut the car door, I pivoted, finding Liam leaning against the driver's side, watching me. "Got a bit flustered about it."

"No, I didn't."

His mouth quirked. "A bit. Especially when your director thought Finn was your kid."

I didn't know what to say. Because I was flustered by the assumption—and the recognition that I *did* want to be part of their family.

He shrugged, closing the already short distance between us. "It is hard to tell the difference," he murmured, his fingers finding mine. "Anyone can see how much you love Finn. It's an easy mistake to make…thinking you're his mom."

"But I'm not, so…"

"Doesn't make what you feel any less true or real."

I blinked rapidly. God, I was so emotional tonight.

"I'll see you at home," he said and kissed my temple. "We have some talking to finally do."

I lowered my chin, fighting a laugh at his stern tone. "Yes, Professor."

"Kennedy."

I met his gaze, innocent. "Hm?"

He rubbed his thumb over my lower lip. "I hope this smart mouth is still as brave when I get you alone tonight. No more hiding from me."

I swallowed past the sudden rocks in my throat, knowing whatever was going to happen later would change everything.

There was no going back now.

TWENTY-ONE
LIAM

Kennedy arrived home not long after I did with Finn. As I got him ready for bed, she showered, then popped back into his bedroom to say goodnight. She was dressed in loose black-and-red plaid pants and a tight long-sleeved shirt, her wet hair in a braid down her back. I was already in Finn's bed, lying on top of the covers, and she had to bend over me to kiss him on the head, the sweet weight of her on top of me for a too-short moment, her breasts and belly brushing my thighs before she straightened. And since she wasn't wearing a bra, I could make out the shape of her hard nipples through the black cotton.

"I'll see you tomorrow morning," she whispered to Finn then started to turn away, but I caught her hand, and when she glanced at me, I tipped my head in the direction of the hall.

"Go to my room."

She shot her gaze to Finn, but he wasn't paying attention, already halfway to sleep. It was way past his bedtime.

After she nodded at me, I released my hold on her, watching as she walked out of Finn's bedroom and swung left to my room, instead of right to hers.

"All right, guy. You need to sleep now." I curled my arm

behind Finn's head and tried to relax. I held still, even as my fingers ached to move, as my legs threatened to take me up and away, toward Kennedy.

Who was waiting for me.

It was excruciating.

Though, I'd waited this long to finally have her. I could wait another ten minutes.

Or, rather, fifteen. As soon as Finn was well and truly unconscious, his breathing deep and even, I untangled myself from him and crept to the hall.

When I opened my bedroom door, my breath caught at the sight of her lying on my bed. She was still clothed, but even the mere idea of getting her completely naked had my stomach in my throat and my heart nearly beating out of my chest.

I closed the door behind me, and she sat up against my headboard. Both of us staring at each other.

There was so much to say, yet my mind was completely blank now that it came time to lay it all out there.

Kennedy was the one to speak first. "You don't have any vases in this house."

Surprised at the random observation, I huffed a laugh. "Never had the need for them."

"Well, you do now since you bought me the biggest bouquet I've ever seen."

I crossed the floor to the foot of the bed. "Could've been bigger. The woman put a bunch of flowers together for me since I didn't find any satisfactory."

"You're the only person I know who'd grumble about flowers not being up to your *satisfaction*," she said with a teasing smile and uncrossed her legs.

"I wanted to add more, but she said it would look bad. Something about the flowers not matching."

"Any bigger, and I wouldn't know what to do with it."

I rocked back on my heels as she crawled toward me. "I think you'd figure it out eventually."

She kneeled in front of me, breathing out a coy, "To your satisfaction?"

I tugged on the end of her braid, hard enough for her to inhale sharply through parted lips, and she might as well have screamed "more" for how my skin prickled and my cock twitched. I wrapped her hair around my hand, gently angling her head back. She stared up at me. So pretty. So perfect.

"Everything you do satisfies me," I said and bent to kiss her, barely a taste, a graze of my mouth on hers. When I pulled away, she reached for me, curling her fingers into my shirt, but I shook my head. "We have to talk first."

"Do we?"

I swept my thumb along her lower lip, like I had in the parking lot after her show. "I told you before, you aren't hiding from me anymore."

"I'm not used to talking…to guys," she said quietly, like she was embarrassed.

I released her hair and slanted my chin, silently directing her to make room for me on the bed. "That's because you were with boys before." I settled on the mattress, and we both stretched out on our sides, facing each other. "You're with me now, and I'm a man. I'm not afraid of what you have to say to me."

"Wow. Just…came right out and said it."

"That I'm not afraid?" I slid my hand across the mattress to her waist, dipping my index finger under the elastic of her pants. "I'm afraid of a lot of things. Of getting hurt. Of hurting you. Of losing the best thing that's ever happened to me, but no, I'm not afraid of finally hearing the truth from you."

"Oh god," she wailed, throwing herself to her back. "That's not what I meant, but oh my god, how am I supposed to respond to that?"

I couldn't help but laugh. "What did you mean, then?"

She dragged her hand over her face like she was being tortured. "I meant you came right out and said we're together now."

I let out a long, irritated breath. "I don't randomly hook up with people, Kennedy. I wasn't that person before Finn, and I'm especially not that person now. So I need to know now if that's what you want."

She turned back to me. "See? That's exactly what I mean. You're so buttoned-up, and you told me yourself you don't let out emotions, but here you are, letting it all out with me."

"Because that's what mature adults do, but you're used to little asshole boys."

She smiled, tracing a button on my shirt. "Real men have feelings, huh?"

"Real men want to make their partners happy. You don't do that without communication."

She undid the button and moved on to the next one. "I admit I haven't always made the best decisions, and I was afraid to talk to you because I didn't want to hear that *you* wanted what happened to be a one-time thing."

I smoothed my hand over her hip to her ass and yanked her closer to me. "I've been afraid you'd think I was taking advantage of you."

"Please, Professor, I know you're not the rule-breaking kind."

I leaned down, kissing her, plying her lips open with my own, both of us melting into each other. I groaned when she wound her fingers into my hair, tugging on it, and I pushed her to her back, holding myself up over her. "I'd break every rule for you."

"Then what are you waiting for?" she asked in her siren voice. "Let's break all the rules."

I didn't need to hear any more. I lowered on top of her, ducking my head to her throat and settling between her legs as she wrapped them around my waist. I ground my swiftly hardening cock against her warm center and licked her skin that smelled of sugar and flowers and tasted of something wholly new and innately Kennedy.

She yanked at my shirt, pulling it from where I'd had it

tucked in my pants, unbuttoning it to push it from my shoulders, whining impatiently when I didn't help her.

"I want to touch you," she said, and I wasn't about to make her or myself wait for that pleasure. I sat back on my knees to strip off my shirt, tossing it to the side, earning a delighted sigh from her. *"Finally."*

I made a home on top of her again as her hot little hands roamed over my sides and back. "I love your tattoos. I never expected you to have them." She traced the infinity symbol on my pec. "What's this for?"

"My mom. She always tells us that she loves us to infinity."

"That's sweet." She smiled and placed her palm on my shoulder blade. "And this is for your family?"

"My brothers and I all got it done."

She curved her other hand on my ribs, right over Finn's footprints. "This one is the best of all."

I agreed with a hum as I bent my head to kiss the hollow of her throat, dipping the tip of my tongue in it before dragging it up to her chin and sucking on a spot under her jaw. Her short fingernails lightly scratched up my neck and over my scalp, as her mouth trekked across my jaw, nibbling and sucking, drawing a growl out of me when I couldn't take it anymore.

"My turn." I backed up to the foot of the bed and took her hand in mine, towing her with me. "Stand up, angel."

She slipped off the mattress and stood between my legs, so I could hold on to her hips. "Take your shirt off."

She responded immediately, without hesitation, and I had a hard time reining in what that did to me. Not that I expected her to be submissive to me in any way, but I liked when she followed my directions. Especially when she did it with that beautiful smile on her face.

Her breasts were big, heavy in my hands, with nipples that were golden brown and begging for my mouth. I licked at one, unable to restrain the groan from my throat when she whimpered, her knees giving in slightly. I wrapped one arm around her, holding her up securely as I lapped my tongue over her other nipple. She latched her fingers into my hair, holding me to her—not that I was planning on going anywhere—and I let my other hand trail over her round stomach and up between her breasts. I took my time, pressing kisses around them, gently scraping my teeth over them, worshiping them like they were meant to be.

"Feels so good," she murmured, and I brushed my thumbs over her tight, wet nipples.

"You like me playing with them?"

She moaned, the corner of her bottom lip between her teeth, her eyes heavy-lidded, and I dipped my head back to her, licking and sucking until she became restless, her hips swaying, thighs rubbing together.

"You think you're good and wet yet?" I asked, slipping my hand under the elastic band of her pants and underwear to roughly grip her ass cheek. She squeaked in surprise. "I want you naked."

"What about you?"

I squeezed her lush backside again. "What about me?"

"I want you naked too."

I shook my head. "Only if you're good."

She blushed. "What does that mean?"

"It means you do as I say, and I say I want you naked. Now." She started to bend, reaching for her pants, but I inclined my head. "Over there. I want to watch you."

She hesitated a moment, and I raised my brows humorlessly, which had her smiling. "Yes, Professor."

"Good girl," I said once she'd stepped away from me, hooking her thumbs into her waistband. "Spin around. Let me see that ass of yours."

Her lips pursed like she didn't want to laugh. "I didn't know you could be so bossy."

"I can be a lot of things," I said, leaning back on my hands, enjoying the show as she slowly circled around and tossed me a coquettish look over her shoulder.

"Yes. I'm learning that."

"Show me what else you're learning." Again, I motioned for her to stop teasing me and continue with her show.

Slowly, so fucking slowly, she turned away from me, the length of her braid hanging between her bare shoulder blades, the golden expanse of her back on display with its gentle hills and valleys. Then she curled her hands over the elastic band of her pants and slid them down her legs, baring more of her glorious skin to me, her thick, dimpled thighs and shapely calves. When she kicked them off, she started to twist back around, but I stopped her. "No. Now, your underwear."

They were cute little shorts with a thick waistband, and maybe I'd admire them on her another day. Today, right now, I needed them off.

As she began to pull them down, I told her, "Bend over. Lemme see."

She did as I instructed, folding nearly in half to tug them off her legs, one at a time, but before she could straighten up, I said, "Hands on your ass cheeks. Pull them apart for me."

Again, she followed directions, and I inhaled tightly when she revealed the seam of her backside and the shadowed heaven between her thighs.

"Spread your legs," I ordered, unbuckling my belt to lower my zipper, my cock like granite as her pussy came into view. "God," I muttered, shoving my pants and boxer briefs down far enough to wrap my fist around my erection. "You're so fucking sweet, you know that?" I gave myself a few experimental tugs, then spat on my fingers. "Stay like that, but touch yourself. Show me how wet you are."

She wrenched back, whipping her head over her shoulder to face me. She gasped when she laid eyes on me, with my dick in my hand.

"Kennedy," I said in my sternest voice.

"What're you doing?"

"Waiting for you to follow my directions."

"You…you're…"

"Trying to get off. Something you should be doing too."

Her forehead wrinkled, but instead of answering any of her silent questions, I pointed at the wall. "Turn around and show me your pussy."

"But I thought… Aren't we going to have sex?"

"Not tonight. I don't have condoms. Now, are you done asking questions, or do I need to spank your ass till it's red?"

She rubbed her thighs together, eyes widening.

Fuck, she was killing me.

"You like that idea, huh? If you're a good girl, I'll give you what you want."

She let out an audible breath and faced the wall, spreading her legs wide as she bent over again. "Liam."

My name on her lips was barely a whisper.

"Hm?"

"Are…" She angled her head, attempting to meet my gaze even from her position. "Are you going to touch me?"

"Are you having a hard time following instructions?"

"Obviously," she said unabashedly, and I couldn't help the low chuckle that escaped my throat.

"Don't laugh," she whined. "I want you to touch me."

I wiped all the humor from my face and voice. "I will, angel. I promise. But first, I want to get off looking at you, at your body, and your sweet fucking pussy. I've been imagining this for months, so give me it, and then I'll give you what you want. What you need."

She licked her lips, the hint of a smile playing at her mouth.

"What?" I asked, dragging my hand up and down my shaft.

"Your accent makes everything you say sound even dirtier."

"You like it?"

She nodded as she reached between her legs, dragging two fingers down her slit, and I let out a long breath. "That's it. That's my good girl."

She played with herself, fingers working her clit, while I tightened my grip on my length, not wanting to come so fast, yet wanting to come right now, all over her back and ass.

It was agony, this push and pull, needing to stay in this moment yet desperate to fast-forward and get her on her back, my mouth on her pussy. I could see it glistening, hear her intake of quick breaths. And with every swivel of her hips, I ached for more. I should have thought ahead and gone to the store, but then again, I wouldn't have had the opportunity to be here, in this position, with Kennedy putting herself on display for me.

"How does it feel?" I asked her, twisting my palm over the tip of my cock. "Nice and wet?"

"Mm-hmm. I wish it were your fingers, though."

"I know. It will be. I'm almost there."

She shifted, rocking her hips side to side, opening herself up to me even more, and I groaned.

"Can you come with me?" I asked her. "Can you get there too?"

She answered by lowering her head, her braid falling over her shoulder, as she circled the fingers on one hand on her clit, placing the other on the wall in front of her. Her back arched, her ass jiggling slightly with every movement, and I knew when I finally did sink inside her, I would never want to leave.

"Fuck, Kennedy, tell me how it feels."

"Like I'm dying."

"You're not dying. Not unless you take me with you," I ground out, pumping harder and faster. "Take me with you."

She let out a series of short moans, glancing over her shoulder at me. "I'm there. I'm there."

I spoke through clenched teeth. "Me too." My breath was short, my skin tight, heart racing, but I refused to close my eyes even as my vision blurred. I didn't want to lose sight of Kennedy while adrenaline and pleasure shot out of me. "I'm coming too."

She moaned as her knees bent like she might crumple to the floor, and I threw myself off the mattress, wrapping my arms around her, holding her back tight to my front, my come rubbing between us. She sighed, dropping the weight of her head against my chest, and I bent to kiss her head and temple.

"How do you feel?" I asked against her ear, and she smiled lazily up at me. "Not too tired, I hope. 'Cause I'm not done with you yet."

TWENTY-TWO
KENNEDY

Liam's voice sent shivers down my spine, his promise of not being done with me yet full of dark sin, and my body sparked to life, no longer sleepy. He spun us to face his bed and held me tight, kissing along the side of my neck down to my shoulder. He was probably a little over six feet tall, and while he was not extraordinarily muscular, I felt safe in his arms. I would do whatever he asked of me because I knew he would never hurt me. So when he said, "Put your hands on the end of the bed," I happily obliged.

Without looking behind me, I heard him walk into his attached bathroom and return a few moments later. He appeared at my side with his pants pulled back up over his hips but left undone. There was something so erotic about the sight of him in his fitted navy dress pants, unzipped with the belt removed, the top of his gray boxer briefs peeking out. The rest of him was naked and available for me to ogle. His contoured chest and abdomen with that sexy swatch of hair, the perfect amount to feel against my back. He was breathtaking and so heartbreakingly tender.

He gently tucked a few stray hairs that had come undone from my braid behind my ear before swiping a warm, wet washcloth over my back then wiped at his abdomen too. He set it down and dragged his hand along the length of my back to a spot above my left butt cheek.

"You have a birthmark here," he said, and I angled my head to him, my hands buried in his comforter.

"I know."

"I like it. A little heart." He gifted me with an amused half smile before smoothing his palm lower. "When I said I'd spank you, you liked that idea, didn't you?"

I bit back a smile. Liam O'Neil was endlessly surprising. "Yeah. I liked that idea."

"Do you want me to?" he asked, and I licked my dry lips.

I'd never been ordered around in the bedroom. When Liam said I had been with boys before, it was true. None of the guys I'd been with had the knowledge or confidence to come right out and say what they wanted or, better yet, ask what *I* wanted. They assumed and tried, and I pretended it was good but was often left completely unsatisfied.

I'd never been told to masturbate, let alone to let them watch and get off on it. It was the hottest experience of my life.

Up until right this second, apparently.

Liam slid his hand back up my spine, and I arched into his touch like a cat. That was when he took hold of my braid, tugging on it.

"I asked if you want me to spank you."

Still positioned with my hands on the bed, completely naked and bent over, I was at his mercy. "Do *you* want to spank me?"

"I want to make you feel good, and I will do everything and anything to make you feel good. So, yes or no to turning this sweet ass red?"

My inner muscles clenched. Primed from one orgasm already, I knew it wouldn't take long for a second. "Yes. Please."

He quirked a smile. "I love hearing you say please."

"*Please*, Liam," I said, and he closed his eyes for a moment like he was in ecstasy before opening them up to me again. He let go of my hair and moved closer, pressing his thighs against my side and curling one hand around my waist, holding me steady.

"You have to talk to me," he said, massaging one of my cheeks and then the other, his fingers plumping my skin like he was priming it. "We don't need safe words or signs. You just tell me how you feel, okay?"

"Okay," I croaked, clutching the thick comforter tight in my fists, trying to stay relaxed as I felt him shift, knowing what was coming. Yet when his hand landed on my left ass cheek, the rush of air that left my lungs wasn't from pain, but from relief.

It stung. And I liked it.

He raised his hand again, this time hitting below where he landed the first smack, and I let my head fall to the bed. It was freeing to know the sharp crack was coming, comfort in being able to control how and when it happened.

There was so much I couldn't control about my body, but this pain? I wanted it.

Needed it.

To know I'd asked for it, could deny it, alter it if I chose to. And because I could, I did.

"Harder," I said, and he rubbed his palm softly over my left cheek before raising his hand and spanking my right side hard enough that I lurched unexpectedly up the mattress and breathed out a ragged gasp.

Liam kissed my birthmark, his breath hot on my back when he asked, "Too hard?"

I shook my head and stretched my arms out long. "More."

He raised his hand again and again, spanking me over and over, never hitting the same spot twice in a row, occasionally stopping to check in.

I greedily accepted each strike, giving in to the sensation, letting the ache roll through me, settling in my core. I could feel I was getting wetter, and I guessed Liam could too because he slowed, gentling his slaps to my thighs and eventually stopping after one last smack between my legs, his fingers connecting with the wet flesh.

"Oh god," I moaned, and he echoed the sentiment.

"Christ, angel, you're drenched." He slipped two fingers through the seam of my pussy, rubbing my arousal around my clit. "You did like that, huh?"

I could barely speak, so I nodded instead and felt him move behind me again, this time both of his hands on the backs of my thighs as he spread me open with his fingers. He licked up the length of me, and I cried out, both from pleasure and from the shock of his tongue on me.

He growled against me. "You're so sweet. Such a sweet fucking girl."

Then he was sucking on my clit, sinking his fingers into me, while his other hand soothed over my hip and butt to the front of my thigh, which he squeezed, hard and possessive. It only heightened my senses, knowing he loved what he was doing, desired me as desperately as I desired him.

I pushed backward, and he hummed in pure satisfaction, so I did it again, searching for more, for another release, but before I could get there, he stood up and patted my hip. "On your back."

It took me a moment to connect my mind to my body, and I was slow to roll over. Although when I finally did, he placed his hands on either side of my head, levering over me. "I want to see your face when you come this time."

I scratched at his jaw, at the day-old bristles, combing up into his unruly waves. "You always so bossy in bed?"

He tipped his head to the side and skated his hand down my side, his fingers still wet from me. "Not always, but you seem to like it, so…" He drifted his hand over my hip and between my legs, cupping me. "Tell me what you like, and I'll give it to you."

"I like you touching me."

His eyes blazed. "Besides that."

"I like using vibrators when I'm by myself."

He froze with his fingers over my clit. "Have you used them while you've been here?"

"Yes."

"*Kennedy.*"

I was all innocence. "Yes, Professor?"

"When? How often?"

"I don't know." I laughed. "I don't keep track."

"What do you think about when you use your vibrators?"

"You, obviously."

He momentarily dipped his chin toward his chest. "I've been torturing myself, feeling bad that I've been masturbating thinking of you, when this whole goddamn time, you've been two doors down, using toys on yourself thinking about *me*. Jesus."

"Sorry," I said, giggling a little drunkenly.

"You're going to pay now." He narrowed his brows at me. "Where are they?"

"In a bag in my bedroom."

"Be specific, angel."

"A purple case in the drawer of the nightstand."

Without another word, he marched out of his bedroom, his hands in fists at his sides. He disappeared down the hall and returned a minute later, the zipper of the cotton pouch already open. Without looking at me, he asked, "Which is your favorite?"

"Depends."

Standing at the foot of the bed, he met my gaze. "On what?"

"How much time I have." I lifted one shoulder, taken aback by how easy it was to talk about this with him. We were chatting about my vibrators like we would the meals for the week. "If I know I only have a few minutes, I use the rose."

He lifted it up, inspecting the red silicone vibrator, shaped like a rose, then set it down on the bed. He held up another. "And this…microphone."

A laugh burst out from the back of my throat, and I slapped

my hand over my mouth. He smirked and pressed a button, turning on the white wand that did indeed look like a microphone.

"It has fifty settings," I said proudly, and he went through a few. The mere sound of the vibration drew goose bumps over my skin. My breathing sped up, and I became restless, shifting my hips and legs.

Liam eyed me as he stopped it then set it on the bed before lifting the purple rabbit. "Mmm. This one, I think." He tossed the bag down and pressed the vibrator against my stomach. "Feet on the edge of the bed and spread your legs."

I swallowed thickly, feeling the cool air against my heated and damp flesh. He swept his gaze over me, clearly liking what he saw from the way he scraped his teeth over his bottom lip. He bent to suck on one of my nipples then the other and slowly lowered the toy, pausing briefly at my belly button, and then lower, skimming it back and forth over my pelvic bone as he pressed his knee into the mattress, depressing it slightly at my hip.

When I tugged at the ends of his hair, he lifted his head to concentrate on gliding the tip of the vibrator up and down my sex. He let out another hum that echoed deep inside me, and I pulled his face to mine, kissing him wildly, all teeth and tongue, until finally, he slipped the toy inside me, the curve fitting inside just right while the "ears" positioned against my clit.

And then he powered it on, eliciting a gasp from me. I was already swollen and close to climax; I couldn't contain my mewling pleasure. I grasped uselessly at the comforter and unconsciously tried to close my legs because it was too much, though he pushed them back open.

I sighed and whined and shook my head back and forth, the rotating shaft hitting perfectly inside me while the vibrator worked my clit, and it was all too much.

"I can't… I can't…"

"Yes, you can," Liam said in a low purr, switching the setting to a harder thrust. "You can take it."

"No… I… It's…" I panted, my words lost on a moan.

He simply nodded his approval and ran his hand over my temple, pushing hair away from my face. As he loomed over me, his eyes lit with fire. A single-minded focus that I knew he only reserved for his work. But I guessed I was his work now. And god, it felt good.

Too good.

"You're almost there," he murmured, his hand moving to my breast, tweaking my nipple. "Come for me like a good girl."

My back arched, and I squeezed my eyes shut tight at the onslaught of tension suddenly racking my muscles and bones. Fire spread out from my belly, and I cried out when my orgasm crested.

"That's it. That's my good girl." He slowed the vibrator down but didn't shut it off, lazily easing it in and out of me. "Look at me, angel."

I tried. I really did, but I couldn't. Even the weight of my eyelids was too much. He lightly kissed my mouth, my chin, my jaw, behind my ear. "Come on. Let me see those big eyes of yours."

He shut off the vibrator and set it aside, firmly planting both hands on either side of my shoulders, and I eventually opened my eyes to him. He smiled warmly. "There she is."

"That wasn't like when I'm by myself."

"If it were, I think I would have heard you."

I scooted up, glancing to his bedroom door, worried. "Do you think Finn heard me?"

"No." He laughed. "But next time, I might have to turn up his sound machine."

"Was I that loud?"

He shrugged, unconcerned, and offered me one more kiss before turning away from me. He removed his pants and tossed them into the laundry basket, so I took that as my cue and started to gather up my clothes to dress.

He noticed. "Where are you going?"

"To…my…room."

He shook his head. "You can get dressed, but you're sleeping in here." Then he stalked off to the bathroom, where he brushed his teeth. I'd already done that, so I threw on my pajamas and slipped under Liam's gray comforter. He didn't use a top sheet, only a fitted sheet and comforter. How I liked it.

After he finished up in the bathroom, a half smile graced his lips when he saw me in his bed, and he gathered up all my vibrators, zipped them in the pouch, then tossed it into a drawer. I guessed they lived in his room now.

He snuggled in bed behind me, in only his boxer briefs, and curled an arm around my waist, kissing my shoulder. "Night, angel."

"Night, Professor."

And I think I wanted to live in his room now too.

TWENTY-THREE
LIAM

I hadn't considered what it would be like to wake up with Kennedy in my bed. Didn't even think about what it would mean for Finn. And I didn't know what kind of shitty father that made me, that I'd lost all sense of time, space, and responsibility. Because all I wanted and cared about was getting a taste of Kennedy, making her so thoroughly satisfied she'd never think about another man again.

Yet having Finn bound into my room and jump up onto the bed plunged me back into reality like being thrown into a pool.

"Addy!"

I shot up, blinking and holding out my hand so he didn't crash into a still-waking Kennedy. "Hey, guy. Careful. Careful."

"Ken-dee!" He crawled over to her, settling between us with a big grin. "Ken-dee!"

She rolled over, glancing at me with a crease between her brows. She apparently hadn't considered the repercussions either. "Hey, babes." She smiled at my son like nothing was wrong. "You're full of sunshine and rainbows this morning." She brushed his hair across his forehead and kissed him. "Where're your glasses?"

Instead of answering, he snuggled into her side, throwing his arm across her middle with his face smooshed against her chest, and she closed her eyes as she curled around him like peas in a pod.

My heart split in two. One half for my son. One half for Kennedy. "I'll get your glasses," I murmured, kissing the back of his head. "And maybe make waffles for breakfast."

Kennedy opened her eyes to me, deep brown and still hazy with sleep. "Mm, waffles." Then she whispered against Finn's ear, "Did you hear that? Daddy's gonna make us waffles."

I turned, heading out to Finn's room as she continued to murmur to Finn, nothing I could hear, but whatever it was made my son giggle. Inside his room, I placed a stuffed dinosaur onto his bed, collected the sippy cup from last night, and grabbed his glasses from a shelf next to his bed. Returning to my room, I paused in the doorway to watch them tickling each other, Kennedy shrieking in fake laughter whenever Finn's tiny fingers scratched her shoulder. Then she would poke him in the belly, earning big, leg-shaking cackles from him.

After a moment, during one headshake, Kennedy spotted me and smiled. "Come on, Finnie. Daddy's got your glasses. Let's put them on and go brush our teeth."

She stood and held out her arms so he'd jump into them. She positioned him on her hip before walking over to me, and I put his glasses on him, kissed his cheek, then kissed her cheek. I figured it was okay since Finn didn't seem to notice or care.

While they brushed in their bathroom, I slipped into a pair of sweats and a T-shirt then brushed my own teeth, wondering how we would move forward. As far as I was concerned, I could clear out some drawers and space in the closet for her, though I wasn't sure how we'd fit all of her makeup into my bathroom.

Then again, maybe she wouldn't want to make my bathroom *our* bathroom.

In the kitchen, Kennedy had Finn seated with some orange juice and one of their ugly homemade hand puppets. This one was…a nutcracker? When I laughed, she raised her eyebrows at me. "What?"

I refused to answer, proceeding to gather a bowl and the waffle mix. I wasn't a great cook, but I could mix up some batter with the best of 'em. Two years ago, my mother had gifted me a Belgian waffle maker, and I tended to pull it out for special occasions.

As I poured a ladleful of the mixture into the iron, Kennedy smoothed her palm down my back. "You laughing at my gingerbread man puppet?"

"I thought it was a nutcracker."

"Oh my god!" She laughed, dropping her forehead to my arm.

"It's great, really. Mine would look even worse."

As the waffle cooked, we both glanced back at Finn, who was quietly singing to himself.

"He seemed fine with…everything this morning," I said, and she met my gaze with a nervous little tic to her mouth. "How are you with everything this morning?"

She lifted her shoulder, her attention on the hem of my T-shirt as she toyed with it. "I'm fine, but I don't want to make anything harder for you."

"You're not making anything harder for me." I grasped her upper arms, forcing her to look at me. "You make everything better. For me and Finn."

"You don't think it'll be confusing for him?"

Again, we glanced Finn's way. He was scribbling a crayon over a piece of construction paper.

"Hey, guy."

He turned to me over his shoulder.

"If Kennedy sleeps in Daddy's room, would you care?"

His forehead crinkled for a moment in thought. "I seep addy's room?"

"No. You sleep in your room still, but Kennedy might sleep in my room. Is that okay?"

He nodded then went back to scribbling, so I faced Kennedy. "Is it okay with you?"

When she didn't answer right away, I cradled her cheek with my palm. "It's okay if you don't want to. There's no pressure or rush."

"I want to go slow," she said with an impish smile. "But I want to go fast too."

I chuckled and pressed my forehead to hers. "We'll take it one day at a time, how 'bout that?"

"Sounds good."

The waffle smelled done, and I opened the iron to fork it out onto a plate for Finn. Kennedy took it from me and cut up an apple to add to the plate before snagging the whipped cream from the fridge. She squirted a small mountain on top of his waffle and served it to him with a flourish, earning an excited shriek.

And I could get used to this. Our little family.

Which reminded me...

"Hey, so, I wanted to talk to you about Christmas." I shut the waffle iron with more batter inside then placed my hand on the counter, pivoting to face her as she bent to retrieve a small pot from a lower cabinet. I ignored the desire to palm her ass and instead sidled up behind her as she placed it on a burner and flicked on the high heat. I kissed the side of her neck. "What do you usually do for the holidays?"

She added a bit of butter, sugar, and cinnamon to the pot. "Depends."

"On what?"

"Sometimes we go with my dad's family, sometimes we go to Mom's, sometimes we do nothing, like last year. I got day drunk on mimosas, and we watched reality shows all day long."

"*We*, meaning you and your sister?"

"Yep." She made quick work of peeling and chopping up an apple.

"I always go to Boston," I said, leaning on the counter to

watch as she added the apple chunks to the pot. "I was wondering if you would want to go with me."

She paused her stirring. "To meet your family?"

I toggled my head side to side. "That wouldn't be the specific reason for you coming along, but, yes, you would meet my mom and brothers."

"That's…serious."

I shrugged and moved backward to take the cooked waffle out and spoon more batter onto the iron. "It doesn't have to be."

She stirred the apples for a few more seconds then poured some of the sweet-smelling warm cinnamon apples on top of the waffle and picked up a fork. She carefully cut off a piece of waffle and made sure to scoop up apples before holding it up to me, expectantly. I kept my eyes on her as I accepted the forkful in my mouth, moaning at the delicious taste.

She smiled. "Good?"

"So good." I took the fork from her and piled some onto it to feed it to her as well.

She licked her lips. "Really good."

We stood there, feeding each other until the other waffle finished, and then I added it to the same plate. Kennedy poured on the last of the apples, and we ate that one too. When we finished, I dropped the plate into the sink, and we both sat at the table with Finn while he picked at his waffle, tearing it into tiny pieces, occasionally eating some of them. Of course, the whipped cream was completely gone. He'd eaten none of the apple slices.

That was when she finally told me, "Meeting your family for Christmas seems like a big step. I don't want to intrude on your traditions."

"You won't be, I promise, but I thought you might like to come along."

She smiled kindly. "What happened to one day at a time?"

I tapped my index finger on the table a few times. "Aside from what happened last night," I started, then reconsidered it because it wasn't only last night. "This has nothing to do with our…attraction. It's about Finn. We'll be up there for a week, and I know he'll miss you. I thought it would be nice to spend the holiday together."

Her attention drifted to the window for a few moments before coming back to me. "I'm touched you invited me, but could I have some time to think about it?"

I tried to pretend it didn't feel like she was letting me down easy and forced myself to smile back at her. "Yeah. Absolutely. Of course." I cleared my throat. "Like I said, no rush or pressure." I turned to Finn. "Right, buddy?"

He made an engine sound as he flew an apple slice above his head like a plane. "Ight!"

"It's only that…" She nibbled on her bottom lip, and I reached out my hand to her because it seemed like she needed it. After a moment, she said, "I tend to rush into things, and I don't want to do that with you." She pointedly glanced at Finn then back at me. "I don't want to mess this up."

I understood. "I don't want to mess it up either."

Her smile was slow to grow, but it was like a rainbow after a storm, the cloud in her eyes gone, and I leaned over to kiss her. Before I could pull away, she curled her hands around my shoulders. "I don't know what your plans are for today, but I was thinking we could go get a Christmas tree since I have a few hours to kill before the show."

As if I would deny her anything. "Yeah. Let's go get a tree."

"It's been so long since I had a real one. Not since I was a kid."

"Then what are we waiting for?" I stood and ruffled Finn's hair. "Let's get dressed and buy a tree."

Finn raced away to his room, while I threw my arm around Kennedy's shoulders. She tipped her head back. "You don't by any chance own any flannel shirts, do you?"

"I think I have one or two. Why?"

She frowned as if I should know the answer. "Spank-bank material."

I smacked her ass with a huff. "Just go get dressed, angel. We can talk about spank-bank material later."

————

NATE

It's Amelia's birthday today, right?

JUDE

Yup.

NATE

Happy Birthday!!!!!!!

You can remember the kids' birthdays, but you can't remember ours?

NATE

I know yours is in January sometime. And Jude's is the end of June.

JUDE

What about Dylan's?

NATE

Dunno.

DYLAN

mother ducker.

DYLAN

duck

DYLAN

FUCK

NATE

Chill, bro.

What are you guys doing for Amelia's day?

JUDE

The usual. Family's coming over for cake and ice cream tonight. We're going to go to an early movie tomorrow.

JUDE

If anyone wants to meet us for a movie and lunch, you're all welcome.

Maybe Finn and I will come. Kennedy's got a matinee performance of her show.

JUDE

Oh yeah, how'd that go?

She's amazing.

NATE

I think I can see your heart eyes through text messages.

DYLAN

messy

NATE

Yeah, how messy is it?

JUDE

What did I miss?

NATE

Liam loves Kennedy

DYLAN

he wants 2 duck his nanny

NATE

🦆🦆

Not funny.

NATE

A little bit.

Nate sent a GIF of ducks fighting.

JUDE

Have you slept with her?

In the strictly technical sense, yes.

NATE

In the biblical sense?

I don't know.

NATE

What do you mean you don't know?

Is cunnilingus mentioned in Genesis?

DYLAN

is what?

NATE

He went down on her.

JUDE

Whoa. That's basically like a proposal for you, huh?

NATE

Look who's talking. You're a monk.

NATE

It's not good to go without sex for so long. Pretty sure you can die from blue balls. That shit builds up.

Yeah? What scientific periodical did you read that in?

NATE

The Blue Balls Bill.

JUDE

Anyway. Count me in for tomorrow.

DYLAN

And me and the kids

NATE

All right. Pull my leg. I'll be there.

Joy.

NATE

NATE

Go see your nanny.

I plan on it.

TWENTY-FOUR
LIAM

Over the next three weeks, Kennedy and I settled into an easy rhythm. She spent every night in my bed, and although I'd gone out and bought condoms immediately after our first night together, we had yet to actually have sex…biblically. I was satisfied learning how every time I licked the crease of her thigh, she let out a high, keening sound because she was ticklish there, and that she had no problem riding my face.

Because she was perfect.

We focused on building a solid relationship, which was much easier after my semester ended. We spent a lot of time talking and experiencing all kinds of firsts with Finn together, like meeting Santa—hated it—and his first hot chocolate—loved it. We decorated our real Christmas tree, and she convinced me to make a hand puppet—my snowman was not any better than theirs.

So, it shouldn't have surprised me when she'd wrapped her arm around my waist while we'd lain in bed a few days ago after putting Finn down, but I'd been pleasantly startled when she asked, "Is your invitation still open to go home with you?"

I had pressed my answer into a kiss against her mouth. And then lower.

Now, we were on our way to Boston in my car with four bags of gifts, three packed snacks, two suitcases, and a partridge in a pear tree.

It was okay, for the most part, and we only had to make two stops. Finn slept for a few hours, leaving Kennedy and me to chat about our childhoods. We discussed memories of our fathers. Hers was tall and dark-haired and, apparently, a doting husband and father. I told her how mine was gruff but loving, in a silent sort of way, never one to be physically and verbally effusive. But we'd all felt it, his support and protection. It was why Seamus felt the need to assume the role of taking care of the family. The only problem was he went about it in all the wrong ways. He'd been arrested for illegal betting and aggravated assault, and when he was finally let out of prison after a year, he'd found himself back behind bars a few months later. But he'd eventually found himself a job welding and walked the straight and narrow now, especially after he'd met his wife and her daughters. I explained that Brian was currently living with Mom after a divorce, and that Collin was the wild child of the family. We never knew what he would do next, where or when he might pop up. He never responded to our group text message about Christmas.

My family was a lot, but I didn't want her to be surprised by anything, including the cursing and possible arguments.

"You ready?" I asked as we pulled over in front of my childhood home, the beat-up corner twin in historic South Boston, only two blocks from the water. And it showed on the house, the peeling blue paint and crusted-over shutters. Brian had said he was going to be helping Mom out with redoing it, but he needed to pick it up a bit. Looked like shit, including the tiny patch of grass next to the brick steps that needed a good power-washing.

Not to mention, someone had made Mom's reindeer look like

they were mounting each other. Probably some little neighbor-hood asshole.

Kennedy plucked at her sweater. "I'm a little nervous."

"You'll be fine. Besides, it should only be my mom and Brian tonight."

She nodded and slipped into her coat, the weather up here a lot nippier than Pennsylvania. As I pulled everything out of the hatchback to pile on the porch, she got Finn out of his seat, and together we stood in front of the dark-stained wood door, deco-rated with a gigantic wreath.

Before I could even knock, it opened. My mother shrieked and pulled me into her. "My baby!"

"Hey, Ma," I said, once she finally let me get away to nudge Finn forward.

My mother picked him up, smothering him so hard, his glasses skewed sideways. He kicked at her until she put him down, and I motioned to Kennedy. But, of course, Mom attacked her just as hard.

Kennedy laughed. "Hi, Mrs. O'Neil."

"Call me Eileen!" Mom took Kennedy's face between her hands. "Look at how gorgeous you are. Come in, come in." She towed Kennedy inside the house. "Cold as shit outside. Come on!"

Finn ran to the tree in the corner as I carried our bags in, noting how there was no hallway anymore, but one big open floor plan. So, Brian was doing something.

By the time I finished with the suitcases and looked up, Finn had his coat thrown on the floor and was lying on his belly, playing with Nativity figurines, while Mom held both of Kennedy's hands, talking a mile a minute about the house, the new bright-yellow color on the walls, and pointing out different photos and people in them.

"Hey," I said, unzipping my coat, "you know some little asshole messed with your decorations? Made it look like—"

"Some little asshole." Mom pointed to my younger brother as

he entered from the door at the back of the house into the kitchen.

Collin raised his hand to me, grinning. "Thought I heard Mom screaming. Figured her favorite son had returned."

"Brian's the favorite. I'm only the smartest," I said, earning a snort. We met halfway for a backslapping hug. "You out having a smoke?"

He nodded, running his hands through his chin-length hair, then pushed the sleeves of his thick sweater up to his elbows, before opening his arms to Kennedy. "You must be the girl."

"Kennedy," I said, not hiding the edge in my voice.

She accepted his hug, and I didn't like the way he looked her over from head to toe. It was no secret he slept his way around the globe, but he wasn't going to be sleeping with Kennedy.

"You must be Collin," she said, all sugar and spice.

"How'd you know?" He slanted his head to the side, offering her the smile that I was sure had a lot of women falling to their knees. Not mine.

"The forearm knife tattoo, the straggly hair, the cocky swagger…screams chef."

He rubbed his palm over his jaw, smiling good-naturedly. "Hey, baby, long as somebody's screaming something, I don't care. Though I'd prefer it to be you."

"Don't be gross," Mom said, batting at him, and Kennedy moved to stand at my side.

I took her coat. "Ignore him. We all do."

"And you wonder why I don't show up more often." He bent, patting Finn's head. "What's up, buddy?"

Finn held a camel out to him, roaring, and my brother chuckled, splaying out next to him, so Kennedy, Mom, and I had to step around him to head farther into the house. I hung our coats up on new hooks on the wall, and Mom gestured for Kennedy to have a seat at the long table, which separated the living space from the kitchen.

"Where's Brian?"

"At the packie."

"Packie?" Kennedy repeated, and I translated.

"Liquor store."

"Kennedy, help yourself," Mom said, setting down two plat-ters, one of fresh cold cuts and cheese, and another of cut-up lettuce, tomato, and onion. "You must be starving." She pointed to the basket of buns. "Come on, Liam, sit."

"I want to take our bags upstairs first."

"You guys are staying on the top floor."

I grabbed the handles of our bags to carry them up to the finished attic on the third floor, which had, at one point, been everyone's bedroom, except for Mom and Dad. Now, it had two beds, one twin, which wouldn't be too comfortable for Kennedy and me, and one little single on the other side, under the slanted ceiling.

By the time I got everything situated and returned down-stairs, not only was Brian home, but so was Seamus with his wife and kids. Everybody was talking over everybody, and I feared Kennedy would be lost in the middle of it, but she was there, sitting between my mother and Finn, munching on food, and laughing at something Collin was saying while she absently fixed Finn's glasses.

She fit right in.

"Hey, brother." Brian clapped my shoulder.

I accepted the pint of beer he offered me and raised it in his direction. "How's it going?"

"Not bad."

I gestured around the house. "The inside looks good. The outside needs work."

"Hey, man, I got my own shit to do. I can't do it all myself."

"The front steps are falling apart."

"What you want me to do? They're only so many hours in the day. You gonna come fix 'em?"

"I'm just saying—"

"You're just fucking running your mouth about shit like you're the boss. Always on your high fuckin' horse."

"Hey! Boys!" Mom snapped her fingers at us, though I didn't even know how she heard us over all the noise. "No fighting on Christmas."

"It's not Christmas," Seamus pointed out as he made his way over to us.

"Close enough," Mom said, "so don't ruin this for me. I finally have all my boys home."

"Home five minutes and already makin' trouble," Seamus muttered, throwing a meaty arm around my shoulders.

I would be the last one in this family to make trouble, but Brian had been extra sensitive since his divorce. I supposed I would be too if I were thirty-eight and living at home with my mother.

"Keily, turn it down," Seamus told one of his stepdaughters, who held an iPad. Once she lowered the volume on her video, he looked down at me—he had two inches on me—and jerked his chin in Kennedy's direction. "It's serious, then?"

I shrugged, downplaying how much I loved Kennedy being here with my family.

"You've never brought a girl home before," he noted, watching how his wife, Nikki, chatted animatedly with Kennedy.

Collin joined us, popping a piece of cheese into his mouth. "I like her."

"She's handling Mom well," Brian said, probably because it had always been a sticking point with his ex about how over-bearing our mother could be. Especially when Brian and Mom were so close.

"You love her?" Collin asked, but instead of answering, I only sipped my beer.

Seamus grunted next to me while Brian snickered.

Was I that obvious?

I turned to Brian. "How're your kids?"

"Good. I get them Christmas night, so they'll be here."

I patted his back a few times. Mom had planned on selling the house, but when things started falling apart for Brian, she told him to move in. The whole of South Boston was becoming gentrified, prices skyrocketing, so the idea was for Brian to fix up the place, sell it for profit, and find something for himself while our mother could get a little apartment somewhere. But until then, he had his son and daughter spend every other weekend here.

"Hey, one of you open that for us," Mom said, gesturing to the bottle at the end of the table, and Seamus stepped forward, delivering glasses of red wine to her, Nikki, and Kennedy, who smiled at me over the rim of her glass, her eyes bright, cheeks flushed.

Yeah, I loved her.

I should have known. Dean did warn me. *She loves hard, and it's impossible not to fall in love with her right back.*

Hours later, when Finn was fast asleep on the other side of the room, and Kennedy and I were finally tucked into the bed that was way too small, I curled myself around her, whispering, "How was it today? Too much?"

"Not at all." She laced her fingers with mine and pulled my arm more firmly around her waist. "I really like Nikki and Seamus. I love that they met because she was his tattoo artist. And your mom's so sweet. Really adores you."

"She really adores *you*."

"I have a feeling she'd adore anyone you brought home."

"I've never brought anyone else home."

She angled her head to look at me over her shoulder. "Not even Tessa?"

I shook my head. "Mom's met her a few times, and they get along, but it's not like…" I lifted my shoulder. "I've always been preoccupied with school and work. I didn't date a whole lot, and when I did, it wasn't serious."

She reached back to skim her hand over my hair and cheek,

her face faintly highlighted by the tiny night-light in the corner, though her smile still glowed. "So, you're serious about me?"

"I'm so fuckin' serious about you."

"Yeah?" she teased in her ridiculous Boston accent. "Wicked serious about me, huh?"

"No makin' fun of me or you get no Dunkies tomorrow."

"Oh no, not the Dunkin'," she said with a stifled laugh as she turned back on her side, burrowing under the covers. I kissed the back of her head, her neck, her shoulder, and pulled her right against me, her soft ass tucked against me. I knew I'd be tortured all night.

But even with the stiffest hard-on known to man, I easily fell asleep.

Only to be woken up with wet heat around my cock. I shot up, blinking blearily as I reached for my glasses. I didn't need 20/20 vision to know Kennedy was between my legs, but sweet baby Jesus in the manager, I wanted to see her.

"Where's Finn?" I asked, putting my glasses on, and she tipped her head up as she continued to smooth her fist up and down my length, twisting her hand at the top, exactly how I liked.

"Downstairs. We've both been up for a while."

"I..." I cleared my throat, raw from sleep and lust. "I didn't hear."

"I know. I took him down for breakfast, so you could sleep." She swirled her tongue around the tip, already weeping. "You deserve it."

I groaned and propped my head up on a pillow to watch her working her mouth up and down. "This my Christmas present?"

It was only Christmas Eve, but Santa sure as hell couldn't bring me anything better than Kennedy and her sweet mouth. I sucked air through my teeth when her hand ventured up my thigh, past my balls, pressing right behind them. She'd done all this before. I'd had her mouth on me before, but being in my mother's house made it more frantic, more illicit, and my blood pounded in my ears.

She shifted, her hips restless, because she always got wet giving me head, and I reached out, searching under her T-shirt and the flimsy cotton bra, to palm her breast, pluck at her nipple. She practically purred, hollowing her cheeks as she sucked. I loved when she offered to go down on me. Her eyes always got glassy as she took me all the way to the back of her throat, sloppy and so fucking perfect.

"Turn around so I can taste you," I said, and she released me with an audible pop and worked her hand up and down my soaked shaft.

"No. There's not enough time."

"Says who?"

"Says your mother who told me to come wake you up."

I groaned, knowing in a few minutes, Mom would be yelling for me to get my ass downstairs. There wouldn't be enough time. I loved going down on Kennedy, but I usually lost track of time and couldn't do that here.

So, instead, I raked my fingers through her hair, gathering it all up between my hands, holding it tightly. "Don't move, angel." She braced herself, with her hands on either side of my thighs, and I thrust up into her mouth, curling my lips to bite back a moan at the crude sounds she made, the suction and slight gagging. "Christ, Kennedy, you're such a good girl. My perfect good girl."

I dropped my head back to the pillow and squeezed my eyes shut at the onslaught of sensation, the buzzing at the bottom of my spine and the back of my head, the overwhelming need to tell her she was everything I could hope for. She was joy and sunshine, sexy and sweet, generous and so goddamn tender-hearted, it killed me to think about how she had been hurt in her past. If I could, I'd wipe it all away, anything that ever broke her heart.

And I would do anything in my power to make sure she never cried tears of pain again.

Because I loved her. I loved Kennedy.

It was with that last thought that I exploded in her mouth, only a moment after I warned her I was coming. She climbed over me, her cheeks pink, lips swollen and shining with a bit of my come at the corner. Pulling her to me, I devoured her mouth, savagely licking and biting, attempting to show how much I felt for her. Because I'd be damned to tell her now, at my mother's house, after she'd given me a really great blow job to wake me up.

No, she deserved more and better than that.

So, kissing her would have to do for now, and when her hair was messed up enough and she was sufficiently out of breath, I let her go with a smack to her ass. "Be down in a minute."

She stumbled, a little dazed, and combed her fingers through her hair, tying the mass of dark locks up on the top of her head, as she smiled at me.

I would never tire of it.

TWENTY-FIVE
KENNEDY

was beat. There was no other way to put it. Liam's family, while wonderful, was exhausting. There were so many people, too many loud voices—which was really saying something, as I wasn't exactly quiet. But the O'Neils were a whole other level.

They argued as much as they got along. They teased one another relentlessly, and I didn't know how Eileen managed to cook so much food. There was never a day when she didn't have something prepared, but it did give me a good opportunity to bond with her since I enjoyed being in the kitchen too. She told me about how she'd met Jack, her dearly departed husband, through her brother and admitted that she had so many kids because she kept trying for a girl. Instead, God blessed her with "a hoodlum pack of boys."

Even though it was lovely to meet everyone, the thing I enjoyed the most was being guided around town. Liam took me on a walk of historic Boston, where he said he'd spent summers working as a tour guide. He nerded out as I complained about how cold I was, to which he responded by placing a searing kiss on my lips. We ate at all his favorite spots, took Finn to the aquarium, and went out drinking one night with Seamus and Nikki when I tried my first car bomb. It was awful.

While the week had been amazing, I was happy to be home.

We'd staggered into the house, bleary-eyed from the car ride, and practically fell asleep as soon as we shuffled upstairs. Today, we did all the boring and horrible post-vacation things like laundry and grocery shopping. Though, I did manage to snag a bottle of champagne last minute to celebrate New Year's.

"Hey." Liam dove onto the sofa, his head in my lap, after tucking Finn in bed since we'd celebrated the New Year with him and Tessa earlier via FaceTime. "What're you doing?"

"Emailing these to Tess." I showed him the photos and videos on my phone that I'd captured of Finn playing with his cousins, falling asleep on the couch in the middle of the day, and ripping open presents. I had promised to send them to her. "It keeps telling me to resize them, though."

He held up his hand. "Lemme see." He fiddled with my phone for a minute. "I'm downloading the Dropbox app. What's your Apple ID?"

"Uh." I stared off in thought. "I can never remember. Look at my notes app. I have all my passcodes listed."

"Are you kidding?" He huffed and sat up with a perturbed glance in my direction. "What if someone found or stole your phone? They'd have all your information."

I waved off his worry and switched positions so my head was in his lap as he continued to work on my phone for another minute before passing it back to me. "I downloaded the app and sent the files, but you need to do something about all your log-ins and passwords."

"Yes, Professor," I said, earning a playful pinch on my thigh along with a smacking kiss to my mouth. "You want to open that?" I pointed to the champagne I had resting in a bucket of ice alongside two regular glasses since Liam didn't have any flutes.

"What? No party hats or any of the usual Kennedy Novak flare?"

"Not tonight." I extended my arm up, curling it around the back of his neck for a kiss, and he skimmed his hand up and down the inside of my leg before cupping my sex. I loved that he felt so much ownership of my body because I felt ownership over his. Whether it was lacing our fingers together, skating my hands over his torso, or slipping my hand into his boxer briefs, I wasn't afraid to show him how I felt.

And I loved knowing he wasn't either.

Right now, what I felt was the hot thrill of possession.

"How can we celebrate the new year without any of your sparkle, hmm?" He coasted his hand up to my breast, kneading it, and I sucked in a sharp breath when he pinched my nipple.

"I trust you can think of something," I murmured into another kiss. "Especially with that box of condoms we have yet to open."

He nipped at my bottom lip. "I'll take care of opening the champagne if you go grab them and find a good playlist."

I scampered away, not wanting to waste any more time, and nabbed the condoms before connecting my cell phone to the Bluetooth speaker in the living room to play Niall Horan. Meanwhile, Liam had opened the champagne and muted the television, which was tuned to the countdown. He offered me one of the glasses, watching me over the rim of his as he drank.

The champagne was crisp and tart, the fizz settling on my tongue like the bubbles in my belly. I licked my lips after downing all of it and held the glass out for a refill. Liam smiled and poured more. "You better slow down. Make it last a little longer."

"What's the fun in that?"

He ticked his head to the side. "Didn't you ever hear anticipation makes it better?"

And I ticked my head to the side. "Didn't you ever hear that ladies can get blue balls too?"

He let out a soft chuckle then took my glass from me before I even had a sip to set them both down on the coffee table. "Dance with me."

He wiggled his fingers in my direction and hauled me off the couch once I placed my hand in his. He led me to the open space in front of the TV, cleared of toys, and wrapped one arm around my waist as he kissed the back of my other hand and held it in his against his chest. I tipped my head back, staring up at him, as he swayed us in a circle. I could feel his heartbeat behind my hand, a stable and soothing rhythm. Like him, stable and soothing.

I could spend the rest of my life looking, but I knew I'd never find a better man than Liam O'Neil. And yet, I couldn't tell him. Because even though he made me feel safe and secure, like I could do or be anything I wanted, I didn't know if I was enough for him. He was on his way to being a tenured professor, and I was Finn's nanny.

If Liam and I were to solidify this growing relationship, it would leave me jobless yet again. I couldn't rely solely on him. Not to mention, my epilepsy always hung over me like a rain cloud before a storm. My specific type was genetic, and I wasn't crazy about the idea of having my own kids and passing it on to them. Seizures were terrifying, and I wouldn't willingly put anyone else through that, but Liam was still young and if he wanted to, he could have more kids. He could choose another woman, one who wasn't flighty or so high-maintenance, one who had a steady job and didn't suffer from epilepsy.

It was impossible to take that next step and offer myself to him when I knew what I had to offer wasn't all that great.

"What're you thinking about?" he asked, the hand at my back tensing ever so slightly, his fingertips pressing into my spine.

"You."

"What about me?"

I motioned to the condoms. "I have an IUD, but I always insist the guy wears a condom because I can't get pregnant."

Liam stared evenly at me, as if he knew I had more on my mind, so I went on, "I can't take birth control pills… I mean, I *could* take birth control, but one of my medications negates it. And if I were to get pregnant, another one would cause severe birth defects, and a *different one* would make it almost impossible for me to carry to term because of what it would do to me."

He nodded solemnly. "I understand why you're so cautious. I'm glad you are."

"Besides my neurologist, I also see a cardiologist because sometimes one of the pills causes heart problems, and if I ever want to change any of the medications, I have to see all my doctors to make sure they all sign off that it's safe for me."

We'd stopped dancing, but I hadn't realized until Liam stood in front of me, holding my face between my hands. "You never have to—"

"What I'm trying to say is that if I ever want to have children of my own, I'd have to go off some of the medications I'm on now. And it would take months or years to find ones that would allow me to, first, become pregnant without having seizures and, then, not have complications for me or the baby. And then there's the possibility of the kid inheriting epilepsy from me. And I'm not sure I want to go through all of that or put anyone else through it either."

He bent to me with a soft utterance of "Angel" and then an even gentler touch of his lips to mine. I curled my hands into his shirt, leaning heavily into him because I knew he'd always hold me up. But I didn't know if I wanted to put him in that position for the rest of our lives. He deserved so much more than that, being a crutch for me.

His lips brushed over my cheek as he angled my head, allowing him access to my throat, to suck and bite at it until I couldn't take it anymore and batted his hands away. I reached for the hem of his shirt, intent on removing it, but he stopped me. "I want you to dance for me."

I stepped away from him. "What?"

"I want a striptease from you."

"Why am I always the one doing the work?" I put my hands on my hips, earning an arch of his eyebrow because this man did *a lot* of work.

He made himself at home on the couch, his knees spread wide, one arm thrown on the back of the cushion, his other hand lifting his champagne to his mouth. After a gulp of it, he raised it in my direction. "Go on."

As usual, his gentle but demanding command left me breathless. But when I brushed my hair behind my shoulders, his eyes sparked to life and heated as they drifted down the length of me while I swayed my hips to "Slow Hands." The sensual lyrics and melody made it easy to dance, and I skated my hands over my sides and hips then back up to my breasts.

He watched me with his top teeth dug into his bottom lip, the growing bulge of his erection clearly outlined under his gray sweatpants, and I bit back a smile at how sexy he made me feel. I tugged my oversized sweatshirt over my head and swept my hair up above my head, letting it fall back down to my shoulders. Never taking his gaze off me, he absently bobbed his head to the song and took another sip of his drink.

I worked my leggings down to my ankles, but there was no attractive way to peel them off, so I sat on the edge of the table and held my bare feet up in the air, giving Liam the opportunity to remove them for me. With one deft tug, he had them in his hand and thrown to the floor. I stood, spinning away from him to undo my bra and let it slip from my fingers as I sent a flirtatious smile his way over my shoulder. He adjusted himself with his free hand while he licked his lips, his desperation palpable.

I faced away from him again and slipped my underwear down my legs, making sure to bend over since I knew he loved that position, and held it for a few moments. Long enough for him to rasp, "Get your ass over here."

Naked and warm, I sashayed toward him, but before I could settle on his lap, he pushed me to lie down on the couch so he was over me. He took one last sip of his champagne then flipped the glass upside down. Staring at the hollow of my collarbone, he slowly dripped a line of the bubbly liquid between my breasts, down my stomach, to my belly button. He set the glass on the table behind him and ducked his head, licking up the trail he'd made, and I was unable to keep from squirming, spilling some of the champagne on the couch.

I gasped out an "Oh no," but he caught it between his lips while he drifted his hand over my wet skin, smearing the champagne over my breasts and nipples, up my throat, and down between my legs. Then his hot mouth was there, licking and sucking at all those same places.

"Liam," I moaned, sifting my fingers through his hair, wanting him on top of me, to feel his weight over me as I finally learned what it felt like to be filled up by him. But he barely moved a few inches, merely enough to pluck an ice cube from the bucket. I let out a squeal of surprise when he touched it to my nipple, circling the already hard tip to an even tighter peak. My breath caught in my throat. "Oh, oh god. Oh my god."

He replaced the ice cube with his mouth, and the change in temperature unfurled waves of pleasure and pain through my core. My back arched off the sofa, my hips lifted aimlessly, and I felt him smile against the soft flesh of my breast. Then the ice cube was at my other nipple, and he started the torture all over again.

He alternated using the ice cube and his mouth until it melted, and when I thought he would give up, he reached for another to continue.

It was madness.

It was bliss.

It was *everything*.

"Liam," I groaned, my internal temperature so high I didn't understand how my skin dotted with goose bumps.

"Yes, angel?"

"I need you to touch me."

"I am touching you," he said with so much humor, I whined in frustration.

"*Please.*"

"Okay, sweet girl, okay," he murmured against my throat, briefly gliding the ice cube between my legs so that I sucked in a ragged breath. Then he popped the ice into his mouth and dragged his wet, cold fingers along the seam of my pussy.

It was the best and worst thing I'd ever felt. "Oh *fuck.*"

He hummed, sucking on that godforsaken ice cube as he drove his fingers into me, immediately drawing shudders from me when he stroked the spot against my front wall. I was already on the edge, barely clinging to my sanity, and all I required was one touch of my clit to go flying.

He was wicked.

He was wonderful.

He was *everything.*

I closed my eyes as an orgasm racked my body, but he wouldn't even give me a respite from that because then his cold tongue was on me, licking around my nipples, sucking at my neck, nipping at my earlobe until the chill faded from his mouth, and I slowly came back down to earth.

"Don't move," he told me—as if I could—and straightened up, tugging his shirt over his head and pushing his sweats down, along with his boxer briefs. His erection stood out, one thick vein running along the length of it on the side, and I was tempted to trace it with my tongue, but he swiftly covered it with a condom. Then he was on top of me, settling between my legs, staring down at me with eyes so full of love, I almost couldn't bear it.

To be the object of his attention, it was both powerful and disheartening. To be the center of his world, and yet not feel like I deserved it.

"Lift your legs, angel."

I brought my knees toward my sides, giving him more room to move, and he held himself up on one forearm as he positioned the head of his cock at my entrance, soaking it with my arousal, sliding over my clit before dropping down to both forearms and finally plunging inside me.

We both let out heavy breaths, and I wrapped my hands around the backs of my knees, wanting more of the exquisite fullness. After each slow pull-out, he thrust back in hard, and I arched my neck, refusing to give in to the primal scream threatening to escape my throat.

But Liam didn't keep quiet. "That's my good girl. Taking it like you were made for me."

I loved that Liam voiced his desire. If he wasn't making himself known with actual words then it was with low grunts and animated hums, like he did now, offering quiet *uh-huh*s against my throat. Like it was so good for him, he couldn't find his words at the moment.

And god, it was so good for *me*, I didn't have words either.

Except three little ones waiting for their time in the spotlight.

Instead, I sewed my lips shut and slid my hand between us to circle my clit, and he sighed. "You there? You close?" When I nodded, so did he. "You feel so perfect. I'm gonna lose my goddamn mind when you come."

He pushed up to his hands and repositioned his knees to drive into me faster and harder. He dipped his head, focused on where our bodies met, where my skin was so wet, my fingers kept slipping, and I watched him watching us. His cheeks were ruddy, his chest heaved, and his abs tightened with every stroke inside me.

"Liam," I cried a moment before the dam burst. My muscles went taut with tension then relaxed just as fast, releasing all that built-up pressure, and he muttered a curse, digging his knees into the cushion, his thrusts becoming wilder and wilder like he was trying to hold on.

I scratched my nails down his back. "Let go. Give it to me."

"Ah fuck, angel," he breathed and dropped his head with one last plunge into me then collapsed, panting against my neck.

I kissed his shoulder, tangled my fingers in his hair, and curled my legs around his waist, keeping him close even as he shifted to look down at me.

"You doing all right?" he asked, and my nose stung with emotion.

He was so sweet, too sweet to me. How could I not fall in love with him?

But I nodded anyway, and he gave me one quick kiss before pushing off me, careful when he pulled out. I might have been embarrassed at the sight of the sticky white evidence of my orgasm all over the root of his shaft and the condom, but with the way his eyes flared, I couldn't be. He was aroused by it.

And I was sure that before the ball dropped, he'd make me come at least a few more times.

I excused myself to use the bathroom, and by the time I returned, he had the music off, the volume of the television up, and our glasses refilled. I started for my sweatshirt, but he shook his head. "Don't even think about it."

He lifted the blanket from his lap, a silent invitation to sit next to him. So I settled in, both of us still naked and warm. He wrapped his arm around my shoulders with a kiss to my temple, and I rested my head against his side. "Happy New Year, Professor."

"Happy New Year, angel."

TWENTY-SIX
KENNEDY

Life returned to normal after New Year's. Even though my show had only been one weekend, I wanted to perform more, so with Liam's encouragement, I planned on auditioning for the next one, which was a few weeks from now. Until then, I intended to spend all my time with Finn and Liam. While his semester didn't start until mid-January, he was taking on a new class for a faculty member who'd had a baby, and he wanted to get a jump start on the curriculum, hiding away in his office for hours at a time. But since it was his birthday, I had something special cooked up, one of his favorite meals plus homemade cupcakes.

After picking up Finn from school, I made a pit stop at the store then we headed home, where I made everyone lunch. Liam took a break and played with Finn for a bit then put him down for a nap, only to return to me in the kitchen.

Wrapping his arms around my waist, he nuzzled my neck, but since my hands were covered in flour, I couldn't swat him away. Instead, I crooked my head back to meet his roguish gaze. "What do you think you're doing?"

He slid his hands down my thighs, scratching his fingernails back up them in a delicious taunt. "What do you think?"

"I think you're trying to sidetrack me."

He started for the button of my jeans. "Correct."

I attempted to wriggle out of his grasp. "Do you or do you not want your birthday dinner made?"

"I do, but I also want you." He brushed his mouth along the side of my neck. "C'mon. Take a break."

"Take a break?" I laughed, showing him my hands. "I just started. Pour more flour down for me, please."

He did as I asked, dropping a scoop of flour onto the wooden cutting board where I kneaded the dough together for the gnocchi. He stayed glued to my back, watching everything I did.

"You ever think about going to culinary school?" he asked quietly, almost like he didn't want to disturb me, which was funny because not even a minute ago, he'd been trying to get in my pants.

"Thought about it briefly, but I'm not cut out to work in a kitchen. I don't think I'd survive."

"Why not?"

I rolled the dough out into lines. "I don't know. Chefs are all kinds of pretentious. They can be really mean and rude."

I felt his smile against my shoulder. "Collin's a chef."

"Exactly," I said, and we both laughed. Collin was definitely full of himself and didn't seem to care about who he offended with his words or actions.

Liam clucked his tongue, his mouth near my ear as he landed a smack on my backside. "You're sassy today."

"Because you won't leave me alone. I'm trying to do something nice for you, and you're disturbing me."

He rubbed his palm over my butt. "It would be really nice if you took your clothes off right now."

I sighed, half turning to him. "You can have fifteen minutes now, or you can wait like a good little boy and get hours later."

"Good little boy," he muttered with one last swat. "I'll give you good little boy later."

"Looking forward to it," I said with a cheeky smile in his

direction as he ducked out of his kitchen, finally leaving me to get the gnocchi finished before Finn woke up.

Which wasn't very long.

I'd boiled all the gnocchi and placed them aside for now so I could get Finn situated. I promised he could help make the cupcakes, and since he really liked the mixer, I wasn't going to deprive him of his favorite part. I set him up on a chair and let him have at it while I took some photos and videos. Then, together, we scooped the batter into the tray and put them in the oven.

We headed to the living room to play while the cupcakes baked, and I caught up with my mom, chatting about her upcoming trip to Sedona, as Finn created a racetrack for his Hot Wheels that involved jumping over dinosaurs. When the timer dinged, I removed the cupcakes from the oven and hung up with my mom, knowing I'd have to give Finn my full attention to make sure he didn't make a mess.

We frosted the cupcakes together, and I took more pictures, especially when he curled his lips between his teeth in concentration, exactly like his dad. Too cute.

"These look great, Finnie. Want to go watch TV so I can finish dinner?"

He scooted away, and I popped sausage and broccoli rabe into a pan to fry up with the gnocchi. I'd just finished cleaning everything up when Liam strolled into the kitchen, stretching his neck side to side. "Smells so good in here."

I reached up to rub at the muscles in his shoulders and neck, knowing he always got tense when he sat for too long, and he thanked me with a kiss long enough to make my toes curl.

We ate at the dining room table because I'd tied balloons to the back of Liam's chair to Finn's utter delight, and when we finished, I slid the tray of cupcakes in front of the birthday boy with the thick 3 and 7 candles lit up. Finn and I sang to him, and I filmed a video of him blowing out his candles then biting into a cupcake Finn handed to him.

It felt right, all of us here together. Like I was meant to be here. Like I was meant to be a part of Liam and Finn's family. And when Liam gazed up at me with sparkling eyes, I brushed my thumb over the corner of his mouth, swiping a bit of blue icing off his lip. I stuck it in my mouth, and he winked playfully at me before turning to grab Finn, tickling his sides.

Without fully thinking it through, I edited the video to the few seconds of Liam smiling and winking at me after I wiped his mouth, added some music, and posted it to my TikTok. I wasn't active on it by any means, but I mostly posted outfits of the day and, more recently, clips from *Hairspray* rehearsals and the blinking lights of the Christmas tree with Mariah singing over it. I posted the short clip of the #HotProfessor and then pocketed my cell phone to enjoy one of the cupcakes Finn had overloaded with sprinkles.

It wasn't until after Finn was bathed, brushed, and in bed with his dad that I kissed his head and made my way to Liam's bedroom, checking my cell phone.

As I sat on the bed, I replied to a text from Taylor about getting together with her on the weekend then checked my other notifications.

The *hundreds* of notifications.

"Oh my god," I whispered to myself, scrolling through the comments.

That daddy, though!

Yes, Zaddy!

Find someone who looks at you the way the hot professor looks at whoever's taking this video.

Going to stand in traffic.

Hot Professor strikes again!

What classes does he teach?

Lord, I've seen what you do for others…

Commenting for the algo to do its thing.

What's the story here? Someone link me pleeeeaaaase!

He's not even that hot tho

THAT'S MY PROFESSOR OMG I'M DYING DYYYING

I didn't bother to read the rest, feeling like I might throw up.

I couldn't believe—I mean, I could believe. I didn't *want* to believe—that in only a few hours, it had been liked and shared thousands of times.

Sure, Liam looked super sexy and flirty, and yeah, that's why I'd posted it, but it was a stupid, silly video. There was no reason for it to be so popular.

I stared at my phone, my heart rate spiking at my carelessness. After everything I knew about Liam and what he'd shared about trying to minimize what'd happened with the interview, I'd gone and made yet another viral video featuring him.

Panic swelled in my chest as more comments and shares rolled in. I swallowed hard and breathed through my nose in an attempt to calm my racing heart.

"He's asleep. Faster than usual. Almost like he knew his father had plans to get you naked." When I looked up at Liam, blinking back tears, his brow furrowed. "What's wrong?"

Dread churned my stomach. I didn't want him to be mad at me. "I'm sorry."

"What happened?" He sank to his knees in front of me. "What's wrong?"

"I know you're going to be upset with me, and I…" My voice cracked, and I cleared my throat, though Liam's face was pained.

"I can't promise I won't be upset, but I need you to tell me what's wrong."

I lowered my attention to the case of my phone as I scraped at the Holy Cannoli sticker. "I didn't think about what I was doing."

With his index finger, he tipped my chin up. "Just tell me."

"When we were eating cupcakes, I took a video of you and posted it to TikTok. It was only a few seconds, and I didn't think…" I couldn't meet his gaze as I rushed out my explanation. "It was stupid, I know, but you looked so hot smiling up at me, and I guess, I don't know. I guess I was proud or something, that *you* were looking at *me* like that, and I didn't think about what might happen if I posted it. I was stupid. I'm stupid."

"You're not stupid," he said, sitting beside me on the bed.

"I am."

"You're not, Kennedy. Stop saying it."

I handed him my cell phone with the app open so he could see for himself, and he blew out a big breath.

"I'm sorry," I said, and he handed me the phone back.

"Can you delete it?"

I immediately deleted the video, although I feared the damage was already done. And from the way he stayed quiet, I assumed he thought the same.

"I'm really sorry, Liam."

A few moments passed before he looped his arm around my shoulders, tugging me into him. "I know you are."

"I didn't do it on purpose. Truly, I wasn't thinking and—"

"I know." He kissed the top of my head then moved his hands to my arms, holding me away from him, forcing me to meet his eyes. "It was a mistake. You don't need to beat yourself up about it."

"But—"

"But nothing. You deleted the video, and all we can do is hope it ends there." He shrugged. "Now, it's my birthday, and I would prefer not to spend it with you crying." He offered me a quarter of a smile. "Unless it's from so many orgasms you can't take it anymore."

I let out a watery laugh. "Okay."

"And please, don't let me hear you call yourself stupid again."

I agreed, but he clearly didn't believe me.

"Or I'll take you over my knee. You won't like it."

That pulled a grin out of me. "Won't I?"

With one arch of his eyebrow, I stood up and started to remove my clothes. The corner of his mouth hiked up. "Such a good girl."

TWENTY-SEVEN
LIAM

strode out of my last lecture of the day, Political Theory, and looped my messenger bag around my shoulder as I thumbed my cell phone on, headed back to my office. But an email from the provost had my steps slowing to a stop.

He wanted to see me. *Immediately.*

Of course.

I knew what this was about. Feared it ever since Kennedy had posted that video. But I had hoped it wouldn't be that big of a deal. The last clip had been captured on national television, so it was no wonder it went viral. This one was just a stupid six-second video of me, barely anything to look at.

With a sigh, I changed course and made my way across campus to the administration building. Stopping at Wendall Assman's closed office door, I took a deep breath and knocked twice.

"Come in."

I opened the door and stepped inside the spacious room filled with dark walnut furniture and a bookcase along the right wall. The fading sun streamed in through the two windows behind Wendall, and I surreptitiously wiped my palms down my pants as I stood in front of his desk.

"Have a seat," he said, turning his computer screen toward me. Before I even got a word out, he asked, "Care to explain this?"

I curled my lips over my teeth, staring at his screen with Facebook open and a video posted there. The same six seconds played on repeat, me smiling up at Kennedy like a love-sick fool. Hearts practically floated out of my eyes.

I had no excuse or explanation, so I went with a clarification. "I didn't post or share it."

"But you participated," he said as if having a personal life was a fatal flaw. "You knew you were being filmed."

"It was my birthday, and my girlfriend never expected the video to be so popular."

"I don't care about intent." He sniffed. God, he was such an ass. "I care that this type of digital presence is unprofessional and unacceptable."

"The video was deleted as soon as we realized that—"

"Not soon enough, apparently. Students are commenting and sharing this. It's appalling."

I didn't like what he was implying. That I was somehow relishing this, or worse, developing relationships with students outside of my classroom. "I have not interacted with any students outside of my classes, and when I have, it's been through email. I have never and would never cultivate an inappropriate relationship with a student."

His eyes bored into me. "Your tenure review is coming up soon, as I am sure you're well aware, and I know Dr. Lang has already spoken to you about the standards we hold for our faculty."

I kept my mouth shut, realizing that no matter what I said, I wasn't going to convince him of anything.

"I will not hesitate to pull my support of your candidacy."

I didn't know what his issue with me was, but it felt like he would find a problem with me no matter what I did.

"I won't withstand another embarrassment like this," he said, and I curled my fingers into fists in my lap. This video wasn't an embarrassment. It wasn't any different from what anyone else would post, and I couldn't control what people said or did. Although, he did hold my future in his hands, and I had to make him understand I took my job seriously.

"I'm committed to upholding this university's values and my own personal standards, and I feel like I've proven my leadership and academic capabilities over the last few years that I've been here."

He didn't argue otherwise, merely rotated his computer screen to its original position and leaned back in his chair. He crossed his hands over his stomach. "Don't let your internet notoriety override your impressive track record. Am I clear?"

"Crystal."

He dismissed me with a curt, "That'll be all, Dr. O'Neil."

I stood with a mumbled thanks and closed the door after me, leaning against it to make sure my heart rate came back down. I wasn't used to getting called down to the principal's office. I didn't get in trouble, and while I knew it wasn't Kennedy's fault, I couldn't help but be annoyed that she'd accidentally caused trouble for me.

During the drive home, I replayed the conversation with Assman. That condescending tone drilling into me about propriety and values, basically accusing me of courting internet fame. As if I enjoyed the attention.

I exhaled harshly, guiding my car into the driveway, and unclenched my jaw as I stepped out of my car, hoping to relax once I stepped inside my house. At the sound of Finn's chatter, my shoulders dropped, my frustration easing. I hung up my bag and coat, and I kicked off my shoes in time for Finn to throw himself at my legs. "Daddy!"

I picked him up. "Daddy? Did you just say Daddy with a D?"

"Daddy!" he repeated, wringing his arms tight around my neck, and my nose burned. I'd been Addy for so long, I wasn't sure I'd ever hear the full word.

"Hey, guy." I kissed the side of his head. "Daddy's got you."

He didn't let me hug him long and butted his head against my shoulder.

"Ah. God. Can you please be a human and not ram me like a rhino?" I set him down on the floor and held out my hand to keep him from bumping me again by palming his forehead.

"Come on, Finnie!" Kennedy called. "Dinner's ready!"

Finn and I both made our way to the kitchen, where Kennedy turned to us with a pot in her hand. She smiled at Finn and then me. "Go ahead. Sit down."

Finn climbed on the chair as she scooped out rice and chicken onto three plates, but instead of sitting, I grabbed a pint glass from the cabinet and opened a Guinness. Kennedy eyed me. "You okay?"

I motioned to Finn. "He called me Daddy with a D."

"He's really doing great with speech, isn't he?"

"Yeah," I said, trying on a smile that didn't feel quite right. I was proud of Finn yet weary from today. After the three of us sat at the table, I picked at my food, more interested in drinking my beer.

"What happened?" Kennedy asked, her big brown eyes filled with worry.

I had difficulty meeting her gaze. "I got called into the provost's office today."

Her face paled. "Because of the video? Because of me?" She set her fork down, curling her hand around my wrist. "Liam, I'm so sorry. I don't even know what to say other than I feel awful about everything. I can—"

"It's not your fault." I interrupted her self-flagellation with a shake of my head. "But, yeah, Assman tore into me about it. Said it was unprofessional and embarrassing."

Her eyes went glassy. "I never should have posted it without asking you. I'm so, so sorry."

"It's really not that big of a deal," I told her, which was both true and false. "It was an innocent video, and if anyone else had posted it, nothing would have happened."

She blinked, and a single tear streamed down her cheek. "Are you in a lot of trouble?"

I caught the tear with my thumb. "No, but I have to make sure I don't piss him off again. So, maybe cool it on posting anything with me in it. No matter how hard that might be."

She didn't smile at my joke, only sniffed. "No more posting anything. I promise."

I tipped her chin up. "No more crying, okay? You didn't mean any harm. Wendall's an ass. Literally."

Her laugh was waterlogged, but at least she wasn't crying anymore. "I'm just scared. I don't want to screw anything up for your job."

I let go of her and went back to the dinner she'd prepared. Because she was amazing.

But I was scared too.

My career was at stake, and while I'd always been good at staying calm and even-keeled, inside, I didn't feel so composed. I'd hired Kennedy to help settle my home life so I could focus on my work, but I was once again making excuses because my home life was affecting my work. Kennedy was good and kind, and life with her would be wonderful. It would also come with occasional surprises.

I wasn't great with surprises.

But we would figure it out. Or, at least, I hoped we could figure it out.

I finished my beer and made sure to polish off my dinner as my mind spun with defensive arguments and possible tenure board questions. I couldn't go into the meeting flat-footed.

After I got Finn down, I found Kennedy in bed, her hair up in a bun and one of my zip-up sweatshirts on. I bent, accepting yet another apology with a kiss from her, but when she lifted the covers for me, I shook my head.

"I'm going to go box."

"Oh." She swallowed noticeably. "Okay."

I changed into shorts and a T-shirt and stepped into sneakers, feeling Kennedy's gaze on me the whole time. I offered her another kiss, and when she begged me with her eyes to explain, I held her chin between my fingers. "We're okay."

"Promise?" she whispered.

"Promise."

TWENTY-EIGHT
KENNEDY

We were not okay.

It had been a very weird week. Liam was stand-offish, boxing every single night, and even though he still kissed and hugged and cuddled with me, his smile very rarely made it to both sides of his mouth, and he was quieter than usual. I knew Liam was worried about his job, and no matter how many times he reassured me that it was fine, I could tell what I'd done was weighing on him.

Which made me feel awful.

Not to mention, Finn had caught another germ from school, and the poor kid was a snot factory. A sick kid made everything more difficult, especially figuring out a time to have an I-love-you-please-love-me-back-even-though-I-know-I-messed-up-and-you-could-have-anyone-else conversation.

But I didn't know if I wanted to cross that bridge just yet. Not until Liam's review, which was only three weeks away. It wasn't like I was going anywhere.

Not when I was already trapped on the sofa.

I held my fingers out to Finn, counting down. "Three...two...one! The floor is lava!"

Finn erupted into giggles as he took off, leaping from one

pillow to another, avoiding touching the floor. Lately, he'd become obsessed with the television show and game, constantly asking to play, and with the freezing rain outside, we didn't have much else to do.

"C'mon!" He scooped up the stuffed pterodactyl and plastic rhino from the floor. "Floor is avaaaa!"

I laughed, waving him toward me. "Hurry! The lava's rising! Hurry up, Finnie!"

He skirted the coffee table and jumped up onto the sofa, tackling me in the process. I hugged him tight, smacking kisses all over his head, plying more giggles out of him. "I love you, babes."

"Love you, Ken-dee."

I kissed him once more then righted us, catching my breath. "What do you say we clean all this up and have a snack? Daddy'll be home soon."

He held up three fingers, pouting. "More minutes."

I rolled my eyes playfully. "Fine! A few more minutes then we're cleaning up. Got it?"

He stood up on the couch, wobbling a bit on the cushion, so I held on to his legs. "Careful. Careful."

He raised his arms up. "Free! Two! One! Ahhh!"

I shook my head in amusement as he jumped down to a pillow on the floor, hopping up and down in delight that he'd made it without falling in the lava. He waved to me, silently telling me he wanted me to get in on the fun, so I stood on the sofa. "Both of us this time. Where should we go to?"

When he pointed to the recliner, I joined him, shouting, "Three…two…one! The floor is lava!" We both took off, me stepping from one pillow to the next, taking the long way around the coffee table, so I wasn't facing Finn to see what actually happened.

All I heard was a thud and a scream.

I fell to the floor. "Oh my god. Finn!"

His cries were earth-shattering, enough to raise the fine hairs all over my body, and I reached for him. "What happened? What hurts?"

His little face flushed bright red, his mouth open wide, as he continued to bawl and writhe around on the floor in pain. Though he did cover the side of his head with his palm, and that's when I noticed.

The blood.

"Oh my god," I breathed, feeling my own blood drain from my face even as it rushed in my ears. "Finn, I need…" I carefully slid my arm under his neck, half laying him in my lap. "Try to take a breath, Finn. I need you to try to take a big breath, okay?"

His eyes were still closed, tears overflowing from them in a constant and steady trek, but I breathed deeply, so he might hear it through his crying, feel it through his rocking. "Try to breathe, babes. Please, please, I need you to try to breathe."

I cradled him close to me, wrapping my hand around his head, over his hand covering the injury, but I could already feel the oozing, see the red stains in his sandy brown hair, the same color as his father's. A pool of blood soaked into the carpet at my feet, his ear and neck slick with it, and my eyes burned with pain and terror. I kissed his forehead, whispered nonsense to him, keeping him as close to me as I could, attempting to calm him. It took a few minutes, but he eventually stopped wailing, though he didn't stop crying.

"Can I look?"

He hiccupped and offered me a barely perceptible nod, but when I tried to move his hand away, he flinched.

"I won't touch it, I swear. I just want to look. I promise I won't touch."

He slowly turned to me, whimpering, and pulled his hand away from his head a few inches. I couldn't see anything but hair matted with blood.

There was so much blood.

Bile rose in my throat, and I swallowed thickly, pushing it

down. I couldn't get sick. I couldn't panic. But I had to do something.

Except I froze, my stomach in my throat and my heart on the floor.

I pressed my hand to my chest, my breaths coming too fast, my vision blurred with tears. I wasn't sure if I felt like I was about to have a seizure or a panic attack.

Maybe both.

I shook my head, struggling to clear it of fog. The last time I'd seen so much blood in person was when I was fourteen and woke up on the kitchen floor, my arm sliced open from the glass I'd dropped when I fell because of my seizure.

I was bombarded with images, smells, emotion.

Terror. Pure terror.

But it wasn't me this time. It was the little boy who had stolen my heart from the moment I'd met him. The little boy I'd do anything for. Give anything. Sacrifice anything.

"Babes," I said, my voice breaking, "we have to get you up, okay?"

I blinked a few times and wiped my wrist over my eyes, before taking a few ragged breaths to get myself under control. I kept my arms around him as I pushed to my knees then up to standing, never letting go of Finn.

"We're going to go to the kitchen and get a towel then put on our coats to go see the doctor."

He didn't like that idea and started sobbing again. He knew the doctor was where he got shots.

"I know, I know. But we have to. We have to help the boo-boo on your head."

"Kiss it," he said in a tiny, heartbreaking voice, and again, my eyes flooded with tears.

"Oh, babes, if I could fix it with kisses, I would." I kissed him anyway. Brushed my palm over his cheeks. "You can have as many kisses as you want, but I need you to try to be brave. Should we bring one of your dinos?"

He whimpered, and I snatched the pterodactyl from the floor. He tucked it under his chin with one hand, the other still on his head. Which was fine with me. I didn't want him to see the blood. It had soaked into his shirt, into the sleeve of mine too.

"Okay," I whispered. "We're okay."

I carefully carried him to the kitchen and sat him on the counter while I dialed Liam on my cell phone. He didn't answer, so I called again. But when he didn't answer for a third time, I shoved it into my back pocket and took hold of two kitchen towels, giving Finn one to hold to his head and wetting the other. As best I could, I wiped away the blood, but I feared putting a clean shirt on him wouldn't go over well. Instead, I helped him put on his coat, careful not to let the towel drop, and slipped into mine too.

After I had my keys and purse in hand, we were out the front door, Finn still in my arms, still crying.

"I know, babes. I know. I'll try to drive quick, okay?"

The freezing rain was *freezing*, and I was soaked by the time I had him buckled up in his car seat, but I had no time to waste and sped out of the driveway before the car was even warmed up.

It was almost four, and we hit all the after-school traffic, driving behind the slowest bus known to man. "Come on," I whined, "move."

Behind me, Finn sniffled. "I urt."

"I know it hurts, babes, but you'll be okay." I didn't know that for sure, but I promised anyway. "You'll feel better soon."

Liam finally called through the Bluetooth when I was stuck at a red light. "Hey, what's going on? You—"

"Finn's hurt."

"What?"

"He hit his head and…" I could barely get the rest out. "There was a lot of blood."

"Jesus fuck," he snapped. "Where are you?"

"In the car. I'm going to the hospital—"

"Go to the urgent care. It'll be faster, and it's closer to campus. I can be there in five minutes."

My hiccupping breath stole my words.

"I'll meet you there," he said then hung up.

Minutes later, I pulled into the urgent care parking lot, not more than seconds before Liam, who came running to my car.

Liam opened the car door and picked up his son. "Hey, Finn, hey. It's okay." He clasped the back of Finn's little head in his hand, his other arm banded around Finn's waist, and he carried him to the entrance.

I wiped my eyes and sank back against my door, not caring about the rain.

Until I'd seen Liam, I hadn't fully comprehended how scared I was, but now that he was here, all the guilt, shame, and embarrassment came crashing down.

I was supposed to be taking care of Finn. Protecting him.

And I failed.

In the worst way.

I'd rather have put my own head through the table than ever have Finn experience a moment of pain, and yet I'd let it happen.

Worse, I shouldn't have been upset that Liam didn't acknowledge me, but I was disappointed.

Like a selfish bitch.

We were here, at a medical center, because Finn was hurt. Not because I needed to be coddled and indulged.

What kind of person was I that I was worried about Liam's reaction to *me?* Me, who was perfectly fine.

Instead of his son, who was bleeding from his head.

I shuffled through the rain and into the small foyer of the urgent care. It was better coming here; there weren't so many people.

Liam and Finn were already seated in the waiting area, and I shook off the raindrops from my coat and hair as best I could before sliding into the chair next to Liam.

He didn't look at me as he asked, "What happened?"

I licked my lips, chapped and bitten from stress. "We were playing the Floor is Lava in the living room, and he fell."

Liam angled his head to me, meeting my eyes with a narrowed, pained gaze, but he stayed quiet.

"I didn't actually see it, so I don't know for sure what happened, but I think he slipped on the pillow and hit his head on the corner of the coffee table."

Liam's nostrils flared, his shoulders visibly rising and falling with a deep breath. When Finn whimpered, he ducked his chin, whispering, "I know it hurts. I know."

"I'm sorry, Liam."

"Been saying that a lot lately," he muttered, jaw tight.

It felt like a knife carved beneath my ribs.

"I'm sorry, I—"

He flicked his eyes my way. "We'll talk about it later, all right? I can't…" He shook his head, focusing his attention somewhere on the ceiling. "I can't do this right now."

It wasn't a surprise that he was angry with me. I'd hurt his child. And yet, hearing his cold dismissal, feeling how rigidly he sat next to me, I worried whatever we had was gone. He'd put his trust in me to keep Finn safe and secure, and I'd all but shattered his faith in me.

"O'Neil," a young Asian guy in scrubs called from the door, and Liam immediately shot up. I didn't know if he'd want me back there with them, but I followed anyway. Liam answered intake questions about Finn after being escorted into a small room, a curtain closed after us.

"What side of the head?" the nurse asked.

"Left."

He typed it into the computer and shifted as if to get a look, so Liam removed the towel, and the nurse gently sifted through bloody hair as Finn kept his face tucked into his dad's chest.

"Mm-hmm. We'll get that fixed right up."

The relief I felt was momentary because once the nurse left, the room was silent, save for Finn's quiet sniffles.

I leaned against the wall, not daring to take a seat on the chair. I didn't deserve one, and Liam didn't make a motion or sound, telling me to take it.

So instead, I searched my purse for a tissue. When I found it, I ventured the three steps it took to get to the gurney and bent to Finn.

"Can we try to blow your nose?"

A few moments later, he twisted in Liam's arms and faced me, pushing his chin out so I could hold the tissue to his nose. He still struggled with the idea of how to do it, and I didn't want to force him, so I lightly wiped his nose, mouth, and cheeks, a mixture of tears and snot covering most of his face.

"Better?" I asked, attempting a smile, but he merely buried his face into Liam again.

I took my place against the wall and waited until the doctor entered the room, a gray-haired white man who didn't appear terribly friendly.

"I'm Dr. Thompson." He peered over the top of his glasses at Liam. "We have a head injury, correct?"

"Yes, left side," Liam said.

The doctor put on gloves then started prodding at Finn's head without warning, which only made Finn flail and cry.

"Please try to keep him still."

Liam didn't respond, but with the way his mouth was set in a straight line, I imagined his molars were ground down to stubs.

I tried my best to help and stepped closer. "I know it hurts, babes, but the doctor will make you feel better."

Except at the moment, he wasn't. This doctor was torturing him. Torturing me.

"It's a straight cut, but too deep and long to be closed with glue. He'll need stitches or staples."

"*Staples*?" I shrieked, or at least I thought I did from Liam's and the doctor's reaction.

The doctor waited for Liam's answer.

"Whatever's faster."

"Staples," the doctor said with a decisive nod, and it felt like my chest was caving in.

"Is there anything else you can do?" I asked. "Just, like, a big bandage or something?"

The doctor huffed. "No."

"Well… Okay. Is…is everything else all right? He doesn't have a concussion?"

He procured a few things from a cabinet. "No. He'll be fine. Head wounds bleed a lot, but he shows no other signs of trauma."

I stared at Finn, my chin quivering. "You sure?" The doctor sighed impatiently, but I couldn't help pointing out, "There's a lot of blood."

"Head wounds bleed a lot," he repeated and peeked around the curtain, calling for the nurse, who entered and instructed Liam to lay Finn down.

"We'll need to hold him," the nurse said. "I'll get his legs and right arm, if you get the left and keep his attention. We need to keep him as still as possible."

I went hot all over, feeling as if I might throw up. I probably should have taken hold of Finn somehow, but I didn't have the heart or stomach for it.

The doctor kept the staple gun—literal staple gun—out of sight as he approached Finn on the table.

"Look at me, Finn," Liam instructed quietly, offering his son a small smile. "When we're all done, I'll get you the biggest ice cream, but first, you have to be brave and be as still as possible."

Finn didn't respond, his eyes wide and shifting all around as if he knew something was up. He should be scared.

I was so scared.

The doctor quickly and silently cleaned the area then set one hand on Finn's head and held the gun to the wound. With one quiet *click*, the first staple was in, and Finn screamed, kicking his legs, and arching his back.

"That's one," the doctor said. "Five more."

The nurse adjusted his hold while Liam moved even closer, attempting and failing to soothe Finn.

I wasn't sure my heart could break anymore, but watching Finn thrash, shouting to get away as the doctor clicked the gun, I felt it crumble to pieces.

Bile rose in my throat again, but this time, I had trouble keeping it down. I whirled away, squeezing my eyes shut, and dropped my head, trying to regulate my breathing, though it was impossible when I was crying.

Crying for Finn.

For Liam.

For myself.

For what I knew was the end.

I couldn't be with Liam. I couldn't continue to be Finn's nanny.

Not after this. Even if there was a slim chance Liam didn't hate me, I hated myself.

They both deserved someone better, someone who knew what they were doing, someone who could give them more than I could. Someone who was smarter, stronger, more capable. Someone who was less needy and not so dependent on *them*.

Someone who wasn't me.

Before the last click of the staple gun sounded, I ducked out of the room to the shattering echoes of Finn's cry.

TWENTY-NINE
LIAM

could barely keep my eyes open, unable to focus on my son while he was in such agony. But I forced myself, holding on tight to his hand and shoulder, even as he begged me to help him with garbled cries.

"You're doing such a good job," I told him, though I doubted he could hear me through his wailing. "Almost done."

With one last *click*, the doctor finally released his grip on Finn and moved away from the table, stripping off his latex gloves in the process. Finn immediately threw himself at me, so upset he lost the D when he cried for me. "Addy! Addy!"

I kissed his head, held him tight. "All done. You did so good, buddy. I'm really proud of you."

I glanced over my shoulder to ask Kennedy for a tissue, but she wasn't there. I spun in a circle with Finn still clinging to me, thinking that she'd pop up from a corner, but the room was probably only ten by ten feet. If that.

I figured she'd stepped outside since she was squeamish.

Dr. Thompson typed something into the computer then hit a button, printing out directions for us. "You'll need to come back in two weeks to get the staples taken out. Don't get the wound wet for at least forty-eight hours. After that, clean gently around it. If it gets itchy, you may use a little bit of Vaseline, but avoid anything else." He handed me the slips of paper. "Do you have any questions?"

"No. Thank you."

With a brusque nod, the asshole ducked out of the room, leaving only the male nurse, who pulled out a stack of stickers. He spoke gently to Finn. "You were really brave. Would you like some stickers?" He flipped through them. "I have Mickey and Minnie, *Frozen*, flowers. These ones are animals or rainbows…"

Finn peeked out from my shoulder, pointing his index finger at the ones he wanted.

"Animals? That's a good choice." He peeled off two stickers, one of a sloth and the other a toucan. "I hope you feel better." Then he offered both Finn and me a smile before opening the curtain, motioning that we were free to go.

"Time to go, guy." I stepped into the hall, kissing the top of Finn's ear. "I love you so much."

He moved in my hold so his legs were wrapped around my waist, his chin on my shoulder. He whimpered, "Quirt?"

My adrenaline crashed now that the crisis was handled, leaving me drained. The last thing I wanted to do was go get some ice cream, but I'd promised. "Yeah, we'll get ice cream with squirt."

I'd been paralyzed with fear when I'd gotten out of class and noticed how many calls I'd missed. I knew in my gut something bad had happened.

I half expected something worse.

God knew the kid was a walking accident waiting to happen. I was honestly surprised it had taken this long for his first incident requiring stitches or staples.

Didn't mean it didn't scare the shit out of me. I think my stomach dropped clear out of my body when I heard Kennedy's voice, breathy and broken. She must have been terrified, but I was so grateful she took good care of Finn. I probably should have thanked her earlier, but I was too worried to think about what I *should* do and functioned strictly on what I *needed* to do.

I'd make it up to her.

Add it to my IOU list.

I could buy her the entire Ulta store and it wouldn't be enough to repay her for what she'd given to Finn and me.

With a deep breath, the tension in my back eased, and I pivoted to the side, expecting to find Kennedy leaning against the wall, but she wasn't there. I craned my neck, searching for her.

"Quirt," Finn repeated, tugging at my hair.

"I know. I know. We can go as soon as we find Kennedy." I met my son's eyes, still red but no longer full of tears. "Maybe she's in the waiting room."

We headed that way, but when she wasn't there either, I checked down the hall to the bathrooms and waited for a minute. Then I asked the receptionist if she'd seen Kennedy.

"She's short with long brown hair. Had on a white coat and big black purse…came in with us."

The receptionist nodded. "She ran out of here a few minutes ago, crying."

I winced, motioning to Finn. "He had to get a few staples."

She offered a smile of understanding. "Yeah. Sometimes moms are more upset about their kids' injuries than the kids are."

I didn't correct her. I didn't tell her that Kennedy wasn't Finn's mom. Biologically, she wasn't, but I knew Finn loved her just as much as he loved Tessa. And I knew Kennedy loved him right back. She didn't have to tell me. I witnessed it every day.

Kennedy was Finn's mom in every way that counted.

And what a gift that was for my son. To have two women in his life who loved him more than anything.

I carried Finn out to where I'd parked my car, but Kennedy's silver Volvo wasn't next to mine. It wasn't anywhere. I buckled Finn into his seat then got behind the wheel, dialing her number. She didn't answer, so I hung up and immediately tried again.

"Come on," I mumbled into the mouthpiece of my cell phone. "Why aren't you picking up?"

I hoped she was okay.

"Quirt!"

I eyed my kid in the rearview mirror. He didn't appear at all like he'd just had six staples put into his head. "I know. I'm trying to find out where Kennedy is so we can get you ice cream. I need you to stop kicking at my seat."

He picked at goldfish that he'd found in his cupholder, and I rolled my eyes, trying her one last time. When she didn't answer, I left a voice mail message. "Hey, it's me. Where are you? I'm nervous that you're not answering your phone. I hope you're okay. Please call me back. I'm taking Finn for ice cream, but I need… I'm feeling really anxious. First with Finn, and now I don't know where you are. Call me."

Even though it was the middle of winter, I bought Finn the biggest sundae the place had with extra whipped cream and sprinkles. He ate all of the whipped cream and left me the ice cream, which I shoveled down my throat from stress.

I kept my phone next to me the whole time, but it had yet to ring, so I bundled Finn back up, tucked him into the car, and drove home as fast as possible to see Kennedy. But all the lights were off, and when I opened the front door, there was no sign that she was home. The pillows were still on the floor, along with a giant red stain on the carpet.

"Kennedy! You home?"

Finn ran to the kitchen, wriggling out of his coat on the way, and I followed him to be sure she wasn't upstairs anywhere.

Uncertainty simmered inside me.

Where was she?

Why wasn't she here?

Where the hell would she have gone?

She wouldn't have left Finn alone after what had happened. And I couldn't imagine her wanting to leave me to deal with the fallout by myself.

Would she?

Settling down, I cleaned up Finn as best I could then made him some toast and let him play on the iPad for a while as I scrubbed at the stain in the living room, spraying spot remover on the dried blood. Though, at this point, I thought I'd rather rip the whole goddamn carpet out.

When I finished, the spot was still pink, and I was exhausted and irritated, incapable of pretending like everything was fine when it wasn't.

Kennedy wouldn't disappear on me. Something had to be wrong. A car accident. A seizure. *Fuck.* A seizure.

Falling onto my butt, I called her phone number again, knowing I'd get her voice mail. "I need to know you're okay. Call me. Or text me. Or I'm going to start calling around. I don't know your sister's number, but I'll find it. Get Nate to give me Dean's. I'm worried."

I stabbed the red button with my thumb and tossed my phone on the coffee table. It was almost Finn's bedtime, but at this point, I didn't even care. I didn't have the heart to make him sleep alone. Even if he wanted to, *I* didn't want him to sleep by himself. He could stay in my bed. Preferably between me and Kennedy.

My cell phone buzzed with a text, and I snatched it off the table.

KENNEDY

I'm fine. Don't worry about me.

Where are you? Why aren't you calling me back?

She didn't answer, and I nearly growled as I pressed on her name to call her. But she didn't answer. Again.

> What the hell is going on? Why aren't you answering your phone?

It was a while before she texted me back.

KENNEDY

I'm at my sister's.

> Why? I'm going out of my mind. What's going on?

KENNEDY

I'm fine. Don't worry about me. Just take care of Finn.

> I am worried. I'm fucking worried, Kennedy.

> You disappeared. You can't do that.

KENNEDY

I'm sorry, but I couldn't be there. And I knew you didn't want me there.

> What are you talking about? Why wouldn't I want you there?

KENNEDY

You barely looked at me.

> Yeah, because I was freaking the fuck out. I'm still freaking the fuck out.

> You're freaking me the fuck out.

I tore my fingers through my hair, waiting until she responded.

KENNEDY

I'm sorry. I'm so sorry. For everything.

KENNEDY

I never meant to hurt you or Finn.

You didn't hurt him.

KENNEDY

I didn't protect him like I should have. And I'm sorry.

I started typing a message, telling her that she had to stop feeling so goddamn guilty all the time. She had to stop apologizing. Not everything that went wrong in life was because of her. Sometimes shit luck was simply shit luck. Sure, she made mistakes, but so did I. So did everybody. But she couldn't get past them. She let them rule her.

Before I could send her any of that, her next message came through.

KENNEDY

I know I'm not what you or Finn need. I'm going to come back for my stuff another day.

"Another day? What the hell?" I hit the call button. Of course, she didn't answer.

Fucking pick up your goddamn phone, or I'm coming to your sister's house. I'm pissed off now.

KENNEDY

I know you are, and I'm sorry. This is all my fault.

"Stop fucking saying that," I nearly shouted as I clumsily stabbed the letters.

> what happened today isn't your fault and I swear to christ i really will be pissed off if you apologize one more time. come home so we can talk about this.

KENNEDY

I'm sorry. I quit.

"No. No, you don't." I typed out another quick message.

> You're not quitting.

I threw my cell phone onto the couch and curled my knees up, resting my elbows on them to drop my head between my hands.

I didn't understand how this had happened. How she could suddenly want to leave.

I knew the past week had been strained between us, but I'd been feeling a lot of pressure from all sides. I didn't want to take anything out on her, so I'd specifically made sure I had time to box and keep my anxiety about work separate from her.

Then today happened.

Everything was falling apart.

And she couldn't just quit.

Then again… I rubbed at the back of my neck. Memories from a conversation we'd had months ago floated through my brain like dust motes, and I closed my eyes to concentrate. To remember.

We'd been talking about failing and how she often abandoned jobs.

"You've quit a lot?"

"I wouldn't say a lot, but I was in the 'if it doesn't bring you joy, get rid of it' camp long before it became popular."

I breathed heavily and rubbed at my chest again. It felt tight, like someone was sitting on it.

If she quit, did that mean she didn't find joy in being with

Finn and me anymore? It wasn't just her feeling guilty? Or, maybe, she felt so much guilt, she couldn't be happy here anymore.

Either way, I felt sick and stood up, raising my arms, locking my fingers at the back of my head to expand my chest, breathing in my nose and out my mouth.

"But you're sorry," I said out loud, like Kennedy was in front of me. Anger beginning to sprout up through my despair. *"You're sorry."* I huffed.

Sorry didn't begin to cover it.

This couldn't be fixed with a fucking texted apology.

Sorry didn't help Finn, who adored her, who would be heartbroken when he found out she'd bailed on us.

Sorry didn't help me. I had to go to work tomorrow. What was I supposed to do? She was leaving me in the lurch.

I fucking loved her, and she was *sorry*.

Fury had me pacing.

How dare she try to leave us without an explanation. Without even saying goodbye.

Rage propelled my feet as I pivoted from one end of the room to the other.

She didn't get to cut us out of her life, not after these last few months, after how far Finn had come, how we'd all grown together as a family.

She said her piece. But I was going to get to say mine whether she liked it or not.

I picked up my cell phone once again, planning on pocketing it before dressing Finn in his coat to go to her sister's house and talk to her.

But I stopped, frozen at the message she'd texted while I was busy losing my cool.

KENNEDY

I don't want to be with you. I can't.

KENNEDY

Don't make this harder than it already is. It's better this way, you have to see that. I'm so sorry.

And all the fight whooshed out of me as I sagged against the wall.

She was convinced the right thing to do—the only thing—was to leave, and as much as I hated it, I couldn't force her to stay.

I couldn't make her do anything.

She'd proudly admitted she quit things all the time.

I just never thought she'd quit *me*.

THIRTY
KENNEDY

"You're watching *Mary Poppins* again?"

I curled onto my side, tugging the blanket up under my chin. "So?"

Taylor sat by my feet. "I feel like you're spiraling out a little bit, and watching a movie about a singing nanny isn't going to help."

I sniffed. Of course it wasn't going to help. Watching Julie Andrews sing "A Spoonful of Sugar" was like picking at a scab. It didn't feel good, but it did make me feel *something*.

A reassurance that I'd done the right thing. I was no Mary Poppins, and Finn deserved someone so much better than me.

"You could vary it a bit. At least put on *Sound of Music*."

I lifted my shoulder. Maria ended up with Captain von Trapp, and I didn't think I could handle that.

When I had turned up at Taylor and Dean's house with wet hair and swollen eyes, Dean'd immediately put on his shoes, ready to go to battle for me. Until I'd spat out a rushed explanation of what had happened: Finn had hit his head and needed staples, but I couldn't stomach being there.

That was when Dean had kicked off his shoes and opened up

a bottle of wine, setting it and two glasses on the table in their living room, along with an open bag of Doritos.

I loved him so much. And I didn't deserve my sister's boyfriend taking such good care of me.

I didn't deserve *anyone* taking such good care of me. Not when I couldn't repay them for what they'd all done for me.

Two days later, and I still hadn't found the courage to turn on my phone. I couldn't handle seeing Liam's texts or listening to his voice mails.

I was already so in love with him, but sometimes love wasn't enough.

I had failed him.

And I couldn't face it.

Taylor plopped down by my feet. "Do you want to talk about it yet?"

I rubbed at my stinging nose. "There's nothing to talk about."

"You're right. Only that you're here on my couch instead of at Liam's house, doing whatever it is people madly in love do."

"The same thing you and Dean would be doing if I weren't here on your couch," I said, and Taylor leaned her elbow on the back of the couch, holding her head in her hand with a quiet snicker.

"We're in a fight."

I tossed her a bland look. "You're always in a fight."

"He wants to get married," she said on a sigh, like it was the worst thing ever.

"Oh. The. Horror."

She bit back a smile. "I have things to do."

"Things you can't do while you're married?" I asked, setting my feet in her lap.

"Well…no, but I feel like we finally found a good rhythm in our work and home life, and I want to enjoy that more, instead of jumping right into marriage. We haven't even been together a year."

I lifted my shoulder. "But when you know, you know."

She shook her head at me. "You're too romantic."

"And you're too pragmatic."

"So let me solve your problem with Liam, and you can pick out my wedding dress."

I sat up. "That means you'll say yes."

"Eventually, yes. Not right now."

I blew a raspberry in her direction. "But you two are perfect for each other."

Her eyes took on some faraway glint as her lips tilted up slightly, and even though I was so happy for my sister, I turned back to the TV, my stomach in knots again.

I watched Mary Poppins help Bert and the kids jump into his chalk drawing—my favorite part—but right as Bert started dancing with the penguins, Taylor nudged my thigh. "So…"

"So?" I grumbled, refusing to look away from Bert and the penguins waddling.

"So, I understand you're upset Finn got hurt, but what I don't understand is why you're still here, acting as if a couple of staples is the end of the world."

"Don't be so flippant," I snapped, removing my feet from her lap to sit up straight. I draped the blanket around me like a shield. "This isn't a joke," I said, my voice losing its hard edge when it wobbled. "It's… It's…"

Taylor leaned in, curling her hand around my shoulder. "It's what?"

I shook my head as my eyes filled with tears, unable to get it out.

"You know what happened wasn't your fault, right?"

"It is." I wiped at my face. "I was supposed to be watching him, and… You didn't see. There was so—" I hiccupped "—there was so much blood."

"Oh, Kenny." Taylor pulled me to her, hugging me. "It was an accident. Kids fall over all the time, especially Finn. That's what you told me, right? That he's so accident-prone."

"Yeah, but…" I inhaled deeply to try to contain my sniffles

and stutters. "Not like that. You don't understand what it feels like to see someone you love like that."

She held me at arm's length, her thin eyebrow arched high. *"Don't I?* I wouldn't know what it's like to see someone I love on the floor, covered in blood, thinking they're dead." She let go of me and brought both of her legs up onto the couch, crossing them, and folded her arms over her chest, finishing with a sarcastic, "No. I wouldn't know *anything* about that."

I didn't have much memory of the night of my first seizure, and although I knew what my sister had done for me then, what she still did for me now, sometimes it was easy to forget that she was the one to find me. She was the one who called the ambulance, who cleaned the blood up off the kitchen floor, and held my hand in the hospital.

Taylor was my overbearing sister, the one who told me what to do and gave me advice even when I didn't want or ask for it.

But she was also the one who took care of me, who I knew loved me more than life itself.

Exactly how I felt about Finn.

My sister blinked a few times, like she might start to cry, but Taylor Novak didn't cry. Ever.

"It was horrible," she said eventually. "The worst thing I'd ever seen and probably will ever see. Sometimes…" She stared at me like she was unsure if she wanted to go on. "I don't think a lot about Dad or how he looked at the end. I don't have nightmares about that, but I do have them about you. That night haunts me." She lifted one shoulder. "I suspect it will forever, so, yes, I know *exactly* what it feels like. Helpless and hopeless and like you can't breathe. Guilty and ashamed and like you would give anything to take it away or rewind."

I nodded. "I keep hearing his screams, and I…"

When I covered my face as I cried, Taylor pulled me to her once again, this time rocking me like I was a child. "It's not your fault. It only feels like it is because you love him and you're responsible for him. I suspect when he loses his first tooth or gets in his first argument with a friend, you might also find a way to think it's somehow your fault."

That tugged a reluctant smile out of me. "No. I'm not you."

"No." Taylor smoothed my hair away from my face. "You're not. You love so easily. You see the best in everyone, even when they don't deserve it, so I don't understand why you don't think *you* deserve the same."

I swiped my sleeve over my cheeks. "You told me not to fall in love with him."

She wagged her head side to side with a pinched brow. "Not *all* of my advice is good."

"I heard that!" Dean called from the kitchen.

"Shut up, you!"

I sniffled a laugh, but my good humor quickly faded. "Liam hates me."

"He doesn't hate you."

"Yes, he does. You didn't see his face."

"Kennedy," Taylor said with a roll of her eyes, "not everything is about you."

I socked her in the arm, and she laughed.

"He was devastated," I said, and she dropped her chin, like *Yeah…?*

"Of course he was devastated. He had to hold his kid down while somebody put metal into his head. Who wouldn't be devastated?"

"And it was my—"

"I swear to god, if I hear you say it was your fault one more time, I will burn all of your makeup."

I wrenched my head back. "You wouldn't."

"I would."

"But Liam bought me this really nice case for Christmas. The outside's quilted and soft." I petted the air like the luxurious case was in front of me. "And it has pockets for all my brushes. He also got me a mirror with a light around the…" I trailed off as Taylor glared at me like the know-it-all she was. "What?"

"He loves you."

"No, he…he couldn't. Not after…"

"You finally found a good guy, and you run away. Explain that to me. You stay with all these assholes, yet willingly let go of the one who actually loves you." When I shook my head, she went on. "I saw it. Jesus, after your show, you two might as well have worn signs around your necks. He *loves* you, and he's a *good* guy. I know you think you have to prove yourself to the people around you or some other asinine belief that has to do with your self-worth, but for once in your life, let go of the baggage." She took hold of my hand. "I promise, everything gets so much better once you do."

"It can't be that easy."

"It's not easy, but it is better. Plus, I have a really great therapist. I don't know why you never called her." She pulled her cell phone from her back pocket, tapping on it. "I'm texting you the contact again." Then she seized my cell phone and powered it on before tossing it in my lap. "First, call the therapist to make an appointment, then call Liam."

One, two, three, that was what Taylor did. Broke life down into steps, crushing each and every one under the sole of her heels. One day, she might take over the world. Until then, I supposed she'd continue to rule this tiny pocket of the world that included Dean and me.

"Can I finish watching *Mary Poppins* first?"

She tipped her head back to let out one single patronizing "Ha!" Then she snatched up the remote to stop the movie. "Call now."

I took a deep breath and lifted my phone, dialing the therapist's number. Since it was the weekend, I knew no one was going to answer but left a message anyway. I turned to Taylor. "Satisfied?"

"Not until you talk to Liam."

That one was harder to accomplish, and I scratched the sweatpants I'd borrowed from Dean. "What do I say?"

She shrugged. "Whatever you want. But you need to start the conversation."

I tried to outline ideas in my head.

I'm sorry.

I know you tell me not to apologize all the time, but you and Finn are the two people in the world I would never ever want to hurt. I love you, and I'm sorry.

I'm not good at thinking I'm worthy, but I'm going to work on it. I want to be worthy of you.

You're worth it. Finn is worth it. The family we built is worth it.

"Okay," I said, more to myself than my sister. "I'm calling him."

With trembling fingers, I hit his number and held the phone to my ear. It rang only once before he answered, his voice a mixture of shock and hurt. "Kennedy?"

"Hi." My pulse kicked up. "How… How are you?"

He sniffed dismissively. "Really? That's what you're going with right now? After you walked out two days ago, ignored me, ignored all my messages, you're going to ask how I am?"

My courage plummeted. "I know… It's just… I don't know what to say."

"Apparently there is nothing to say. Isn't that what you told me? It was better this way. Don't make it harder than it already is."

I couldn't answer even if I wanted to because he spoke right over me.

"That's what you texted me. You *texted* me, Kennedy. You broke up with me over a text."

The fact that he even considered us something to be broken up stole my breath and thoughts.

"I know, and I'm sorry. I…"

In the background, I heard Finn happily chattering away, and my heart flip-flopped at the sound.

"How's Finn doing? How's his head?"

"Seriously?" Liam's harsh scoff had me leaning back into the couch cushions, as if I could retreat from him. "You refused to talk to me for two days, but suddenly you want to check in on him?"

"I know…" I rubbed at my forehead. "I don't know what else to say besides I'm sorry. I'm worried about him."

"Finn's not your concern anymore." Liam's normally smooth and warm voice was icy, his Boston accent full and harsh. "*You* quit on *us*, remember?"

My eyes went blurry with tears. "I know, and I never should have left like that, but I want to fix it." I bit my lip, waiting for him to say something, but his silence spoke volumes. "Can we meet? I would really like to talk in person and explain."

"I don't know what you could explain. You keep apologizing, but your sorrys mean nothing to me."

I covered my mouth with my hand in an attempt to hide my gasp.

"We're all dealing with shit in our lives and trying to do our best, so I don't know why you think you can continually walk away from something whenever you feel like it. Life is hard, Kennedy. You can't keep quitting because you don't like it or it doesn't feel good."

"I know, Liam. I'm going to do better."

"Better than what? Walking out on me and Finn without a goddamn word and then acting as if a couple of texts are enough of an explanation? It was incredibly immature, and I thought you were better than that." His words hit me in the soft spot under my ribs when he said, "And how am I supposed to trust you after this?"

This was what I'd expected. Why I felt so awful. Because he'd trusted me to take care of his only child, and I'd failed. "You don't trust me with Finn anymore?"

"I don't trust you with *me* anymore," he corrected. The fight drained from his voice, and the pain was worse than the anger. So, so much worse. "Goddamn it, Kennedy. I thought I loved you, but I don't know how I could've fallen for someone who could be so careless. Who didn't consider the repercussions. You were everything I wanted, everything Finn and I needed, but I guess I was wrong if you can do a one-eighty and bail at the tiniest sign of trouble."

I openly wept now, not bothering to cover it up. All the things I'd been insecure about were true, but because *I'd* made them true.

Even though Liam loved me and thought I was perfect for him, I didn't believe it. I was the one who walked out and didn't want to listen because I was afraid to confirm everything I already thought was true, but I should have known better.

I should have trusted Liam to love me like I loved him.

But it was too late, and this time, it was he who apologized. "I'm sorry. I can't do this anymore. I gotta go."

The line went dead, and I stared at my phone for a while until Taylor took it out of my hand. With one look at her, I fell into her open arms.

"He said he loved me," I got out between sobs. "but he's done with me."

She stroked my head and hair, letting me soak her sweatshirt, and then I heard Dean's voice behind me. "Who do I need to kill?"

"You know, I don't understand where all this big-guy bluster comes from," Taylor told him. "You're only 5'11", your cardio is shit, and last I checked, you gave up on 75 Hard."

"First of all, there is no *only* 5'11" because it's a perfectly respectable height. My cardio is shit compared to yours, but you're a fucking machine. And yeah, I gave up 75 Hard because it was fucking hard. No one can drink that much water in one day."

"Poor baby." There was not one ounce of sympathy in her words.

"I hate you so much," he said, but I was uncomfortable with the amount of lust embedded in that sentence.

I moved out of my sister's arms so I didn't get caught in their verbal foreplay. "I'm going upstairs."

"Sit down." Dean pushed on my shoulder when I started to stand. He squished in next to me. "What happened?"

I relayed as much of the conversation as I could while Dean and Taylor both listened intently.

"You hurt him," Dean said when I finished. "That's why he said what he said."

Taylor agreed. "Yeah, I don't think he meant any of that."

"I broke him. I broke us. How can I come back from that?"

Dean folded his arms over his chest, nudging me with his elbow so I'd meet his gaze. "The thing you need to realize about life is none of us knows what we're doing. I think *you think* everyone else except you has their shit together, which is completely false."

"I have my shit together," Taylor muttered under her breath, and Dean sent her a dry look before smiling at me.

"I love you like I love my own sister, and I hate that you're so hard on yourself. I wish you could see yourself the way everyone else sees you."

Taylor snuggled in close to my other side, sandwiching me between them. "Dean's right."

He cupped his hand around his ear. "Say that again. A little louder, if you please."

She ignored him. "Liam loves you. All you have to do is remind him why. If he's upset you left, show him you won't leave him again. Even when you're scared or don't trust yourself, you have to show him that you trust him with your heart. Because you do, right?"

I reached for a tissue from the box on the coffee table. "But how do I show him that I trust him to take care of me like I want to take care of him? I won't leave again if things get hard. How do I prove that? Ask him to marry me?"

Taylor rolled her eyes, and Dean shrugged, both of them speaking at the same time.

"Don't be ridiculous."

"If you want."

That pushed a laugh out of my lungs, and…actually, that idea didn't seem all that bad to me. I loved Liam. I loved Finn. I wanted to be with them for the rest of my life. Then again, I didn't want to rush with him like I did with everything else in my life. I wanted to be thoughtful about my decisions, like Liam was.

I wrapped my arms around both my sister and Dean, yanking them in for a group hug. "You two are the best, even if your flirting is super weird. I love you."

"Love you too, Kenny," Taylor said with a squeeze to my cheeks as she backed away.

Dean pointed his finger at me. "You know I warned him, back in September. I told him he'd fall in love with you. Told him it was a little too easy with you." When I flung myself at him, he laughed. "Love you, Ken."

"You're the best brother-in-law a girl could ask for."

"Tell your sister that."

Taylor stood with an irritated wave of her hand. "Oh my god, you two. You're the worst."

Dean and I grinned at each other, enjoying our little team.

"So, you want to finish *Mary Poppins* or what?" he asked, picking up the remote.

"Absolutely." I leaned into his side, both of us bopping along to Bert and the penguins dancing.

THIRTY-ONE
LIAM

"This better be good," Dylan said, slumping down in a chair next to me at Walt's. "Genevieve was in the middle of getting naked when I got the call."

Nate dropped his head back to his shoulders. "Dude!"

"She's been gone for six months, Paige has the kids, and all I want to do is bury my face between her legs, but—"

Nate thumped down a beer in front of Dylan. "Seriously. I don't want to hear details about what you're doing with my sister."

"You were the one who called me. We thought something was wrong," Dylan said as he lifted his beer to his mouth.

"There is something wrong." Nate pointed to me, and Dylan's eyes widened as if seeing me for the first time.

"What happened to you?"

I didn't bother answering, only took another gulp of my Guinness.

From the other side of me, Jude leaned his elbow on the bar, saying, "Kennedy left him."

"Shit, man, I'm sorry." Dylan furrowed his brows. "Where's Finn?"

"I dropped him at Jude's to play for a bit," I said. "I need to figure out what to do for childcare. *Again.*"

"My mom's watching the kids," Jude explained. "I told him we could come here and talk it out."

Dylan pulled his baseball cap off to scrub his hand over the back of his head then put it on backward. "Okay, what's the plan?"

"I told him he needs to get Kennedy back." Nate shrugged as if I could snap my fingers and get her back. "He said Finn's been asking about her a lot."

"She left me," I said through clenched teeth, hating to repeat myself again. "She quit through a text."

"Yeah, but you did say she called you," Jude noted, always trying to find the bright side.

As far as I was concerned, there was no bright side.

"She called you?" Nate inclined his head, his hands on the bar. "You didn't tell me that detail."

I lifted my glasses up to rub at my eyes. "Because I don't want to keep rehashing it."

"Start from the beginning," Jude said. "Let us all hear it, and then we can go from there."

With a breath, I set my glasses back on my nose and dragged my hands through my hair. It needed a trim. I hated the thought of anyone else touching my hair besides Kennedy.

I inhaled in a rough breath before I started in on the story. "Everything was going great. I took her up to see my family. They all loved her, she loved them, everything was perfect. And then she posted a video on my birthday that stirred up more of the viral BS."

Dylan picked up his phone, mostly likely to search for the video because he liked to give me shit about it, but I whacked his forearm. "She deleted the video, but it'd gotten around a bit before that. Made its way to some of the students at the university."

Nate sucked air through his teeth as Jude winced. "They're pissed?"

"The provost is pissed. He's an asshole, but he's the final say on if I get tenure or not, so even though I didn't technically do anything wrong, he's got it out for me."

"When do you find out if you get it or not?" Jude asked.

"The board review's in less than three weeks, which is why… this whole thing could not have come at a worse time."

Dylan drew a line on the bar top. "Well, how'd we go from the video to her leaving?"

"The other day, Finn fell and busted his head open on the coffee table in the living room. I got out of class and had, like, ten missed calls from her. He was bleeding pretty bad, and I met her at urgent care. They put six staples in his head." I scraped my index finger on my scalp at the same place Finn had had cut his open. "He's fine, but Kennedy… I don't know. She freaked out and disappeared. I turned around to talk to her, and she was gone. She didn't pick up when I called her, wasn't answering my texts, and when I got home, she wasn't there. I thought…" I winced, remembering the fear that had clutched my heart at the thought of Kennedy hurt. It was as bad as the idea of Finn being hurt. "She's got epilepsy, and all I kept thinking of was her in a car accident or having fallen down the stairs because of a seizure. Every worst-case scenario raced through my head."

Silently, Jude gripped my shoulder, squeezing it. He understood because he had experienced a worst-case scenario with his wife, Mira.

"She was fine, but she'd run away to her sister's place. She texted to tell me she quit."

"She quit?" Dylan repeated.

I nodded.

"I still don't understand why," Jude said.

I shook my head. "I don't either."

"What *exactly* did she say?" Nate asked.

"Nothing, really. She kept apologizing and saying she never meant to hurt Finn. Which is ridiculous. I always told her she had to stop thinking she needed to apologize for everything. She constantly feels like she owes people." I held both of my hands up at different levels. "Like she's down here and everybody else is up here, and she doesn't deserve whatever people deign to give her." I curled my fingers into fists and crossed my arms. "I hated it, that she felt like she was below anyone. Because she's fucking perfect, and, if anything, everyone else owes *her* something."

We all sat quietly for a moment until Jude said, "But then she called you yesterday, right? What happened?"

I closed my eyes and heaved out a breath. "I was an asshole, and I unloaded on her. But I'm mad, you know? She left me for no reason. She left Finn. How could she do that?"

"Uh…" Dylan cleared his throat, briefly met my eyes, then stared down at his beer. "I, uh, can understand. Whatever's happened in her past, if she thinks she doesn't deserve love, I get that." He lifted his shoulder and cleared his throat again, looking at each of us in turn. "It's hard to learn to accept anything good when you think you're going to fuck it up. So, you run away instead because it's easier than facing the truth…that you *will* mess up. But it's a matter of knowing you can fix it that changes things."

I took in my friend's words, thinking about all the times Kennedy had shown me how she loved me, by making dinner and buying silly gifts and taking such good care of Finn and me, but then had trouble accepting the same from me. "What do I do?"

Dylan took a breath deep enough to raise his shoulders as he rolled his pint glass around on its edge. "Keep showing up. Keep telling her you love her. I think that's all you can do."

I curled my lips over my teeth in thought. Sure, I could do that, but in the meantime, I needed to do something with Finn. "I'm back to square one with childcare."

Nate placed a napkin and pen in front of me. "Make a nanny list again?"

I let out a derisive laugh and scratched out a few words. *Wanted: Kennedy Novak. Must love me and Finn.*

From over my shoulder, Jude read my sad scribbles out loud, and Nate chuckled. "Awfully specific there. I don't know if you can find exactly that."

"I don't know," Dylan said into his beer, his eyes focused over Jude's shoulder. "You might be surprised."

"My name's Kennedy, and I hear you're in need of a nanny."

Except for Dylan, the rest of us whipped our heads in that direction to find Kennedy in all her glory, glossy hair curled and spilling over his shoulders, wearing my favorite pair of dark jeans and a snug sweater under her white coat with her big black bag over her shoulder. She took my breath away, even if her smile wobbled.

"Can we talk?"

Dylan set down his beer, not even half drunk, and pulled his keys from his pocket as he stood. "I'm gonna head home. No one talk to me for the next three days. I'm going to be too busy fucking."

"Bro!" Nate turned on him. "Don't think I won't swing on you again."

"Your sister'll be mad."

As the two continued to bicker, with Dylan walking toward the exit and Nate talking trash from behind the bar, Jude slipped his coat on. "I'm going to go relieve my mom."

That left Kennedy and me alone.

Being a Sunday afternoon, the bar wasn't very busy to begin with, but we might as well have been in a vacuum, her and I staring at each other. Even though she wore her usual makeup with thick lashes, dark eyeliner, and what I knew was blush and bronzer because I'd studiously watched her do it so many days, I could tell she was tired. It was in the way her smile didn't reach her eyes and in the set of her shoulders. I wondered if she wasn't sleeping well. Like me.

I gestured to the stool next to me, and she gingerly sat like she wasn't sure if she was going to stay or not.

I motioned to the taps. "Do you want anything?"

"No, I..." Her throat lifted on a visible swallow. "I'm so nervous, my stomach's upset. I'm worried if I drink something, it might not stay down."

I felt like shit. I didn't want her making herself sick. "Want some water, at least?"

"No, really..." She shook her hands in front of her. "I got myself all psyched up to go to your house, and then you weren't there, and I didn't know what to do because I wasn't sure you'd answer if I called or texted, and I figured I might as well check the one or two places I knew you went," she said all in one breath.

"Where did you go?"

"I went to Imagination and looked around then decided to come here, in case you were here." She turned her palm up to me. "And you are, so it all worked out, but also not because now we actually have to talk, and in all the times I practiced this monologue, I didn't imagine it at Walt's, and it's kinda throwing me off."

"You're not auditioning for me," I said, hoping she'd stop and take a breath.

Which she did, and then she hung her purse over the back of her chair and removed her coat.

"If it helps with your nerves, you can picture me naked," I offered, earning a reluctant smile that transformed into a frown when she started crying. "Hey, hey, please don't cry."

She dug through her purse, plucked out a small plastic dinosaur and a single sock, belonging to Finn. She was such a *mom*, especially when she plucked a tissue from a little packet she'd located. She wiped at her nose and eyes then focused her gaze on me. "Sorry. Hearing you make a joke… It hit me in the gut, you know? I'd convinced myself that there was no way you could ever forgive me, let alone joke around with me."

I opened my mouth to speak, but she held up her hand. "I know you're about to tell me not to apologize, and I'm going to work on that. But you and Finn, you are the two people I should apologize to."

"I don't want it. What I do want is an explanation."

She licked her lips, toying with the tissue, mumbling, "I guess the long and short of it is… I love you. I love Finn. I—"

"You love me?"

She nodded, and I wrapped my foot around the leg of her stool, dragging it right up against mine then sank my hand under her hair to curl around her neck. The scent of sugar and flowers surrounded me. I didn't know how much I'd gotten used to her smell until it was gone. "Say it again."

She blinked a few times as if confused.

"I want to hear what you just said, but this time, I want you looking me in the eyes when you say it."

She slowly tipped her chin up, lifting her beautiful face to mine, the smallest of smiles gracing her plump lips. "I love you, and I love Finn. I love you both so much that I was afraid to face my insecurities and have it confirmed that I wasn't good enough for either of you. It was terrible of me to walk away from you and not communicate. I know—" She dropped her gaze to her lap, where she fidgeted with her hands. "I know it was imma-ture, and I know how upset you were. You had—have—every right to be angry with me, but I need you to know that I won't ever do it again."

I gently squeezed her neck, urging her to look at me. "How do I know? I want to believe you, but how do I know you won't get scared and run away?"

"Because I know what it feels like to be without you, and I don't want to feel that again. Plus, what would I do with all this?" She twisted away from me for her purse and took out a shopping bag, from which she set items on the bar top: a pack of brown bags, yarn, googly eyes, sequins, markers, and three bottles of glitter paint. "Finn and I have a lot more hand puppets to make."

That pulled a laugh out of me, and I shook my head in amusement.

"Plus, Finn has a playdate next week that I know he was really looking forward to. It's with Van from his preschool class, and I really like his mom, so..." She held up her index and middle fingers, crossing them. "I really want it to work so I have some mom friends."

"Mom friends?" I repeated, my heart clanging around in my chest. My pulse doubled in speed with every word she spoke, with every second she sat in front of me, offering herself up, open and honest like the Kennedy I knew and had fallen in love with.

Her teeth briefly passed over her lower lip as she bit back a smile. "I talked to Tessa."

"You did?"

She sat up tall, like she was excited about this part. "We Face-Timed this morning, and I told her what had happened. I figured you'd emailed her about the staples, but I wanted her to hear it from my mouth. She was so understanding and sweet, and we had a really great conversation."

Tessa was a sensible, intelligent, and good person. There was no reason why she and Kennedy wouldn't be friends, but what came out of her mouth next almost knocked me off my stool.

"We talked about me being a permanent person in your life, in Finn's life. I asked her if, when the time came, it would be all right to call myself Finn's stepmom."

"You *what*?"

"I told her how much I love Finn and explained that I wanted to spend the rest of my life with you, but only if we were all on the same page. I wanted to get her blessing."

My mouth went dry. My mind spun, so I couldn't quite grasp what was happening. "What are you saying?"

"I'm saying I want you to know I am very serious about you, about us and our life together. I'm trying to be mature and communicate…you know the thing you said grown men do."

I bit back a smile, letting her continue.

"I know I have some work to do on myself, and I don't want to rush into marriage, but that's what I want eventually. I want you and Finn forever. I love you, and even though you haven't said it back, I know you do. I feel it every single day, and the past few days wouldn't have been so agonizing if we didn't love each other."

She was a dozen years younger than me, but in some aspects, Kennedy was more mature than me, certainly in giving people grace and consideration. I only wished she'd allow herself some too.

"So you're saying you're not planning on leaving me again any time soon?" I asked to tease her a little bit.

"No." She shook her head, blinking at me so sweetly. "Now, can you say it back to me?" When I didn't answer immediately, she pouted and slid her hands around my shoulders. "Please?"

I clucked my tongue. "Well, you know how much I love it when you say please." I bent, leaning my forehead against her. "I love you, Kennedy. Maybe from the night you first walked up to me at this bar and convinced me to hire you as my son's nanny."

She laughed. "Best spur-of-the-moment decision I've ever made."

"Me too." I kissed her once, twice, three times on the lips. "I'm sorry I snapped at you on the phone yesterday. I was surprised and didn't know how to handle everything I was feeling, but I should never have said that your sorry didn't cut it. You were trying to talk to me, and I shut you down. That was on me. We could've had this conversation yesterday," I said, motioning to her props on the bar. "Without all the art supplies."

"Yeah, but I think it gave my speech some extra flair." She

shrugged, and I released a long breath, happy that she was happy.

Cupping her face in my hands, I smoothed my thumbs over her cheeks. "You are everything I want and need in a woman, partner, and parent for Finn."

"Are you okay if I don't want to have more kids? That was one of the things that I worried about. I don't want you to give that up because of me."

"If you don't want more kids, I don't care. If you decide you want them in the future, fine. But I am giving nothing up. Your health and happiness are the most important things, so I don't want you to ever think you're less because of that. Or any reason. I love you exactly as you are, high-maintenance, dry-clean directions, and all." I followed the line of her bottom lip with the pad of my thumb. "It's my privilege to take care of you. Like you take care of me."

Her reddening eyes and tip of her nose alerted me to her coming emotions, and I smiled into a kiss. "Before you get weepy again, you ready to get out of here? We'll have to pick Finn up from Jude's, but you want to go out for dinner?"

"Yes, definitely. I haven't been able to eat much the past few days."

I stood and held her coat open so she could slip her arms inside. I swept her hair back over her shoulders so it didn't get caught then zipped it up to her chin. "I missed you, angel. And even if you hadn't walked in here tonight, I would have found you. I would've gone over to your sister's house eventually and stood outside playing Broadway songs on a speaker until you talked to me."

She snickered as she cleaned up her art supplies. "What was going to be your first choice of song?"

I thought on this while buttoning up my coat. "I could probably only name a few from your show, but I liked that one you were singing in the shower the other day. It was about coats and kisses."

She turned to me, her purse on her shoulder, a purple beanie on her head with a ball on top. "'I'll Cover You.' It's from *Rent*."

"I'll Cover You." I wrapped my arm around her shoulders. "I like that one."

She leaned her head back, offering me her lips for a kiss. "I like that one too."

THIRTY-TWO

KENNEDY

had ravioli with homemade sauce simmering on the stove and a bottle of champagne chilling in the fridge. Or whiskey on the counter…in case of bad news.

But it wasn't going to be bad news.

It was going to be good news. I was manifesting it.

"Good news, right, Finnie?"

Finn followed me as I paced, thinking it was a game. He'd tried to slow me down or trip me up by pretending to be a rock or dinosaur or crashing a Matchbox car into my feet like he was doing now. "Good news!"

"Yes, that's right." I patted out a nervous beat on my thighs as I avoided the plastic track Finn had laid out on the floor. "Good news. Daddy's going to have good news."

Liam had been insisting his board review would be fine, but I knew he was nervous. Even with all the amazing work he'd done. I told him he had to let his insecurities go, like my therapist had told me. Write them down on a piece of paper and get rid of it. Rip it up and throw them away. Don't give them power.

But it seemed my good-luck blow job this morning did more for his confidence than any information I'd passed on from my few therapy sessions.

It had really been helping me, and I'd never been happier, being with Liam and Finn. I, of course, was no longer being paid to be his nanny, but my job hadn't ended. For now, I was still with Finn full time, although I planned on finding a hair salon to work at a few hours a week. Liam said I didn't need to work, but that only solidified my decision. Knowing I didn't need to work meant I could really think about what I wanted to do, and it turned out I really wanted to get back into cosmetology. I loved talking to people and genuinely loved making people happy with their appearance. When I had asked Liam if that sounded silly, he'd said, "Everyone needs to get their hair cut at some point. Why shouldn't it make you happy to do it for them?"

Then he'd smacked my ass and told me to get on all fours.

He had a real knack for driving the point home.

Below me, Finn dropped a heavy dinosaur on his face, which he'd been flying in the air above him. He cried out, and I bent to pick him up. "You okay, babes?"

"My chin," he said clearly, and even though I didn't want to smile because he was hurt, I couldn't help it. He was doing so well with his speech, his beginning sounds improving every single day.

"Your chin hurts? Want a kiss?"

He nodded, and I rubbed my palm over it a few times then kissed it.

"All better?"

He nodded again and squirmed for me to put him down.

"Why don't we pick up? It's a mess in here. One of us is going to get hurt when we step on one of these toys."

He sat on the floor, gazing up at me, confused. "Hurt toy?"

"The toys will hurt our feet if we step on them. So come on, let's pick up." I handed him one of the canvas bins, but as I began to toss toys into another, the front door opened.

I startled and stood, my heart racing as Liam stepped inside.

"Daddy!" Finn raced to his father. I wasn't far behind.

We threw ourselves at him, and he laughed, catching us both in a hug. "Quite a welcome home."

"How'd it go?" I asked, skipping pleasantries. "I've been dying."

"*You've* been dying?" His mouth crooked in the half smile I loved so much.

I thumped his shoulder, but I already knew the answer from the way his hands curled around my waist. "Did you get it?"

He answered with a grin.

"Ah!" I threw my arms around him, squealing. "Congratulations. I'm so proud of you!"

"Up! Up!" Finn whacked my leg, demanding to be picked up, so I grabbed him and smooshed him between us in a group hug.

"Did you hear that? Daddy got tenure! That means he's really smart and a good teacher."

Finn held his arms up, hands curled into fists as he cheered. Liam and I laughed, alternating kissing his cheeks, which only made him giggle and wriggle around.

"Okay." I put Finn down and clapped a few times. "I'm going to open up the champagne. Finn, you keep cleaning up. We're going to have dinner in a few minutes."

I skipped up to the kitchen and popped the champagne, pouring it into the flutes I'd bought since I'd convinced Liam we'd be hosting parties and needed them. Not that he'd say no to anything I wanted. I could tell him I wanted to paint the whole house pink, and he'd bring home samples for me to choose between salmon or rose.

Really, he spoiled me.

I set the table and called the boys up. "Dinner's ready!"

I waited, and when I heard laughter instead of footsteps, I poked my head around the wall, peering downstairs. "What are you two doing? Come on."

"I'm being attacked by a triceratops," Liam called, and I smiled to myself as I dished out the ravioli.

A minute and a few screeches later, Liam appeared with Finn on his back, both of them roaring.

I propped my hands on my hips, taking in my boys with their matching smiles and wavy, overly long hair, their heads tilted at the exact same angle. "Only humans get to eat ravioli. Dinos can't hold forks."

"You hear that? We have to be humans again."

"Avliolis!" Finn shouted, and Liam nodded.

"Yeah, if you want ravioli, you have to be a human." Liam stage-whispered to Finn, "Kennedy says so."

I playfully whacked at him then took Finn in my arms, smooching his cheek before sitting him down in his chair. "I think we should celebrate tonight and watch a movie," I said, setting a plate down in front of Finn. "What do you think, babes? What movie should we watch?"

He didn't answer, instead diving straight into the food.

I circled back around to the stove and started to dish ravioli onto plates for Liam and me, but he interrupted with a kiss to my neck. "You know the later we stay up with a movie, the less time *we* have to celebrate."

I nudged him back with my butt against his groin, and he groaned quietly. Biting my lip, I deposited the plates on the table then twirled around to pick up the flutes, handing one to him. He tugged me close, drifting his free hand over my hip and ass. He took a sip of the bubbly then twisted the glass in his hand. "I'm surprised you didn't get these printed or monogrammed with something."

"'I'm with the Hot Professor' is a little too long to put on a glass."

He waggled his head side to side. "A T-shirt, maybe?"

I sipped from my drink. "There's an idea."

"Or a tattoo?"

I jerked back. "A tattoo?"

He nodded. "I want to get a tattoo. I have one for all the most important people in my life, but I'm missing yours."

I was both touched and horrified. "Are you, like, gonna get my face or something?"

He laughed into a kiss. "Actually…" He skimmed his hand down along my side. "I want to get this." Then he squeezed my ass.

"You want to tattoo my butt on you?"

"I want to tattoo your silhouette on me." He pulled his cell phone from his pocket and brought up a picture of a simple and minimalist design, then flipped through a few more.

"They're beautiful, but how…"

"Later on tonight, I'm going to take some pictures to make sure I get a good likeness of you."

I slapped at his chest, laughing, but…he was completely serious.

"Liam. You're going to take pictures of me naked and show them to some guy to tattoo you with it?"

"If by some guy, you mean Nikki? Then, yes."

"Oh." That made me feel better about the whole process. And getting a tattoo did sound really romantic.

"She's done all my tattoos," he said, and I tipped my head to the side.

"Maybe I'll get one too."

"Yeah? What would you get?"

I didn't hesitate. "Two matching dinosaurs, but a daddy and a baby."

Liam's grin was positively radiant. "For me and Finn?"

"Of course. Who else would it be for?"

He shrugged and pulled me into him. "Maybe you really like dinosaurs."

I tilted my head back for a kiss. "Maybe I really like you."

"And thank god for that." He turned toward the table, where Finn had made an absolute mess. "Feels good to be home."

There were never truer words.

EPILOGUE

LIAM

"Hellooooo!" Finn ran into Imagination Station, greeting our friends, but I wasn't too far behind.

"Late again," Jude noted as Dylan shook his head, tsking at me. The last few times we'd made plans to hang out, I'd shown up late.

But it was real damn hard to leave Kennedy sometimes, especially this morning, when she'd come so hard, I'd needed to cover her mouth with my hand.

Finn had interrupted us after he'd woken up by flinging himself into our bed, and while he hadn't *seen* anything since Kennedy's head was under the covers, I was left hanging.

So we all had breakfast, and then we sat him in front of the television with *Toy Story* and his drum kit as we scurried back into our room, where I ate her out while she sucked me off and then I used her microphone vibrator until she screamed my name.

It was a great morning.

"Sorry not sorry," I said and handed each of my friends a hardback copy of my book.

"Oh, man. This is awesome." Jude flipped it over in his

hands, admiring it. "I thought it didn't come out until next week."

"Author copies," I said by way of explanation.

Dylan pointed to the back flap. "Got your face on it and everything."

"Sign it." Jude thrust his back to me, but I didn't have a pen.

"You got something to write with?" I asked, and he shook his head. I didn't even bother asking Dylan. "If Kennedy were here, she'd have four different markers in her Mary Poppins bag."

It got bigger and bigger every week.

I was sure she'd be yanking out lamps from it soon.

"Well, you can sign it another time," Jude said, thumping his fist against my arm. "But this is very cool. My friend wrote a whole book."

"Yeah," Dylan agreed. "Congrats."

"I don't expect you guys to read it or anything."

Jude flicked through a few pages. "No, I want to. I'm going to."

Dylan shrugged. "I probably won't, but Gen's got me into audiobooks lately. You gonna have an audiobook?"

"Um, not sure," I said and sipped from my coffee, but curiosity got the better of me. "What kinds of books do you listen to?"

He tugged on the bill of his baseball cap and turned his head side to side, as if making sure no one would hear. "We listen to them together, and we're in the middle of this fantasy series with these fairies and wars and whatever." He leaned his elbows on his knees and angled in closer to us. "Which was fine, but then they got, like, spicy."

Jude tipped his head to the side as I laughed into my fist. "Spicy?"

"Yeah, man. They were soul mates, she made him soup, and all of a sudden, they were..." He mouthed the rest. "Fucking."

Jude raised his brow. "You listen to romance books?"

"I mean, they're not full romance, but yeah. We're not done

with this series yet. They're about to have a big battle." He sat back and shrugged. "I like them."

"Kennedy reads romance. She sends me portions to read…" I deliberately inclined my head. "Sometimes she'll read them out loud to me." I lifted a shoulder. "They're hot."

Jude toggled his gaze between Dylan and me. "You're telling me you're both into romance books?"

"Smutty romance books," Dylan said, but I held up my hand.

"I think that's a derogatory term."

Dylan waved his hand to where Scarlett and Amelia were playing, or rather, appearing like they were tussling over a fake hair dryer. "Hey, girls. Share." Then he turned back to me. "Genevieve calls it smut."

I considered this, my hand already on my cell phone to text Kennedy for her opinion. "Maybe it's one of those things where they reclaimed the word?"

Jude blinked a few times, his voice low so only we could hear him. "I can't believe you guys read your porn."

"Give it a shot," I said. "You might like it."

He swatted away the idea. "I have no one to read it with."

"You want someone to read it with?" Dylan asked, and Jude shook his head, quickly changing the subject by elbowing me.

"So, how's it going with you and Kennedy?"

"Perfect. She's perfect. Everything is perfect."

Jude grinned. "Good for you."

"Her mom's coming to visit in a few weeks, and Tess will be home in June. It's all working out."

Dylan tossed me a smirk. "Exactly like you planned, huh?"

I huffed in amusement. *"Exactly."*

Although I never could have planned for Kennedy and how she'd changed my life, I would always be grateful. She was it for me, and while we'd agreed to wait on making it official, I'd caught her looking at monogrammed towels and matching Mr. and Mrs. coffee mugs a time or two.

And that made me happier than I ever thought it would. So I wasn't going to wait *too* much longer on making her my wife.

I absently rubbed at my bicep, where I'd had Kennedy's silhouette tattooed during a quick trip up to Boston over my spring break. Finn was obsessed with the dinos she had inked on her forearm. It was adorable each time he traced them and the little heart between with his finger.

But then Jude pointed to the side, where Finn had his head shoved inside the plastic mailbox. Yet again.

Not so adorable.

I sighed, standing up, mumbling, "I love my child. I love my child. I love my child."

———

So glad you've made it to the end! **Want to celebrate Father's Day with Liam and see how spicy it gets with Kennedy and some sundaes?** Click here for a bonus epilogue delivered straight to your inbox!

BONUS EPILOGUE

LIAM

Growing up without a dad had always made Father's Day weird until I had my kid. Then it took on a different meaning.

It was a day to appreciate this new light in my life. Finn was now four-years-old, and sometimes I still couldn't believe this brilliant, funny, and terrible kid was mine. Last year for Father's Day, Kennedy put on a big to-do with my favorite dinner, a banner, and a mug that revealed a picture of Finn when I poured coffee into it. That was aside from the card Finn had created with Kennedy's help. It had been covered in dinosaur stickers and spelled out I love you in big letters, some of them backward.

But this year, it was my turn for a big to-do. Even if she didn't know it yet.

As promised, we didn't rush into it, no matter how badly I wanted to. We spent the last year finding our way as a couple and family. Kennedy hit her stride, working part-time in a salon and volunteering at the local community theater. She was routinely cast in their shows, yet still found time and ways to shower Finn and me with her Kennedy sparkle, from matching family pajamas at Christmas to daily homemade dinners. She'd also become close with Tessa, the two of them talking regularly about things that had nothing to do with me or Finn, meeting for pedicures and brunch every few weeks. Apparently, Kennedy was determined to find Tessa a guy, and while Tessa had reservations, I knew Kennedy got whatever she put her mind to.

For my part, I fought the urge to ask her to marry me every damn day.

But finally, I was giving up on the waiting.

"Who's ready for sundaes?" Kennedy called from where she leaned against the kitchen counter, licking whipped cream off her finger.

Memories flashed through my mind. Over a year ago, when my attraction to Kennedy first became a problem after she so innocently brought out the whipped cream, using it to help potty train Finn. Then to when I'd brought it into our bedroom for her birthday in February. I'd sprayed it over her, licking the sweet cream off my sweet girl. And I thought about a few weeks ago, when we'd found Finn on the floor after he'd attempted to climb the shelves on the inside of the refrigerator for the can.

I bit back a laugh at the image of my son and walked into the kitchen. I wasn't nervous at all for what I was about to do, though my adrenaline was high, and I cleared my throat to make sure it didn't come out squeaky.

"We're here," I said from behind Kennedy, and she spun around, slamming my hand to her chest.

Her fear faded immediately. "When did you sneak up here? Scared me."

I smiled, easing closer, wrapping my hand around her hip. "Sorry. Finn has something on his shirt he wanted to show you."

I waved Finn forward, and she bent to him. "Did you spill more applesauce on it? I told you, you gotta eat...up..." Her words trailed off to an eventual gasp as she read the words on his shirt.

Will you marry my daddy?

She immediately started crying, even though she couldn't have been surprised. We'd already talked about our wedding, especially since we'd attended Dylan and Gen's wedding two weeks ago. Kennedy had said she wanted something smaller, which surprised me. Neither of us were ever married, so I had assumed she would want the big white wedding thing. But, no. She wanted an intimate ceremony. Maybe somewhere we could take a brief vacation with Finn.

I tugged her hands from her face and held them in mine as I dropped down to one knee. "Finn and I had a chat not long after you moved in here. I asked if he loved you, and he said yes."

She sniffled, and Finn—the amazing boy he was—handed her a tissue, pulling a laugh from the both of us. She kissed his head as she accepted the tissue, and I waited until she wiped her cheeks and met my gaze again.

"I think I loved you then too. You were meant to be with me. Meant to be with Finn."

She sank down to the floor, wrapping her arm around Finn as he smacked his shirt, all proud. "Ken-dee, marry me!"

She breathed out a water-logged laugh then looked back to me, so I went on.

"Since you've come into my life, everything has been better. You're thoughtful and kind, patient and funny. I love that you make conversation with strangers, and you're always thinking about what you can do for others. You're generous with your time and spirit, and you make me a better person, father, and partner. So, please, angel, marry me?"

She brushed her long hair behind one shoulder, managing to be sassy even as her chin wobbled. "You know how much I love it when you say please."

I shook my head, biting my lower lip to keep from telling her how I would have her begging later, and opened the ring box.

She blew out a breath at the sight of the diamond ring with little amethyst gems on either side, giving it the appearance of a flower. And because I thought head, I'd already purchased the matching wedding ring.

"So?" I asked, ring poised at the tip of her finger, and she nodded, grinning.

"Yes! Of course!"

Finn cheered, and I slid the ring on over her knuckle before standing and pulling her into me, cradling her cheeks in my hands to kiss her head, her temple, and her perfect mouth. She wrapped her fingers around my wrists, smiling against my lips. "You know I'm going to get us matching T-shirts, right? I'm going to be so annoying. Mrs. Hot Professor, what could be better?"

I lifted her left hand, brushing my thumb over her ring, then kissed her palm. "Nothing," I said, and pressed her hand against my chest. "Nothing is better than this."

"Big hug!" Finn shouted, throwing his arms out to us.

"Come on up here, guy." I lifted him up so Kennedy and I could squish him between us until he squealed with laughter. We covered him with kisses before I set him down. He immediately hopped over toward the counter and the ice cream, sprinkles, whipped cream, and cherries Kennedy out set out.

"Squirt!"

We all filled our bowls and sat at the table to eat, though Kennedy spent so much time grinning at me and her ring that she barely touched her sundae. Finn wolfed his down, so I tipped my head toward the steps. "Want to go get ready? Mommy'll be here soon."

Kennedy frowned at me. "She will?"

I nodded. "All part of the plan."

Finn pumped his fist, sprinting off. "Goin' to da park! Goin' to da park!"

His speech had come so far, and I was so proud of him. Still hadn't lost that feral side of him, though. A thump sounded from upstairs and then, "I'm okay!"

Kennedy leaned over, snickering into my shoulder, and I looped my arm around her shoulder, kissing her head.

"He's going to give me gray hair," I said, stealing her ice cream.

She leaned away from me to comb her fingers through my

hair. "Can't wait for that." When I raised my brow, she tugged on the ends of the strands. "Silver fox."

I swallowed down the last of her sundae and pressed a kiss to her mouth, slipping my tongue along her lower lip. But before I could pull her into my lap, Finn came literally roaring back into the kitchen.

"Want to run around outside until Mom comes?" I asked, and he swung right back around, heading to the front door. I held my hand out for Kennedy and laced our fingers together as we walked through the front door. We spent a few minutes counting for Finn, timing how long it took him to run from one end of the yard to the other. Because, as he liked to remind us, he was "very super fast!"

When Tessa showed up, she gave us each a hug of congratulations and talked animatedly with Kennedy for a while about the ring and the date Tessa had gone on last night, then made plans to get together next week. I was basically the third wheel now.

"Mommy!" Finn wrapped himself around Tessa's legs. "Let's goooooo!"

"Yes, yes, okay, okay." She leaned in to kiss my cheek then Kennedy's and gestured for Finn to do the same. "Say bye to Daddy and Kennedy. Say we'll see you in a few days."

He hugged each of us, repeating, "See you in a few days!"

After they drove away, I followed Kennedy back inside and upstairs to the kitchen, where she began to clean up, cringing at the now melted tub of vanilla and chocolate ice cream. "I forgot to put everything away before we went outside."

I shrugged, taking it from her as I swatted her butt. "Still useful."

She put the dishes in the sink. "As what?"

I shot her a look of disbelief. As if she didn't know me. As if I wouldn't use any and every tool at my disposal. "Angel…"

She put the whipped cream away and leaned against the closed refrigerator door. "Yes, Professor?"

"Strip."

Her teeth bit into the corner of her bottom lip, but she didn't hesitate, lifting her tank top over her head, tossing it at my face. As I held the thin cotton material in my hand, an idea sprouted, and I watched with growing lust as she unzipped her jeans to pull them down her legs, setting them on one of the kitchen chairs. She pivoted away from me to remove her bra and underwear, glancing over her shoulder at me in that same teasing way she's perfected. Drove me wild.

"Stay like that," I told her and used her tank top to bind her wrists together at her lower back. I could hear her breathing, see the goosebumps that rose on the skin of her arms. Knotting the material, I asked, "You like this?"

She nodded, shifting so her soft ass pressed back against my groin.

"Stay just like this," I said, and sucked on her shoulder, tugging on her binding. It wasn't tight, and she could break out of it at any time, but I knew she wouldn't. "My good girl," I rasped, trailing my hands up her arms to her breasts, gently rolling her nipples. I stepped right up behind her, lining her lush body against mine, and she dropped her head back to my chest, angling her neck so I could kiss and lick it how she liked.

Before long, she was shifting back and forth, rotating her hips, searching for something. For me.

Knowing we'd get dirty, I shucked off my T-shirt then guided her to turn around and reached for the tub of ice cream. I coated my index finger with the melted dessert and held it up to her lips. "Open."

She obeyed, and I stuck it in her mouth. Her hot tongue touched the tip first, a moment before her lips wrapped around my finger, sucking hard. It sent a jolt of pleasure down my spine, and I inhaled sharply.

She grinned wickedly. She knew exactly what she was doing to me, and I growled into a kiss, dipping two fingers into the ice cream and caressing her skin with it. I continued painting her until my finger prints marked her, covering her neck, chest, and belly. When I stepped back to admire my work, blood rushed south and my dick swelled in my pants.

I set the tub of ice cream down and wrapped my hands around her waist, holding her still as I dragged my tongue over the wavy line of the sweet cream, licking every bit of it off her skin. I nibbled on the curve of her breast, traced the delicate bump of her collarbone, and sucked on both of her nipples.

"So sweet," I murmured against her stomach, laving her belly button with my tongue before licking over her sweetly rounded belly, digging my fingers into the soft skin of her hips. I kneeled in front of her, tucking my nose and mouth into the cleft of her sex, inhaling deeply. "My sweet girl," I said, staring up at her for a moment, her eyes half-lidded and silently beginning.

But of course, my angel always used her manners. "Please, Liam."

I smiled and licked into her, drawing a long sigh out of her. She relaxed against the refrigerator door, her head back, hips tilted out toward me, and I grabbed a handful of ass cheeks, pulling her even closer to my mouth.

I concentrated on her clit, feeling her muscles tense with every hard suck on the sensitive bundle of nerves. But it wasn't enough, and I pulled away from her, extending my arm up, offering her my fingers, still sticky from the ice cream. "Suck them clean."

Her eyes sparkled, and she bent her head to take my fingers into her mouth, circling her tongue around them before bobbing her head up and down, mimicking how she sucks on my cock. And I had to look away or I wouldn't be able to last as long as I wanted to.

Jerking my fingers from between Kennedy's lips, I trailed them down her torso to the sweet heat between her legs. I teased at her soft, damp flesh until she whined. Only then did I dip them inside of her, finding the swollen spot against her front wall. She bucked against me, so I wrapped one arm around her to hold on her wrists and pinned her hips back with my other forearm before sucking on her clit.

She alternated between loud moans and almost inaudible murmurs of *yes* and *please* and *oh god*. It only spurred me on to work her harder, to push her over the edge until she cried out, soaking my hand with her orgasm.

I ignored the ache in my knees and stood, not wasting any time in pushing my pants and underwear down before directing Kennedy in front of me. I released her hands and towed her up against me, kissing her shoulder and neck as I massaged her wrists for a few seconds. "You okay?"

She nodded, peering up at me with drowsy eyes.

"Hold on to the counter," I said, and she complied, spreading her feet and showing off the gorgeously round and dimpled backside I loved so much. I rubbed at it, pressing my fingertips into her skin, and gave into the desire to bite her ass cheek, just below her birth mark.

She tossed me a siren smile over her shoulder because my dirty girl loved it when I was a little rough. I smacked her thigh. "You ready for me?"

"Of course, Professor."

I lined my erection up at her entrance, rubbing it along the seam of her pussy, coating my myself in her wetness before plunging inside.

"Hold on tight, angel." I gripped her hips. "This is gonna be fast and hard."

"Yes, please."

I fucked into her over and over, staring at where my hips met her ass, watching as my cock repeatedly disappeared inside her body. She felt so good, so tight and wet. Nothing was better than this.

After many discussions over the last year, I'd gotten a vasectomy because we'd decided not to try for any biological children, but we hadn't ruled out fostering and adoption. As Kennedy always said, she loved being a mom and wouldn't mind a whole brood. I wouldn't either.

But these last few weeks since the procedure, I'd become obsessed. Insatiable.

Although, I doubted I'd ever get enough of her.

I folded over Kennedy, circling my fingers over her clit, making sure she came one more time. Her skin flushed pink, inner muscles clamping around me, and after a few more thrusts, I let go, both of us groaning in release.

It took me a few moments to collect myself, but once I did, I gathered her hair up in my fist and kissed the top of her spine. We were both breathing hard and slick with a mixture of sweat, ice cream, and evidence of our sex. "Shower?"

"Yes, definitely," she said, and I carefully pulled out of her before not so carefully swinging her up into my arms. She shrieked in laughter and draped her arms around my neck as I carried her upstairs to our bedroom, depositing her down in the bathroom.

I flicked the taps on, holding my palm out under the spray of water. "So, Mrs. O'Neil, we have the—"

"Mrs. O'Neil." She grinned. "I like the sound of it."

"Me too," I said, helping her into the shower with me.

She stood with her back to the water and skimmed her hands up chest and over my shoulders, tracing her fingers over each of my tattoos, physical reminders of all the people I loved most in the world. She ended on the one I got for her, scratching over the shape of her on my bicep. "How soon can we make it official?"

I rubbed my thumb along the tattoo she'd had done for Finn and me, and smiled into a kiss. "As soon as you want."

"Tomorrow?"

I huffed a laugh. "Tomorrow might be a little too soon. Maybe a few weeks. As long as it takes to get the paperwork completed."

She nodded and accepted a kiss on her lips. I tunneled my fingers into her hair, holding her head as the water saturated the dark strands. "How 'bout after we clean up, we take my laptop into bed and figure out where we want to do it?"

She smiled, sunshine and rainbows. "Always planning ahead."

"With you, I have to. Can't let you get away."

Her gaze drifted down to her left hand, and she wiggled her fingers, admiring her new ring.

"You're stuck with me now," I joked, reaching for the soap, and Kennedy grinned up at me.

"Exactly how I planned it."

I clucked my tongue and laid a smacking kiss on her smiling lips. "Devious little Mary Poppins."

"You just wait," she said, spinning around to douse herself with the water. "One of these days, I' m gonna come home with a talking parrot umbrella and full on Mary Poppins dress. Then what're gonna do?"

"Not a damn thing." I wrapped my arms around her, ducking my face to the side of her neck. "Except maybe lift it up and go down on you for a while."

She tossed her head back and laughed.

My perfect, sweet angel.

ACKNOWLEDGMENTS

Indie publishing is a wild ride. Thank you, reader, for coming along with me.

I wouldn't be able to put out these books if not for the encouragement of my friends and the guidance of people much smarter than me, in particular Diamond Dogs of publishing. Big shout out to Echo Grayce for the amazing cover and to Libby and Lisa for editing my brain vomit into an actual book. I'd especially like to thank my street team for helping me spread the word about my books. I'm forever grateful.

If you'd like more information about me, you can find it at https://sophieandrewsauthor.com/

ABOUT THE AUTHOR

Sophie Andrews is a contemporary romance author who writes steamy books that will leave you smiling. As a millennial, she's obsessed with boybands, late 90s rom-coms, and will always be team Pacey. When she's not writing, she's most likely trying to wrangle her children or drinking red wine. Or both at the same time.

ALSO BY SOPHIE ANDREWS

Tangled Series

Tangled Up

Tangled Want

Tangled Hearts

Tangled Beginning

Tangled Expectations

Tangled Chances

Tangled Ambition

Single Dads' Club

The Rehearsal Fling

The Nanny Tenure

The Dating Pact

The Bartender's Baby

Stand-Alones

How to Ruin a Wedding

Love at a Funeral and Other Awkward Conversations

Hart Brothers Novellas

Made Over by Meredith

Wrapped Up in Holly

Collections

Tangled Series books 1-4